HEIRS *of the* DEMON KING

UPRISING

BY SARAH CAWKWELL

WWW.ABADDONBOOKS.COM

An Abaddon Books™ Publication
www.abaddonbooks.com
abaddon@rebellion.co.uk

First published in 2014 by Abaddon Books™,
Rebellion Intellectual Property Limited,
Riverside House, Osney Mead, Oxford, OX2 0ES, UK.

10 9 8 7 6 5 4 3 2 1

Editors: Jonathan Oliver & David Moore
Cover Art: Andrew Evans
Design: Simon Parr & Sam Gretton
Marketing and PR: Michael Molcher
Publishing Manager: Ben Smith
Creative Director and CEO: Jason Kingsley
Chief Technical Officer: Chris Kingsley

ISBN: 978-1-78108-223-2

Printed and bound by CPI Group (UK) Ltd, Croydon, CR0 4YY

SARAH CAWKWELL

HEIRS *of the* DEMON KING

UPRISING

For Beatrix Moore,
who came into being at the same time as this book.
May the rainbow always touch your shoulder.

A Treatise on the Kings of England and the Rise of Magic: The Plantagenets

by Brother Edmund of the
Order of St. Aidan, Royal Archivist
from his greater text A History of the Demon Kings, *second edition (1694)*

IN MARCH OF the Year of Our Lord 1194, Richard the Lionheart returned to the people of his kingdom following years of captivity. He brought with him tales of the Crusades; captivating and bold tales of fierce warriors whose strength in battle was unmatched until the Christians brought them low. He told tales of arcane wonder. Beyond all these, he brought something else. Something that would change the direction of our great country forevermore. The forgotten, whispered words of eastern mystics.

Richard returned with a thousand words of ritual, mysterious incantations and sweet-smelling incense. He brought back knowledge of runes of great power to invoke the spirits of the elements. This was a rare gift granted to Christendom from the wise men of the east. In Richard the Lionheart, they saw a strong man; a leader to whom the power could be entrusted. Richard's well of gratitude ran deep and he was eager to share the knowledge with his kingdom. He chose, rather poetically, to call it the Eastern Promise.

It was the gift of magic.

England already knew about magic in its simplest form. Herbal poultices and preparations have aided the English people since before records were kept. The stripped bark of a willow tree is known to ease aches and pains. Adding particular herbs to hot water produces calming and comforting brews that aid the sick and ailing. Man has long worked with the forces of nature; the planting and growing of crops is dependent upon the seasons, just as the rise and fall of the tides is connected with the phases of the moon. The people who walk upon this country's green and blessed shores know when to reap and they know when to sow. This is knowledge garnered over many years, the result of trial and error.

What Richard brought back was magic in a purer form. He travelled back with the best of intentions, to share this wonder with his people. Good intentions, as we all know from our schooling, are the stones that pave the road to Hell, and it is tragic that this rang true in the case of King Richard. The truth of what happened was the product of a kingdom made greedy and the results were far from the glory Richard Plantagenet saw for the future of his people.

Richard the Lionheart learned, on his return from the Crusades, that his absence had led to a loss of control over the running of his English kingdom. When he called a council to discuss the Eastern Promise, there was great dissension. The King yearned to share the secrets of magic with all of his people, but the priesthood and the nobility of his court argued that such power should be held only by those best qualified to do so. They feared that with the gift of magic at their disposal, the common folk would turn against their betters. The country could ill-afford another revolt, they said.

Eventually, the King relented and placed the gift of magic into the hands of the nobility. Those who became party to the secrets of the Holy Land found themselves in possession of something more wonderful than simple mastery over the elements. The Eastern Promise unlocked a whole new world. It was a world terrifying and overwhelming in equal measure—but it was also a world of limitless potential. A world where every mystery conquered rewarded the magic user with fresh knowledge... and still more mystery.

King Richard oversaw the rise of this mystical power in his lands and he was pleased. The men he had chosen to wield the arcane gift were just and loyal, and they did not abuse their new-found power. Content that his kingdom was secure in their hands, he retreated to his beloved Aquitaine.

The words of magic began to slowly trickle down. The first

magicians chose to share their gifts with friends and family or favoured apprentices. Slowly but surely, magic became part of the culture, seeped into the everyday, and the people of England knew it and embraced it gladly.

With magic now part of everyday life, the crime of witchcraft that had once so persecuted country healers was no longer treated as such. Healers no longer lived in fear for their lives, and were able to practise their herbalism and healing without challenge. But it was not long before things took a turn for the worse.

It became clear that some people were naturally gifted; a connection with magic that made them stronger. Such people were considered remarkable and were fiercely prized by their communities. Some, it was whispered, were so skilled with magic that they could summon demons from the pits of Hell with nothing more than a word. But even if these rumours held truth, such practices were not commonplace, and any demon-summoning was performed in secret. The Church worked tirelessly to stamp out the rumours.

By the time of Richard's death, five years after his return, and the ascension of his brother John to the throne of England in 1199, magic had firmly taken root. England, France, Spain and Italy in particular were greatly altered by the whispers of the eastern mystic who had spoken with Richard at the gates of Jerusalem.

So the gift of magic flourished for a time. With each mystery solved, a new benefit for the men of the west was granted. Summers became longer, with those now known as *magi* able to summon the rains on request to feed the crops. Harvests grew richer. The bounty of the seas multiplied. Illnesses were cured, injuries healed. Under the guidance of the House of Plantagenet, the country bloomed and swelled in power. These were great days; a time of peace and prosperity.

It was no surprise that the gift eventually spread to the continent as well. In the courts of Paris, magicians demonstrated remarkable sleight-of-hand techniques, artfully aided by dipping into the wonders of the gift. The people of Europe lived in opulent, indulged wonder and magic was embraced.

The Plantagenet line flourished, made rich and strong with the addition of magic to its blood. But King John was not the strong leader his brother had been, and with the signing of the Magna Carta in 1215, the citizens of England regained many of their long-absent rights and privileges. With new and completely unchallenged access to forbidden vaults and archives, the spread of magic through the population was unprecedented. No longer an exclusive and carefully managed thing, magic became tainted and sour. Those who had very little realised that with the right application of magic, they might gain more. By contrast, those at the top, with all the wealth and power, had little desire to lose it. The country began to fall to fighting and swelling greed.

Mainland Europe largely ignored the squabbling in England, leaving the little country be. England, once considered a prize for any prince, soon fell into a state of famine and bitter civil war.

After John's death, Henry the Third took the throne. Only nine years old when he took the seat of power, he was raised by the same priests and nobles who had advised his long-dead uncle. They had come to fear for their lofty positions as the peasantry took to the arcane arts, and during Henry's reign, desperate efforts to stamp out common magic usage and return power to the royal and the noble commenced. The easiest way to make their statement came in the form of public execution. Those among the common folk caught openly practising magic were hunted, tried and summarily executed.

Every scholar knows the pattern of kings from this point. Edward the First, Second and Third came and went, and although they carved out their place in the history books, they never fully succeeded in reclaiming magic as the exclusive gift of the nobility. It is said that the Black Plague, which killed half of the country's population in the mid-fourteenth century, was a direct result of Edward the Third's attempt to channel a higher, forbidden form of rune magic. These claims have never been proved true and should be treated as rumour, not fact.

Richard the Second took the throne, but after surviving the so-called 'Peasants' Revolt,' his luck only grew worse. He was swiftly removed from power, deposed by his first cousin, Henry the Fourth, who brought a new name with him. The House of Lancaster, as the ruling family were now known, still carried the Plantagenet bloodline. As Edward the Third's grandson, Henry was every bit a Plantagenet, even if he hid behind a different name and a different banner. His reign was fraught with uprisings from the magically-strong Welsh, Scots and Cornish people, who sought to fight for the right to use their magic freely.

Before he died, passing the throne to his son Henry the Fifth, the King decreed the re-building of Hadrian's Wall to the north. Later, his grandson would extend the barrier and build visible borders to the Welsh lands and in the southwest of the country. The Celtic people were resistant to this act but could not hope to match the forces of the King.

Henry the Fifth had no magical blood in his body. He was a warrior king, a throwback to a greater, glorious age. It was in him that the first lust to totally destroy magic in its varied forms arose. Unsurprisingly, this did not make him popular amongst those who still yearned to embrace magic to improve their lot. After Henry, efforts continued to end the reign of magic.

The bloodline thinned, but did not completely die out, and by the time Richard the Third took the throne, the country was in dire straits. The prosperous years following the Crusades were long forgotten. Disease once more stalked the lands, hand in hand with famine and death.

But each king knew the true secret. Each of these kings knew what it had cost Richard the Lionheart to bring the gift of magic to the shores of England. They knew the source of the power and they knew the dangers in stretching the limits of that power. Not one of them, not even the boldest, dared to test that limit.

Richard the Third dared.

Prologue

21st August, 1485
Ambion Hill
England

'The truth. Give me the truth!'

The King's fist slammed down onto the table at which the commanders of his army sat. The argument ceased immediately at the sound, and all eyes turned to the man seated at the table's head.

'The truth, sire? The truth is that we cannot hope to hold out against Tudor's forces for another full day.'

'Do we not outnumber them?'

'Yes, sire, by almost a thousand men.' The Duke of Northumberland chose his next words carefully. 'But our numbers will count for nothing. His advantage is too strong.' He drew a deep breath. The King had demanded the truth—and the truth he would have. 'The battle will be lost.'

The words cut through the tense atmosphere like a sword. The King sat down heavily and shook his head. 'That cannot be. I refuse to concede defeat without a blade raised in defiance. Tell me something else. There has to be a way we can defeat him.'

'Short of murdering his vile retinue in their beds...' Northumberland started, but the King interrupted him.

'Do you not think I'd considered that? Assassins have been infiltrating Tudor's forces for days and still he encroaches. Still he brings those abominations before me and seeks to drive me from my throne. Well, he will not have it. There has to be a way, but you *fools* are too stupid to provide me with one...'

The candlelight flickered against the King's furious face. It was not a handsome visage, the features somehow misaligned and uneven as though he had not been put together correctly. The only reminder of his noble heritage was the solid set to the heavily stubbled jaw line and something across his prominent brow that called to mind the Plantagenets who had seized the English throne for their own.

King Richard the Third of England was not a man who cared much about physical appearance. He was, however, a man who cared a great deal about how his kingdom was perceived. This was not a battle he could afford to lose if he was to be seen to be strong. Henry Tudor was within days—hours, if his commanders were to be believed—of taking that throne from him. The expectations of his ancestors fell heavily on his stooped shoulders. He was not a happy man.

Those loyal to his cause were few in number, but utterly dedicated to the Crown. Their King was young, but seasoned and tempered in the fires of battle. Tudor was an untried warrior and largely an unknown quantity, but his sheer presence had been enough to sway the hearts of the weak-willed and the opportunistic. It was a battle that should never have come to pass, a rebellion that should have been over before it had even begun. For months they had known of Tudor's scheming and intentions—for months they'd had time to marshal their forces and march on Lancaster—but Richard had been confident he could dispel the growing threat with words and politics.

He had been too confident. And now the price was being paid in blood and lives in the muddy fields of middle England. Because of Henry Tudor and his followers. Because of the colours and the design of the banner that marched at the head of the enemy and what they stood for. The dragon standard had become synonymous with Tudor's encroachment, an ancient iconography whose boldness of statement could not be missed. All who flocked to Tudor's banner knew what weapon it was that he wielded. Those who marched beneath the white rose of York found out, often too late, what weapon it was that they faced. All of Richard's armies could not hope to best such power.

So numbers had dwindled as fear of the King and his laws was eclipsed by fear of Tudor's arcane might. Lords found excuses to keep their warriors at home or simply ignored the King's summons altogether, casting aside familial oaths to await the inevitable outcome. This campaign had cost many lives, not to mention the great expense to bring the King's diminished army to the field to answer Henry's defiance. If the material or actual costs weighed heavily on Richard's shoulders, it didn't show in his words or deeds. But he was losing, and tomorrow, Richard feared, he would have lost. He would be consigned to the history books as the man who lost the crown of England to a pretender. His hands curled and uncurled as he concentrated on keeping focused and not allowing his burning hatred of Tudor to cause a tirade of impotent rage.

He knew this was more than an attempt on his throne and on the crown. Tudor wished to totally destroy the English way of life. If he ascended the throne of England...

A silence fell across the command pavilion, uncomfortable and unpleasant. The only sound was the rain outside, drumming heavily above their heads, incessantly driving and churning the earth into a gruelling swamp. It should not have been raining; the weather was wholly unnatural given the clear skies. But then, their enemy wielded unnatural power.

There was a coughing at the entrance to the command tent, and seven pairs of eyes turned to the young messenger who stood there.

'Speak.' Richard sat back in his chair, resting his hands on its wooden arms. 'Bring me news I want to hear.'

'Alas, I cannot, sire.' The messenger was little more than a boy, not more than sixteen or seventeen years old. Like Richard, he had seen the army assembling in the fields beyond and knew what it represented. He bore the same air of grim determination that now marked all of the King's men. Richard's eyes narrowed to barely visible slits. The boy's manner did not please him.

'Then speak. What are his plans?'

'Lord Stanley remains neutral. He has positioned his units between our forces. He will take whichever side he sees fit once battle is joined. It seems that unless my lord concedes to his demands immediately, his loyalty will be fickle to the last.'

'His son will remain in custody until his loyalty is proved.'

The Duke of Norfolk, silent until this point, finally spoke up.

'He is one of the few advantages we may yet field in this battle. His loyalty belongs to the King. This posturing proves nothing.'

'This "posturing" will be our undoing,' snapped Northumberland.

'Be still, Northumberland.' The King's voice was soft, but commanding. The man fell silent, glowering. 'Continue, boy.'

'Tudor is in session with his commanders. They have set up camp some two and a half miles from here.'

'The ground is ours.' Norfolk was confident in this. 'They will be forced to fight uphill through the mire while we rain arrows upon them.' His spark of optimism did not catch among the gathering, but guttered and died.

'Tudor's magi...'

The very utterance of the forbidden word drew sharp intakes of breath from everyone present, and the messenger foundered slightly, aware that he might well have transgressed. The men turned to look at Richard, who did not move, bar to crook a finger indicating the youth should continue. He did, cautiously.

'Tudor's magi plan to maintain the weather tonight. The storm will not hinder his forces, and he believes that come dawn, the men will have lost the will to fight and will throw down their arms rather than face death.' He ran his sweating hands down the sides of his stained, muddy tunic. Richard remained leaning back in his chair, most of his face hidden in the shadows. 'The ground—forgive me, my Lord Norfolk—is not ours at all.'

Norfolk set down the goblet of wine that he had barely touched. He leaned forward on the table for a moment, looking around at the expressions on the faces of those gathered. Then he gave a deep, lusty sigh. 'They are probably right.' He leaned back again, folding his arms across his chest. 'Unless we can do something to disarm Tudor before it happens, this war is over.' He shook his head and ran his fingers through his beard. 'The battle is lost.'

'No,' said Richard aloud, drawing looks from the commanders. 'No. I will not let this thing happen. The Battle of Bosworth will go down in history as a victory for the house of Plantagenet, not as a defeat. Tudor must *not* be allowed to take the throne.' He closed his hand into a fist and pounded it down on the table again.

'Those who came before me fought for this throne, and for this crown that I wear. I will not betray their sacrifices and their legacy because of *one man!*' As he spoke, his voice rose in pitch until he was screaming. For the young messenger, it would be the last sound he would ever hear.

Richard drew the dagger he wore strapped to his shin and threw it, with easy grace and deadly accuracy. It embedded itself in the boy's chest and the young man let out a startled cry of pain. Blood drooled from the puncture wound and he pitched forwards onto the straw floor of the pavilion, landing on the hilt and driving it further into his flesh. He thrashed a few times, his limbs twitching in the final throes of death, and then he lay still.

'Get out.'

Richard's tone left no room for question or argument. Those who had declared their loyalty unto death left, one by one, stepping around the stiffening corpse of the unfortunate messenger. Not one of them knew the boy's name. Not one of them cared.

The Duke of Norfolk was the last to leave. He studied his King wordlessly for several moments. Richard raised his head and looked Norfolk right in the eye.

'If you have something to say, then say it,' said the King, rising from his seat and moving to get a goblet of wine from the end of the table. 'Otherwise, begone, before I have your head.'

'What do you plan to do, sire?' The duke asked his question.

'That is my business.' Richard poured the wine, watching the dark fluid slosh into the steel goblet like blood. He raised it to his lips and took a drink. 'Go and rest now, while you can. There is a battle to be fought on the morrow.' Richard stared into the goblet, but Norfolk continued to linger. He had not given his loyalty to Richard without reason, and to see him so concerned tapped a rare wellspring of sympathy. He sought to offer encouragement with a few careful words.

'Understand, sire, that those of us who fight for you do so with every ounce of strength in our bodies. This horror that you fight so hard to destroy... this gift of magic... by the end of tomorrow's battle, it will be driven into the mud. Tudor's head will become the trophy it should be, and this sorry business will be past. Your reign will continue.'

'Past, perhaps,' said Richard, without looking at Norfolk. 'But not forgotten.' He finally raised his head and there was such determination in his eyes that Norfolk took an involuntary step backwards. 'Fetch Mother Sewell. I wish to speak with her.'

SHE WAS A toothless old hag, her mumblings barely audible, bent practically double with age and nameless aches that twisted her fingers into painful claws. The young woman who brought her to the command tent did so with care and obvious respect. Richard looked the girl over as she entered with eyes made appreciative by two goblets of wine. For all his alleged cruelty and visible deformities, Richard had never wanted for mistresses. There were *some* advantages to being the King of England, and a bevy of beauties clamouring to bear his bastards was just one of them.

But tonight, rutting was far from his thoughts.

The old woman sat down on one of the chairs with obvious difficulty, grumbling quietly at the pain in her knees as she did so. The pretty young thing who had brought her fussed over her for a while, ensuring she was comfortable, and then dropped a low curtsey to the King before retreating.

Richard set down his wine and considered Mother Sewell. She had been in his service for six years, during which time her advice had proven invaluable. And she was the closest thing to magic that he tolerated in his court.

He moved back to the table, pausing briefly to kick the corpse of the dead messenger over and retrieve his dagger. He took a seat next to her and leaned forward, briefly resting his head in his hands. Then he sighed heavily.

'I need to know, Mother Sewell,' he said, his words slurring a little. 'I need you to read the omens and weave the threads of the future into something that will give me victory tomorrow.'

She mumbled something incomprehensible in response, but Richard didn't bother demanding she speak up. He'd given that up a long time ago. Mother Sewell made herself understood only when it suited *her*. She was quite mad—of that there was little doubt—but her advice and her visions had proved invaluable. Time and again her premonitions had saved the King's life, or spared him humiliation during diplomatic negotiation.

Mother Sewell leaned forward on the table and held out a gnarled hand. With obvious difficulty, she uncurled her stiff fingers until her palm was as flat as it could be.

'The price, Richard.' He did not comment on the familiarity; Mother Sewell said what she wanted to say when she wanted to say it. And she was perfectly understandable when she wanted something. Richard sneered only a little as he drew the blade of the blood-stained dagger across his own palm. A line of deep scarlet welled up in the wake of the blade, and the King clenched his hand into a fist, hissing at the stab of sudden pain. Holding his hand above Mother Sewell's, he watched as the blood dripped slowly into her open palm. Five. Six. Ten drops of blood.

'You smell of fear, Richard, son of Richard. Is it death that you fear?' She brought up the finger of her other hand and smeared the King's blood in rings on her liver-spotted skin.

'No. I do not fear death.' His response elicited a deep cackle and he scowled, snatching his bloodied hand back. He took up the water pitcher and poured the slightly brackish fluid over his hand, washing clean the self-inflicted injury. There would be another scar on his palm come the break of day, but if Mother Sewell guided him well, the price would have been worth it.

'What do you see?'

'Patience,' was her infuriating reply. 'You must be patient. The skeins of fate twist and converge. Teasing free a single thread is no simple task.' There was a faint lilt to her accent; she had been born in the valleys of Wales.

The gnarled, bent forefinger of her left hand continued to trace the King's blood across her palm, and then she let out a low moan, as if she were in terrible pain. Richard did not start at the noise; he had witnessed her reading his future often enough.

'The seed of Tudor will sit upon the throne,' she said.

'Not whilst I draw breath,' Richard snarled instantly, his hand instinctively closing around the hilt of his dagger. 'Is defeat certain, then, witch? Will he take my crown?'

Mother Sewell looked across at Richard, her rheumy eyes not meeting his, but looking somewhere across his left shoulder. 'His forces will slaughter yours. Their magic will prevent your victory. Before the sun has set tomorrow, the House of Plantagenet will be no more. The Tudors' light will rise in the east and the day of your family will be done.'

Her words chilled the blood in his marrow and he shook his head. 'This cannot be,' he responded. 'There must be something that can be done.'

Mother Sewell looked at him then. Her cataracts caught the flickering candlelight and she gave a toothless grin. Her crooked finger jabbed into her bloody palm.

'Indeed there is,' she said. 'I see it plainly enough.'

'Tell me. What must be done? How can I rid myself of this would-be usurper?'

'The answer, Richard, son of Richard, is the one you already know.'

The King's heart began to pound painfully in his chest and he reached for his wine. He took a long drink and the silence stretched out for an eternity.

'Speak the name of my mistress, King Richard. Taste the possibilities.' Mother Sewell's voice was like a fly buzzing around his head. He yearned to reach across to her, to grab her by the neck and slam her skull into the table. It was a primal urge that filled him simultaneously with bloodlust and a terrible, terrible shame.

'I... cannot.' He put the goblet down, attempting to hide the dreadful shaking that had started in his hands.

'Speak the name, Richard. You know it is your salvation. Speak the name.' For such a frail creature to hold such command in her tone made Richard sensibly wary.

What she asked of him, thought Richard, was something that could not be undone. Once the word was spoken, it could not be unsaid or taken back. Once that dreadful name was uttered, then he was going to a place from which there could be no return. For good or ill, he would be sacrificing everything in the name of victory.

Three syllables. That was all it would take to condemn him.

He drew a deep, shuddering breath as though it would be his last. The word, when it left his lips, came tinged with anticipation, fear and more than a little regret. All the years of keeping the knowledge secret, of guarding it more closely than even the crown that Henry the Second had taken so many years before, crumbled into dust.

'Melusine.'

The word left his lips as a whisper, but it seemed to him that he might just as well have shouted it from the top of Ambion Hill.

'Again, Richard.' The old woman's coaxing permeated the shroud of horror that he felt drawing in around him. He closed his eyes and drew a deep, deep breath. The word came again, stronger this time but with just as much hesitance as the first.

'Melusine.'

Richard had not thought it possible to grow colder than he was right now. On this August night, when the night outside the pavilion should have been balmy and pleasant, the unnatural rain conjured by his foes drummed down. It crept beneath the edges of the canvas, turning earth and straw into a sucking slurry. It was the kind of rain that seeped into everything, that drove your spirit from you. Since they had set up camp, none of them had been truly warm.

But now, Richard's veins were like ice.

'Speak the name again, call to her.' Mother Sewell's voice was completely clear now. Gone was the broken rasp. Gone was the stuttering madness. The King watched the old woman with growing horror as the cataracts melted from her sea-green eyes. The wrinkles smoothed from her ancient skin, the liver-spotted complexion replaced by something both less and more hideous.

'Melusine.'

Coarse, steel-grey hair lengthened and coloured before his eyes as the old woman's body straightened from its arthritic stoop. The hair was a blaze of copper, tresses that curled around a face of ethereal beauty. The full lips curved into a sensuous smile as the demon Melusine spoke through a human form once more. The air around Mother Sewell squirmed with energy and Richard found it difficult to breathe. His skin itched as though he were crawling with insects and he saw the sodden earth of the pavilion come alive with writhing worms and bugs as they blindly strove to flee.

'What have I done?' Richard let out a terrible moan of despair and his head dropped forward into his hands. Dark blood began to drip from his nose; the gore spilled from the dead messenger began to blacken and crackle as something pushed its way into the world of men.

'What you have done, Richard Plantagenet, is claim your rightful victory.' Melusine—he could no longer see this beautiful, awful creature as the old woman—rose from the seat with feline grace and moved towards him. 'You need the means to defeat Tudor. I can grant you that.' Her fingers tickled across the back of his neck and he shuddered in response. Her touch invoked too many emotions. Too many things that confused him. Soft, warm flesh; sweet breath; hot iron; the rough hide of a reptile. He pulled away and she laughed, honey-sweet and alluring. She remained behind him, where he could not see her, and that unnerved him even more.

'I cannot let him win. He cannot take the throne.' Steely resolve crept back into Richard's spine and he sat up straighter. 'He has magic on his side, and we cannot hope to match that on the open battlefield. If the bastard only fought with men and steel, we could take him and his army and bury them in the mud before noon.'

'It is a shame your family chose to turn their backs on the gift of the magi,' she said, trailing her fingers across his neck once again. 'You could have been more than this. You could have taken the known world by now.' She clicked her tongue against her teeth in a loud tutting noise. 'But you will do. I can see the thirst for victory burns bright in your breast.' She placed a hand on his breastbone. 'I feel the beating of your heart as it strives for victory.'

'Then give me what I want. Give me what I need to make England mine again.'

'What is your request, my little king?' She was mocking him, and Richard had never taken well to such things. His hands curled into tight fists. 'What is your request?' She leaned forward until her lips brushed his ear. 'And more importantly, what will you give me in return?'

The ice in his veins burst into flame, and a near-insatiable lust drove through his twisted body. His initial revulsion at the demon's presence melted away under the searing need for victory and the desperate desire to serve her. And only her.

He knew in that instant the answers to both of her questions. Turning in his seat, he stared into the raging depths of her oceanic eyes, tumultuous and perilous. He stared into them and was lost in their depths. He gave her the answer.

'I will give you anything.'

'Of course you will,' she said. 'You are hungry for power, Richard. You dare where Henry Tudor would not.'

'You... petition my enemy?'

'His ambition was a small thing, just power for his magi. But such power is easily taken, it will be his downfall. You have the sense to see what our union can bring.'

Yes, screamed that inner voice. *Death. Destruction. Carnage on an unprecedented scale.* Richard quelled the voice. He had passed the point of caring a long time ago now. The only way he could go was forward. His eyes met hers.

'Name your price.'

'I will give you the knowledge to conquer all before you, and your family line will become... gifted,' she replied. 'With the blessings of my blood. Your line will grow beyond the understanding of men, your might unchallenged. Down the generations, each first-born son will be greater, stronger, and mightier. And in time will come a pure vessel. He will be unmatched in all ways, a perfect soul to usher in a new age, a conqueror of nations and master of all. Many generations from now, one of your line will be the greatest, strongest king this country will ever know.'

After she had spoken, she leaned into him and her lips met his. His brief second or two of anguished ecstasy gave way to pain as she bit through the tender skin of his bottom lip, drawing blood.

'You offered this to Tudor?' Richard reached a dazed hand to his lips and stared at the blood that came away.

'He refused. He wants nothing for himself. His sense of honour will be the one thing that damns him. Do we have an understanding, Richard Plantagenet?'

He had no choice. Deep, very deep in his soul, the last light of Richard the Lionheart's ancestral fire sputtered and faded forever. He nodded, once.

'Done,' she said in her dulcet tones. 'Shall we seal the deal, my king?' She leaned in and kissed him again, revelling in the taste of his blood.

Richard had no power to resist her. And the entire time she was taking her fill of his lips, the whole time she lapped up the blood she'd drawn from his flesh, he could not lose the image of the bent old hag that she actually was. The thought turned his stomach, but the deal was sealed. The battle, come tomorrow, would be won. Without his magic, Henry Tudor would become a stain on the history books. He'd be remembered only for his defeat.

Finally sated, the demoness stood back. 'Bring the corpse,' she said. 'It contains blood enough still for the ritual.' She did not wait for a reply, simply strode out of the tent into the deluge. Richard, weakened and dizzy from drink, blood-loss and her sudden absence, leaned down and scooped the corpse of the messenger boy into his arms and, ducking through the canvas, stepped out after her.

DAWN.

There was little birdsong in the damp morning air. The rains had stopped two hours past midnight, bringing some relief to the beleaguered army, but the ground remained sodden. The grey reaches of the night would soon give way to pale morning sunlight.

Under other circumstances, the setting would have been idyllic. There was humidity in the air; the late summer heat that had been held at bay since Tudor's magi had brought the storm had finally returned. Water vapour steamed gently from the leaves of the trees and the air was thick with the scent of turned earth and the lazy buzz of insects.

Even the spirit of Nature seemed to be aware that a crossroads in history was being reached.

'Why stop the rain now?' Norfolk had barely slept. His tent was cramped and uncomfortable, and his anxieties had kept him awake into the small hours. He had taken the time to pray and to hope, but he was not optimistic. His mood was sour as he emerged into the damp August morning. 'What new devilry has Tudor planned?'

There was a buzz of activity in the King's camp. Battle smiths worked furiously, effecting last minute weapon and armour repairs. War horses stamped impatiently in anticipation, their harnesses and barding clattering. The infantry and archers were already lining up, mustering for the battle under the guidance of the King's most loyal men.

'Where is the King?' Northumberland had had just as appalling a night's sleep, and stretched aching limbs with a sour expression on his face as he joined Norfolk. 'He is not in the command pavilion.'

There was a ripple of activity on the far side of the camp, and Norfolk caught sight of a running figure pushing its way through the massed armies of King Richard. Another of the young message bearers; Norfolk recognised his nephew.

'Uncle!' The youth's face was pink with exertion. He had clearly been running for some time.

'What's the matter, William?' Norfolk grabbed hold of the boy as soon as he came into range and dragged him forward. 'Speak!'

'Tudor's army is in chaos, uncle. Three of his supporters have withdrawn from the field, taking their soldiers with them.'

Norfolk narrowed his eyes at his nephew. 'Are you certain of this, boy?' he said. 'Tudor is no fool, could they not simply be attempting to flank us?'

'I am sure, Uncle.' William nodded vigorously. 'The Earl of Oxford has been seen this very morning retreating south, his troops with him. He is most certainly abandoning Tudor. Two more are said to be leaving, but they have not yet broken camp.'

'Take scouts. Go and confirm these rumours, but do not spread word to the men just yet. False hope can break a man's back.' The boy nodded and bowed his head. Seeing the light of dawn beginning to creep above the eastern horizon, Norfolk found himself daring to hope. 'And William,' he added as the youth made to leave, 'find the King. We *must* find Richard.'

'Can this be true?' Northumberland moved a few steps towards Norfolk, keeping his voice as low as possible. 'If Oxford has truly gone ...'

'We can but hope, my friend.' Norfolk felt a strange tingling in the pit of his stomach. He did not recognise the sensation, but had he been pushed to put a name to it, he would have called it relief mingled with hope, as if fate had stepped aside and offered another choice. 'Perhaps Tudor may now be open to negotiations, although I do not believe the King will settle for words. Not after Tudor's betrayal. But before we can consider any course of action... we must find Richard.'

THEY FOUND HIM wandering to the south of Ambion Hill, in a state of what seemed to be drunken confusion. But there was no taint of alcohol on his breath. His skin was grey and clammy, and the flesh of his forearms and chest was laced with shallow lacerations. A physic was sent for, but Richard waved him away.

'To arms,' he said, vaguely. 'I must ready myself to meet Tudor.'

'Sire, listen to me. There is word from the camp of the enemy.' As succinctly as he could, Norfolk relayed the news William had brought, and watched for the King's reaction.

There was none save a brief flare of triumph in the King's dull eyes. He nodded his head.

'The day will be ours,' he said, his energy slowly returning to him. 'We must be ready to attack within the hour.'

'Sire, I thought... perhaps you might wish to negotiate with Tudor? Perhaps there may still be room for an allia...'

'When I want your advice, Norfolk, I will ask for it.' Richard's interruption came in a harsh tone that belied his sickly appearance. 'The time for negotiation has passed. Henry Tudor made his claim on my throne, and I...' There was a pause—less than a heartbeat—and the King corrected his own words. 'Henry Tudor made his claim on my throne and we will refute it with everything that we have. But try not to cut him down in the field. He doesn't deserve anything so honourable.'

A wild gleam came into Richard's eyes, enough to send a shiver of dread down the necks of the lords surrounding him. 'He will answer for his actions. The whole country will be made to understand the price of treachery and the danger of consorting with witches.'

The irony burned on his tongue and he fell into sullen silence.

THE HEAT OF the early morning gave way to a scorching August day. By the time the troops were fully mustered, the soggy grass was visibly steaming, days of endless rain evaporating into thin mist. Sure enough, within the hour, there had been the expected petition brought to the camp of Richard from the camp of Tudor. A plea for discussion. A chance at peace.

'"Lives could be spared if you will only meet with me,"' Richard read aloud, scorn in his voice as the anxious messenger waited for his response. '"Do not throw away this chance to save the lives of our countrymen."'

'Your answer, my lord?' Norfolk sat on his horse beside the King, now fully armoured and holding himself rigid in the saddle. The certainty and sense of confidence he radiated was completely infectious and the previously demoralised armies of the English King were now ready and willing to do battle.

'We will deliver our answer to Tudor personally,' said Richard, crumpling the hastily penned note. 'Let him hear it from the blades of our swords and the points of our arrows.' He glanced mockingly down at the runner. 'You have the time it takes to return to your master's side and warn him. We will be right behind you.'

The boy scampered down Ambion Hill, heading for the furrow between the two armies. To the side, Richard spied the forces of Lord Stanley and sneered. The fool still had not decided where his loyalties lay. The time had come to demonstrate to the doubting lord exactly who held power in England. 'Execute Lord Stanley's son immediately,' Richard growled. One of his officers looked as though he was about to object, but a warning glance from the King silenced any protest before it could begin.

'Loose arrows,' he said, levelling a finger at the fleeing messenger.

'Tudor will have our reply.'

A thousand arrows rose into the morning air, briefly darkening the sun and casting a grim shadow across the boy as he scrambled towards the camp of his master. He looked up, his expression filled with dread as the first of many arrows punched into his face. He screamed briefly, the shrill sound dissolving into a gurgle as his mouth filled with blood. Dozens more shafts sliced into his body, pinning him to the damp earth and hammering into the shields and men of Lord Stanley's force. Henry Tudor had his answer.

With a rallying cry, the troops of King Richard the Third began their assault.

When did I lose control?

Henry stood at the head of discomfited men, who had once formed perfect ranks of valiant warriors but who now clustered together as though they could somehow find safety in one another's proximity. Henry's closest advisor and master of his magi stood with his head bowed. Communing, no doubt, with the powers that had fled in the night.

The man's name was Hywel. He had promised victory through the application of magic both subtle and powerful, and Tudor did not doubt his ability. He had witnessed a taste of Hywel's phenomenal gift when he had conjured a creature from what the mage evasively called 'beyond.' It had worn the face of a woman and was full of whispered promises, but Tudor had not been fooled. He had asked only for magic to fuel his mages' spells and had given his little finger in tribute to seal the pact. With mastery over the weather and Richard's dread of the arcane he was confident it would be enough to ensure victory.

For three days a handful of Tudor's magi had ensured the rains fell. For three days and nights, working in shifts, they had murmured their eerie, arcane words and the skies had answered with rain and thunder. The plan had been to mire Richard's great army and fill them with the same fear as their King. And it had been working. Then, shortly after midnight on the eve of battle, the rain stopped.

'My lord. The spell will not answer us.' Hywel stood just outside his tent, deferential in his plain robes. His gentle accent was filled with an uncertainty that Tudor had never once associated with him. Hywel usually carried himself with the ease of a man who knew he could not be directly challenged, a man who knew that his power would protect him. Now his face, with its silvery-grey beard, was troubled.

'Hywel, you are not filling me with confidence.' Henry tried to inject some calm into his voice, to counter the panic he sensed lying just beneath the surface. Tudor was a personable young man, and people had flocked gladly to his banner. He had little experience in war, however, and had gladly deferred leadership of the army to Lord Oxford. It was a decision he was beginning to regret. With the failure of the magi and the greater numbers Richard had brought to the field, Oxford was in full retreat.

'The ritual was undisturbed and the words spoken, but the spell does nothing. The rains will not answer us.' Hywel looked deeply unsettled as he spoke, and it was clear that this was completely outside his experience.

'Then try again,' Tudor insisted.

'My lord,' the mage replied, 'we have tried again, and again. The spell no longer works, and I am at a loss to explain it.'

Further explanation was cut off by a scream from the hillside, as the hapless messenger was cut down by a storm of arrows. A huge wedge of knights bearing the King's own colours thundered from the crest of the hill toward the forces of Lord Stanley, followed by marching blocks of spearmen. The King had obviously decided to force the indecisive lord's hand or grind him into the mud.

One way or another, it would not be long before those knights and spearmen were bearing down on what remained of Tudor's army.

'To arms!' Henry roared as the first sounds of combat echoed across the field. Welsh and French soldiers hurried into formation, shields to the fore followed by a bristling forest of spears. Tudor returned his attention to Hywel. 'It would seem the time for subtlety is past. Use different spells, Hywel. Pull lightning from the heavens or fire from the winds and scour Richard's army from the hillside. I will win this battle, but I need your magi to do it.'

Hywel bobbed his head in assent and turned to his brothers. Together they made their way into the front ranks and began to call upon their magic, while Henry mounted up beside his personal guard. The scrum of fighting around Stanley's position was embarrassingly brief, and it was only a matter of minutes before Stanley's colours fell in beside those of King Richard.

'Hywel!' Tudor snapped at the mage. The drone of arcane words filled the air as the magi summoned their power and prepared to unleash the fury of the elements on the approaching army.

There was a pause, like an intake of breath, and then one of the magi exploded. Meat, blood and splintered bone painted the horrified warriors on the front line, who began pushing and shoving to get away from the grisly sight. Another mage burst into flames, rainbow-hued fire burning his robes to ash and immolating his flesh like a human candle. He howled in agony and staggered back into the ranks, scattering soldiers as he went. Tudor could only look on in horror as awful, unnatural fates consumed more of the magi, and his army dissolved into chaos.

The order to retreat was drowned out by the roar of King Richard's army and the growing thunder of hooves.

A Treatise On the Kings of England and the Rise of Magic: Bosworth and the Aftermath

by Brother Edmund of the
Order of St. Aidan, Royal Archivist
from his greater text A History of the Demon Kings, *second edition (1694)*

The history books would record the events of that day as the 'Bosworth Massacre,' and for good reason. The forces of King Richard destroyed those of Henry Tudor with no remorse and no mercy. The would-be usurper's men were slaughtered where they stood and Richard's army put them to rout.

The order was given for Henry Tudor to be taken alive, but it was not to be so. Neither was his death ever confirmed. The victory was complete less than three hours after King Richard's archers had loosed their first arrows on the enemy and despite the best efforts, Tudor's body could not be found amongst the dead.

Tudor had not been seen fleeing the field of battle, and his banner was found trampled and bloody among the bodies of his retainers. Scouts and huntsmen failed to find any trace of him in the lands beyond. It was decided, amidst much celebration, that Henry Tudor, usurper and traitor, had come to an unnatural end, and Richard's heart lifted with the joy and knowledge that came from his victory.

Only four prisoners were taken from the field that day. Each was a mage, and all of them mad and raving about their magic betraying them. Richard decreed that each be tried publicly, their torture and executions to be held variously in York, Ipswich, Warwick and London: the four cornerstones of England. To a man—or in one case, to a woman—each of the magic users raved about a great evil abroad in the world and that it would wear the crown of England. Their tormented claims and screams of denial served only to confirm their guilt and further condemn them.

King Richard's reign continued unbroken. By 1495, ten years after the Bosworth Massacre, he had fathered several strong, robust sons and a number of daughters and restored the name Plantagenet. In order to commemorate the House of York, he retained the symbolic rose, but he stained it forever black. He added four crimson drops of blood to the flag—*ad perpetuam memoriam*, so it is said, to the victory over the magi whose works had threatened to undo his great deeds upon the battlefield.

Richard remained hale and hearty, ruling a country that shrank back once more from the practice of magic and instead grew wise in the ways of strange, new sciences. A treaty of sorts was called with the French, and for five years, trade prospered between the two countries. It could not hope to last. Richard's eldest son, Prince Edward, led the troops of England in a successful campaign, winning the hearts and support of the English people as he did so. When Richard died in 1500 and was buried amidst much pomp and ceremony as was a king's due, his son was eagerly accepted as the nation's new ruler.

Edward was a force to be reckoned with; a warrior king who truly deserved the name. Like so many of the Plantagenets past, his soul burned with the desire to conquer, and he sought to make France fall under the yoke of British rule. His greed and ambition proved costly, and he died on the field of battle, murdered by a French magus, barely fifteen years after he took the throne.

The mantle passed to his son and namesake, Edward the Seventh, but the family curse took hold once more. Never as healthy as might have been desired for a man destined to be king, Edward's health failed within six months of his coronation. Despite the best efforts of the court healers and their alchemy, he died in his bed at the age of eighteen, giving rule of the country over to his younger brother, King Richard the Fourth.

From the moment he took the throne, the sixteen-year-old Richard made it quite clear that he was neither a weakling like his dead brother, nor the warrior king his father had been. Instead, he brought cunning and wisdom to the throne; a need to impose order on a country still crippled by disease and civil war. He took control of the great halls of power and nobility, including the influence of the Church itself.

Naturally, this drew the ire of Rome; the Pope demanded this upstart young king attend him immediately. Richard quite deliberately kept him waiting for five years. In 1530, following what are described best by other historians as 'extremely painful' negotiations, he dissolved the Crown's connections with the Roman Catholic Church. He stated that his people were free to worship however they wished, but as head of state, he ruled that no money would be granted to the Church from his coffers. Churches became poor, surviving on the charity of the faithful. The King decreed the cathedrals be stripped of their wealth, and the money used to fund the creation and development of the Royal Halls of Science.

Some of the money, however, went to the creation of the King's Inquisition. The men he recruited into its ranks were fervent enemies of magic in all its forms, and King Richard tasked them with rooting out those who dared to continue its vile practice. Farcical trials were held, which almost always ended in public executions not so different to the deaths of the Bosworth Four.

The King's Inquisition drew the cruellest, hardest-souled men in England. Latterly, women were also embraced into its ranks, despite widespread protest. By the time the King died at his own son's hands, the practice of magic had been recognised as a crime of treason. Trials became routine and then irrelevant, the word of the Inquisition becoming the word of the King, although a handful of Inquisitors clung to the tradition.

King Richard the Fifth ascended to his rightful place as heir to the throne of England in August of 1550, sixty-five years to the day after his ancestor slaughtered the armies of Henry Tudor.

The reign of the demon kings continues.

One

April, 1565
Horsham
England

Everyone agreed afterwards that the execution had been one of the most entertaining in years. The perpetrator's head had needed six powerful blows of the deliberately blunted axe before it parted from the body, and the King's Own Executioner had played to the caterwauling, hungry crowd with every stroke. Each blow was more theatrical and exaggerated than the last, and the gathered townsfolk had howled and jeered in adulation.

The headless corpse finally lay still, blood pulsing from its ragged stump and pooling on the wooden stage. In due course, two dull-eyed women arrived to clean the worst of the mess, but the old boards soaked up far more than the crones could ever hope to scrub away. The platform was worn and smooth, and the block itself stained ruddy from use and the countless lives that had ended upon it.

There were many memories in the wood of that stage. If only it could speak, people used to say, what tales it could tell. Whispers of things best left unsaid; of things that should never have been permitted.

After the execution was over, after the King's Own had hung up his crescent-bladed axe to await the next poor fool to violate King Richard's sacred law, everyone approved. A painful death was the only thing for heretics and traitors.

Arrest to execution had taken less than four days, one of the fastest the town of Horsham could remember, perhaps because of the nature of the man's crime. There had been no case for appeal.

The prisoner had freely acknowledged that the accusations were true. He had denied nothing and admitted everything.

William Eynon had once been a greatly respected citizen of the town. A talented alchemist and physic, his knowledge of the human body was unsurpassed for miles around. Whether treating simple coughs and sneezes, or healing a young boy with strangulation sickness, Will Eynon's medicinal skill was a precious gift to the people he treated. He had been a quiet, introverted man with a wife and young son to whom he was devoted. His generosity was well known and his compassion a rare gift in a time of hardship.

William Eynon, now cruelly beheaded before a baying mob. Public executions were intended to remind the people that Richard had ultimate power over every life in his kingdom. William Eynon may have been beloved in his community, but his grisly death served to remind people that nobody could commit treason and escape the law.

Treason.

The word held such terrible connotations. It seemed unlikely that a young physic the likes of Eynon could ever be found guilty of treachery against the King. But an Inquisitor had deemed his medical knowledge more than simple herb-craft and learning. More than the medicine practised by village midwives and wise women, with their salves and poultices. The accusation was that his talent had been bolstered by something greater. Empowered by that which King Richard feared above all else: the gift of magic. Or the curse, as was more commonly believed.

For one young woman, the execution represented much more than a man being brought to the King's justice. As she stood in the town square, long after the crowd had dispersed, Elizabeth Eynon could do nothing but stare with blank eyes at the spot where her husband's life had ended. He had sought her out in his last moments, his eyes fixing on hers before the executioner had pushed his head down to expose his neck. He had looked for her in the thronging crowd and he had found her. There had been nothing but love in her husband's final glance. Love, and an apology.

Forgive me, Bess.

He had spoken to her without words, just as he had done so many times throughout their courtship, and later, their marriage. She had never even truly noticed it. She had just—naively, it transpired—believed that their bond was that strong. Her initial reaction to the discovery that Will had been a practitioner of forbidden magic had been revulsion. But her deep-rooted love for the kindest man she had ever known, the memory of how many lives he had saved and how much pain he had relieved over the years...

I forgive you.

She mouthed the words silently as clouds gathered overhead, as if to mirror her sorrow. Will was no longer here to listen to the absolution, but she knew that somehow he would understand. His head had been taken by the Inquisitor to return to the court of King Richard. There it would remain, mounted on the walls of the Tower, until nothing of her handsome husband remained but a featureless skull. Such was the fate of the magi.

A breeze whipped the rough fabric of her skirts around her legs, and she paid it no heed. She stood staring at the stage with her hands clenched so tightly that her nails drew blood, but the pain was a welcome distraction. It balanced the grief that transfixed her and reminded her that life went on. She was beyond tears, the pain having already passed beyond that simple expression of grief and into an aching, iron band around her heart.

So she stood. Even when the rain began to fall, she stood, not knowing what to do or even where she could go that would be an escape from her loss. Had it not been for her young son, presently in the care of her sister, Elizabeth would have thrown herself on the mercy of the Inquisitor as well. But he had had no interest in her beyond interrogation. He had simply asked her questions—embarrassing, indecent and horrifying in equal measure—over and over again, while consulting with a little copper medallion. It had been enough to establish that William had been alone in his crime. She and Mathias would still suffer for it, however.

Mathias.

Thinking of her boy forced some kind of sensibility back into Elizabeth's numbed senses. She had to hold body and mind together, for his sake. He was barely a year old and already his life was marked with tragedy. The family home and assets had been seized by the King's Treasury, and other than the clothes on her back and a paltry sum of William's modest wealth that had been granted back to her, she had nothing. Her son, once poised to inherit the family holding, was now little more than a homeless pauper.

Her tears began to fall again, mingling with the rain that pooled at her feet in a mockery of the blood that had spilled on the stage only a few short hours earlier. Elizabeth took a shuddering breath and turned away from the only life she had ever known.

SEVERAL MILES AWAY from the now-deserted square of the small Sussex town, a group of men were returning to London. A broad, heavyset man in a dark, hooded cloak led the group, his body swathed in leather armour and looped with belts. Numerous pouches, pockets and purses jounced around his frame, filled with trinkets and esoteric devices of his trade, and he openly wore a heavy sword and pistols at his waist. He rode with his head down against the driving rain, while behind him trailed his small retinue, six thugs who muttered and bickered amongst themselves. Despite the sturdy cobbles of the King's roads, the weather had forced them to slow from a gallop to a walk, and their crude banter was becoming a distraction to Charles Weaver's thoughts.

One of only eight people in the entire kingdom to hold the position of King's Inquisitor, Weaver was a snarling brute of a man. He had joined the Inquisition, fiery and ambitious, at the age of sixteen, and in the five years he had served his masters had ripped his way through the ranks with unsurpassed ferocity. Still young, he was formidable and unequalled: nobody had delivered as many heads to the feet of Richard the Unyielding as Charles Weaver.

They called him humourless, but never to his face. Weaver thought nothing of disposing of those he considered weak or ineffective. The trail of the dead in his wake consisted of more than just those he hunted. Those who dared speak against him, against the King or just out of turn met a swift end.

'Yer honour?' The voice belonged to one of the mercenaries who were so often an unwelcome necessity in his pursuits. Weaver preferred to travel alone and despised the casual blasphemy and petty vice of others, but sometimes his prey would try to run, and every huntsman needed his hounds, however odious they might be.

'Excuse me? Yer honour?' The wheedling voice spoke again and Weaver turned to regard the approaching rider. An errant breeze whipped the hood from the Inquisitor's face, revealing green eyes glittering behind a featureless iron mask. He said nothing, but the movement was enough to acknowledge the speaker's presence. The scraggly-bearded man who had spoken scratched at his thin, pointed nose. The mercenary clearly didn't want to speak to him, but had been bullied into the task by his comrades. It was in the stance, the way he shuffled uncomfortably in the saddle. In the way the narrow eyes squinted at him with such anxiety. Charles Weaver had devices at his disposal for drawing out the truth and revealing the unseen, but he was also very good at reading people. It was part of what made him so very good at his job.

'Yer honour, me and the lads was just hoping that we could maybe... find an inn or something? It's a bit... well, it's miserable, an' we're soaked through.' He indicated his soggy clothing.

Weaver's head moved a fraction more, turning to fix the sodden group whose notably less expensive mounts were plodding along the road behind him. Then he turned back to the speaker, who persisted gamely.

'We're all a bit, well, cold, yer honour. And hungry, tell the truth. Ain't eaten since before the execution.' The speaker twisted his damp tunic in his hands. 'Something hot inside us wouldn't go amiss.'

The King's Inquisitor blinked slowly. There was something unsettling in the gesture, briefly closing off the link to the human beneath the mask. The spokesman suppressed a shiver not entirely brought on by the cold. He never knew a blink could convey such contempt.

'Inns are a cesspool of corruption and heresy,' Weaver said eventually. His voice was slow and ponderous; a deep, bass rumble that could be heard even across a crowded room. The iron mask added a hollow, sepulchral tone that chilled the blood. Charles Weaver had not once been heard to shout. He did not need to. 'If I find reason to suspect any of you are involved in vice or villainy, then I will scourge the wickedness from you personally. Am I understood?'

'Yes, yer honour.' The spokesman's eyes lingered on the tools of Weaver's trade, hanging from the richly-tooled leather belt at his waist. More were stored in the saddlebags, but Weaver knew the importance of first impressions. Few things created such a good first impression as a serrated-edged torture knife. 'Perfectly clear.'

'Then ride ahead and find an inn. And be sure that it is a clean one. Inform the innkeep precisely who it is that you travel with and that we are not pilgrims to be fleeced by moneysnatchers. I am certain that will make them more accommodating. Stables for the horses, food and a bed for the night. We will depart at dawn.' Weaver pulled the hood back up over his head, reached within the folds of his cloak and tossed a bag of coins at the man.

'Why do you tarry? Go.'

'At once, yer honour.' The snivelling toady bowed and galloped away. Weaver turned his attentions back to the road ahead and ignored the excited whispering from behind him. They would no doubt end up in the kind of establishment that the men thought suitable for a man the calibre of Charles Weaver. Lice-ridden mattresses, rats in the kitchen...

It didn't matter. Not really. The task had been completed. He had rooted out another heretic and the execution had been satisfactory enough. The mage's head was packed in a sack tied to his saddlebags, and by this time the next day, he would kneel before his liege-lord and present it. Richard would reward him handsomely and send him out on the hunt again. It was what Weaver lived for. Not the money or the vast estate in Kent where he never spent any time. The reward he hungered for came with the blood of magi and the praise of his King.

The rain continued to pour, washing the countryside in shades of grey and slicking the cobbles so that they shone in the failing light. A pall of darkness hung in the sky to the north.

London.

* * *

Whitehall Palace
England

'COME BACK TO bed, Richard.'

King Richard the Fifth of England, Richard the Unyielding, stood at the open window of his bedchamber. Dirty rain sluiced from the palace roof, streaking the walls with ash and soot, the refuse from the many chimneys and fire stacks that pierced the London skyline. Even at this hour, the ring of metal and the hue and cry of chain-gangs echoed in the streets, keeping the foundries burning. Pools of pale light dotted the palace grounds, crystal globes of lambent gas fastened to iron spars casting an eerie glow in the evening gloom. Richard dreamed of a day when such wonders lined the streets of every English town and village, the light of science casting out the shade of magic once and for all.

The King wore only a loose shirt to cover his nudity, and even then only barely. Behind him, his queen was stretched out languidly on the soft feather pillow, unashamedly naked. He glanced at her appreciatively. Her full figure, admired by so many, had softened over the years. The birth of their five children had given her a pearly network of marks on her belly, and had forced her girlish curves into those of a woman. Her meticulous attention to her appearance caused sensations at court; any number of young noblewomen sought to emulate her style, but none succeeded.

Tresses of a striking shade of burnished copper fell to the middle of her back when she wore her hair loose. Right now, her hair lay over her naked breasts, sending a new wave of desire through the King. He adored her.

For a fleeting moment, Richard took the rare opportunity to forget his troubles and simply enjoyed looking at her, the smooth, alabaster flesh of her body laid bare for him to do with as he pleased. Their lovemaking had been more gentle than usual this evening. Richard was a harried, frenetic lover, servicing his wife with the focused energy that he applied to most things. But he had needed some comfort this night. Anna had given him that.

Strange how it had turned out. It had been a marriage of convenience rather than of desire; she was the eldest daughter of the present High Lord of Scotland, and his father, King Richard the Fourth, had arranged the marriage as a part of the treaty. Richard had been disgusted at the thought of marrying into the barbarous apes of the northlands. He had raged against his father's decree for months, whilst around him, his younger siblings married whomever they desired.

But he had changed his mind the moment Anna had stepped from the carriage that had brought her down from Scotland and delivered her into his life. A beauty even at the tender age of fifteen, she captivated him, and it soon became apparent that she possessed a startling intelligence and quick wit that matched her new husband easily. Necessity had swiftly given way to the kind of deep, abiding love that Richard had never thought possible.

Over the decades, and through careful marriage, some of the physical deformities had been bred out of the Plantagenet line. King Richard the Fifth was just coming into his prime, and unlike his oft-derided ancestor, he was passably handsome. He was taller than his father had been, with a rangy set to his muscles. Portraits of the long-gone Henry the Second could have been swapped with his own and few could have told the difference.

Richard John Edward Plantagenet had come to the throne at the age of twenty-four. For fifteen years he had reigned, a hale, healthy and vigorous man, during which time the face of England had altered dramatically. Advancements in everything from weaponry to construction, combined with blueprints obtained at great cost from Italy, had allowed his country to develop faster than he ever could have dreamed. The English fleet, bolstered with ironclads and dreadnoughts, was the terror of the seas.

Being gifted with an inherent ability to understand and appreciate engineering, Richard spent long hours in meetings with the land's greatest architects, smiths and builders, working with them to realise and improve da Vinci's designs. Workshops, foundries and shipwrights worked day and night, producing ever more potent and terrifying weapons for his army and navy. When England returned to France, it would be an invincible machine, ready to roll across Europe and free it of the yoke of magic.

And the time *would* come. Of that, Richard had no doubt.

'Richard?' Anna moved to stand behind him, her arms wrapped around his waist. 'What's wrong?' Her soft voice was accented lightly, the Scots burr having faded in her time in the English court. She still had all the Celtic fire that so endeared her to him, though.

He turned around and looked down at her, her pale skin contrasting strongly with his own tanned flesh. Richard was not the kind of man to sit idly at court all day while streams of courtiers curried for a word or boon. He left that business to others. He planned and studied, he trained with the armies. He spent as much time as possible away from the throne his ancestors had fought so desperately to take.

Because he was acutely aware of the price that had been paid for that throne. A price that might one day be exacted from his own flesh and blood. He had learned the truth from his father in those fateful minutes before he had wrung the last breath from the old King's body. He recalled the pride in his father's eyes as the light had faded from them. He had borne aloft the dagger that had killed a long line of illustrious kings and he had tasted the power in his blood, the power in his very soul.

'Nothing of note, my love,' he replied, the lie coming easily to his lips, as every lie did. 'Let's go back to bed. Weaver should be returning tomorrow with the head of the Sussex witch. There will be feasting and celebration.'

'I do not like him.' Her rosebud lips pouted prettily and he smiled indulgently. If this strong man, this solid king had one weakness, she was standing right before him. He patted her cheek fondly.

'Charles Weaver is a great Inquisitor,' he said. 'He will drive the shadows out of my kingdom. He will pave the way for the advance of enlightenment free of the infernal magi and their arcane superstitions.'

'He is evil,' she persisted, and Richard's pat on her cheek became something entirely less friendly. She shrank back and he pulled her to him, immediately contrite.

'So are they, my love,' he said and led her back to the bed, reaching up to pull the curtain around them. 'So are they.'

Two

August, 1589
Portsmouth
England

ISAAC BONNINGTON KNEW that the *Indomitable* was unlike any other vessel in the King's Fleet. The fact gave him great pride. He had brought the initial designs to court and stood, visibly trembling, whilst the King had pored over them in mute reflection. Isaac was not a brave man, but he knew how to build gunships. He understood the workings of black powder weaponry with fine precision, and when he had come to choose his career, he had wavered between becoming a shipwright and taking an apprenticeship at the Hall of Science. The apprenticeship had won out in the end, and in time, the position of Royal Engineer had come to him.

But ships had ever been his first love, and it was the shipyards of the south coast that were now his home. He was a quiet, intelligent man in his late forties, with a balding pate and a rat-like face that was incapable of concealing emotion. Women and children had entirely failed to feature in his life, and so he devoted every waking moment to his craft and, of late, to the *Indomitable*. When she was launched, when the French fleet felt the bite of her cannon and broke before her prow, the world would know of Isaac Bonnington's work. This ship would immortalise his name.

Who knows, he thought with uncharacteristic bitterness, he might even get paid. He was certain that if he approached the King and asked for an advance, he might find himself replaced with someone King Richard considered more patriotic and less materialistic. Others had ended their days in the Tower for less.

Since he had taken the throne of England, Richard the Unyielding had proven himself to be a man gifted with drive and determination. Blessed with a fierce intellect that grasped the principles of construction and engineering, the King possessed knowledge of the sciences quite beyond the most gifted scholars. Heavy industry had flourished in the cities of England. The cannon of the *Indomitable* had been cast far from Portsmouth and transported down from Liverpool by ship, while the plates that armoured her hull were beaten in a forge in Manchester.

There was no shortage of bodies to work the furnaces, swing the hammers and dig the mines, as criminals and the homeless were pressed into service. Shackled work gangs toiled in shifts to pull iron, copper, tin and coal from the earth and feed the fires of industry. Labourers and artisans worked the forges and foundries to produce the wonders of Richard's kingdom. It was dangerous work, but not without its benefits. Those free men and women in service to the Crown were well paid for their efforts, though it was argued by some that the risks outweighed the rewards. Richard did not tax his vassals heavily, but he taxed them all. Farmers, once exempt from the need to present their annual accounts, now had to employ the literate and numerate to control their spending. Failure to provide to the Crown guaranteed a stint in a work gang.

Freedom was a thing long forgotten in England. But Isaac didn't mind. He was happy in his little office with its tiny window that let in the reek of the port. The odour of the shipyards clung to him; the constant smell of tar, metal and brine. He had grown so accustomed to it that he no longer noticed it, although it was the *first* thing his visitors noticed.

From the comparative comfort of that snug office, Isaac sighed heavily, dragging his eyes back from the window overlooking the expansive docks, and turned his attention to the pile of missives that had mounted up in the past few days. Money, while certainly important, had never been a preoccupation of Isaac's. He craved immortality—he wanted to be known and remembered, like a great playwright or poet—and his work would be his route to that dream. It was a constant frustration that others did not share his enthusiasm. Casualties among the chain-gangs working on the hull had made them surly and intractable. The labourers fitting the guns had not been paid on time. An engineer responsible for the labyrinthine engines had lost both hands in an accident. They were still on schedule, but the cost had been heavy. Isaac's eventual fee was going to be a fraction of what it had been at the beginning.

He sighed again and pushed the invoices to one side. Money was a terrible necessity. Instead, he let his attention drift out of the small window and fix on the iron spars of the *Indomitable*. He had wanted to name her the *Lady Jane*, in tribute to his long-dead mother, the woman who had once stood with him on these very docks marvelling at the beautiful ships that came and went. He had even once seen a barge full of prisoners, being taken off to serve in the King's Navy as oarsmen and loaders.

But the King had vetoed his suggestion, insisting on something that conveyed the spirit of the vessel. In his heart, Isaac still called her the *Lady Jane*.

The *Indomitable* was still in dry dock, but the modified design of her carrack body was beyond a doubt the single most beautiful thing that Isaac had ever seen. She had been delivered into his hands as plunder from a naval action in Portuguese waters, whole and complete, and had saved both time and money by providing a stable base from which he could develop something unique.

When she had come into Isaac's possession, she had been blessed with seven decks and thirty-two guns. Now she had only six decks, but thanks to Isaac's designs, she had more than doubled in size and arsenal. The ship was massive. Some even considered it to be impossible that so much iron could take to the waves. But smaller ironclads had already proven themselves, and would spearhead the fleet with their armoured hulls.

Isaac watched as one of the vessel's massive cannons was lowered slowly onto the upper deck. They had yet to be tested at sea, but he had attended a demonstration on the royal estate and the results had been terrifying and astonishing in equal measure. When Richard grew bored of his treaty with the French, their naval forces would be crushed. With the *Indomitable* at their head, the English would be invincible; heathen magic would yield to the purity of science.

Word at court suggested that the war that was inevitable was barely months away. The pressure to ensure that the *Indomitable* was seaworthy was immense.

Thinking of court provoked a pang of guilt. Isaac had not attended the King for several weeks now, claiming that he was needed at the docks. Before long, he would receive the kind of summons that came in person, and was not to be ignored.

He refused to dwell on it. Instead, Isaac gazed at the armoured flanks and bladed prow of the vessel. The *Indomitable* would put to sea in the spring and would claim the Channel as her own. Nothing would stand against her, and seafaring folk the world over would speak Isaac Bonnington's name in hushed whispers. But his thoughts didn't rest on one thing for long, and soon, he was poring over the blueprints for another, different project. A project unlike anything else.

When he completed the *Lionheart*, the King's power would be absolute.

Hampton Court
England

'GIVE ME THE monthly tally.' King Richard crooked the little finger of his right hand at the black-clad man standing before the throne. Charles Weaver bowed deeply and took a piece of parchment from the hands of one of the minions crouched behind him. He cleared his throat and began to speak. His voice, distorted as always by the faceless mask that was the mark of his office, read out the figures in a calm tone.

'In the month of June, in the county of Sussex, following twenty-seven accusations of open practice of witchcraft, fifteen resulted in execution. The remainder were given the choice of re-examination in the Tower or industrial servitude. All chose the latter.'

He continued reading from the parchment, each county broken down accordingly. Forty in this county, six in that. The city of London had seen only two executions. The practitioners of magic had long since fled to the country, in the mistaken belief that Richard's Inquisition would not find them.

As head of the Inquisition, Weaver imposed an iron rule that execution was never the only possible outcome of an accusation. It was too easy for the greedy, the cowardly and the vindictive to point the finger of treason, so Inquisitors were very thorough in their investigations. A man innocent of witchcraft might find light cast on other deeds worthy of punishment, and some charlatans claimed to possess the gift of magic to enhance their status or business. Most offenders chose industrial servitude for their transgressions, a punishment shared by those who made false accusations. Left free, false accusers were ridiculed and often murdered by their own former friends, disgusted by their lies.

In total, well over two hundred executions had taken place across the breadth of Richard's kingdom in June. Ten more than in May. Nearly fifty more than in the same month of the previous year. The King nodded as Weaver finished his report. The Inquisitor rolled the parchment back up, sliding it into the ornate scroll case that he usually wore on his belt.

'The problem remains and continues to grow,' he concluded.

'And what of the highlands and valleys?'

'They remain troublesome, my lord. Those that flee your good justice are embraced by the north and west. The Inquisition alone cannot scour every hill and cave, and the people remain hostile to our presence. Work on the Wall has been delayed due to the recent rains, but it will pick up pace as soon as the weather turns.' Weaver's voice took on a faintly irritated tone. 'If we were to use the army, we could sweep the heathens from our borders forever. Could the move on France not be delayed...'

'No.' Richard interrupted Weaver's question. The High Inquisitor had asked every month, and every month the King gave him the same answer. 'The invasion will go ahead as planned. A few dirty hedge magi on the borders are a mere nuisance beside the threat posed by the French and their neighbours.' He paused for a moment, irritated that he was unable to completely purge his own isle. His instructions for the timing of the invasion had been quite explicit, and while supreme power rested with the King, it was not the only power at work in England.

'Thank you for your report, Inquisitor Weaver. Your concern is noted, I will grant the Inquisition more men for the prosecution of their duties, that they might better bring our justice to the barbarians. Now please be seated.' All eyes watched the big masked man as he took his seat. Silence reigned for a moment longer and then Richard turned his attentions to more pleasant matters.

'I have received word from Isaac Bonnington,' he began. Bonnington's sporadic attendance at court had birthed a quiet joke that the engineer was nothing more than a figment of the King's imagination. 'Progress on the flagship has continued apace and we should be in a position to strike at France before summer ends.' A slow smile crept onto his face. 'The ironclads will sweep the French fleet aside and deliver our armies onto their beaches. The country will be ours. And we will strike them at their very heart.'

Weaver raised his masked head, hungry for the words to drop from his King's lips. This was the very thing toward which he had been working for so long.

'We will stamp out magic across the continent. And then, when they have all been brought to heel, we will turn our attention to Rome. We will bring the light of purity and reason to that nest of magi.'

The King's words brought a pleasing murmur of assent from the assembled nobles. For many years, England had been hovering on the edges of hostility with the rest of Europe. She had grown increasingly isolated, rejecting magic and shunning the Church in favour of Richard's vision of a secular nation.

More pleasant matters. Everything was relative when you were the King of England.

Gloucestershire,
England

THE TOWER OF London was Charles Weaver's base of operations, but he rarely remained within its walls for long. The home of the

Inquisition had become the most terrifying edifice in England. King Richard had granted the Order the fortress to use as barracks, prison and workshop. To most it was simply referred to as 'the Tower' and was a byword for fear and suffering. Iron brackets lined its walls, adorned with decaying heads, a horrifyingly graphic demonstration of the consequences of treason. No prisoner taken within its walls had ever been released, and it was rumoured that its deep dungeons rang perpetually with the screams of the tormented.

They were fanciful tales that the Inquisition did nothing to discourage, but for all its fearful reputation and dark history, the Tower was as much a place of invention and learning as it was a gaol. The Inquisition employed the best smiths, artisans and alchemists outside of the royal court, all turned toward the singular purpose of documenting and hunting magi. The Inquisitors' masks had been forged within its walls under the instruction of the King, offering intimidation, protection and anonymity.

The influx of fresh mercenaries presented an opportunity not to be missed, so only a day later the High Inquisitor was glad to be on the road again with thirty men at his heels, heading for the Welsh border. A community near the site of Richard's wall had been brazen in their use of the arcane, but had been allowed to go unpunished for want of men. The time had now come, however, for them to face the King's justice. Treason could not—and would not—be tolerated.

The settlement was home to a handful of families. Crudely built roundhouses, large enough to house a dozen people each, were secreted on the edge of woodland scrub. A clear brook bubbled at the edge of the village and snaked away down the fertile valley to feed a small, scrubby stretch of patchy fields.

Weaver shook his head at the stupidity of the people. That they sincerely believed that they would not be caught was an affront to his profession. That they did nothing to conceal their crime was an insult to his office. If they attempted to excuse their actions, it would offend him personally.

Many of the people in this place possessed magic. Weaver knew it the moment he approached. The air prickled with it. Over the years, he had come to recognise its taint. Just as black powder weapons gave off a distinct odour, so did the use of magic. He didn't even need to employ his tools to identify the people as magi, though the blue sparks that crawled over his copper talisman said as much.

'Please, my lord. Do not do this. Have mercy on us, I beg you.'

Weaver sat atop his destrier and gazed down at the desperate villager. He was healthy for a peasant, his skin browned by outdoor work and his rough clothing of better quality than the Inquisitor commonly saw among the lower classes. A small nod encouraged the man to speak further, and he did.

'There are only a few families living here. Six babes in arms, my lord. Six babies, and some older children. We do nobody any harm. We are peaceful. We grow our crops with our magic, nothing more. Please, my lord. We want and expect nothing from the Crown. Please, leave us be.'

'Do you practise magic openly?'

'No!' A hesitation before the unfortunate man changed his mind. He looked beyond Weaver to the retinue he had brought with him. Thirty strong men on horses, armed variously with crossbows and swords. 'Yes,' he amended. 'But we only do it here, we don't teach it to others. I thought that if we kept quiet, looked to our own, that we might be left alone, too. We use magic, yes. But we keep it to ourselves and only use it for good...'

Weaver snorted. Then he spoke in his deep, rich tones. 'And who, pray tell, are you to judge what is good or otherwise? The law of the land is quite clear'—Weaver looked down at the scroll he had taken from the Tower—'Master Edward Mason. Yet you not only ignore it, you openly flout it. You think to wave your notion of "good" at me as though it is some kind of defence?'

Weaver rolled up the parchment and slid it back into its case. He reached up, and for a moment, Edward Mason thought he would remove his mask. But Weaver's fingers only touched its contours, a gentle caress down the featureless metal. He invested his next words with all the authority at his disposal, yet still with that tone of bored disdain. 'By order of His Majesty King Richard the Fifth of England, it is my duty to confirm that, in the sight of the most Royal Inquisition, this village has sinned. Its evil will be cleansed from the land by fire and the curse of magic cast out. By order of the King...' He leaned forward and dropped his voice to barely more than a whisper. 'By order of the King and by order of the Lord Inquisitor.'

'Magic is not a curse.' The man's passion was evident in every syllable as he allowed his fervour to overtake his fear and desperation.

Several of Weaver's retinue sucked in their breaths loudly and shook their heads. Mason ignored them and forged on. 'Magic is no curse. It has blessed us. Through our magic, our crops have grown strong. See!' He gestured down the valley to the fields rippling in the wind.

'Hoarding food is a crime. Keep going, Master Mason. With every word you forge the nails for your own coffin. Keep speaking.'

Mason pressed on, desperate now. 'It has cured sickness and given us healthy children. We live quiet lives. We're no threat to the King or anybody! None of us would know how to do harm with magic. It only protects us, and brings food to our tables.'

'You say that you have no intent to cause harm to others with your curse.' Weaver's laugh was not a pleasant sound. 'But it can be turned to such an end. Magic is a weapon as much as it is a tool. Do you know the minds of every man, woman and child here? Who is to say that they will not turn against the King? There are traitors everywhere, Master Mason.'

'Yes, but there are none of them here! We are peaceful, truly. None of us has the capacity to harm the King, neither would we wish him ill.' Mason drew a shuddering breath and began a fresh bout of pleading, albeit with noticeably less conviction than before. 'Please, my lord. Reconsider. The children! I beg you to think of them. Would you truly see them left alone? Left abandoned in the woods to die? Or do you intend to slay innocents as well?'

These were poor words to choose and Weaver's hand curled into a fist. 'I do not slay innocents, Master Mason. You further damn yourself with every word you utter, but I promise you this before this ends. Your children will not die. There is ever a need for more hands in the King's mines and foundries. With their own hands, your children will lay the foundations of King Richard's new world.'

'You intend to steal our children from us?' Edward Mason was not a violent man. His life was forfeit, that much he knew, but if he could spare the others, or even just the children, the horror of what awaited them, then he would be satisfied.

A peal of thunder rumbled somewhere in the distance and Weaver looked up from the conversation and stared out over the darkening horizon. Rain was falling on the hills and crags a few miles away, grey curtains sweeping the tops and shrouding the end of the valley with mist. It would be here soon.

'You are mistaken,' he said, his voice distant. 'I plan to collect the orphans when this village is no more.'

The last word Edward Mason ever uttered was little more than a hoarse whisper.

'Please.'

The Inquisitor kicked the peasant in the throat, the toe of his boot suddenly sprouting a blade as he did so. 'I grow weary of your hollow pleas. This village is guilty.' He turned with cold indifference from the dying man. 'Burn it all. Take the children. And bring some of the stronger ones alive.'

Weaver always tried to take some alive. Sometimes they knew about other magi and could be persuaded to part with the information. The dungeons of the Tower were deep, and at least some of the rumours concerning them were true.

DEMONS: MYTH OR TRUTH?

by Brother Edmund of the
Order of St. Aidan, Royal Archivist
from his greater text A History of the Demon Kings, *second edition (1694)*

LEGENDS OF DEMONS and monsters have existed as long as Man has walked these isles. The Church writings claim that demons are creatures from Hell; spirits of evil, cruelty and destruction. But the myths are older than Christianity. In pagan texts, demons are just one of many terrible and fantastic creatures. Fairies. Imps. Pixies. Will-o'-the-Wisps. All have their own curious tales.

Much is simple folklore, but many cling to it even in these more enlightened days of science: the maid puts out milk for the pixies to keep them from stealing children away, for example, while the smith nails a horseshoe over the door of his forge to ward off evil. The stories are believed by many, and the superstitions are practised by the peasantry in their thousands. Educated men and the nobility scoff at such fanciful and archaic notions, but is there any truth to the claims of ghosts and ghouls, devils and demons?

There are written accounts of folk suffering visits from what they call ghosts. Most of these stories suggest an unquiet spirit of the dead, a soul denied the peace of the grave, who returns to haunt people and places familiar to them in life whilst they seek restitution. Absolution for their sins, perhaps, or as some fancifully believe, just the right to ensure their families are faring well without them.

Many of these ghosts seem benign, others less so. There are tales of a murderous coachman who returned from the dead and prowls the roads of Kent at night. There is another concerning a headless horseman, and still others of the dreadful *beann-sidhe* and ghostly wraiths who haunt churchyards, ever yearning for their eternal rest. It is also a sad (but factual) truth that many of those who have claimed to witness these phantoms were peasants who were latterly declared to be mad.

Demons and devils, though, are something apart from these little tales. The Church names them as the minions of Satan, creatures of wickedness to be feared and reviled, tormentors of fallen souls. There is great power in names. Is it not possible, for example, that *demon* is merely another name for something that others would call a 'ghost'? Or a fairy, pixie or hobgoblin?

One thing is for certain. All of these things, should they exist, are not of this world, which begs the question—where *are* they from?

Some folklore suggests the existence of another world; one which lies between life and death. A place through which the spirits of the dead pass on their way to their eternal rest. Sometimes, they cannot find passage, and return to the only world they know—the origin, perhaps, of ghosts. What would such a place be like? Would the shades of the dead and mostly-dead walk freely as we do? Would it be as the world we know, or subtly different? Would good and evil exist in a way we understand, or would they be given form by those who name them demon or angel?

A long dead magus once suggested that this 'other world' is closer than we believe, and is the source of all magic. He warned that no good could come from meddling too much in what we did not understand. He chose to call it the *Aetherworld* and I find the term pleasing.

Those who claim to speak to the dead tend towards being charlatans who ply their trade to bring comfort to the recently bereaved. It is highly unlikely that they truly speak with those who dwell in the Aetherworld. It will likely forever be a mystery, and perhaps, if the magi are to be believed, that is as it should be.

THREE

August, 1589
Cwm Heddychol
Wales

'YOUR MAGIC IS good, Mathias Eynon.'

The young man at the 'business end' of the cow looked up from his task and shook his head. 'No magic here, Llewellyn. Just patience and understanding.'

The older of the two men in the cow's barn shook his head. 'No,' he disagreed. 'She wouldn't settle for me. Just one pat from you and she calmed.' Indeed, the cow was contentedly chewing the cud whilst Mathias focused on the extremely physical task of rearranging the tangle of limbs inside her womb. Had he not arrived when he did, the cow would be dead now. She had been struggling to birth the calf, which had been lying badly. Mathias's efforts had not only calmed the frantic, panicking creature, but had prepared the calf for a more normal delivery. It was hard, heavy, extremely messy work, but Mathias did it anyway. The heifer carried on chewing, her labour pains apparently forgotten whilst the young man worked.

He had always had a way with animals, and it was that ability which had finally given him a skill with which he could return the debt he owed to the small Welsh village in which he resided. He had a ready eye for herbs, and could put together poultices that soothed fractious cattle or horses. He knew instinctively what was wrong with a creature just by sitting quietly with it for a short time. No animal, people laughed, could resist the charms of the friendly young man.

'It's her time now, Llewellyn. Do you want to help her with the birthing? I could use a break.'

'Sure, lad. Go clean up in the water trough. Will you stay close, though? Just in case...?' The heifer looked up as the two men swapped positions, her soft brown eyes calm. She had birthed two dead calves in the past, and Mathias knew that Llewellyn feared for this third. It had certainly felt very alive to him.

He had stripped his clothing from the waist up on arrival, anticipating the task, and so it was an easy thing to plunge his arms into the trough and let the liquid pour, cool and soothing, over his aching body. He was not particularly large or even particularly strong; 'all rabbit and little beef' was a phrase commonly employed to describe him. Llewellyn may not have had Mathias's way with animals, but he had breadth of shoulder. He took over the delivery with ease.

Mathias knew he had bent the truth just a little. He *had* used magic to calm the beast. His gift with animals certainly ran far deeper than mere understanding. His instincts were too sharp and well-honed to be natural. But his mother, dead nearly twenty years, had told him of the fate met by a father whose only crime had been to help others, and even here, amongst people to whom magic was a gift and a blessing, Mathias kept his own counsel.

'She had the calf yet?' A girl's voice, much-loved, pulled Mathias from his reverie. He looked over the stall fence to where Tagan, the blacksmith's eldest daughter, stood. She was still wearing her leather forge apron, and her pretty face was smudged and dirty. With a complete lack of self-consciousness, she gave him a beaming smile. Her dark hair, cut boyishly short, clung to her scalp and face with sweat. The smile woke the dimples in her cheeks and Mathias smiled back. He loved her; she loved him. In an otherwise complicated and frequently confusing world, that was the one certainty.

'Not yet,' he reported, 'but it won't be long.' He nodded towards the cow, who had engaged in a sort of push-pull match with the farmer. The big man had his hands around the calf's legs and was tugging with all his might. The cow seemed reluctant to release her offspring to the world.

Tagan leaned on the wooden stall, watching with bright blue eyes. Mathias allowed himself the luxury of admiring his betrothed.

When she and Mathias had first met as children, they had hated one another with a passion. He was quiet and preferred to keep to himself—a product of his mother's paranoia. Tagan, the eldest of six girls, was boisterous and playful and used to pester Mathias. They fought and argued, scrapped and squabbled and by the time both of them were young adults, it was clear that they were destined to be together.

He adored her. She was everything he was not. Fiery—which, given her magical ability, was not so surprising—and feisty, gregarious and confident, and pragmatic enough for the both of them. She was able to pull Mathias free of the brooding moods into which he frequently slipped, and for that alone he loved her.

'Here we go!' Llewellyn couldn't keep the joy from his voice as the calf slid from its mother onto the straw beneath her. It lay still for a few moments and then four long limbs began to twitch. 'Well done, old girl!' Llewellyn patted the cow's flank. 'A fine little heifer!'

'Oh!' Tagan breathed as she witnessed the calf's first moments. All of them had seen many animals born over the years—cattle, horses, even cats and dogs—but the miracle of new life never failed to bring joy. 'Oh, Mathias, she's lovely!'

'Thank you, lad.' Llewellyn watched as the little calf struggled to her feet and stumbled blindly for a moment or two before finding her mother and beginning to suckle noisily. 'Thank you.'

'Don't thank me,' Mathias said, watching the mother and daughter for a moment as he gathered his things together. 'She did all the work. She should be fine, but sprinkle some of this on her feed. It'll keep her milk rich and give the little one strength.' He handed over a pouch, which Llewellyn took gratefully. 'I'll look in on her tomorrow.' His gaze roved over to where Tagan stood, her eyes held by the beauty of the little creature, and Llewellyn smiled.

'Sure, lad.' The farmer paused for a moment, then lowered his voice to a gentle tone that was rare for him. 'Your mother would have been proud.'

* * *

The words had been simple, but it was clear to Tagan that Llewellyn's parting sentence to Mathias had left an impression. She didn't really recall Elizabeth Eynon that well, and Mathias rarely—if ever—spoke of her. Today, prompted by Llewellyn's words, she felt a moment of bravery.

'You never talk about her much.'

Her arm was linked through Mathias's. They were walking down from Llewellyn's farm to the village. Nestled in a dell deep within the Welsh valleys, the settlement lived in the shadow of craggy hills on three sides. Several streams splashed down from the moors, often swollen by the rains, and gathered in a pond in the centre of the village before flowing away down the valley. The current was not naturally strong enough to turn a mill, but it did so anyway, with a little arcane encouragement.

He looked at her, pulled out of his reverie. 'I wasn't that old when she died. I suppose I don't really remember that much about her. She was happy when she came here, though. I remember that. I understand why.' They were walking alongside one of the brooks, going slightly out of their way so they could steal a few precious moments together. Mathias paused to reach down, trailing one hand through the cool running waters. A few sticklebacks flitted about anxiously, disturbed by the motion, then settled back into lazily drifting along with the current. A little way up-river, Mathias knew, was a small settlement of monks who used the pure water in their brewing process. The ale from the monastery was unsurpassed in the region.

The summer had been hot and dry everywhere in the country that year, but the hanging trees alongside the brook offered some relief from the stifling heat of the day, and for Tagan, the heat of the forge.

'Do you think she is happy for you? I mean, do you think...' Her hesitant question brought a laugh to Mathias's lips.

'Sometimes you confuse me, Tagan. You're so strong, and yet there are times when you seem as shy as a little girl. But to answer your question, yes. She would have loved you.'

'How can you be so sure?' Tagan knew what his answer would be, but she pushed for it anyway. Mathias stopped walking and reached over, stroking a finger down the line of her jaw. For months she had pulled away from him, unable to believe that Mathias liked her that much. Time had worn down her natural defence and shyness and now she turned her head to rest it in the palm of his hand.

'I'm sure that my mother would have loved you, Tagan, because I love you.' She'd expected the reply, anticipated it. It was artless and without poetry or drama. But the truth of the answer still filled her with joy. That Mathias Eynon, the most intelligent man she had ever known, had chosen her above the other girls of the village... it still left her breathless. And when he acknowledged it with the words, her heart stood still.

The two of them sat down beside the small brook and she revelled in the moment. His words filled her often restless thoughts with calm, as they always had. They sat in companionable silence for a little while, and then she found her answer.

'I love you, too,' she replied in as soft a voice as she could manage. Her usual rough voice, constantly hoarse from shouting to be heard over the cacophony of the forge, was not easy to repress, but she tried. To her eyes, Mathias deserved a proper lady on his arm. So she tried to overcome her tomboyish tendencies and to be more ladylike. What she had never realised, in all the time they had been together, was that Mathias loved her for precisely who she was.

'Watch this,' she said, made embarrassed by her sudden display of emotion. 'I've been practising.'

She turned to a small pile of dried grass, which she had absently gathered and laid between a couple of small rocks. She reached into the pocket of her leather apron and pulled out flint and tinder. She struck them together expertly and the dried grass ignited immediately. She blew gently on the burgeoning flame until the tinder caught properly.

Mathias watched the fire, then stole a glance at Tagan. Her expression was a picture of concentration. He allowed a brief smile to flicker onto his face. She flattened out her palm, passing it through the flame of the tiny fire. She moved her hand back and forward and then Mathias felt it. The rush of air as though the world itself drew a breath, ready to exhale something.

Tagan's flat hand closed into a fist and she drew it closely to her chest for a moment. Her eyes closed and her lips moved silently. Then she slowly unfurled her hand. In the centre of her palm, the flame that had been born from dead grass and a single spark from her flint twisted and turned, a living thing that she controlled through fierce determination.

Carefully, she began to shape the fire into something else. Fascinated, Mathias watched Tagan as the flame in her hand stretched and twisted according to her will. When she was done, a few moments later, a fiery butterfly lay in her palm. She closed both hands together, creating a cage of sorts, and the fire-butterfly began to flit against the bars of her fingers. It did not seem to singe her flesh.

The year before, Tagan's spirit walk had resulted in her happily confirming what everyone had long suspected. The butterfly had chosen her. *The spirit of change. The spirit of joy and colour*. Tagan brought joy and colour to the lives of all she came into contact with, just as Mathias brought peace and calm.

When Mathias had attempted a spirit walk of his own, he had failed to find a guardian creature. He had been sorely disappointed. He still tried from time to time, but the spirits could apparently never agree amongst themselves. He stared at the fire butterfly and a beaming smile lit his face.

'Tagan, it's beautiful. You are finding the shaping of the fire so easy, now. Your skill is growing by the day.'

'No,' she replied candidly. 'No, it's never easy. But it is... always a pleasure.' She opened her fingers and the fire-butterfly hesitantly broke free of its fleshy prison. It was caught instantly in a rogue breeze and broke into a trail of smoke.

'The more I can control the fire,' she said, watching the dark trails of her creation as it dissipated into the day, 'the more I can control the forge. And the more I control the forge, the better the goods are that I make.'

Tagan sorely undervalued her own skill. Mathias knew from having watched her work that the remarkable young woman could turn untempered steel into an axle for a cart in under an hour. Or refine it into a sword for a warrior in two. Sometimes she employed her exceptionally artistic side and would create a bracelet or brooch for a gift. Her talent for creating fine jewellery was rare, and one which brought the family prestige and wealth.

She had also, so she told Mathias, crafted their wedding rings. She would not let him see them.

'There need to be *some* surprises between us,' she always said.

'I am jealous,' said Mathias eventually. He slid his hand into Tagan's. 'All I can do...'

'Shut up, Matty.'

She kissed him.

Their hands entwined, the two young people sat in contented silence for a while, the sound of the brook and the occasional whisper of the hanging leaves the only sound that intruded on their peace. They were content like this, safe in each other's company and with no demands or expectations on them.

Sadly, the peace was not to last.

'Tagan! Mathias!'

The voice pulled the idling pair from their comfortable reverie. It wasn't so much the volume—which was considerable—as the urgency in the tone. It was a young voice; female, heavily accented. Tagan's youngest sister, fourteen-year-old Angharad. She pushed her way through the overhanging willows until she emerged by the waterside. She was blonde and lissom where her sister was dark and square. Stand the two girls side by side, and one would have been hard pressed to spot the familial relationship between them. Except for the eyes. Both girls had their late mother's eyes.

'Wyn needs you,' she said. She was breathless, having run from the village without stopping. Her eyes were deeply anxious and there was something close to fear in them.

Mathias didn't wait for an explanation. Already he was back on his feet, ready to head back to the village. Tagan also rose, but held back a little. 'You go,' she prompted. 'If you need me, you know where I am.'

'Are you sure?'

'Go, Matty. He's your da.' It was rare that Tagan used the

diminutive of her betrothed's name, a child's nickname that did not entirely suit the man he had become. But occasionally it slipped from her lips.

Wyn was Mathias's adoptive father, to be completely accurate, but the relationship cited by Tagan was close enough. Following Elizabeth's death when Mathias had been only a small boy, Wyn—even then an old man—had made a promise to the dying woman. He would care for the boy until such time as he could care for himself.

It had been a task taken on with great reluctance but as the years wore on, the two developed a deep and genuine affection for one another. For twenty years the pair had shared the same living space. Wyn had taught Mathias everything he knew, and in return, Mathias had brought joy to a sour old man's life.

'All right,' said Mathias, cautiously. 'I'll find you later.'

'I know you will.' She kissed his lips gently, ignoring Angharad's pointed snigger. Oddly, the sound brought some comfort to her. If her little sister could still find humour in a situation as everyday as her older sister kissing a man, then Wyn's summons was not likely to be for anything too serious.

Realising Mathias was still standing, waiting for some sort of formal dismissal, she gave him a gentle shove. 'Go.'

He nodded, and left. Tagan sighed and ran her fingers through her hair. There was a sense, deep down, that something was about to change. Clouds had begun to gather in the formerly blue sky, stealing some of the light and warmth of the day. In the distance there was a low-pitched, ominous rumble.

'Storm's coming,' she observed.

IN THE TWENTY years of their relationship, Mathias had always called Wyn by his given name. Never *da*, or *father*. But there was no denying the bond that connected the two men. Thrown together by the tragedy of Elizabeth's premature death, they had stayed together through mutual respect and responsibility, and latterly, shared affection.

Mathias ducked into the low doorway of the small cottage he shared with the old man. It consisted of only two rooms: a main living area, where they had passed many an evening in companionable silence or engaged in learning, and the small room off to the side where Mathias slept. Once, Wyn had slept in that room, but as he'd aged and the chill in his bones seeped further in, Mathias had insisted on swapping. The larger room always had a fire in the hearth. It was always warm.

The embers of the fire were barely glowing this early in the evening, but Mathias didn't stoke them. He knew full well that if Wyn wanted them stoking, he'd do it. Like Tagan, one of the old man's seemingly endless parade of magical talents leaned towards the elemental. Unlike Tagan, he exhibited little fine control over it. There had been times during arguments, of which there had been many, when nearby fires flared up uncontrollably in response to Old Wyn's temper. The winds would rattle around the eaves, and Mathias swore he once felt the ground lurch beneath his feet.

'What took you so long, boy?' The old man lay on the pallet that served as his bed. It was comfortable enough; the feather mattress had been painstakingly stitched together by some of the village women as a gift for the elder. 'I've been calling for you for the whole day.'

'I was delivering Llewellyn's calf, Wyn. Then I was down by the brook.' Mathias's first reaction on hearing the grumbling complaint was abject relief. He knew, perhaps more than anybody, that Wyn could not live forever. It was said that he had seen as many as seventy summers, an astonishing age for the people of the valleys. There were none now living who could remember Wyn as a young man. 'Do you want tea?'

'Aye, brew us a drink. We have to talk. I have a tale to tell you, an important one. One more lesson for you from an old man.'

Mathias paused in the act of collecting the mint leaves from the earthenware pot on the side where they were kept. Wyn was not a man to waste time in idle chatter; if he said it was important and had been calling for him all day, then it was most certainly going to be important.

'Tea, boy!' Wyn snapped him out of his reverie and Mathias shook himself alert. The familiar actions of filling the pot with water and setting it onto the coals of the open fire, the silence whilst he waited for it to come to a boil before dropping in the mint leaves to steep, were a comforting routine. He took Wyn his cup and sat down on the floor, cupping his hands around his own tea.

'Much better.' With arthritic slowness, Wyn sat up. He was a wiry old man with a shock of long, fine white hair that flowed down past his shoulders. Coupled with blue eyes that were still bright and alert despite the advance of old age, he still cut a straight-backed figure when he walked in the street. He was the most respected elder in the village, and with good reason. He sipped on the brew and sighed.

'Have you been with that girl again? I smell the forge on you.' He narrowed his eyes at Mathias, but the younger man merely smiled. He knew that Wyn, like Tagan's father, approved of the match. 'She'll bring you nothing but misery, lad. That's the job of women, you know. To make our lives more complicated.'

Unsurprisingly, Wyn had never married.

'Are you going to tell me this important tale of yours, Wyn?' Mathias's patience when it came to Wyn and the subject of Tagan was limited.

'Mm. Yes. The story.' Wyn's eyes narrowed as if struggling or reluctant to recall. While he might have been old, Mathias knew he was still as sharp as a pin. 'Is there more tea in the pot...?'

'Wyn.'

The old man snorted with mixed amusement and annoyance. 'You always were so easy to irritate. You should learn to rein that in, it will get you in trouble one day. Is the door closed tight?'

'Yes, Wyn.'

'Good.' He set down his cup and leaned forward, the joints in his arms cracking audibly as he did so. Mathias made a mental note to mix him some more of the joint balm later. Out of the corner of a room, a cat materialised from the shadows. Wyn encouraged cats into the cottage and it was not uncommon for three or four of them to be curled up in various nooks around their home. This one slunk into the centre of the room to take a spot beside the fire. Mathias reached out and stroked its tabby fur. It flopped over onto one side at his gentle touch and began to purr, a low, steady thrum.

'I had hoped to spare you this for a little longer, but it seems that I may no longer have a choice, so listen well. The things I am about to tell you nobody else here need know.' He waved a liver-spotted hand vaguely to encompass the village. Wyn was a natural storyteller, but Mathias had never heard the old man sound so grave. There had been many nights that he had sat in front of the fire—as a boy, and then as a young man—listening to the tales spilling from Wyn's lips, but this was different.

'What things?' He heard the breathy catch in his own voice and felt a little embarrassed by it. *What things, Wyn? Tell us another story, Wyn.* The piping voice of his childhood gently teased him within the confines of his head. The young man focused. He was a child no longer.

'Things about our past, boy. Things about magic that you need to know.' Wyn's voice lowered so that Mathias had to lean forward to hear him. 'About King Richard and the evil that lives within him.'

WYN CLAIMED TO have been a travelling bard in his youth, and said that he had walked the length and breadth of the isle and beyond. He had told his old folk-tales and stories in inns and taverns from York to London, and the people would gather around, ply him with beer or wine and eagerly listen. Sometimes, when he had finished, they would press money into his hand. He rarely accepted it, he said, or he would have been a wealthy man.

When Mathias had been small, back when his mother still lived, he had trailed Wyn around, shadowing the man every bit as faithfully as the cats that stalked after him. When Elizabeth had died and Mathias had cried himself to sleep over her still body, it had been Wyn who had gently picked him up and carried him to the bed that became his for nearly twenty more years.

He'd told Mathias a story on the night of Elizabeth's funeral. A child's tale, naturally. A story of fairies and elves, of nature's magic and all things bright and beautiful. A tale woven into a comforting blanket of peace that cocooned the bereaved, orphaned boy and brought a smile back to his face.

Whether there was any truth to Wyn's bardic past was unclear. He did seem to possess an unlimited capacity for folklore and fables, and could tell them in a way that was utterly captivating. But Mathias had never been entirely convinced, certain that Wyn had never left Cwm Heddychol and possessed his knowledge simply by virtue of being old. At least, that was what he had believed until now.

Wyn took a deep breath, pressing the palms of his hands together. Mathias was about to ask the old man what he was doing when the fire leapt into life. It was brighter than it should have been, and as the young man looked around, colours, sounds and smells became sharper, more vivid than they ever had been before.

'What's happening?' Mathias asked, slightly dreamily.

Wyn didn't answer him. His eyes closed and his brow furrowed in concentration. Curling shapes formed in the flickering shadows cast by the fire: cavorting figures, beasts and birds wheeling through a bewildering parade of actions. They were hypnotic, one shape falling into the next, looping upon themselves.

Then Wyn opened his eyes, revealing pits of light that swallowed the world.

Where are we?

Mathias found himself standing beneath a copse of trees on a grassy hillside. It was early, the warm sun only just peering over the horizon and drawing mist from the sodden earth. Everything smelled damp and clean, as if heavy rains had only recently departed, but there was not a cloud in the sky.

England. This is an illusion. It will show you what you need to see.

Wyn's voice came from everywhere and nowhere. No longer cracked by age, it was strong and firm, possessed of a resonant tone of command. Mathias had never seen such powerful magic before, and Wyn had never given him any reason to believe that he could perform such miracles.

You have never done this before.

I have never needed to, and there were reasons not to. Now hold your tongue. This is difficult.

Sounds filtered into the idyllic scene, half-heard and distant. They were sounds with which Mathias was mostly unacquainted, although he clearly recognised the ring of metal on metal. He heard voices shouting in defiance, voices crying out in the kind of terrible pain he had never known during his secluded upbringing. He heard screams and the gurgling agonies of dying men. He did not like it. The sounds of battle were alien to his ears and filled him with fear and horror that he had never experienced.

Stop.

The noise was relentless, running together into the long, discordant wail of warfare. Mathias covered his ears, but it made no difference; to his horror, he realised he could not see himself. He was simply an observer to events outside his control, forced to look on until the illusion had run its course. The roar of battle was joined by the coppery stink of blood, the stench of opened bowels, sweat, turned earth and hot metal. Beneath it all lay an incongruously sweet summer breeze, more horrible for the contrast it presented.

Stop!

But Wyn did not stop. The illusion continued, relentless and punishing, saving the awful sights for last. A mass of squirming, armoured bodies hacked at each other in a frenzy. Knights wheeled and charged their horses, trampling bodies into the sodden ground and opening them with blade and lance. Blizzards of arrows descended on the rear ranks, cutting men down indiscriminately around the banners of their lords. Most horribly of all, robed figures ran screaming through the mob, burning, bleeding and wailing in agony. Even among the press of flesh and steel men struggled to get out of their way, preferring death to the curse of their touch.

Where is this?

Bosworth. England. Many years ago. A century past. Wyn's voice was strong and resonant, but there was a quiet sadness to it, an undercurrent of loss. ***I was not there, of course, but others were. These sounds, these memories are theirs and not mine.***

But why here?

Because this is important, Mathias, in ways you have yet to understand. That is Henry Tudor's army being slaughtered. Such a waste. So many lives, destroyed by betrayal. Those are his magi. Mathias's attention was drawn again to the tormented, burning figures as they mindlessly shrieked in agony.

What's happened to them?

She *has happened to them.*

Mathias didn't have to ask who *she* was. An ethereal figure strode languidly through the scrum of battle, unhindered by man or horse. It was clearly a woman; she was so achingly beautiful that he yearned to go to her, to press his lips to her, to serve her in any way he could. But as she came closer, his fascination turned to dread. The stench of blood grew stronger at her approach and he had the impression of slithering things, a sulphurous stink and the red ruin of open wounds. No longer did he want to kiss her. He wanted to run.

You cannot flee. You are not really here.

He knew that, but he tried anyway. It was like an old nightmare in which he was being hunted, but no matter how fast he ran he was unable to escape. He watched helplessly as the woman dipped her ghostly fingers into the chest of one of the magi and gave a delicate tug. The man collapsed, his flesh bubbling and running from him as he was wracked by terrible change. Fronds of tortured flesh peeled from his bones and lashed out at the horrified soldiers surrounding him. Mercifully, the twisted ruin of a man did not live long and was hacked to pieces by warriors of both sides. Mathias had never imagined anything so vile, but in his disembodied state had no outlet for his revulsion.

Her name is Melusine, but she is no woman born of this world. She is a demon wearing the face of an angel, and she was there, walking unseen across the field at Bosworth that day.

Mathias watched her walk, her movements fluid and graceful. She did not so much walk as *prowl* the battlefield, like a lioness stalking its prey. He watched as she moved behind another of the unfortunate magi and burned him to ashes with a touch. He didn't ask what she was doing, but Wyn's commentary continued.

She stalked Tudor's magi and she killed them. She turned their magic against them. The more potent the magic, the more terrible the destruction. Had they but known the danger...

It was, quite simply, horrific. His eyes remained glued to the scene whilst Wyn's words continued in his mind.

She walked unseen on the battlefield, but all felt her presence. King Richard the Third, who sullied his family name with demonic blood, grew in strength even as Tudor's armies failed. He loved her for the power she gave him, and yet he was afraid.

Mathias watched her in horrid fascination. He could understand the dichotomy. Her beauty was unsurpassed and yet she was somehow completely repulsive. She appeared fair, yet her presence invoked revulsion.

Richard bought his success that day and gave power to this creature even as she gave power to him, but the price was unspeakable. For as you know, Mathias, all things must have balance. For every action, there must be an opposite. Without balance, the world...

...falls into chaos. Mathias nodded. The lesson that had been one of the first he had learned, coming to his lips as easily as breathing. He watched the demon winding her way through the battlefield. *But why are you showing me this now?*

Because you need to understand what is to come, Wyn's voice boomed. *Richard bought his victory with blood, but that was not all. He tainted the royal bloodline, and that taint has only grown stronger with each generation. Melusine is no petty spirit who barters for favours, she is a great power that seeks to enter the world of men and claim it as her own.*

But if what you're showing me is true, she entered our world at Bosworth Field, didn't she?

No, she did not. What you see here is just a hollow shade of the demon Melusine. Mathias sensed a certain frustration in Wyn, as if the old man needed him to understand more but lacked the time to explain. *However, a time is coming when she will be able to enter our world, and the King will lament the day his ancestors made this dark pact.*

I still don't understand what this has got to do with me.

The scene of battle dissolved just as Tudor's defeated forces were attempting to flee the field, pursued by Richard and his army. This time Mathias was standing on a small patch of dark earth surrounded on all sides by black, glistening rock. The circle of sky above was a smear of unfamiliar stars and deep, rich blue. A female figure was silhouetted in the glassy surface in front of him, its exaggerated femininity revealing who it was that lurked beyond, or within, the peculiar surface.

Few outside the line of kings know this secret. The reach of the Inquisition is long and their methods ruthless. Melusine has given Richard the tools and knowledge to hunt down those who know the truth.

The presence within the stone pushed forward, swimming into terrible focus. A doll-like visage with smoulderingly dark eyes and rosebud lips that pouted beautifully at him. She ran a perfectly pink tongue over those lips, revealing tiny fangs beaded with blood.

I am old, lad. Wyn's strong voice had dropped to an anguished whisper. ***All these long years I have turned my magic to hiding. Keeping myself, these people and this village as safe as I can.*** There was a long pause. ***Keeping you hidden. But I am old.***

The glassy rock parted like liquid, revealing the pale visage of Melusine. Her scent poured into the little space: jasmine, honey, blood, iron. This close, she was overpowering, and Mathias knew that had this been more than an illusion, he would have been lost in moments. Soft skin, moist flesh, the taste of bile, flowing silk, the touch of a blade. A wave of agonising, conflicting sensations washed over him.

She has found me.

Mercifully, the illusion melted away. Mathias became slowly aware that he was in Wyn's house, sitting on the floor by the fire. He was trembling and sweating and absently noticed that he had spilled his tea. He glanced up and over at the white-haired man he considered a father. Wyn's head was drooping to his chest in weariness. Without being asked, Mathias crossed to the fire and poured another mug of the rejuvenating brew. He pressed it into Wyn's hands without comment and the old man nodded his thanks.

A silence passed between the two men. Wyn was regaining his composure and Mathias was too shaken by far to intrude on his thoughts. Eventually, the old man raised his head once more and a sad smile flickered onto his face.

'I had hoped for more time,' he said. 'I had too much faith in my own power and wanted to spare you this knowledge as long as possible. I have... been remiss. There is so much that I have not told you. So much that I *should* have told you.'

'I do not understand, Wyn.'

'No. You don't. And that is my fault. The truth of the matter is that Melusine's pact, seeded with Richard all those years ago, is on the cusp of bearing fruit. Evil comes to this world, my boy. Real evil, the likes of which man cannot begin to understand. It has to be stopped.'

Mathias laughed without humour. 'You are surely not expecting me to... don't be silly, old man. I am not some kind of great warrior or magus...'

Wyn shook his head.

'You are a quiet champion, my boy. The most worthy kind.' When Mathias simply looked confused, Wyn patted the boy's shoulder with great affection. 'I have great power. You know that now. But I am old. Too old now to protect you from what is coming. I chose you a long time ago, for a reason, but we must act fast. Now that Melusine has found me, the Inquisition will be coming.'

'But...' Mathias saw the expression on Wyn's face and knew that asking any further questions at this point would be a waste of time.

Hampton Court
England

'RICHARD, WAKE UP.'

Anna shook him vigorously, and as the King's eyes opened, he reached out as though he would claw at her face. She ducked his attack and held her distance until her husband's senses restored themselves. He gasped loudly and sat upright. Sweat rolled from him in steady rivulets.

'Another dream?' Her voice was filled with genuine concern and sympathy. She reached over and stroked back a lock of greying hair that had fallen into his eyes. He slapped her hand irritably and nodded.

'Was it *her* again?'

Still the King did not speak. The dream had been too personal to share. He stared at his wife for long moments, then waved a hand. 'Bring me wine,' he ordered. When she didn't move straight away, his imperious tone became something entirely more demanding. 'Go! Now! And send for the seer. I must speak with him.'

'The seer?' The distaste in Anna's voice made Richard look at her sharply. He knew that she, like many of the nobility, thought it deeply hypocritical that the King should keep a magus in the employ of the court. But he did not care to listen to whispers of accusation. Josef was little more than a madman, but he had his uses.

He roared at Anna. 'I said *now!*'

She scurried away, casting a glance over her shoulder to the King in his bed, his head buried in his hands. Yes, it had been another dream. More to the point, it had been the same dream that had woken him every night this past week. Richard knew that there was no way he could ignore it. Not any more.

JOSEF WAS ONLY in his twenties, but his wasted body, and the loss of most of his teeth, made him look much older. He was brought before the King, who was now clad in a night robe trimmed with finest ermine. Shackles were bound about the seer's hands and hobbles stopped him from moving at any great speed. He abased himself before the King, and looked up as Richard spoke.

'I dreamed,' he said. 'You will help me understand the revelations.'

'I live to serve, my King.' Josef giggled inanely and Richard glowered. He hated the creature, hated him with a passion, but he needed him to make sense of the dreams that plagued him. He relayed the words of the woman who haunted his sleep, carefully omitting details of her identity. For six nights now she had come to him, stirring his rage, his lust, and his desires. For six nights he had dismissed her. But the raw power of last night's vision could not be denied. He needed to untangle his thoughts.

'She told me that the Vessel is ready.'

Josef cackled and clapped his hands like a delighted child. Richard felt an overwhelming urge to choke the infernal creature. The seer continued to cackle for a little longer, rolling around the floor, and then rose up to his knees. He lifted his bound hands, the chains clinking in emphasis.

'The Vessel comes, Richard Plantagenet? Why, it's your son. Your first-born. So pure. So pure! Anybody can see if they have eyes to see it! He comes of age in a few months, and she comes to claim her long-awaited prize. The time is coming for the line of kings to pay the debt of their rule.'

Richard's mouth went dry and he stared at the seer. His eldest son, his namesake. His heir. A boy he loved with every beat of his heart and with every breath in his body. He would be damned before he turned him over to anybody.

'It is clear to me, your majesty,' Josef said, his sing-song voice grating on every nerve in Richard's body. 'She has given you her power and whispered her secrets into your ear, and now she wants what is hers!'

'No,' said Richard. 'No. There must be some other way.'

'She is a demon, a creature of magic and deceit. You are bound to her as she is bound to you, you cannot escape such a thing.' Josef shrugged. 'Unless the Inquisitors have wiped out all magic in the realm.' The seer prodded experimentally at himself for a few seconds, then giggled to himself. 'No, they haven't!'

Richard got to his feet and moved to the window. 'There *must* be some other way,' he repeated. 'I need you to find me an answer.' He glared at Josef. 'I will *not* give her my son.'

'It seems to me,' said the seer, 'that if you want to rid yourself of a magical threat, you get rid of all the magical... things.' He waved a hand, struggling to find the word he wanted to use.

'The magi? The Inquisition... yes. Yes.' Richard's hand curled into a fist. 'I will have them work harder. We must purge the taint of magic still lingering in this country. If there is no magic, then she cannot be summoned. My son will be safe.'

He pulled a slim knife from beneath his robes and advanced on the cackling seer. 'If I must slay every magus with my own hand then it will be so.' The King glared down at the maniacal seer. 'Starting with you.'

Cwm Heddychol
Wales

BRING TAGAN. MEET *me at the Circle.*

The instruction had been simple, and still reeling from the things Wyn had revealed to him, Mathias had considered disobedience. But he was a good man and a loyal son, even if he was not truly of Wyn's blood.

The Circle lay beyond the village borders, on one of the windswept hilltops overlooking the valley. There it was that weddings were held, and last words were spoken of the dead. It was nothing more than a rough circle of flattened grass surrounded by innocuous rocks of varying shape and size. The view from the top on a clear day was spectacular, the rolling crags and valleys of South Wales stretching away in every direction. This evening it was far from clear. The distant storm had closed in, gusting around the hilltop and driving a thin drizzle before it. Mathias approached the Circle, Tagan's hand in his.

He had collected her from the forge, to her father's great disapproval. When he mentioned they were going to the Circle at Wyn's behest, the blacksmith had merely nodded. His eyes flitted between Mathias and his daughter.

'Take care of her, Eynon,' was all the taciturn man said, and it seemed unnecessarily *final* to Mathias's ears.

I'm imagining things.

Wyn's story had shaken him far more than he realised. As he and Tagan walked from the village to the Circle, she had not asked him a single question. His serious manner and quiet demeanour had been enough for her to comply with his request.

He looked sideways at her. She was only an inch or so shorter than he was, and usually she walked close to him, their shoulders touching. Today, however, she was keeping a slight distance. Mathias knew exactly why this was. They were heading to a meeting with six of the most revered members of the village, and her father frequently told her that her open familiarity with Mathias was behaviour unbecoming of a young woman.

When she spoke, it broke the silence alarmingly.

'Are you marrying me?'

Tagan's question shook some of the darkness from the corners of his thoughts and he glanced at her with a quick, nervous smile. 'Of course, my love,' he replied quietly. 'Only I hadn't exactly planned to do it this evening.'

'Good,' she said. 'Because I'm hardly dressed for it.' Her smithing apron had been removed and she wore a simple linen shift. 'My wedding dress is still in pieces on my father's floor.' She was nervous, he realised, talking about inane things to calm herself, and he gave her hand an experimental squeeze. *I am here,* he hoped to convey. *Don't be afraid.*

In response, she squeezed his hand back. It made him feel better. She smiled at him, the dimples in her cheeks making her even prettier than usual, and for a moment, all his own anxiety drained from him.

'Mathias,' she said in a tiny voice as they approached the Circle. 'Mathias, why are they dressed like that?'

He looked where she pointed. There they were. Six figures, each seated on one of the flatter rocks lining the Circle. Wyn spotted them and raised a hand in greeting. He had changed into druidic robes, which was a startling enough sight, but as they climbed upwards, it slowly became apparent that all six of the elders were wearing similar outfits. Mathias had seen Wyn's robes before. Usually, he wore them only for weddings and funerals, and other rites performed within the Circle.

'Welcome and greetings, Mathias Eynon,' said Wyn in the most formal tone the young man had ever heard him use. The old man's eyes turned to Tagan and softened slightly. 'And Tagan. Welcome and greetings to you also.'

'Greetings and thank you, Elder,' said Tagan formally, and she curtsied. The gesture surprised Mathias and he mumbled an echo of her response, dropping a respectful bow of his own. Wyn smiled at both of them, but there was not much joy in it.

'We must discuss the defences of the village,' he said. 'In light of what I have told you, Mathias, we can expect the Inquisition here soon. As such, we need to invoke powerful, ancient magic. We need your help. Both of you.'

There was a grumble of thunder as if in response to Wyn's ominous words, and the sound echoed around the valley. Mathias's fingers remained locked with Tagan's, and the two young people exchanged glances.

'You are owed explanation,' said Wyn. 'And it will come. For now, though, please. You must assist us.'

'Of course, Elder.' It was Tagan who spoke and Mathias felt a creeping shame as she did so. 'What must we do?'

'Step inside the Circle,' said the old man, his eyes on her. 'We don't have much time.'

The road to London
England

THE JOURNEY BACK from the village was, by necessity, much slower. A ragged chain of children and a few surviving men and woman followed Weaver's mercenary band, their hands and feet shackled. They had done with sobbing and pleading, now, and simply trudged behind the horses in weary resignation, dull-eyed with horror at the fate that awaited them.

The rain had caught up with them, a fine drizzle that quickly soaked to the skin and turned the ground into a quagmire. Seated on his horse at the head of the miserable procession, Weaver was supremely indifferent to these facts as he quietly pondered where the next raids should be targeted. With the influx of men, the Inquisition would be able to push deeper into the valleys than had previously been possible.

The pain, when it came, was so shocking and unexpected the Inquisitor couldn't even cry out. He arched his back, his mouth open in a silent scream of anguish as knowledge, bright and hard, seared itself directly into his brain. Emerald light danced beneath his mask and spilled from the eye holes, and his horse and those around him reared in sudden panic.

He suddenly knew, with absolute certainty, that on a hilltop to the west a group of magi were soon to perform a ritual. A ritual that absolutely had to be stopped, and he had until sundown before it would be too late.

The agony faded and Weaver felt the warmth of blood beneath his mask as it leaked from his nose. He shook his head and gasped, the absence of the pain as shockingly sweet as its arrival had been terrible. When it was obvious that the Inquisitor was not dead and that the incident had passed, one of the mercenaries dared to approach.

'Are you all right, my lord?' The big man's question was hesitant.

Weaver turned slowly in his saddle to stare directly at the speaker. 'Pick five of the men to stay and escort the prisoners. The rest of you are with me. We ride west; there isn't much time.'

'My lord?' The warrior wasn't convinced that the Lord Inquisitor had not gone suddenly mad.

'You heard me; *go!*' The Lord Inquisitor was not entirely sure, but he believed he caught the lingering scent of jasmine, tinged with hot blood.

Cwm Heddychol
Wales

INSIDE THE CIRCLE, the air was shockingly calm. The wind rose, driving the rain in sheets across the hilltop, but Mathias and Tagan blinked in wonder as the storm roared its fury overhead yet failed to touch them. Wyn did not allow them to wonder for long.

'Mathias, Tagan. I wish there was more time to explain what is about to happen. But you must believe me when I say what you are going to learn—over the next few weeks, months, maybe even years—is of the utmost importance. The fault lies heavily on my shoulders for not speaking to you about this sooner. I had... hopes, I suppose. Hopes that the Vessel would not be forthcoming during your lifetime.' Wyn sighed. 'I was wrong.'

Around the Circle, the five other magi were murmuring in soft voices as they drew strange, angular symbols on their rocks using coal and chalk. Tagan watched them whilst Wyn spoke, and then leaned into Mathias.

'Do you understand what they are doing?' Her voice was a harsh whisper. The young couple were standing in the centre of the Circle, as directed by Wyn. They had not let go of each other's hands the whole time. Mathias, his eyes very firmly fixed on his adoptive father, shook his head slowly.

'Only that it is great magic, and I've never seen it before.'

THE KNOWLEDGE BURNED in Weaver's mind like a brand, a terrible certainty that if he did not reach the village of the magi before sundown, he would be too late.

Hooves thundered across the ground, saliva flew from the mouths of twenty panting, snorting horses that were being ridden to the very edge of endurance. The men atop them drove them harder, switching at the flanks with crops and digging their heels in. The Lord Inquisitor had made it clear that they would kill the horses if necessary, and none of the mercenaries had argued. It was unwise to argue with Charles Weaver.

They had entered the valleys an hour earlier. Their objective was within reach, but five of their number had already been lost to the mad dash. Two horses had collapsed, their riders left behind, while three more had been killed when their steeds had stepped badly in the rain and rugged terrain. Weaver didn't care as long as he made it with enough men to do the job.

Time was slipping away. Acutely conscious of the vital importance of their task and not wishing to draw Weaver's ire, they rode west toward the darkening hills.

* * *

'Sit down, Mathias.' Wyn made a vague gesture with his right hand and Mathias could feel the magical compulsion to sit come across him. Uncharacteristically, he attempted to resist, suddenly feeling rebellious. It was about as effective as a mouse pressing against a boulder, and he felt his knees buckle before he sat down, hard, on the flattened grass of the Circle. The bump startled him and he blinked in hurt surprise at Wyn.

'You too, Tagan.' Wyn's tone was kinder to the young woman, and she made the choice to do as the old man said. 'I'm sorry, both of you. I had hoped that this burden would not fall to you. I have grown fonder of you, Mathias, than I should have done, and sought to shield you from the danger that now bears down on us.'

'You told me about the demon,' Mathias said. 'Melusine. Does this have something to do with her?' Tagan gasped at the word 'demon' and made a warding gesture across her chest.

'It has everything to do with her.'

'I still don't understand.' Mathias shook his head. He could sense that Wyn was afraid, and that, more than anything, filled him with dread. 'What is it that you expect me to do?'

'Time is running out, Wyn.' One of the magi spoke in a low, urgent voice. 'We must perform the sending now. While we still can.'

'Mathias, Tagan, listen to me.' Wyn took a hurried step towards the couple in the Circle. 'We are going to use the power of the Circle to send you to one who can help. Find him, you will find them all. You will need their power.'

'I...'

'...don't understand. I know that. But mark these names well. The Shapeshifter. She Who Sees. The Pirate King. The Wanderer. Seek out the Shapeshifter, Mathias. His power is as yours. Earth calls to earth. Remember that, my boy: earth calls to earth. You *will* find him. I know you will.'

'Wyn!' Mathias caught at the old man's hand as he made to step backwards. Wyn hesitated, then touched the back of his free hand to Mathias's cheek.

'If I had been granted a son,' he said, 'I could not have been prouder. Now close your eyes. It will make the sending easier for you. For both of you.'

'What is the...'

'Close your eyes!' The roar in Wyn's voice was loaded with terrible power, and light blazed from his eyes.

THE HORSES COULD run no further. Their riders dismounted and made the rest of the journey on foot. To the west, the storm had swallowed the light. It was impossible to tell, through the gloom and driving rain, if the sun had set or not. It was barely possible to know which way was up and which was down. Their goal was minutes away.

'Destroy the village. Burn it to the ground and kill them all,' demanded Weaver. 'No prisoners, no mercy. For King Richard and England!' He drew his pistols and, head down, began to run as hard and as fast as he could.

EARTH CALLS TO earth.

Mathias didn't claim to understand the words Wyn had spoken, and yet he found something strangely comforting in them. His power, such as it was, had never grown like Tagan's. Not for Mathias the ability to bend fire to his will. Not for Mathias the skill of Wyn's mighty illusions. He had always simply assumed his talent was a small thing; that he just had a way with animals.

Wyn's barked command that Tagan and Mathias close their eyes had been irresistible, but they remained locked together, his arms around her, holding her to him. Her head rested on his chest and he knew that she was crying. He had never, in the years he had known her, seen her cry, and he was glad, his eyes tightly closed, that he did not see her crying now.

His hand stroked her back gently and he breathed in the scent of her. Fire and forge and flowers; the three things he associated with her. Nothing that was happening made sense.

Sense.

His senses were altering. Changing. He could feel and smell Tagan in his arms, and that was comforting. The compulsion to keep his eyes closed had otherwise blinded him to what was occurring around the Circle, but he could hear the voices of Wyn and the others. They were chanting, speaking words he did not know or understand.

The air began to crackle and Mathias tasted the metallic tang of potent magic; as he had during Wyn's illusion, only many times stronger. The hairs on the back of his neck and arms began to tingle and the tri-fold smell of Tagan began to fade. Gone was the smoke, the smell of cooling metal, of the flowers that she carried in her pockets. In its place came something else.

Something... familiar. Something comforting. The smell of rich peat and loam. Grass and trees. The smells of the woodlands and the valleys that were his home. Mathias felt his fears begin to ooze from him despite the strangeness of the situation.

'They are coming!'

The shout came from somewhere at the foot of the hill and Mathias yearned to open his eyes, to see what was happening. The chanting did not break, and neither did the chanters add any urgency to what they were doing or saying. They maintained the spell they were weaving, drawing on more and more power. The smell of the earth grew stronger, joined by the sensation of sinking.

They are burying me alive. Why am I not afraid?

Wyn's voice came to him, more to his thoughts than to his ears.

Earth calls to earth, Mathias Eynon. Remember that. We will not meet again in this life. Remember me fondly and forgive me. Protect Tagan. Her journey is tied to yours, but the time will come when she needs you more than you can ever know.

Wyn, pleaded Mathias softly, trying to reach out to the man. *Father.*

Aye, lad. That I am. Find the Shapeshifter.

Mathias opened his eyes just as the earth closed around his face. He opened his mouth to call out in panic as a masked man crested the hill, pistols levelled at the man he loved as his father. Then a great weariness overcame him and, heedless of the mouthful of earth he swallowed, sleep took him. Just as it had already taken the woman in his arms.

* * *

'BRING THEM BACK.' The Inquisitor's weapons remained levelled at Wyn as he approached. 'Undo the ritual you have performed, traitor, and bring them back.' The mask he wore to hide his features distorted his voice grotesquely.

'You are too late, King's man.' Wyn stood his ground. 'The sending is complete.'

'Where have you sent them?'

Wyn's eyes burned with light. 'Your King's line will fall!' He began to laugh, a mad sound.

In response, Charles Weaver shot him, the *crack* of the pistol shockingly loud in the still Circle. The bullet blew the back of Wyn's skull off and he toppled backward into a spreading fan of blood. The Inquisitor noted with disgust that the old man was still smiling. With Wyn's death the bubble of calm contained within the Circle collapsed, letting in the storm. A tongue of lightning lit the figure of Weaver in hellish monochrome and thunder crashed around the hill as he turned his gaze to the surviving magi. The first screams and sounds of battle drifted up from the valley below, and a few of the mercenaries struggled up the hill through the driving rain.

'Kill all but one,' he ordered. 'And destroy the stones.'

FOUR

September, 1589
Bavaria
Germany

MATHIAS WOKE WITH no idea how much time had passed since he had fallen into magically-induced sleep in the ritual circle. His face was pressed into damp, fragrant leaf mould, and as he sat up, blinking sleep out of his eyes, pine needles clung to his face and clothes. He brushed them away, and saw that the earth was thick with a carpet of moss and the littered debris of a forest's evergreens.

The air was heavy with the clean, crisp scent of conifers and he inhaled the unfamiliar scent deeply. He knew trees, of course, but the smell was entirely different from home. It was cold and fresh, like it was at the tops of the crags in autumn. He looked around, trying to work out where he was, but all he could see was more trees. They stretched away on all sides, their trunks close. The forest floor was punctuated with outcrops of rock, thick moss and broad ferns. It was dark and it was forbidding.

Where am I?

Mathias blinked a few more times. His eyes felt gritty, but this was not the usual grit of sleep. This felt as though someone had thrown a handful of dirt into his eyes. He remembered...

'Wyn!'

He called the old man's name, but there was no response. His voice was swallowed by the forest; only leaden silence remained when the word died away. He scrambled to his feet, the suddenness of the movement leaving him dizzy. Swaying unsteadily, he reached for the nearest tree. Its trunk was sticky with sap and its needles rustling. He felt as though they were whispering words, but he lacked the skill to understand them. He was also, he realised as he looked down at his body, filthy.

Perhaps, he thought as he desperately tried to piece together his fragmented memories, *perhaps I am simply dreaming? Or perhaps I am dead.* But he knew neither of these was the case. Everything here was too real. He took several slow, calming breaths before crouching down, placing a hand flat on the spot where he had woken. The ground beneath his palm was black and hard; not the soft loam that he had expected to feel. The sensation of being swallowed up by the earth had been something he could certainly not forget.

'Mathias?' Tagan's voice. He stifled a sob of relief and looked around. The young woman lay, much as he had, amidst a pile of brown, fallen needles. They clung to her face, her hair, her linen dress. For a wild moment, Mathias thought he had never seen her looking so beautiful. He edged across to where she was and looked over her with concern.

'Are you all right? Are you hurt?'

'No, I'm fine. I'm...' She rubbed at her eyes, then stared up at him. 'What's happening? Where are we?'

'I don't know,' he answered, honestly. 'But... I remember Wyn sent us here to find someone. Do you remember what he said? The Shapeshifter?'

'He did actually say all those things, then? That we need to find those people?' Tagan's re-adjustment to reality seemed to be far less arduous than his own. Her pragmatic nature extended, apparently, to the oddities of arcane travel. Mathias remembered the masked man coming over the hill too, his weapons aimed at Wyn, with a lurch. It did not seem like a good time to share that particular recollection with Tagan.

'He definitely said them,' Mathias confirmed. He stood up—more carefully this time—and held out a hand to help Tagan to her feet. She half-stumbled, half-rushed into his embrace and buried her face in his shoulder for a brief moment.

'I don't understand,' was all she said, her voice muffled by his clothing. 'I don't remember what happened. I fell asleep, or fainted or... something. I remember hearing Wyn say something about finding the Shapeshifter, sending us to where we might find him, whatever that means.'

'Yes,' said Mathias, stroking her close crop of dark hair thoughtfully. 'All I can guess is that we are there. Or, in fact, *here*.' He pushed her away a little. 'Look. What do you see?'

She blinked at him and squinted into the gloom. Amongst the looming pines were tall menhirs, swathed with moss and lichen. Tagan made a little noise of understanding. 'A stone circle,' she said, spotting exactly what Mathias had seen. 'We were in a stone circle back at home, and now...'

'The elders sent us here,' Mathias said. 'Some great earth magic. The ground itself held us in its embrace. Brought us here...'

'We have nothing with us,' she said, her eyes bright with tears. It made Mathias uncomfortable to see her this way. He stood and watched her, feeling as helpless as a day-old kitten. There was nothing he could do, nothing he could say that would explain any of this—because he didn't understand it either. 'No food, no water... only the clothes on our backs... we don't know who we're looking for!'

'Other than he's the Shapeshifter. Or she.' Mathias sighed. 'I wish I could say something to help, Tagan, but... I suppose all we can do is look. See what we can find. We're in a forest. We can find berries, roots... hunt small game. You can make a fire. We will be fine. And we're together, at least.' He spoke the words confidently and there was enough conviction that she nodded, wiping away the unshed tears.

'We know nothing about this Shapeshifter,' she said after taking a few moments to compose herself. 'Can't we just... call for him, or something? Maybe he'll come out here...' She paused. 'Or her. Oh, Mathias, this is utterly foolish. We don't even know what this person looks like! How will we recognise them?' Her hand remained locked with his. Despite the situation, Mathias liked it when she did that.

'I am fairly certain that standing here shouting will serve little purpose other than to make us look lost and confused,' he said, attempting to inject a little levity into the proceedings.

'Mathias,' she said in a familiar tone. 'We *are* lost and confused.'

'Yes,' he agreed, shooting her a smile which, to his delight, she returned. 'We are.'

Their hands firmly clasped, they walked deeper into the forest, and all sound disappeared into a silence that called to mind a church at prayer. The light turned from a pale, pre-dawn grey to twilight gloom.

'It's really quite beautiful,' Tagan said in a breathless tone and Mathias nodded. All the creeping uncertainty that had plagued him was swept away in the sheer glory of nature unbound. This forest was wild, pure and untamed, and it was, as she said, beautiful. He had half expected there to be no birdsong at all, but it was there; a background buzz muffled by the bristling canopy.

A sense of peace and stillness stole across him as they made their way quietly through the forest. Apart from the distant, muted sound of the wind high above them and the unseen birds, the faint crunch of needles as they walked was the only thing that Mathias could hear. No rustle of small animals accompanied their passage, and after several minutes, that fact began to bother him deeply. He opened his mouth to break the quiet, but found he could not do it. It was too peaceful.

Too perfect.

'We're being watched.'

Tagan seemed to lift the thought directly out of Mathias's head. She let go of his hand, stopping dead where she was. She looked around, turning in a half-circle, and peered into the trackless woods. Nothing but trees and gloom looked back.

'We're being watched,' she repeated, her voice catching in a breathy, slightly frightened way that was not in keeping with her usual brassy confidence. Mathias narrowed his eyes and looked in all directions, including upwards. He could see nothing, but he was sure Tagan was right.

'Yes,' he agreed, keeping his own voice low. He wasn't sure why he did that. There was something sacred about this place. Speaking aloud bordered on the sacrilegious. 'Stay close to me.'

A skittering amongst a patch of drooping ferns caught his attention, and he swung around to see the fronds trembling slightly as something moved beneath them. He caught the barest flash of the tip of a furry tail. Too big to be a squirrel. Far too big.

Instinctively, he moved to stand in front of Tagan and then

wondered precisely why it was that he had done that. He was no warrior; he understood animals and plants, not swords and combat.

'Tagan, keep close to me,' he repeated, without turning to see his betrothed. 'There's definitely something there.'

'Yes,' she said in a voice so tiny that it barely carried on the breeze. 'I know.'

Something in the way she said it caused Mathias's heart to sink; he took a deep breath before he turned to face the same direction as Tagan. There, standing beside a tumble of rocks, was an enormous dog.

Easily as high as Mathias's waist, the creature's rough fur coat was a dark charcoal grey. Its fangs were bared in a threatening snarl, sharp teeth studded along a massive jaw that was perfectly suited to ripping flesh. Huge muscles rippled beneath its skin, tensed and ready to spring.

'Stay perfectly still,' Mathias said to Tagan, who was caught in the animal's amber-eyed glower. The hackles on the back of the dog's neck slowly rose and Mathias felt his own come out with it in some kind of sympathy.

'Do you think this is the Shapeshifter?' Tagan forced the question out around a desperate urge to turn and flee. She had never liked dogs that much, not even the peaceful ones that slunk around the village back home. This dog radiated feral menace. Mathias blinked. The thought had not even occurred to him.

'I... don't know,' he said in response. The dog continued to stand where it was, its teeth still bared. The faintest of growls rumbled from its throat and slowly—very, very slowly—Mathias took a step backwards. The dog took a step forwards. Stalemate.

'Try talking to it,' Tagan urged. Still she wanted to run, but did not dare move. The animal, should it pounce, could tear out her throat in a heartbeat.

'What?'

'Talk to it!' Tagan snapped, and the dog's eyes blinked very slowly, startled. The growl grew louder and Tagan swallowed nervously.

Feeling astonishingly ridiculous, Mathias held his hands out in an open palm gesture. 'Greetings,' he said. 'Hello. Ah—do you understand me? My name is Mathias Eynon,' he said in slow, careful tones. 'I seek the Shapeshifter. Are you him?'

The dog's amber eyes closed and opened again as its huge muzzle turned in Mathias's direction. The young man felt a sense of panic rising in him and then shook his head. His gift had always enabled him to keep even the most furious animals calm. He took a step forward, ignoring Tagan's indrawn hiss.

'Do you understand me?' He slowly lowered one hand. The dog growled more loudly and took a step backwards, away from this intruder. Unperturbed, Mathias moved forward again. 'Are you the Shapeshifter? Here, see? I will not hurt you...' He lowered both hands and stood completely still.

An age passed between the two, man and dog. Mathias did not ask his question again and the dog seemed not to wish to approach him.

'You waste time talking with her.'

The voice came from behind Mathias, but he did not turn to look, acutely aware of the growling animal. Tagan, however, did turn.

Standing directly opposite the dog, clad in animal furs and leather, stood the broadest, stockiest man she had ever seen, at least as wide at the shoulders as he was tall. Whilst short in stature, he more than made up for this with an alarmingly powerful presence. His arms, which were bare beneath his furs, were strong and heavily muscled. His hair was wild and dishevelled and as bright a shade of red as she had ever seen. A beard of the same colour covered the majority of his face. What skin could be seen through the hair was tanned nut-brown and two intelligent, dark brown eyes bored into the pair as though taking the measure of them. Then he grunted and repeated his words.

'You waste time talking with her.' The stocky man's voice was thickly accented and very deep; a voice like stones grinding together, yet it carried through the woods as clear as a bell. 'She speaks no words of English.' He narrowed his eyes, looking from Tagan to Mathias, who finally allowed himself to take his eyes off the animal. The man looked back at the dog and chuckled deeply. 'Also, she is just a dog.'

Having made this pronouncement, the man barked at the dog.

Tagan and Mathias both stared; it was a true bark, much as every dog they had ever known had made. The wolfhound barked in response and then bounded towards him, her tail wagging fiercely. Gone was the fierce beast of seconds previously. In its place was a puppy, keen and eager to play. Mathias realised how tense he had been as his whole body relaxed. Had the dog chosen to attack him, he had little doubt as to who would have won.

There was a sudden shifting in the air, something both Mathias and Tagan recognised. It was like an inward rush of a breeze, or of water in a sudden eddy in the stream, and with it came the metallic scent of magic. Where the stocky man had stood was a second dog; also a wolfhound, but that same bright shade of copper that his hair and beard had been.

'Mathias!' Tagan was staring. There had been no gradual transformation. No extending of limbs, or changing of the face. No sprouting of fur and a tail. There had been a man, then there was a dog. There had been, in fact, a shifting of shapes. Tagan had never seen such powerful magic. Unable to hold back the reaction, she clapped her hands together, delightedly, like a little girl.

The two dogs romped around in circles for a few moments until the female finally stopped and sat on her haunches, her tongue lolling and her mouth open as she stared at Mathias with the most unnervingly human expression he had ever seen on an animal.

Another rush of air, another inexplicable sense of the world bending inwards, and the red dog was gone.

'I am Warin, called the Red.' He made this pronouncement as though daring them to dispute it. 'Welcome to my home.' He stamped a little way away from them, then stopped and turned around. 'Well? Come? Stay? Makes little difference to me.' He continued striding away, the wolfhound trotting along beside him. Warin rested a hand on the dog's neck and scratched affectionately as he walked. He didn't cast a single backwards glance to see if he was being followed.

Tagan and Mathias exchanged glances and followed him. It didn't seem as if they had a lot of choice in the matter. Their fingers interlocking once more, they moved deeper into the woods, to the very depths of the forest where a true silence reigned supreme. Here and there, bright flowers tried to force their way through the needles; hardy little things that grasped weakly at the wan light.

After a while, the tantalisingly familiar scent of wood smoke joined the mingled scents of earth and pine. Warin walked a little further, pushing aside branches with effortless ease. He didn't once stop to ensure that his companions were following, and several times Mathias had to duck as tree limbs sprang back in his wake. The great dog loped along at Warin's side, occasionally dropping back behind the two stragglers, herding them along. Once, Mathias attempted to engage the stout man in conversation. It was not particularly productive.

'Where are we going?'

'To talk.'

'Where are we?'

'You are in my land now. The lands of the Teuton.'

That, it seemed, was that. Mathias pressed on, his thoughts churning with the impossibilities of the past few hours. Days. Months... It had occurred to him that he had no idea just how long it had taken for him and Tagan to get wherever they were now. One thing seemed right, though. Warin was the one they had come here to find. That was without doubt. *The Shapeshifter,* Wyn had said, and they had witnessed Warin's magic. Exactly what his intentions were remained to be seen.

Beside him Tagan kept going, gamely struggling through the increasingly thick undergrowth. She was strong and robust, but he could see that she was tiring. The lingering effects of Wyn's spell were beginning to take their toll on him as well. He felt tired, the same bone-weariness that he remembered assailing him as the earth had swallowed him.

Instinctively, he sensed that tiredness would irritate Warin and he felt a spark of defiance ignite deep in his soul. He simply tightened his hold on Tagan's hand and hoped that she could draw on some of his own fading strength. She looked up at him, gratitude in her eyes.

'There's food and drink up ahead,' said Warin. His spoken English was easy enough to understand, once you worked past the thick accent, but every sentence was as abrupt as the last. This was a man who did not choose to speak often. 'And rest.' He looked over his shoulder and his dark eyes took in the slowing figure of Tagan. 'Not far.'

Mathias sensed he was trying to show some sort of empathy for the blacksmith's daughter with those last two words, but even they were barked rather than spoken. Tagan, too, bewildered and—although she was doing a fine job of not showing it—frightened, nodded gratefully.

'Thank you, Master Warin,' she said respectfully.

'"Warin" is fine.'

She visibly deflated and Mathias hid a smile by looking down at the forest floor. When he looked up, they were approaching a ramshackle building that might have fallen together by accident.

It was open to the forest at one end, the three solid walls rising up to support a thatched canopy that sagged threateningly in the middle. One large open room seemed to contain everything that a magus of Warin's considerable talent apparently required.

'Sit,' the Shapeshifter said, indicating the uneven forest floor. Tagan immediately sank down, stretching her legs out in front of her. They ached more than she could ever remember, and she had stood for hours before the forge. She reached down to rub ruefully at her stiff calves and closed her eyes for a moment. Mathias, on the other hand, remained standing. Warin stared at him, the dark pools of his eyes narrowing suspiciously.

'I said sit,' he repeated, his tone commanding. Mathias blinked, feeling a strange compulsion to do exactly as he was told. He recognised the power, having experienced it at Wyn's hands. In that moment, he suspected that there was more that connected his adopted father with this bizarre woodsman.

Either way, he sat down next to Tagan. The red-haired man levelled an accusatory finger in his direction.

'You will want food. Drink, too.' It was not a question. Warin patted the dog at his side—the animal once again sat on her haunches, panting up at him—before entering the strange forest house. 'I can provide both of these things. Then you tell me why you come to speak with Warin the Red, eh?' His expression softened, at least as much as the face of a man mostly hidden behind a shrubbery of beard could. 'No harm will come to you here, *waagehenkel*.'

'Wa...' Mathias blinked, not having a clue what the strange word meant. Warin considered him for a moment, then moved to a table in one far corner of the room. He picked up a platter with cold meats and a half-eaten loaf of some kind of dark bread.

'*Der waagehenkel*,' he repeated as he offered the plate to Tagan first. She fell on the food with pleasure, her stomach overriding the fleeting concern that this strange man might be trying to poison her. 'In your language...' Warin managed to convey extreme distaste at having to translate. 'In your language, you would say—uh—the hook on which the balance hangs. Fulcrum? Yes. That. *Der waagehenkel*.' He stared at Mathias, daring him to question it.

Mathias did not.

Warin relaxed his stance slightly and crouched before a still-smouldering cook fire. He blew on the ebbing flame in an effort to rekindle the fire, but it stubbornly refused to catch. He began to mutter to himself in what was presumably his native language. Neither Mathias nor Tagan understood a word, but the suggestion was clear. Tagan passed the plate of food up to Mathias, who took it and ate absently.

'Here,' she said, softly. 'Let me.' She crouched down beside him and gave him her most winning smile. Warin considered her suspiciously for a moment, then nodded. '*Ja*,' he said. 'You do it. I smell the flame on you.' He sniffed pointedly in her direction.

Not questioning his odd choice of words, Tagan focused on the tiny glowing ember at the bottom of the cook fire and tipped her head to the side before she held out her hand palm-down in front of her. She turned it upwards and lifted it slowly, as though coaxing the fire to rise with her. The flames crept up through the wood as if drawn on an invisible thread. Tagan straightened her head and smiled.

'Burn,' she said in barely more than a whisper.

The damp logs that had refused to catch light began to crackle merrily at her command and she dropped back to rest on her heels, admiring her handiwork. So did Warin. He let out a huge roar of approval.

'Red has not seen such skill with flame for—oh—many years now. You are more than you seem, are you not?'

'We are all more than we seem,' came Tagan's soft reply. It was a remarkably philosophical thing for her to say, given her propensity for plain talking. Her eyes were still caught in the heart of the fire. Mathias wondered if she were taking some comfort from the white-hot core of the little blaze; some faint reminder of her distant forge. She pulled her attention from the fire to see Warin move across the room to fetch a kettle filled with water, which he set down on top of the flames.

'You are the most powerful magician I have ever seen,' she said to the stocky man. 'How is it that you aren't able to do something as simple as light a fire using that talent?' Mathias winced inwardly, half expecting an angry response. Warin shrugged. As he spoke, the two young people grew more and more used to his accent until his broken sentences became easier to understand.

'My power is of... the earth,' he replied. 'Of the trees and the ground, of the crops, of the animals... and of the sun. When the sun is at its highest, then my power is at its greatest. When the sun is not in the skies... then I am wary. That is the time of those who act in the cover of darkness. It is how I knew where to find you. I felt something in the bones of the earth, something coming.' He looked up at Mathias. 'You and I,' he said, 'are the same. Your power is of the Mother, too.' He nodded as he poked the kettle on the fire. 'I could sense it when you arrived in my forest. Were you bigger, I would fight you for my territory.' He let out a short, barking laugh. 'Like badgers. It is what the children of the Mother do.'

'The Mother?' Mathias looked at Tagan and she shrugged.

Warin stared from one to the other. 'Have the people of your land become so ignorant of what you are? From where your magic comes?'

'Magic is... not well tolerated in our country any longer, Warin,' said Mathias. Warin's hard expression softened to something akin to regret. 'Those of us who can use magic well are forced to hide in the fringes of the kingdom. We hide what we are for fear of our lives.'

'So it has ever been since the days of King Richard. Who sits on the throne now?'

'King... King Richard.' Mathias felt the need to add, 'Not the same one. Obviously.'

Warin stared that animalistic, unblinking stare. 'Do I look,' he said, 'like a man who would think otherwise?'

'No, sir.'

'Sir?' Warin seemed pleased. He poked at the fire, studying the two young people before him. 'Now you tell Warin why it is that you come to his home, hmm?'

Mathias looked at Tagan and he sighed. 'I don't know, Warin,' he said eventually and there was resignation in his voice. 'My... father led some kind of ritual to send us here. He said that we were to find the Shapeshifter and some others, too. But he seemed confident that we would find you here.'

'Who are you sent to find? The words exactly, boy.'

'It is hard to recall. I feel as though I am walking in a dream.'

'Then wake up and answer me. Who are you looking for?'

Mathias wrinkled his nose with the effort of recall. 'The... the Shapeshifter,' he said. 'Which we appear to have done. What were the others? The Pirate King. The Wanderer. There was a fourth. Another name.'

'She Who Sees.' Warin said the last name with something like venom colouring his tone. Mathias didn't notice; he nodded eagerly.

'Yes,' said Mathias. 'She Who Sees.'

'Then you will fail. I will go nowhere if... *she* is going to be there.' He folded his muscled arms across his chest and rather comically thrust out his lower lip, as though he were a child refusing to carry out a chore. Tagan put a hand to her mouth to hide her sudden smile.

Mathias studied Warin for a while. He looked across to Tagan who gave a slight shrug of her shoulders. Without speaking, she implied that this task was Mathias's to deal with.

The young man blew a lock of hair out of his eyes and looked at the Shapeshifter in growing despair, wondering where in the name of all that was good and holy he was ever going to find enough charm to move the unmovable.

FIVE

Whitehall Palace
England

KING RICHARD WAS not a happy man. Neither was the messenger knelt before him. It was difficult to tell, at that moment, who was the more worried.

'Repeat your message.' Richard didn't quite know why he made the demand. Self-flagellation, perhaps. He trusted the Inquisition to deal with the magi and arcane threats across the isle but it seemed, on this occasion, that they had failed him.

The messenger cleared his throat. 'The village was destroyed along with the standing stones and the people put to the sword. The magi were also slain, but the Lord Inquisitor spared one for further questioning. There was a ritual...' The messenger's eyes filled with anxiety as Richard's stare bored into him. The King had a way of looking through you that made you shrivel to your soul.

'What about the ritual?' he asked calmly, his manner controlled. The messenger felt a spark of hope that perhaps his life might not be forfeit.

'The Inquisitor arrived too late to stop some kind of rite. Lord Weaver reports that he saw two bodies in the ground as he approached, but when he reached the stone circle, they were gone.' He shuddered at the thought. 'They dug down several feet in the wake of the circle's destruction, but they found nothing.'

'I see.' Richard leaned back in the throne, his hand reaching up to rest against his bearded chin thoughtfully. 'And the survivor?'

'In the Tower, my lord. Under the guard of the Inquisition.'

'Very well, I trust Lord Weaver will extract some answers. You are dismissed.'

Apparently granted his life, genuinely surprised, the messenger kissed the floor with his forehead before backing out of the chamber.

Richard watched him go. He knew the man had expected some kind of retribution. The fear had been written across his face. The King knew a moment's discomfiture at the thought. Did his people truly see him as so very tyrannical? He knew that he was not a benevolent man, not by a long stretch of the imagination. But still... the dread on the young man's face filled the King with uncertainty.

The doubt fired Richard's anger. After all, he was used to being completely in control. He had no real understanding of the heathen practices of the magi, and by his own order had branded such knowledge heretical. Those who still practised magic within the borders of England did so on pain of death. The use of a stone circle was something he had not encountered before, though. He worried at the thought, turning it over in his mind in an attempt to fathom out what conspiracy was at work. He felt a twinge of regret that he could no longer consult Josef on such matters, but crushed it savagely. No magi could be tolerated, for any reason.

His fingers closed around the pendant he wore at his neck. No magi could be tolerated, but Richard had higher powers he could call upon, though his skin crawled at the thought.

Rising from the throne, the King straightened his tunic. It was time to go hunting.

USUALLY THE ROYAL hunts were occasions of pomp and spectacle; petty nobles and minor lords vied for his attention, their obsequiousness eclipsed only by their greed. This was not one of those occasions. Today, Richard rode alone.

The announcement that he was going hunting was received with the expected resistance. The guard felt it a dereliction of their duty. The court thought it unseemly. The Inquisition considered it dangerous. All of these arguments and more were brought before him as he prepared to ride and made his way to the stables.

Eventually, following a message informing the King that hunts were important affairs that required weeks to prepare for the catering alone, that they were special events that the King of England should arrange for the most political of reasons, Richard turned his smouldering gaze on the unfortunate footman who had delivered the news.

'Yes,' he said. 'I am the King of England. And that is precisely the point.' He glared at the man, who wore the livery of Norfolk, and he seemed to visibly shrink. 'I am the King of England. This is *my* kingdom. My domain. If I choose to visit it alone, then that is precisely what I shall do. There will be time after this war is won for frivolity. Return to your master and tell him that in future, if I want his advice, I will ask for it.'

RICHARD RODE THROUGH the thick woodlands bordering the royal estate, his expression morose and his thoughts dark. Most of the expansive grounds surrounding the palace were carefully cultivated and sculpted into flowering gardens, clipped mazes and ornamental ponds. An army of serfs was employed to tend to the land, keeping the industrial refuse of London outside its borders, but some of the woods had been allowed to grow wild for the King's sport.

For his entire life, Richard Plantagenet had known, like his father, that a day might come when he had to answer for the actions of his ancestors. The price of Richard the Third's success on the battlefield that day so many years past was something that could never be spoken of outside the line of kings. If it became known that the royal family consorted with demons, then not only would it spell doom for the house of Plantagenet—it would see the fall of England alongside.

Like our souls are not already damned.

He rode deeper into the heart of the forest, where he could detach himself from the reality of what he knew must surely come. He was King of England, but he was also a husband and a father, and entirely capable of separating his roles. He devoted himself to his children whenever he had the chance. They had been born, every one of them, strong and healthy, robust and beautiful, and they represented the future of his bloodline. He feared for them now, for what their future might hold. Things were moving too quickly for his liking.

His hand came again to the pendant around his neck. Crafted from silver and untarnished despite its age, it had once belonged to the victor of Bosworth Field. Small and delicate as it might have been, Richard felt its leaden weight hanging around his neck like a millstone. He reined his horse in as he rode into a clearing and reached up to tug the pendant over his head. He turned it over in his hand and studied it.

The symbol stamped onto it was a representation of the rose of his family's heraldry, stained black as the rose in the banner was. Richard ran a finger over the embossed design.

The King dismounted from his horse and tethered the animal. He slipped a set of blinkers onto its head and it began contentedly cropping at the brush. He did not want the beast to be spooked by the sight of the unnatural. Above him, the sky was clear, a few wisps of dirty cloud the only things that intruded on the pristine blue of a summer's day. He could still smell the soot of the forges, but a light breeze pulled the smoke of the fires south, away from the palace.

'Seasons come and go,' Richard thought aloud. The horse raised its head in curiosity at the sound, then returned to the important task of slow deforestation. 'Seasons come and go, but the house of Plantagenet is constant. The bloodline will *not* end with me.'

He took a deep breath and strode to the centre of the clearing. He knelt down in the dew-damp grass and inhaled the heady scent of loam. Since his ascension to the throne, he had performed this ritual only four times. It should have been more, many more, but by the time his fifth child was born, he could no longer bear it.

He took a dagger and a strip of cloth from his belt. He set the cloth across his thigh and took the dagger into his right hand. He drew a deep breath and cut swiftly into the meat of his palm. Red blood welled instantly and he closed his fist around the pendant. He winced at the sting of the injury, but held his hand aloft. This was the critical part of the ritual. He felt a horrible twinge of guilt at what he was doing. How many had died for performing arcane rites like this? How many magi had gone to the Tower for lesser crimes?

A great many. And I am a hypocrite.

He shook himself from his reverie and focused on what he was doing. Three drops of blood. Three drops alone. Too few and the ritual would not work; too many and the consequences could be dire.

A single scarlet bead oozed from between his clenched fingers and dripped to the ground. As it hit the grass, staining the green with crimson, he murmured the name.

'Melusine.'

One more drop. And a third. With each drop, the King said the name. When the ritual was complete, he wrapped his injured hand immediately in the cloth to stop any more blood flow. Then he waited. There was nothing else for him to do.

Time ticked by, slow and ponderous. It might have been hours before a quiet sigh stirred the air. Strands of black and crimson curled from the site of his sacrifice and wove themselves into a female form. It was thin and insubstantial, but the presence still made Richard's heart contract with fear. The dreams had been bad, but they paled into insignificance beside the shade.

'An early summons, my King? It is not yet time, and yet it has been so very long.'

By tradition, each king since Richard the Third's victory at Bosworth summoned Melusine on the anniversary of the pact. The practice had become largely ceremonial, and often the demon chose not to appear at all, but the current King had grown to dread the rituals. Melusine had appeared to him every time.

He tried to speak, but he could not find his voice. The demon walked up to him and knelt in the grass at his feet. She took his hands in hers and looked at him with her head tipped to one side. She was so beautiful. He felt the passion for her stirring in his blood. Passion and revulsion. All his resolve, all his determination that he would be able to wring answers from the creature, melted like tallow before a flame.

For some time, all he could do was stare at her, the ache in his loins growing worse with each passing moment. Her grip on his hands tightened even more and he groaned softly, fighting back the conflicting urges to pull her into his embrace or push her away. She tipped her head a little further over and then straightened. With a soft, humourless laugh, she released Richard's hands and leaned back, resting on her heels.

'Is that the spark of rebellion I sense in you, Richard Plantagenet? Do you plan to forsake the promises of your forefathers?'

His voice was returned to him, as was mastery of his treacherous body. He took a few deep breaths, cooling the unnatural ardour. She gave him time to compose himself and waited for him to speak.

'Something has happened,' he said, speaking slowly. He knew that it was important to pick the right words. 'I have summoned you early to seek... to seek your advice. To ask your forgiveness and for your help.' From the moment news of the ritual in Wales had reached his ears, Richard had been worried. There had been no great works of magic since before he took the throne. The last great magi in England had been put to death during the time of his father, and the Inquisition believed only lesser practitioners remained. He did not know what Melusine's reaction would be to the news.

'You have been lax in honouring the pact, sweet Richard, but I forgive you.' The crimson lips turned up in a coy smile. 'For I know I am ever in your thoughts. And your dreams.'

'The dreams you sent me,' he said. 'Josef claimed that... he claimed that you want my son...'

She shushed him into silence and waved a long-fingered hand dismissively. 'There is time for such talk later. First, you must tell me what it is that has happened to worry you so.'

The shade's red eyes glittered with amusement and Richard suddenly felt very foolish, as if this creature knew everything he was about to say and more besides. 'Five days ago, Lord Weaver destroyed a village of magi beyond the Welsh border...'

'This is pleasing and excellent news.' The demon interrupted again. 'Lord Weaver is to be commended for his dedication to duty.'

'Indeed, he is a credit to the Crown.' Richard forged on, a little desperately. 'However, he bore witness to a ritual, and was unable to prevent its completion. Such magic has not been heard of...'

Melusine's ruby smile had crystallised into something sinister and the aura of lust and malice throbbed around the clearing. Richard's horse stood trembling, its animal senses filled with primal fear even without sight of the demon.

'For a very long time.' She finished Richard's sentence. 'I know.'

'You know?'

'Yes, and Lord Weaver really *is* to be commended. The ritual he came upon was a sending, a bridge between two places. It is old magic that no magi now within your kingdom could hope to wield.'

'But if the peasants of a tiny Welsh village have mastered such power,' Richard replied hesitantly, 'then might there not be others who...'

'No. There are no others in this land. With a single shot, Lord Weaver unbound Aethelweard. Now that he is free of his flesh, we are free to hunt him.' Her voluptuous form flickered as she spoke of hunting, just for a moment, and revealed something awful. The blood drained from the King's face and a lock of his hair was bleached white. Then she was a woman again, her gaze fixed on Richard with predatory hunger.

'You must find the ones he sent.'

Richard swallowed hard, his breath coming in quick, ragged gasps. The conflicting sensations rolling from the demonic shade were consuming and bordering on overpowering. Honeysuckle. Jasmine. The snap of bone. A warm tongue. Teeth breaking. 'How... how can we find them? We have no way of knowing where they have gone.'

'Dear Richard,' Melusine purred. She stood and walked in a languid circle around the King, trailing the tip of a finger across his shoulders. 'Aethelweard hid them from my sight for so long. But no longer. He has sent them across the sea, to the lands beyond France. He will be looking for other magi of great power. You must stop them.'

'Beyond France.' Richard repeated the demon's words, realisation slowly dawning.

'You wanted your war, Richard. It seems that you will have it sooner than you believed.' The diaphanous spirit spun on its heel and made a clawing motion with its hand. The King's horse burst like a ripe fruit, painting the clearing with gore and offal. The King could not help but cry out; he covered his eyes just a fraction too late. As Melusine's womanly form became something infinitely more terrifying, she leaned into him. 'War, Richard Plantagenet. I demand it!'

He could not watch what followed.

Six

The Tower
England

Charles Weaver sat at the desk in his study, his head bowed over the ledger, his hand writing the reports from the week's activities in his beautiful slanted script. The Welsh prisoner had yielded nothing of note, but there was time yet for him to break. At his side was a tray bearing his choice of sustenance: bread, cheeses and a few slices of home-cured meat. The simple repast would serve him well enough. A bottle of wine was uncorked and stood before him. But Charles Weaver neither ate nor drank. To do either required the removal of his mask, and until his personal servants retired for the night, he would not take it off. Even then, he had become strangely reluctant to do so.

The reports came in on a regular basis and not all were pertinent. Here there was an account of possible evidence of magic use in a distant English backwater village. There, details of attempts by magicians to receive the support of the Church. So many of these ended without the intervention of the Inquisition, overly-dramatic scenes of self-martyrdom by the desperate and unofficial elevation to sainthood in the eyes of their faithful followers. All these Charles Weaver read, and more. Wherever there was a hint of unusual activity, the Inquisition would follow up the leads.

So many reports. Weaver growled quietly as he read. A plague upon the people of this country. Nothing seemed to get through to them. Threats that were made and carried out served as little more than a temporary bump in the unholy road they persisted along.

'My lord?' There was a tapping at the study door and Weaver raised his head.

'Enter.' He set down the quill and leaned back in the heavy oak chair. One of the staff he had brought from his country estate to work in the Tower as his personal servants entered the claustrophobic office.

'Forgive the disturbance, my lord, but this arrived moments ago. The bearer stressed its importance.' The servant, a faceless serf whose name Weaver had never bothered to learn, held out an ivory scroll case. Rising to his feet, Weaver moved the bulk of his huge body round to the front of the desk. He took the scroll case, recognising the seal instantly.

'It's from the King, isn't it, my lord?' It was presumptuous of the servant to speak without cause, and as the metal face turned on him and he saw the glint in the eyes beneath, he wished he'd remained silent.

'You may leave now,' the Lord Inquisitor replied stonily. He watched the servant scuttle out of the room, taking a quiet satisfaction in the obvious discomfort he had caused. When the door shut, he stepped across to it and turned the key in the lock. He would not be disturbed again.

He opened the scroll case, slid out the parchment within and unfurled it. He leaned against the desk, holding the paper taut as he read the missive from King Richard. It did not take long. There were several lines that discussed the logistics of what was to come, but Weaver's eyes were drawn to the words at the very bottom, above the flourish of Richard's signature.

We will go to war.
You will lead them in my name.

Beneath the mask, Weaver began to laugh, a sound entirely devoid of humour.

Finally, it was going to happen. Finally, the moment he had been waiting for had arrived. He would sweep across France, then Italy. Spain and Portugal. All the countries who wore the badge of magic on their breasts would be crushed. Magic would be driven from the shores of the continent and an English Empire would be born in the twin lights of science and reason.

'We will go to war,' Weaver repeated aloud.

* * *

Bavaria
Germany

AFTER HOURS IN Warin's company, Mathias had come to the conclusion that there had been nobody so stubborn in the history of the entire world. The stocky Shapeshifter was as implacable as rock and about as dense. Mathias had tried everything in his limited power to gain the assistance of the magus but had utterly failed at every attempt.

Eventually, he let it rest. He was tired. Tagan had already curled up in a corner of the peculiar little hut and gone to sleep, a thin blanket of rough hide pulled over her. Warin had vanished off into the forest with the female wolfhound an hour or two earlier as the last of the light began to leave the day. It was a clear night with a velvet sky studded with stars and constellations. Mathias stared up at them, finding a sense of great comfort in their familiarity.

With evening had come a chill that saw him fetch a blanket of his own and wrap it around his shoulders as he sat in the hut, staring at the jumping shadows cast by the fire that flickered in the gloom. The air was fresh and clean, and the sounds of the forest were equal parts strange and familiar. The wind whispered through the trees, stirring the boughs in an endless, gentle song that soothed him.

Flittering wings drew his drowsy attention as a bat made its way overhead in pursuit of some sort of insect. Mathias watched it for a while as it beat its erratic course through the darkening sky. Eventually, however, he was lulled into a light sleep by the sound of the trees.

He didn't know how long he slept. An hour? Maybe longer. But it was the smell of roasting meat that pulled him back to wakefulness. His nostrils flared in response to the scent and his mouth salivated as consciousness returned to him. Just beyond the lip of the hut, Warin sat cross-legged before the fire, turning three plump rabbits on a spit. The wolfhound lay at his side.

Mathias glanced over towards Tagan and was surprised to see

that she still slept. She shivered once or twice and the young man got to his feet, crossing softly to her and laying his own blanket over her shoulders before stepping out to join Warin.

The wolfhound's head rose sleepily, but when she realised that it was only Mathias, she made a strangely contented sort of noise and lay back down.

'Hungry, Englander?'

'I'm Welsh.' The response was automatic and only half-hearted.

'I don't know what that means. You are Englander to me. Answer the question. Are you hungry?'

'Yes,' Mathias admitted. 'I am.'

'Grauenhund and I hunted for you and the girl.' Warin waved a hand at the rabbits. 'Eat what you want, leave the rest.'

'What about you?'

'I said we hunted,' replied Warin. 'I ate my fill then.' He turned his head slightly and a wicked grin spread across his face. 'One of the things about being a shapeshifter is no need to cook your food.'

'You ate your food raw.' It was a statement rather than a question, and if Warin had been expecting Mathias to be shocked, it didn't work. The stocky man deflated slightly.

'It's almost ready,' he said, waving at the rabbit. 'It is not much.'

'Thank you,' said Mathias simply and he took a seat next to Warin. The air of the night was cool and the warmth from the fire very welcome. He reached over to stroke the long, silken ears of the female wolfhound and she cracked open one eye to study the young man. She shifted her bulk a few inches closer to him and Mathias smiled, running a hand over her coarse fur.

'She is a fine hunter,' Warin said. 'My companions have come and gone over the years, but she has been the best. And the most loyal. She is old, of course. Not much longer for this world.' The matter-of-fact way in which he said it did not hide the underlying sadness.

'What's it like? Being able to change what you are?' Mathias took advantage of the melancholy moment to ask the question that had been burning at the back of his mind since he had first witnessed Warin's remarkable talent. 'Becoming anything you wish to be?'

'I wish that I could be anything I wanted to be,' came the reply.

'But my powers are limited by my own nature. I can take the form of any other animal, any of the children of the land. But you know this. You are of the earth. Can you not change your shape also?'

'No,' said Mathias. 'I can't.'

'Did you try?'

The question came out of nowhere and he was startled by it. Yet somewhere in there was a clue as to a way to encourage Warin to open up. 'No,' he said, carefully. 'I didn't. Perhaps, if you travel with us, you could...'

'I will not leave my forest. I will not teach you.' Silence fell again and eventually, Mathias resumed conversation.

'What about other people? Can you take their likenesses?'

'Yes,' Warin replied. 'But I don't. That way leads to many complications. For me. Animals are different, but their natures are predictable. Humans? Less so. I chose to spend less time with them and more time with the children of the forest.'

'The beasts and the birds, hmm?'

Warin's amber eyes blinked up slowly at Mathias. 'Just the beasts,' he said and there was such longing in his voice that it was moving. 'Not the birds. That skill belongs to another.' The tone became faintly bitter.

'She Who Sees? Is she a shapeshifter as well?' Mathias read the reaction cautiously, but clearly he read it well. The by-now customary scowl crept back onto Warin's face and he folded his arms over his chest.

'Something smells good,' said a sleepy female voice. Tagan had woken, the blankets wrapped around her, and was stepping out to join them. Mathias smiled fondly at her, but inwardly cursed her timing. Warin had finally been about to open up, he was sure of it.

'Warin cooked for us,' he said, keeping his voice pleasant. He reached up a hand to his betrothed and she took it, stepping off the hut floor and down onto the dirt and grass of the forest. She sat down easily, crossing her legs and sniffing at the cooking meat.

'Wild garlic,' she observed. 'Thyme.'

'You have a good nose,' said Warin, clearly impressed.

'I cook for my family,' was Tagan's response. 'This is a rarity for me. Having someone else do the cooking, I mean.' Her mood was bright and cheerful. Mathias felt another stab of apprehension as he wondered what had become of the quiet little village they had left behind. He couldn't bring himself to share his fears with her, to burden her with worry and uncertainty when they already faced an uncertain future.

'Mathias tried to cook for me once. He made me a stew. To this day I am unsure as to what meat was in it.'

'Meat,' replied Mathias good-naturedly.

'From what part of the animal?'

'You know the phrase "what you don't know can't harm you," right?' He grinned and for a moment, Warin, the dog, the cook fire and the Bavarian forest slipped away. For a fleeting heartbeat, it was just the two of them. Impulsively, Mathias took the young woman's hand and kissed the back of her knuckles.

She gave a little smile and ducked her head. Caught up in the moment, Mathias leaned forward to give her a small kiss on the cheek.

Warin rather destroyed the tenderness of the gesture by noisily clearing out one nostril onto the fire. The resulting sound was not unlike a damaged bugle sounding a battle call.

'Do you want me to go back out hunting whilst you two mate?' He waved a hand and Tagan flushed bright pink. Mathias blushed even harder and more hotly than she did.

'We certainly won't be doing that,' he said. 'We have *some* propriety, you know.'

Warin laughed uproariously, slapping his hands against his crossed legs. 'Is better with the animals. They don't care so much for prop-ri-ety.' He broke the word down into exaggerated syllables, mimicking Mathias's accent. 'The people of your land,' he said, waving a finger, 'are—what is the word—prune-ish?'

'Possibly *prudish*,' murmured Mathias. 'Thank you for your offer, Warin. You don't have to leave.'

'Englanders.'

'I'm Welsh,' said Mathias again, feeling pleased that he heard Tagan mutter the same. Warin blinked his slow, animal blink.

'So you keep telling me,' he said.

A companionable silence descended, settling over the little tableau like a comfortable cloak. The stars twinkled overhead, like diamonds set against the black velvet of the night. The shadows of the tree canopy moved in a whispering breeze that blew the sweet breath of night into their faces. Warin flensed the meat from the cooked rabbits and passed it to Mathias and Tagan, piled high on a plate of bark. They ate with enthusiasm, tearing chunks off the hard, unleavened bread that Warin had also cooked on one of the firestones.

When they had finished the meal, Tagan begged Warin to shapeshift again. She had been entranced, she said. Never had she yearned for a power so wonderful. Perhaps impishly flattered by her attentions, Warin obliged. He took the form of the wolfhound first, which clearly delighted the other dog, who danced around him, barking in delight. The wolfhound melted away and a rabbit took its place. The rabbit hopped behind a bush and a mouse scampered out and ran up Tagan's arm to sit on her shoulder.

He entertained them this way for some time until once more, the flame-haired man was sat opposite them.

'What happens,' Tagan said, her eyes shining with delight, 'to your *clothes*?'

He gave her a cool stare and a nonchalant shrug of one shoulder. 'The first principle of magic,' he said. 'It is not what you *actually* do, but what you make others believe you do.' He gave Tagan a grin. It was evident that he was flattered, and was happy to answer her. 'Now you show me what *you* can do.' He levelled a stubby finger in Tagan's direction and she looked embarrassed.

'I can't do anything as wonderful as change my shape,' she said, modestly. 'I can work metal well, though. I can forge you a sword or a piece of filigree with equal skill...'

'You can do more,' said Warin. 'To shape the body of the earth using the tongues of flame, air and water is the greatest power there is.' He said this so matter-of-factly that Tagan laughed, thinking he merely sought to return her flattery.

Warin did not laugh.

'You're serious,' observed Mathias. He had enjoyed Warin's little display, but not without the faintest pangs of jealousy. What it must be to be able to effortlessly change your form into something else. What freedom it must bring. As an animal, Warin would have no expectations placed upon his shoulders, no impossible task to accomplish...

And Mathias saw it all with a cold clarity. Why it was that Warin the Red, the Shapeshifter, chose to live in isolation within a dark, forbidding forest. Why he eschewed the company of his fellow men and women and preferred the company of animals. He looked up at Warin and found the man's animalistic, amber eyes resting on him. The next words the red-haired man spoke were in a soft voice, barely hiding an odd yearning.

'When last I walked amongst the world of men,' he said, telling his tale without invitation, 'honour still meant something. The magi still meant something. Warrior kings made war for land or glory, this is true, but they respected the magic. Now, though, magic is a tool to make life easy, or make rich, or kill others. And you tell me now magi are hunted. It is a world to which me and my... to which I do not belong.'

'What *are* you, Warin?' Mathias held out a hand and rested it on Warin's arm. The stocky man stared at it and snatched his arm free.

'I am the Shapeshifter.' He closed up again, his moment of vulnerability vanishing.

'We need you,' said Tagan. She had been stirred to curiosity by Warin's suggestion that she was somehow far stronger in her magic than she even knew, but now was not the time. 'We were sent to find you and others. The Pirate King. The Wanderer. She Who Sees...'

Warin rose and turned his back on Tagan and Mathias. 'You will leave when morning comes,' the Shapeshifter announced. 'And I will not go with you.'

'But...'

'No. I will say no more. I will not leave my forest. It has been too long or it has not yet been long enough.' He waved a hand dismissively. 'Whatever it is, the answer is "no." I have no need to return to the world of men and kings and deceit. No. You leave in the morning.'

'But...'

Warin glared at the young couple and in a heartbeat, he shifted into the form of the wolfhound. Grauenhund barked in joy, delighted to have her playmate back, and the two of them ran into the forest, swallowed up silently by the all-encompassing darkness.

20 miles off the coast of Dieppe
France

SUNRISE BROUGHT A rolling fog that curled around the hulls of more than a hundred ships, each proudly flying the French colours. Scores of hawk-eyed boys, and several magi, stood in the crow's nests, senses strained for any sign of the English who were said to be approaching the coast. A hastily scrawled missive from a spy in the court of King Richard claimed that the King had returned from a hunting trip stained with blood; the result, he claimed, of a failed assassination plot by French agents. He had been so outraged by the incident that he had immediately ordered the army to begin preparations, and the fleet to a state of battle readiness.

Even sped on its way via arcane means, the report had barely reached the ears of King Henri in time to get the fleet in place and the army on the march.

The sound of churning water disturbed the stillness of the morning. It was joined by the chorus of paddles biting at the sea as several dark smears appeared in the fog. The lookouts called out the alert, and within seconds, hundreds of guns were run out in readiness. Every ship was armed and ready to confront the English intruders: the frigates, galleons and carracks presented the formidable firepower of their broadsides.

Crews tensed as the sounds drew nearer. Along with the familiar sounds were other noises—metallic scrapings that were alien to the seas. A dark pall and the smell of tar and soot washed ahead of the approaching vessels. On the deck of the French flagship, a fat-bellied man-of-war dubbed the *Hirondelle*, the master magus and his coven prepared a spell. He firmly believed that King Richard's notorious disdain for magic would leave the English vessels defenceless against the arcane, despite his much-lauded science.

At an unspoken command, the magi throughout the fleet acted as one, their magic pooling and dispersing in unison, ripping the fogbank apart. At the same time, every French vessel opened fire, the thunderous roar of the cannon eclipsing the noisy approach of the English. A great wave of powder smoke billowed from the guns and the crews let out a mighty cheer of defiance as their trap was sprung.

The cry swiftly turned to despair as the smoke cleared and the French saw what was bearing down on them.

Two score vessels, their hulls studded with iron and belching black fumes, churned the sea to foam. They were led by a dreadnought whose bladed prow stood half as high again in the water as the *Hirondelle*, its deck pierced by a forest of masts and chimneys. They were followed by an armada of barques and frigates, loaded to capacity with soldiers and horses.

Fire from the French guns met the hulls of the ironclads with a dull *clang*, buckling plates or turning aside with shrieking sparks but failing to inflict any serious damage. A second volley creased the air, the well-drilled crews reloading their weapons with a sudden urgency born of desperation. A few English ships stuttered, chimneys holed or paddles shredded, but the rest came on, as relentless and as apparently undaunted as the sea itself.

The magi stationed on the masts began to cast their spells, hurling fire and arcs of lightning at the approaching vessels. They were answered by marksmen among the English crew, wielding long rifles and crystal lenses. What had begun as righteous defiance quickly became disorganised flight.

The master magus looked on in despair as his brothers and sisters died, plucked from their perches by unseen snipers. The captain of the *Hirondelle* was bellowing orders as he tried to bring the great ship about, but it was already too late. For something so massive, the English flagship moved with horrifying speed. The mage closed his eyes and whispered a quiet message to the air, infusing it with a little power. The words flew away faster than thought; they would reach the ears of one of the magi assembling with the army. It would be enough to warn them of what was coming.

He opened his eyes in time to see the iron prow of the *Indomitable* towering over him, blotting out the sun. Then it drove into the side of the *Hirondelle* and broke her open. Screams, and the sound of shattering wood, consumed his world.

'INTO THEM!' WEAVER roared.

The Lord Inquisitor sat astride his war horse, taking in the growing scene of carnage spreading along the beach. A line of shields and spears bristled halfway up the sand and was steadily pushing the French line back. Hundreds of arrows rained from the high ground on to the landing boats, but the wood and leather roofs of the boats kept the majority of the men safe until they were able to join their comrades.

Pockets of resistance formed around the French magi, who blasted holes in the ranks with elemental fury, crushed flesh and armour with fists of invisible force or turned the ground to sucking mud with their powers. The English outnumbered the French, but still landing as they were, they were unable to bring their greater numbers to bear.

Weaver frowned behind his mask as a broken warrior sailed through the air and plunged into the sea. Ahead of him a mage had emerged from the ranks and was laying into the English soldiery with a staff. The force of the weapon's impacts was huge, the magically enhanced staff smashing shields to splinters and pulping men with each blow. The Inquisitor drew one of his pistols, sighted and fired in one fluid motion. The newly developed crystalline shot flashed through the air, leaving a greenish trail, and struck the mage in the side of the head, blowing half his skull away. The alchemical bullets were just one of many new weapons that had been bestowed upon the Lord Inquisitor before his departure from England. It had transpired that Isaac Bonnington was not, in fact, the useless creature many had taken him for.

The King had impressed upon him the importance of his mission. Paris must be broken before winter arrived, and Weaver had no intention of disappointing his King. He turned in the saddle as another wave of boats crunched onto the beach, this one carrying more of the esoteric weapons birthed by English science. Several units of archers and fire-lancers took up position behind hastily erected mantlets and began returning fire up the beach. The long rifles were many times more potent than the bows, but were slow to reload, so their wielders had been instructed to look for magi or nobles among the army.

A dragon's-breath team struggled up the sand, two men bearing heavy barrels of alchemically treated pitch following another pair who handled a pump and nozzle. Upon reaching the line of shields, the first man uncovered a tiny gas light whilst the second began working the pump. A jet of black spewed forth and emerald fire raged into the enemy ranks. Men and horses shrieked and died, the flesh melting from their bones, and a pair of magi were immolated where they stood.

The French line wavered in the face of this new assault, their morale beginning to buckle. Then a huge figure descended onto the beach and the defenders gave a cry of elation. Weaver narrowed his eyes in distaste as the creature stomped its way across the sand. It could only be a mage, quite possibly the master magus of the army, but its form was entirely concealed within a hulking body of stone.

The Lord Inquisitor watched as arrows and shot clattered harmlessly from its craggy hide. It pushed through the alchemical fire, streams of burning liquid cascading in its wake, and slammed into the English ranks. Men were scattered like toys before the giant, their mangled bodies crushed into the beach, flipped into the air or broken with contemptuous ease. It stomped on the dragon's-breath team with a crunch of breaking bones and wood, and the barrels of pitch exploded, belching a mushroom of green-tinted smoke into the air.

'My lord, we cannot fight the likes of that.' The armoured Duke of Suffolk looked aghast at the monster. 'We must retreat, and bombard the coast with the ships' guns.'

There was an uneasy murmur among the assembled lords behind the Inquisitor. Weaver turned slowly to regard the Duke. 'There will be no retreat,' he growled, voice echoing in his mask. 'Any man who voices otherwise, be he lord or serf, will answer to me for treason.'

The Duke of Suffolk visibly shrank in the saddle and a number of nobles very obviously distanced themselves from him.

'Bring up the repeater,' Weaver ordered a runner and the boy hastened to obey.

Less than a minute later, a carriage pulled by two straining horses splashed onto the beach from the Inquisitor's own boat. They turned in a half-circle to present the rear of the wagon to the enemy and then the canvas covering the vehicle was pulled back. Thirty miniature cannon, bound together with copper and iron, sat bolted to the floor of the carriage, attended by a pair of soot-smeared gunners. At Weaver's direction, they took hold of a number of crank handles protruding from the rear of the weapon and began to turn, heavily muscled arms pumping in unison.

The noise, even above the clamour of battle, was tremendous.

Not all of the shots struck the stone-clad mage; several smashed through the line, killing French and English alike, while a few more failed to fire altogether, the imperfect mechanisms missing their triggers. The rest hammered the giant to its knees, chewing fist-size chunks from its hide and filling the air with the stink of sulphur and rock dust. Then one of the ballistae struck something at the core of the creature that was soft and yielding.

A mist of gore exploded from the rear of the giant and with slow, majestic grace the creature toppled backward to shatter into rubble on the beach, revealing the broken remains of a grey-robed magus. The shot had cored the man, blasting a huge hole in his torso and hollowing him out. The French broke and began streaming back up the beach toward the doomed village of Dieppe.

'Advance,' Weaver ordered. 'No prisoners. Burn the town to its foundations.'

The invasion of France had begun.

SEVEN

Bavaria
Germany

DAWN, WHEN IT finally broke, was cool and damp and although well-rested, Mathias woke with an ache in the small of his back and a throbbing in his head, just behind the eyes. He sat up and rubbed vigorously at his face to divest himself of sleep.

The Shapeshifter was once more seated by the fire, his broad shoulders hunched over as he stirred water in a pot. He raised his head briefly as he heard Mathias moving about and grunted by way of greeting. Tagan was already awake, sitting by the fire with him. She looked as though she had not slept anywhere near as well as he had, and she gave him a wan smile as she saw him. The blanket was wrapped around her shoulders like a cloak.

Mathias stretched out his aching muscles and stepped out to join the two of them at the fire. He touched his hand to Tagan's shoulder gently and she nodded in response.

'I will take you both back to the circle after you have eaten,' said Warin, clearly not prepared to waste any time—or allow Mathias another opportunity to attempt to reason with him. 'I will send you back to your land. Warin the Red will have no part in this.'

'Warin...' Mathias began, but Warin raised a meaty palm.

'We will not discuss it further.'

'But...'

'Ah!'

'I just...'

The Shapeshifter unleashed a string of Germanic words that Mathias didn't understand, but which he was pretty certain was something less than complimentary. A few moments of silence passed and Mathias's shoulders slumped in defeat. Breakfast, it turned out, was a thin broth that tasted faintly of last night's rabbits. It was hardly filling and probably not all that nutritious, but it was hot and turned away some of the damp that these woods seemed to bring to both body and spirit.

The three of them ate in silence, the she-wolfhound lying with her great head across Warin's lap, soulful eyes gazing up at him. He stroked her silky ears tenderly and looked faintly annoyed when she trotted over to do the same to Mathias. The younger man smiled down at the animal and carefully stroked her head.

'She trusts you.' The red-headed man observed this in a flat, toneless voice and Mathias grasped on the final chance to find some common ground.

'I love animals,' he said. 'I always have done. You said yesterday that there is much about my magic that I do not understand. I would dearly love to learn more.' Warin's eyes narrowed as though he suspected another lobbying attempt to get him to travel. When it didn't come, he visibly relaxed.

'You are old to start learning properly,' he said. 'But not so old that you cannot learn a few important things. Perhaps when you return to England...'

'Wales.'

'Perhaps when you return to your home...' He glared at Mathias and the young Welshman fell silent. Tagan giggled quietly beside him. 'You can get your father—Ardwyad?—to show you the true power that you have locked up here.' He reached over to put his big hand flat on Mathias's chest. 'So much to unlock. He has shirked his responsibilities, yes?'

'His name is Wyn, not Ardwyad,' Tagan said, and Warin's eyes turned to her.

He grunted. 'Wyn, eh? Not what I expected.'

'Why would you expect somebody to have a particular name?' Tagan asked.

'Because that is what he is. To you, anyway. I would usually know him as Adelmo. The men of the north know him as Asmund; those of the south, Alexander. It is who he is. You call me the Shapeshifter, because that is what I am. The Pirate King is just that. The Wanderer...'

A faint hint of reverence came into Warin's voice. 'The Wanderer, he is never where you left him.'

'But what *are* you?' Mathias was feeling bold enough to ask this question again. He still had no idea what Wyn expected of him, or what it had to do with the revelations about the demon. It had seemed to him last night, whilst Warin had been demonstrating his considerable skills, that the Shapeshifter's magic was far, *far* beyond anything he had ever seen in his entire life. 'Please, Warin. If you will not come with us, at least do us the honour of explaining what this is all about.'

'It is not my place. Ardwyad...'

'Enough!'

Mathias had had enough of ignorance and evasive answers. All his life, he had been a quiet young man, placid and good-natured. He had never raised his voice to anybody other than Wyn, and the old man had taught him to respect his elders in return. The simple community in which he had grown to manhood had taught him kindness and compassion. The old man and the village were probably both now gone, and the stress of the last day and Warin's truculence finally overcame him in an explosive outburst.

'All my life,' he said, forcing the words around his sudden anger, 'all my life I have been given half-truths and lies. My mother never told me the truth about my father's death. I had to learn that after *she* died. My adoptive father tells me a tale about a *demon* that he believed was hunting him. I am sent, by magic I never knew existed, to a country to which I have never been, to meet a man who will not be reasoned with and who *continues* to talk to me as if I were a child. Enough! I want answers, and you, Warin the Red'—Mathias levelled an accusing finger at the stocky man—'you are going to start *providing* them.'

Tagan stared aghast at the unexpected outburst and Mathias flushed with indignation. There would be a time, much later, that he would come to regret his demand.

Warin tipped his head to one side and then he nodded curtly before he began to speak, his voice low and passionate. His manner held Mathias and Tagan in thrall from the moment he began. Outlandish as the tale proved, it was spoken with such conviction that there was little room to doubt that he, at least, believed every word he was saying.

'Demons are real,' he began. 'Not in the way that the Church would have you believe, or not entirely. They dwell in a land much like our own. It has forests'—Warin gestured expansively to the surrounding woodland—'it has seas, plains, many things you would understand. It also has many things you would not. It is like a shadow of our world. It is the same shape but is very different, yes?' The two young people nodded. Warin stoked the fire and continued.

'That place has many names: Elysium, Samsara, and Niflheim. Some magi have named it the Aetherworld. It is from there that all magic flows, and it is often closer to us than we think.'

'You mean... the stone circles?' Tagan interrupted. Warin nodded.

'Yes, that is where the veil between the world of men and the Aetherworld is at its weakest. You have heard not to go into a circle at twilight? That is when the worlds are in close. It is where old tales about mushroom rings comes from. Bad things will snatch you away, or carry off your children. The demons, though, they cannot cross over. They are things of magic. Without magic, they are like fish, plucked from the river.'

'But Wyn showed me a vision of a demon. Stalking the battlefield at Bosworth. Killing magi.'

Warin shook his head. 'What you saw was nothing more than a shade. They can be given power in our world for a short time, with blood, or gold, or dreams. A sacrifice of some kind. It differs for each. But they cannot remain for long.'

Warin's hand stroked the back of the dog's ears and she whimpered softly, lying down at the Shapeshifter's feet and gazing up at him with adoring eyes. His tone became deeply sorrowful. 'But always they are trying to find a way, trying to get into our world, to take what is ours and make it theirs.'

Mathias became aware that Tagan's fingers had closed around his and he squeezed her hand in return. Warin stared up at the leaden skies, where clouds gathered, heavy with the promise of rain.

'Sometimes the Church says that a man is possessed, or that a witch has a demon in her, but that is wrong. They say it because it gives them power, not because it is true. A demon cannot wear the flesh of a man. A summoned shade may have the face of an angel, but you can feel its evil, feel its wrongness. You cannot invite that into you. To do so, even for a little while, brings madness. It rots the mind and body, the soul.'

'So, if they can't stay here, even through possession, what is it that they want with us?' Mathias asked. He had only experienced the presence of Melusine through Wyn's illusion, and couldn't imagine what the appalling reality of it might feel like.

'Purchase. Permanence. They need to forge their pure vessel.' Mathias suddenly remembered Wyn mentioning something about a vessel as he had prepared for the ritual on the hill. 'They whisper in the ears of men who lust for power, conquest and war. Men who might forge a dynasty. There have been others before Richard—Caligula, Xerxes, Genghis Khan, Vlad Draculesti—but always people have risen to stop them. Their bloodlines have died or been too weak.'

'But not this time,' Mathias said in alarm. 'Wyn said that he had hoped that the vessel would not be born during my life. What does that mean?'

'It means that after generations, one has finally come who can endure true possession. One who can host a demon without withering and decay. One who will wield magic like a god and force the nations of men to their knees, driven by a master of power beyond reckoning.'

'Melusine,' Mathias breathed. Warin nodded slowly.

'Richard wages war on magic because through his family, she has led him to do so. Magic is the only thing that can threaten her. It is the defence of the world of men against the Aetherworld. And when the time comes, she will use her power to tear down the veil. The demons will spill through and enslave humanity to their will.'

There was a long pause, and Mathias stared in open horror at Warin.

'And you will stand by and just let this happen? Wyn sent us here because he believed you would help us!'

Warin could not meet Mathias's eye. He stared down at the ground, running his hand through the hound's fur. 'The earth will endure. Evil comes and goes, but the earth will endure. It always does.'

'But *we* will not. You are happy to hide in your forest and let people suffer and die as long as your precious earth survives, is that right?' The young man's voice was thick with indignation.

Warin surged to his feet, his face a dark, furious mask. 'And you would be a hero, is that right, boy? Men are weak! They bicker and fight and serve only their own greed. You might have been shown Richard's corruption at Bosworth Field, but did *Wyn* also tell you that Tudor bargained with the demon as well?' There was thick, heavy sarcasm around the name that Mathias's adoptive father had used. The Shapeshifter turned from the pair, shoulders heaving. His voice, when he spoke, was composed once again. 'Kings. Princes. Nobles. Even if this time is different, it will only happen again. There will always be another.'

Tagan got to her feet and hesitantly went to Warin's side. She put a hand on his shoulder. 'Please,' she said quietly. 'At least come with us for a while, tell us what we must do, where we must go. At least for a while.'

For a long time she thought the Shapeshifter would not answer, but then he sighed and turned to look at her. 'Very well,' he said with evident reluctance. 'We will go back to the circle and I will send you back to your land.' Her face dropped, but then he continued. 'But I will come with you back to England to speak with Adelmo. I will see this King Richard for myself.'

'His name is Wyn,' Mathias said, though the relief in his voice was obvious.

'Of course it is,' Warin replied sombrely.

The road to Paris
France

THE ARMY MOVED quickly, considering its size. A huge plume of soot and dust trailed in its wake and mingled with the rising pillars of smoke to the northwest. Dieppe burned. Nothing had been spared. Those few able to escape the destruction fled before the English and a bow wave of terror now spread south ahead of the advance.

Weaver rode at the head of the army. Sir Thomas Thirwell, King Richard's personal banner bearer, rode at his side, proudly flying the royal colours. A number of the nobility had protested his brazen approach, fearing that he would present an easy target for enemy magi should they come upon them on the road. The Inquisitor had silenced them with a word. He would not be cowed. The idea that magi might actively seek him out was an irony he found grimly amusing.

They passed farms and hamlets, all of which bore signs of hurried evacuation. The signs of open magic use were everywhere. Fields tended by animated tools, rain artificially brought to crops, animals corralled by fences of air. At one point they came upon a line of windmills that turned enthusiastically despite the feeble breeze of the day. All were put to the torch in turn, to expunge the stain of the arcane.

The Lord Inquisitor stopped to observe a plough as it turned the earth of an empty field, but waved the army to continue on. There were no oxen in the traces, no man to steer it. The tool simply worked up and down in neat lines of its own accord, following the arcane instruction of the magic that animated it.

'An honest man does honest work,' Weaver growled.

'Shall I send for some serfs to pull the thing apart, my lord?' Sir Thomas said. Weaver thought he detected a trace of scorn in the man's voice, but dismissed it as irrelevant. There were many among the court who did not fully grasp how insidious magic could be.

'No. Inform one of the dragon's-breath crews to melt it down as they pass. That should be thorough enough.' One of the quick-footed messengers sprinted off toward the rear of the column without needing further instruction.

'We cannot scour every magical blasphemy from the land, my lord,' Thirwell said. 'The King expects Paris to fall before...'

'I know what the King expects,' Weaver snapped. Sir Thomas was a bear of a man, like his father and grandfather before him. He was made larger still by the bulk of his armour, and sat astride his horse with the confident ease of a warrior. Yet he seemed to shrink before the Lord Inquisitor. 'And he should not concern himself. We will tear down the walls of Paris before...' Then he stopped, mid-sentence.

Since the incident in Wales, the flashes of inspiration had become more regular and more comfortable. Thus far, they had also proven to be entirely accurate on every occasion. He was suddenly certain that the people who had vanished at the ritual site a few weeks ago were to the east. He was even more strongly certain that he had to find them as soon as possible. The urgency of the knowledge was startling.

'My lord?' Thirwell asked. 'Are you quite well? Should I send for an apothecary?'

'No. No. I am quite well.' He turned to the gang of runners that followed at his heels like ducklings around their mother. 'Send word to the noble lords. I need the ten best from their retinues, stripped of armour and ready to ride.' One of the boys bobbed his head and hurried away. 'You, fetch me the master alchemist.' Another scampered off toward the rear of the host. Weaver turned to regard Sir Thomas again. 'I must leave, and I must do so immediately. Until I return, command of the army and the siege of Paris falls to you.'

The banner bearer looked aghast. 'But my lord, the nobles will not defer to me. There are many amongst them who will...'

'They can and they will.' Weaver cut him off. 'Any that don't will answer to me upon my return. Is that understood?'

Sir Thomas nodded reluctantly and fell back in line with the army.

Bavaria
Germany

THE RETURN JOURNEY through the forest was spent in complete silence. Mathias was still smarting at Warin's attitude, and Tagan was caught up in the dark majesty of the forest the Shapeshifter called home. They pushed through fern-choked dells, up grassy hillsides and over clear, bubbling brooks. They were evidently taking a more circuitous route back to the circle.

The only sounds beyond that of water and wind were Warin's occasional mutterings—in German—to the dog who padded at his side. Once or twice, the animal disappeared into the undergrowth, only to return a few minutes later and continue at his side.

Mathias broke the silence eventually. His anger had cooled now, and some of the things Warin had said sparked his interest. He also wanted to find an opportunity to apologise.

'You said that I could do what you do,' he began. Warin turned and studied him.

'Yes,' he conceded grumpily. 'It is possible. I feel a strong flow of the earth magic through you. But it takes many years. It is not easy. You need the patience of the mountains and the trees, the solid nature of rock and stone. You are too old. Too full of fancy.' He lapsed back into a sullen silence and strode on.

'Wyn never told me that I had that sort of potential,' Mathias pressed on. 'I am keen to learn what I can from you whilst I have the chance. Would you consider...?'

Warin held up a hand that stopped Mathias and Tagan in their tracks. The blacksmith's daughter had been gazing around the woodland, enthralled by its eerie beauty, and collided with the suddenly still Mathias. She opened her mouth to complain, but Warin hushed her with a look that could have frozen lakes.

'Something... is not right,' muttered the Shapeshifter. 'We must go carefully. The circle is close, but it is in pain. The earth itself cries out.' He looked at Mathias, then at Tagan. 'Tell me. Do you feel it?'

Mathias blinked, then remembered the strange calm that had filled the stone circle back home. He was not feeling that now. The air felt charged, like the moment before a predator springs. The forest groaned with the tension. He shook his head slowly. 'I feel... something,' he said in response. 'But I don't know...'

Warin's expression became grim. 'Something is wrong,' he said.

They hurried on, Warin now filled with a cautious urgency. The closer they came to the circle, the more pronounced the sense of disquiet, until they emerged from the trees into the rocky clearing of their arrival. The stones still stood. Moss and lichen clung to their sides. There was nothing obviously different, yet the sense of wrongness was palpable.

'With me,' Warin growled. 'Into the circle.' At his command, they hesitantly stepped between the stones and shuffled through the dead needles and ferns to the centre.

'Warin, how are you going to get us back? Wyn needed all of the elders with him to work the spell,' Tagan asked quietly.

'Wyn... is old. His time is almost over. I am not so old and my strength is greater. The magic is simple enough.' Mathias looked at the Shapeshifter, but there was no trace of arrogance in him. It was a simple statement of fact.

'Now quiet. I must speak with the earth. Then we will be on our way.'

Mathias and Tagan watched with interest as Warin closed his eyes. His lips worked within the burnished hair of his beard, silently mouthing words, and then he grew still. The sense of foreboding that had filled and surrounded the circle slowly drained away, replaced by a stillness that was equally uncomfortable. *The calm before the storm,* Mathias thought.

For several long moments nothing happened. Mathias looked at Tagan, who gave a little shake of her head. Neither wanted to break the awkward silence. Then Warin's eyes snapped open and he gasped.

'Warin?' Tagan took a step toward the man as he staggered, as if momentarily drunk.

'It is gone,' he said hoarsely, his ruddy face pale with shock.

'What's gone?' Tagan, ever sensitive to other people's moods, stepped a little closer to him. Warin stared at her, and to her shock, his eyes were filled with tears. Of misery or of rage, she could not be sure. She reached for him to comfort him in some way, but he stumbled away from her, gasping ragged breaths, his hands balled into fists.

'The circle,' he said in response to her question. 'The circle you came from is gone. The earth. The earth, she weeps for its loss.'

'How can it be gone?' But even as Mathias asked the question, he knew the answer. 'Those men... the ones who appeared just as the magic took hold. They must have destroyed it!' An icy fear clutched at him. 'If the Circle is gone... then Wyn...'

'Dead.'

Warin spoke the single word with leaden finality. He turned back to the pair and there was a fey, amber light in his eyes. 'It is not for the likes of men to uproot the bones of the world.' His voice boomed with power. The stones around the circle came alive with intricate, curving ochre script that pulsed in time with the rhythm of his words. The trees surrounding them groaned and seemed to lean away from the enraged magus.

'This sacrilege will not go unanswered or unpunished,' Warin continued. Mathias felt the ground shake at the proclamation and he recoiled from the Shapeshifter, putting his arms protectively around Tagan as he did so. Then the magus let out a long, shuddering breath and normality resumed. The stones faded and he was once again just Warin.

'Warin... if the circle in Wales has gone...' Tagan's voice was small; tiny and childlike. Mathias looked at her. He had known in his heart that Wyn was dead, and he feared what that meant for the rest of the village. Fear and guilt tempered with a bizarre sense of relief warred within him. Guilt because she had been dragged into this madness, and relief because she was here with him and might have escaped a terrible fate at the hands of the King's Inquisition.

'Then I cannot send you back.' Warin finished the words for her. 'And we have a long way to go.' Gone was the affected cantankerousness. In its place was a man of conviction and focus; someone who had been reawakened to the world and found it not to his liking. 'No man, be he king, mage or pauper, should attempt to unseat the old magics of the world. We need to travel, boy. You, me, her.' He pointed at each in turn. 'We will find the others that you seek, and together this wrong will be righted.'

'But where will we go? Wyn didn't tell us where the others might be. Only you.'

'You would give up so easily?' Warin frowned and peered at Mathias. 'You're a strange boy. I see great pride and strength running through you, yet you deny all that you are. What *are* you?'

Mathias couldn't answer that, but Tagan answered for him. 'He is the man I love,' she said, simply. 'We just don't know how we're supposed to find these people. We don't know who they are, or even what they might look like.'

'Then it is good that I do know, yes? Or at least I know a place to start.' Warin dragged his fingers through his tangled beard and frowned. 'It will be easiest to head south, over the mountains. It is a long way to the sea, but there are lakes between here and there, it is possible that he might be listening...' There was a clear edge of distaste to his words. 'I may be able to get word to de Luna.'

'Who?' Mathias tipped his head at the unusual name.

Warin sneered slightly. 'Giraldo de Luna. Or at least, that was the last name he went by. You mentioned him by another name: the "Pirate King."'

'But how far is it to the sea?' Tagan looked helpless. She had seen the sea once, as a very small girl when she'd accompanied her father to a fishing village on the coast, but she had no understanding of where they were. Warin tipped his head, his lips moving as he worked out which route he would take.

'Many, many leagues,' he said, eventually. 'For us on foot—very long. For two of us on four legs... not so much.' He turned his gaze on Mathias and the solemn expression suddenly became something entirely different. Amused, possibly. 'Well, Mathias Eynon. You wished to learn how to properly embrace your magic, now it looks like Warin will teach you.' His lips curled up in a sudden smile, something predatory and filled with a deep amusement. 'Yes?'

Suddenly, Mathias was no longer so keen on the idea.

The road from Paris
France

THE HORSES THUNDERED across the French countryside, their hooves flying. Every man had been in the saddle for two days, eating on the move and keeping sleep at bay with a foul-smelling and worse-tasting brew supplied by the royal alchemist. The horses foamed at the mouth, pink froth streaming from their muzzles as the potion forced into them kept them running. Weaver had already put leagues between himself and the army as the insistent, inexplicable call to the east drove him on.

One of his chosen warriors, a knight named Sir Anthony, pulled his horse level with the Lord Inquisitor. There were dark circles under the knight's eyes, and despite the alchemy's work, his face was drawn with exhaustion.

'My lord.' Anthony had to shout to be heard over the sound of hooves and the rush of the wind. 'My lord, at this pace we will kill the horses.'

Weaver looked around at the rolling fields, farms and hamlets. Word of the approaching army had not yet reached this far inland, so they occasionally passed shocked-looking peasants at work. Those who failed to get out of the way were run down. Many of the farms had stables.

'So we kill them,' Weaver yelled back over the noise. 'When they are dead, then we will rest. Then we will take more, and we will continue until they die. We stop for nothing else, do I make myself clear?'

The knight did not reply, but nodded grimly. The eleven riders pushed on.

EIGHT

Bavaria
Germany

MATHIAS WAS NOT having a good time. Warin's idea of 'teaching' him how to shapeshift seemed to consist largely of the stocky little man changing into an animal and urging Mathias to copy him. So far he had achieved nothing except a lot of ineffective pink-faced grunting.

'Stop laughing,' he muttered to Tagan, who sat watching, the wolfhound at her side. The dog's tongue was lolling as she watched the two men, and Mathias had the distinct feeling that both Tagan and the dog were laughing at him.

'I didn't make a sound,' came her reply, but there was a twinkle in her expression. 'Do you want me to close my eyes? Am I putting you off?'

'Of course you are not putting him off. Now concentrate. Think... rabbit.' The man's figure shot downwards and was replaced by a rabbit. It twitched its nose at him in what Mathias thought was a decidedly mocking manner. He closed his eyes and took a deep breath.

I am a rabbit, he thought, somewhat self-consciously. *I am a rabbit. I am a rabbit. I am...*

He opened his eyes. He was still Mathias. Warin the rabbit hopped up and down once or twice and then became human again. 'Stop worrying about man things, think rabbit things.' His voice was stern. Mathias flushed even brighter. Warin had obviously gauged the problem with embarrassing ease. 'Just calm yourself. Think rabbit. Now concentrate, Englander.'

'I'm Welsh.'

Warin smirked. 'Welsh men would not have half the difficulty you are having. Stop doubting and start believing, boy.'

Annoyance and frustration rose in the pit of Mathias's stomach and he glared at Warin, who simply smirked again and became a rabbit, hopping mockingly around his feet. Mathias resisted the urge to kick the little animal and closed his eyes once again.

I'll show him, he thought. *I'm a rabbit.* He could visualise the form he needed to take. He considered the size of a rabbit compared to the size of himself as a human. It was ludicrous. How on earth could he possibly fit a man's body into a rabbit's form? He muttered softly to himself and pushed the negative thoughts aside. The irritation gave way to a sense of desperation. Warin said he had potential. Thus far in his life, all he had been was adequate. Something fundamental changed within Mathias Eynon in that moment. Adequate was no longer good enough. He was caught up in huge, terrifying events that demanded more.

I can do this. I must do this, I don't really have a choice any more, came the resigned thought. *But if I'm going to be a rabbit, I'm going to be a better one than Warin.*

A sudden gasp of surprise from Tagan made him open his eyes to look at her. He realised that he had to look up. Then he had to look up some more. He twitched his furry little nose at her and she stared at him with eyes as wide as saucers. There was admiration in those eyes. Admiration, and even a little fear.

Very good. Warin's voice was exactly as it was when he spoke as a human, but it arrived right inside the privacy of his skull. Mathias hopped, startled by this sudden intrusion, and turned to look at the other rabbit. *The ears are little over-long, but you would pass as a rabbit. Now change back.*

Exhilarated, Mathias let the magic envelop him. He had never allowed himself to properly embrace the gift that had been his all through his life. Too afraid of it, perhaps. But here, in a dark forest, far from home and with only his betrothed and a wild magus to judge him, he found that he had power. Real power.

In the heartbeat it took him to once again take on his true form, Mathias Eynon truly grew up.

'Matty!' Tagan got up from where she sat on the grassy bank and flung her arms around him, kissing him gleefully on the lips. 'You did it!'

'I did? I did!' Delighted at his own success, he hugged her back, revelling in the moment for just a while. The events of the past hours had shaken him, left him feeling lost and lonely in a world that he no longer understood. But Tagan was here for him.

'When you two are *quite* finished,' said Warin sourly, 'we must practise more and we must get it right. Whilst you two kiss and cuddle, evil stalks the lands of your home.' He looked carefully at Mathias. He reached a hand up to scratch at his wild red beard, then smirked.

'Consider,' he said to Mathias, 'the horse...'

Troyes
France

THE HORSES FINALLY died thirty leagues south of Paris. They staggered to a halt, their emaciated limbs shaking and their breathing ragged. It became apparent that no amount of beating would get them to move. Then, one by one, they collapsed, little more than skin and bone. All but ruined with fatigue and time spent in the saddle, Weaver and his ten knights staggered the last few miles into the town of Troyes.

It was early morning and the streets were empty of life. The men broke into the first house they came to and collapsed into an exhausted sleep. The Lord Inquisitor felt the ache in his bones, but the potion still thrummed in his veins. Besides, he had found that he needed less rest of late.

'Rest, feed yourselves and find more horses. I will be back in a few hours,' Weaver said to his companions. They all nodded absently before sinking gratefully to the floor and falling asleep with the casual ease of the truly exhausted. The Lord Inquisitor left them to their rest, sneering at their weakness before he walked out into the empty street.

Narrow, half-timbered buildings of white clay lined the cobbled road, but all were quiet, their doors and windows closed. Weaver had a sudden compulsion to explore the town, his curiosity piqued by the absence of life. He walked down the empty street, his boot heels clicking on the cobbles, and headed toward the centre of town, which was dominated by the towering, ornate spire of a church.

The smell of baking bread stopped him in his stride, and he approached the bakery, expecting to see it bustling with activity. Instead, he found it empty, trays of loaves loading and unloading themselves from the clay oven without any intervention required from a baker. The Lord Inquisitor snorted in contempt at such flagrant use of magic to perform tasks that should have been conducted through honest work. King Richard had always maintained that magic made men weak rather than strong, and the evidence was here for anybody to see. There was a scuffling in the alleyway behind him and he spun around, his hand flying to one of his pistols.

An urchin with a dirt-smeared face stared back at him, eyes wide with fear. Weaver relaxed and dropped his hand to his side. He had no doubt that his outlandish appearance terrified the girl-child: huge, dark, masked and thick with the dust of travel.

'Where is everybody?' the Lord Inquisitor boomed. He spread his arms wide to indicate the town and shrugged his shoulders as if puzzled. He knew only a little French, and was under no illusion about his ability to communicate with the girl verbally.

'The people. Where are they?' He repeated the gesture, asking his question just a little louder.

Whether the child understood or not was unclear, but she raised a shaking finger to indicate the church spire and Weaver nodded. Time had blurred since he had started this wild ride and he had lost track of the days. It must be Sunday. He nodded to the child and started to turn away, then, as an afterthought, tossed one of the fresh loaves to her. The girl caught it and blinked in surprise.

'You should leave.' Weaver's voice was little more than a rumble. Again, he did not know if he was understood, but she gave a small smile and took to her heels, disappearing back into the alley.

The Lord Inquisitor strode into the square before the church and looked up at the magnificent building. It was in the process of being expanded, and wooden scaffolding clung to its flanks, boards sagging under the weight of stone waiting to be lifted into place. A statue of Saint Julian sat bound in ropes, awaiting elevation. The muted sound of voices raised in song could be heard from within the building. Weaver advanced on the double doors, pushed one open and slipped inside.

The pews were loaded to capacity and the Lord Inquisitor found himself at the back of the nave, in the area reserved for paupers and peasants. The wealthier residents were seated closer to the sanctuary in recognition of their status. A number of the congregation looked up at his intrusion, uncomprehending of who or what it was that had come among them. The priest at the altar was recounting his sermon in French; the words were lost on Weaver. He recognised the story that was being related all too well, however, as his eyes were drawn to the living illusion being woven for the masses.

The cleric had conjured a scene that depicted the shores of a lake. A great many people surrounded a figure, who was taking food from a basket and distributing it in seemingly endless supply.

'The feeding of the five thousand,' Weaver declared, his sepulchral voice carrying the length of the church. 'I have heard it told many times, but never have I *seen* it. Is this how you keep the people enthralled to your corrupt will?'

The illusion faltered and vanished, and several children at the front gave little cries of disappointment. Weaver slowly paced down the aisle, his steps shockingly loud in the hollow, hallowed space. The priest regarded him curiously from the platform and asked a question in French. All eyes in the hall were now on Charles Weaver and a ripple of whispers passed through the crowd as he approached the altar.

'Magic is a corruption of the spirit. It softens men, makes them weak.' Weaver stopped at the head of the nave, his eyes fixed on the cleric through the slits in his mask. He turned around and looked out at the sea of faces, some confused, some intrigued, a few—mainly those closest to him—afraid.

'You are all sinners,' he went on. 'You are all weak, and have allowed yourselves to be blinded by the arcane to the truth of your lives.' He started to walk back down the aisle, his voice booming out and carrying to every corner of the church.

'Honest people do honest work. They do not grow fat while

spells and sigils work on their behalf.' He stopped near the doors, and some of the peasants shuffled away from him as he turned once again to address the congregation. 'In the name of King Richard the Unyielding, Lord of England and conqueror of Europe, I pronounce this town guilty of arcane blasphemy.'

He slipped his hands into one of the pouches at his waist and withdrew a pair of crystal phials. Lambent blue liquid sloshed within their confines. They were sealed with treated wax and bore the mark of the royal alchemist.

'I condemn you to purification by fire.' Weaver hurled the two phials into the air, and they sailed down the nave to shatter on the steps of the altar. He was already stepping outside as they broke open, spilling liquid alchemical fire throughout the congregation. Muffled screams came from within the church as Weaver walked away. He tossed another phial at the doors as he went, sealing all those inside behind a spreading pool of molten blue fire that devoured the wooden scaffolding in short order before leaping hungrily to the surrounding buildings.

As the sun set, Weaver and his ten rode into the night, Troyes burning fiercely at their backs.

Bavaria
Germany

In the hour since he had successfully shifted his form into that of a rabbit, Mathias had discovered what it felt like to be a fox, a badger, a wolf and finally a horse. Not a particularly outstanding horse; not like the chestnut stallion that Warin effortlessly became. More of a piebald pony, with one eye ever so slightly higher than the other. But the thought was certainly there. Mathias came from a farming community, and his idea of what a horse looked like was evidently very different to that of Warin.

As a horse, the Shapeshifter was a truly magnificent beast. A deep, rich chestnut coat, glinting in the failing daylight, covered the strong, powerful body. A horse like this could run for miles and there, of course, was the purpose made flesh. Mathias's soft brown eyes flickered over to his betrothed. Tagan had watched the whole display with ever-widening eyes and a near-palpable sense of envy. Mathias recognised the expression. He had worn it enough times himself whenever she showed her remarkable talent with fire.

Our time grows short. This form is not as good as it could be, but it will do. The stallion lowered its head and shook its mane. *We have to run, and this is the form best suited to that task. I will carry the girl. I am stronger, more used to it.*

The wolfhound, Warin's constant companion, was running around the legs of the stallion, barking. Clearly this was a form that the dog was hugely unfamiliar with, and as a horse, Mathias could pick up on the delicate nuances of animal fear very clearly. He put a tentative hoof forward. Very quickly, he made a discovery.

Four legs are far more complex to manage than two.

In the hour of changing forms, he had not moved from the spot, apart from the tiniest of hops as the rabbit. The other animals had not made any attempt to move. As Mathias put his long leg forward, the other three immediately became confused and tangled up, and sent him sprawling to the ground with a snort.

The chestnut stallion stared at him, great dark eyes unblinking and holding the tiniest bit of scorn. The piebald pony scrambled to his ungainly legs and fiercely focused his attention until he was able to walk forwards without falling over.

Get used to it quickly, Englander. You have to run.

I am going as quickly as I can. I haven't done this before, remember? The expression in the chestnut horse's eyes softened just a little, which was as close to acknowledging Mathias's circumstances as Warin had come. The Shapeshifter warped back into his human form and reached over to pat the little pony on the neck.

'You have done well,' he said, and there was an endearing awkwardness in his tone that suggested he rarely gave praise. He turned to Tagan. 'Do you know how to ride a horse without a saddle?'

She nodded. Growing up amidst a farming community had given her any number of skills. Everyone was encouraged to learn to ride, and Tagan, ever more adventurous than most, had often gone without a saddle. Warin smiled. 'Then you will ride and we will run. We will stop to rest when you are so tired you fall off.' He roared with laughter at her startled look. 'I joke. We will take a little while to gather some food and water and then we will leave. You'—he pointed to Grauenhund—'are staying here in the woods where you belong.' The hound flattened its ears and whined before jumping up to lick Warin's face. She loitered a moment longer and then prowled off, slinking into the forest. Warin watched her go and sighed. Then he pointed at Mathias. 'You... do not change back. Practise.'

Hampton Court
England

THE KING HAD not slept well since his return from the 'hunting trip,' days ago. His restlessness had driven his wife out to sleep in her own chambers, and he was oddly grateful that she was not close to him. The first night, he had dreamed of strangling her and hanging her body from the rafters. The second, he had smothered her beneath the pillow in her sleep. Tonight, he woke bathed in sweat from a particularly potent nightmare. So powerful had the images in his dreams been that he had woken convinced that she would be lying beside him, her belly torn open and her bowels spilled across the bed. He could even taste the copper of her heart's blood in his mouth.

Richard shuddered and closed his eyes to block out the moonlight that stole into the chamber through the small window. He felt terribly sick; cloistered and oppressed. He knew that these dreams were being visited upon him because of his reluctance to bring his son before Melusine. He didn't know how to begin to broach the subject with the boy; the thought of it made him ill.

The voice, when it came, caused him to cry out briefly but a soft, ethereal hand pressed across his mouth, stifling the sound.

'Hush now, my love,' came Melusine's voice. 'Do not be afraid. No harm could befall you in your own bedchamber, could it?' Her voice dripped with poisoned honey, sickly-sweet and fatal. 'Why do you refuse me what was promised? Have I not given you everything you desire? Have I not given you and your line power beyond measure?'

Richard looked down and realised that the taste of blood was real; scarlet drops ran from his lip and pattered into the blanket. Melusine had summoned herself.

'You have.' His voice was hoarse, dragged from a dry throat like thorns through his skin. The idea that the creature could control him through his dreams, even to the extent of making him summon her, appalled him. 'But... he is my son.' He lay back, exhausted by her toxic presence and the effort of giving voice to his defiance. Her long-fingered nail traced the line of his sternum, and although he could see nothing of her but her eyes, glinting in the moonlight, he knew she smiled.

'Richard,' she breathed in her sultry voice. 'He is *our* son. Without me, he never would have been. *You* never would have been. The line of your family would have been ended by Henry Tudor and would be rotting beneath the earth in a forgotten field.' Her voice transformed from liquid purr to bestial snarl as she spoke, and her ephemeral form flickered in the darkness. Richard cringed back, the buried memory of what he had seen in the forest resurfacing. When she spoke again, it was once again in soft, womanly tones. 'A boy should not be without his mother. You should not worry, my dear Richard. I have no intention of harming him. His care and comfort are foremost in my thoughts. You *will* give him my regards, won't you?'

He nodded. He had never been so deeply afraid of his future, nor so deeply ashamed of his family's past, as he was in that moment. A hundred of years of rule. A century of comfort, of belief that no ill could come of their bargain. War. Execution.

Because a fearful man was too proud to admit defeat.

'I cannot hear you,' she said sweetly. 'I want to know you will bring him before me.'

'I... I will speak to him,' Richard forced himself to say, with a sob. 'It will be as you wish.'

'Do not sound so despairing, dear one. You are so close to greatness. Those that have come before you could never have imagined the heights to which you have climbed—and your son will be greater still.

He will herald a new age for your people. What more could parents ask for than the success of their children?'

Images of people enslaved, caged in black iron, tormented by unseen horrors, filled the tortured king's mind. He cried out in despair and the door to his bedchamber burst open. Two of the Royal Guard barged in and cast about, alert for any intruder. Apart from the King, the room was empty.

'Your majesty, are you well?' One of the guards asked the question carefully.

'It is nothing,' Richard replied, his face pale and drenched with sweat in the moonlight. 'Just a bad dream.'

Mahón
Spain

THE MAN HAD never had a particular fondness for the middle of the day. Usually, he kept such late nights that he rarely surfaced before noon anyway. Night time was when he did his best work. With the night came the darkness, and a thief's best cover had ever been the mantle of darkness.

Today, however, he needed to be outside. Today, he needed to be *seen.* This late in the year the cabin was pleasantly warm, stirred by a gentle breeze, the last breath of what had been a long summer. Motes of dust danced in a shaft of pale sunlight spearing through an open porthole, and the sound of water lapping gently against wood murmured outside. This had been a good season. Long and extraordinarily lucrative. It was because of this good fortune that Giraldo de Luna heaved a sigh, prising himself out of his bed after only a couple of hours sleep.

He disengaged himself from a tangle of lily-white limbs—no fewer than three girls had shared his bed that night—and none of them made any effort to recall him to their soft-bosomed midst. He gazed on the delightful scene as he tugged on his clothes. Life, he decided as he straightened the heavy frock-coat and tightened the belt around his narrow waist, was good.

On the wall of the cabin was a slightly tarnished looking glass, and he paused to check his reflection as he passed. He had heard that vanity was a sin, but then, so were many of his other pursuits. He turned his head this way and that, ensuring that the neatly-trimmed beard set off his high cheekbones and rugged jawline to maximum effect. Emerald-green eyes twinkled with inner mischief, and from time to time, he had to push back the sandy blond hair that artfully flopped into them.

He looked to be in his mid twenties, but he had looked that way for a long time. The styles and fashions might have changed, but the man beneath was the same. Unable to resist, he winked at his reflection. The glass rippled slightly and the reflection raised an eyebrow in mock-despair. 'You, Giraldo,' he said in his musical lilt, a voice that could lull people into a hypnotic state, 'are a handsome man. *Bueno. Bueno!*'

He stooped to pick up his hat from where it was casually discarded on the floor, among the clothing that had once adorned the three sleeping women in his bed. He carefully straightened out the plume set into its brim before placing it at an appropriately jaunty angle on his head. The hat defined him; people saw the hat long before they saw his face, and they knew who came their way. Giraldo de Luna. The self-styled but greatly admired Pirate King.

He needed to stoop before he could exit the cabin, not just because of the ludicrous hat, but because he was at least six and a half feet tall. He was lean with it, which appeared to draw his height out still further. He unfolded on the other side of the door, stretching his long limbs with unfettered delight in the warmth of Mahón's morning sunshine.

'Captain,' came a voice, and Giraldo glanced across to nod gravely at Tohias, his longest serving first mate. Sailors came and went under the Pirate King's command. Very few of them left his employ in what was seen as the 'traditional' way—dying on boarding actions or raids. Usually, they worked for him until their aching bones would no longer allow them to live the hard life of a pirate. When that happened, Giraldo paid them handsomely, thanked them for their service and set them ashore at a port of their choice.

He commanded absolute loyalty from his crew. He instilled fear into his enemies, and yet Giraldo de Luna did not take a life unless it was absolutely necessary. He took money and possessions and he shared the wealth generously with his crew. As long as he had wine in his goblet and women to share his bed, he was the easiest captain any of them ever worked for.

'Tohias,' said Giraldo. 'Has there been any word from our expected guest?'

'Nothing, Captain.' Tohias shook his head, his wobbling jowls stopping a few seconds after his head fell still. 'What makes you so sure he's coming?' The question drew a smirk from Giraldo.

'Call it intuition,' he said. 'A change in the tide. I can smell the forest in the air... he's coming, even if he doesn't have the good manners to let me know. He always was an animal.' He moved to lean on the rail of the ship. The *Hermione* was a stunning specimen of her kind. He had taken her as a prize only a handful of weeks earlier and happily moved himself and most of his crew across. The old ship, whilst it had served him well, was now in the possession of another. Giraldo's taste for ships was as changeable as the tides.

He watched the busy people on the dock for a while. They had been in port for a few days whilst necessary repairs were made to the *Hermione*. 'Necessary repairs' was, of course, Giraldo's term for decorating his cabin with the most beautiful women he could find. His appetite for the opposite sex was quite insatiable and always had been.

'We should head to the market,' he said, his eyes still ranging over the bustling quay. 'There is a promise to be kept.' He pushed away from the rail and stretched out his shoulders. He patted the basket hilt of the sword he wore at his waist and nodded to Tohias. 'Let's go. The Pirate King does not want to keep his subjects waiting, does he? Does nothing for the reputation.'

He grinned, the morning sun glinting off a gold-capped front tooth. Just another day of keeping the peace amongst the thugs of the Mediterranean.

Nine

Bavaria
Germany

After the first two hours of running, Mathias found that his thoughts skipped easily between his life as a man and this new form. The longer he stayed in the form of the long-limbed animal, the more he found he was thinking like a horse. He relished the feel of the breeze that rippled through his mane as he and Warin galloped across the German landscape. They had left the confines of the forest behind not long after setting out, and the land had become rolling, grassy hills. The sense of freedom that came with once more being out in the open air was intoxicating. He pushed himself as hard as he could, and his heart sang with the sheer pleasure of being alive.

Tagan rode astride the Shapeshifter's broad back with self-conscious uncertainty. She was a capable rider, but the fact that she knew the horse she rode was also a man, a hound, a wolf, a rabbit... was somewhat unnerving. Still, it felt good to throw off the uncertainty of the previous night and to actually be *doing* something. She tried to set aside the fact that where they were heading, and what they would be doing, remained a mystery.

She could not help but smile every time she thought of her betrothed as being somewhere in the mind of the small horse that charged gamely a few feet behind them. Warin's stride far outmatched that of the piebald, even when he was consciously attempting to keep pace. *What a marvellous thing,* she thought. *To take on the shape of another living being.*

Warin's constant insistence that her own talent was every bit as worthwhile did not really do much to alleviate the faint air of jealousy. She and Mathias had been raised not to use their magic talents too much. Whilst the community in which they had grown up had encouraged magic and embraced its practical applications, the threat of the country's laws still hung over them with dark menace.

They continued to run for a while, and eventually Warin began to slow his pace and came to a halt beneath the shelter of a large pine tree. He lowered his neck and whickered softly. It was not hard to interpret his request, and Tagan slid ungracefully from the animal's back. Only once she was standing on solid ground did the first aches start to hit her. She knew that more hours of riding lay ahead and set her jaw determinedly. She would *not* complain. She was *not* the kind of woman who demanded sympathy and coddling.

Warin adopted his human form once more and she saw, in his stern face, the joy that being the horse had brought to him. The pony trotted up a few moments after she had dismounted and, without Warin's finesse, also slid back into a human form.

'How are you finding it, Englander?'

Mathias had given up correcting Warin. In fact, he was in no real state of mind to do anything but talk at great length and with great energy about the experience he had just undergone.

After he paused to take a breath, Warin interjected, amusement sparkling in his brown eyes. It seemed to Tagan that the man was more alive now than he had been in the oppressive confines of the Black Forest. 'Breathe, Mathias. Breathe. You are having fun, then?'

'It's the most incredible thing. I was... a *horse*.' He waved his hands in his excitement and Tagan laughed at his animation. He caught her hands and looked at her. 'You don't understand,' he said, earnestly. 'I *was* the horse. There were moments when I forgot I was anything but. It was the most amazing thing! I never...'

'That is precisely why we have stopped.' Warin's tone grew solemn. 'To remain in one form for too long—especially at the start? Is bad.' He shook his shaggy head. 'Very bad.'

His words punctured a little of Mathias's enthusiasm, but he paid close attention regardless. Warin nodded, pleased. 'It is easy to fall in love with something you are not,' he explained. 'Many animal forms are so much more suited to life than the human. But it is wrong to be forever stuck in the wrong body. Eventually your mind will get sick. Drive you mad. I knew a man who took the form of a fox and never changed back.' Warin shook his head sadly. 'Even though he wanted to. The body holds onto the new shape and refuses to listen. So we must take care.'

Tagan nodded. 'I don't really want to marry a horse,' she said solemnly. 'So be careful.' Her words brought a smile back to Mathias's concerned face. Warin stomped away from the pair for a while, scanning the horizon.

'We can get several more hours in today before we should rest. Take time now to eat and drink, and to remember what it is to be human. We will continue south. De Luna should know we come to him soon. If he does not already. I hope he has the sense...' Warin paused and snorted with mock-laughter at his choice of words to describe the erratic Pirate King. 'I hope he has the sense to put his ridiculous boat in a place where we can find him.'

Mahón
Spain

THE PIRATE KING had matters to attend to. Today, his most pressing concern took the form of a grim-faced, dark-skinned man who was not in the slightest bit impressed with Giraldo's easy charm. Even after a round of drinks, compliments and casual jibes, Captain Bachir simply shook his head.

'Your pretty words do not impress me, de Luna. I came here to talk business. To talk money. But I have no wish to waste my breath with...' He waved a hand dismissively. 'A strutting peacock.'

Tohias bristled at the insult to his captain, but Giraldo laid a steadying hand on his first mate's arm. 'Peace, Tohias,' he murmured. 'It seems that Captain Bachir needs to get something off his chest. Why don't we just let him talk?' His smile was warm, friendly, dazzling.

Hypnotic.

'We will just let him talk, Captain,' said Tohias.

'Do continue, Captain Bachir,' said de Luna, turning his attentions back to the other man, who raised one shaggy eyebrow. Bachir reached over and caught de Luna's right hand, stopping its slow, languid movements. De Luna stared down at the huge, filthy paw grasped around his own and then raised his head to consider Bachir with a new level of wary respect.

'Let go,' he said. Now the charm left his voice, and a tone of quiet command took over. To give Bachir his credit, he resisted the order for several moments before his fingers released, leaving marks in de Luna's flesh. Giraldo rubbed at his wrist and resumed his friendly, open expression. Approachable and genial. It usually worked, although it wasn't going so well today.

'Your magic is strong, Captain de Luna,' said Bachir, shaking back the dark, braided hair that fell into his eyes. 'That is impressive. But I've spoken with my boys, and some others, and we are all agreed. It's time for a new King.' He smiled, showing broken teeth that did little to improve his already unattractive face. This was a man who had risen to his position by brute strength and intimidation. Magically, he was completely barren. Giraldo had sensed that the moment the captain had stamped into the room. Easily as tall as the Pirate King, Bachir was broader and stronger by far. Muscles rippled beneath the surface of his swarthy skin, and the tell-tale grazes on his knuckles told of a man to whom the first rule of discipline was violence.

For the first time in years, Giraldo de Luna felt a ripple of uncertainty. He looked Bachir up and down. 'Your message suggested you wanted to talk ways in which we could work together for the good of both. I agreed to meet you. You seem over-aggressive to me.' He offered a carefully-selected dazzling smile. 'We take too much, attack the wrong place, and we will upset someone important, tip the balance. Then one of the navies will be all over us. Maybe *all* the navies. And that's not good for anybody.'

'We are *pirates*, you spineless fop.' Bachir's meaty fist pounded down on the table, setting the tankards jumping. Neither man had taken ale. For de Luna it was because even *he* had standards and did not drink before noon; for Bachir, it was clearly so he could maintain at least a modicum of control. 'We should take what we want, when we want it, and to Hell with those who say otherwise!' His broken teeth parted in a leer. 'It's time we started taking!'

'Ah,' said Giraldo, nodding sombrely. 'Of course. I start to understand you.' He crooked one finger at Tohias, who rose from the table and disappeared from the tavern. Giraldo was left alone, a fact which did not go unnoticed by Bachir's retinue. 'You want a return to the old ways, am I right? Plundering, looting, burning and murdering?' He waved a hand vaguely. 'All that sort of messy business?'

With every word, the light in Bachir's eyes grew brighter, and a palpable lust began to expand from him. He even licked his lips.

'But that approach never ends well for anybody,' continued Giraldo. He leaned back in his chair and crossed his long legs in front of him. Even his boot-tops were immaculate, the leather as shiny and perfect as the day they had first been worn. Although the few who could have seen beyond the veneer of glamour that Giraldo cloaked himself with would have seen a very different picture. 'You have a brief, good run, but then some governor or officer out to make a name hunts you down and sinks your ship. Or hangs you. Probably both. Sometimes at the *same time*. And death is so messy, and often remarkably unnecessary. No, my way is better. We get the plunder and the loot, most of the people get to live and we get left alone.'

'We don't want to be left alone.' Bachir released a wheezing laugh, polluting the air around him with abominable halitosis. 'We want to be *feared*. We aren't merchants, we're the wolves of the sea. Murderers. Robbers. Rapists.' He leaned forward. 'We *get* what we want by *taking* what we want.'

It was a truth that caused Giraldo's heart to sink. This was a man that could not be reasoned with through words or glamour. It was possible that Bachir entirely lacked the empathy required for even the smallest manipulation. He had encountered others like him over the years, but he had won them all over in the end. This time, it seemed, it would be different. He heard several swords being pulled; the rasp of steel against leather and the unmistakable click of a crossbow being readied. His crew was still on board the *Hermione*.

He was alone against a group of very angry men who wanted his blood. He was outnumbered sixteen to one.

The odds, he mused as he slowly lowered his feet to the floor, were not good at all. Sixteen to one.

For a moment, he came uncommonly close to feeling sorry for them.

The road to Strasbourg
France

THE CART HORSES they had taken from Troyes were weaker than the war horses on which they had begun their journey. The land over the last five leagues had become more rugged, the fields and grasses giving way to hills as they pushed ever eastward. Weaver estimated that within a day or so they would leave France behind.

Knowing that they were closing on their objective, the Lord Inquisitor eased the pace, if only a little. The horses would not last much longer, and farms were becoming more scattered, sometimes with leagues between them. By the time the sun set on their second day, both the men and the horses were barely coping. The knights had only managed a couple of hours of rest in Troyes before Weaver had kicked them awake and moved them on. None of them questioned the growing inferno spreading throughout the town. It was no great struggle to fathom what had happened, and none of them cared to question the actions of the Lord Inquisitor.

Near dusk they came upon a substantial farm with a stable and several large barns. To the relief of the party, Weaver called a halt. The men gratefully fell from their saddles, stumbling into the nearest building, too weary to chase the residents from their home. They sprawled in the hay and dropped into dreamless sleep. Even the Lord Inquisitor could feel the compelling lure of rest and the ache in his bones.

Tired as he was, he still forced his way into the house and put the family to flight, sending them running into the gathering gloom with bellowed curses and a shot from his pistol. It did not matter that they would return. By the time they did, Weaver and his men would be long gone.

The Lord Inquisitor sank onto one of the recently-vacated straw pallets and lay back. He only intended to close his eyes for a moment, to rest his back and his throbbing legs. He had been troubled of late, and true sleep had been elusive, but the constant travel, the alchemical potions and the lack of real food finally conspired against him and he was asleep within seconds.

When his eyes opened, he was in another place, an unfamiliar place. The sky above was a deep, rich blue, and smeared with unfamiliar stars. There was no moon, but the landscape around him was clearly visible. The tall, tawny grass in which he lay seemed to glow softly. Weaver got to his feet and looked around, perplexed by his surroundings.

Grassy, rolling plains stretched away in all directions, rippling in a wind he could not feel. Trees dotted the landscape, but they were unlike any trees he had ever seen before. They were incredibly tall, their slim trunks towering over a hundred feet into the sky. Skeletal limbs drooped from them, tapering into twigs heavy with clusters of pale, pearlescent fruit. These too were surrounded by a faint luminescence, like the gas bulbs developed in the workshops of London.

In one direction, the horizon was a mass of knotted black spires, darker still than the sky. In the other direction, at the top of a hill, stood a figure clad in a mantle of white fire. Weaver squinted and managed to make out hints of silver amidst the light, and as many as six arms. The figure was much larger than a man; it would have towered over him, were he stood beside it. The Lord Inquisitor raised his hand in greeting, without fully understanding his own actions. Instantly the thing was gone, faster than he could blink, leaving nothing but wavering grass in its wake.

A painfully discordant wail came from behind him.

Weaver turned to see a fleet of winged shapes spilling across the sky from the direction of the spires, and a terrible sense of foreboding filled him. He looked toward the dark horizon, and to his horror, something looked back.

His vision blurred and he had the sensation of flying across the plains at great speed, the ochre grass and mighty trees racing beneath him. The land became bleak and broken, then alive with a sick light that spilled from deep fissures. Then he was among the spires, razor sharp pillars of knotted black glass flickering past on either side.

A great maw opened ahead of him, and he found himself within an impossible palace, its dimensions defying his understanding and its angles beyond human comprehension. He screamed as the insane geometry spiralled about him, and he began to rise, until he was surrounded by towering pillars of different heights.

He was still screaming, the clawing madness of the place searing his mind until he was sure his skull would burst. He circled the pillars and knew that atop each was something that would surely break his mind if he looked upon it. He squeezed his eyes shut and put his hands over his ears, but even the memory of the palace made him sick.

Clashing, jarring sensations washed over him, every experience the human mind could understand, from its blackest pits to its greatest heights. Every one was tainted. Every one of them was subtly different.

The eighth pillar was the tallest.

He felt his sense of self pushed to the back of his mind, to the very remotest corner of what he knew as Charles Weaver. The thing atop the eighth pillar turned its gaze on him. With only a sliver of power it made him open his eyes.

It was like looking into the sun. Weaver screamed, as his very existence crumbled to ash.

'Hold him!' a voice commanded. Strong hands held his arms and legs and a great weight lay upon his chest.

The Lord Inquisitor thrashed and screamed, and despite his captors' best efforts he cast them aside. He rolled to his feet and clawed at the mask on his face, gripping its metal edges. It wouldn't come off.

He opened his eyes to find his knights standing around him. Some of them had their hands on their swords and were looking at him as if they expected him to attack at any moment. Weaver dropped his hands to his sides and gulped air into his lungs. He was in the farmhouse he had taken. Warm sunlight streamed through the window and a gentle breeze plucked at his hair. He stood there for a moment, disoriented, and then his armour of composure dropped back into place. 'We have rested too long,' he said brusquely.

'My lord, are you... is everything well?' Sir Anthony asked hesitantly. 'We tried to wake you, but...'

'A dream,' Weaver interrupted. 'Nothing more.'

The knights looked at each other, but relaxed a little. They all looked much better for a night of rest.

'Get fresh horses, we leave immediately.' Weaver barked out the command, all weakness banished. Sir Anthony nodded and led the warriors out. The Lord Inquisitor watched them go, his eyes haunted.

Mahón
Spain

THERE HAD BEEN many brawls in the tavern over the years. Some were small, between two men maybe, over a game of cards. Other fights involved entire crews, and spilled out of the tavern onto the street. This one was remarkably one-sided. Afterwards, those who were able to leave the tavern were never quite able to recall all the details. Much later, the 'Legend of the Hundred Man Brawl' would be retold in taverns throughout the Mediterranean; just another story of the notorious Pirate King.

Captain Bachir threw the first punch. That was one thing that was a definite fact. He surged to his feet, overturning the table, and lunged for de Luna. The Pirate King stepped aside, avoiding the clumsy attack. Not a soul actually noticed him get to his feet. Bachir tripped on the vacated stool.

'You don't need to do this,' Geraldo said in a mild tone. Bachir laughed nastily and got to his feet.

'Afraid you're going to lose, old man?'

The Pirate King bristled and drew his sword.

'*Old?* Why, I'm barely a day over twenty-five!'

'Kill him!' Bachir roared, and his crew rushed to obey.

There was a *snap* as a barbed crossbow bolt flashed across the room. Despite the range and the bowman's careful eye, he somehow missed, the shot instead finding its way into the chest of one of his companions. The man grunted and flipped over a table, dead before he hit the floor.

Giraldo de Luna did not appear to move quickly, but he moved with such incredible grace it was as if the thugs were asleep, their movements jerky and lethargic. The Pirate King flowed between them, leaving a blur of colour in his wake. His sword was a living tongue of silver that flashed three times as he crossed the room. Then he stood before the bowman who had only just begun to reload.

'That was unfortunate,' Giraldo said to the wide-eyed thug. Behind him, three men howled in anguish as knives and cutlasses fell from severed fingers. The blade flashed again, cutting the bowstring and slicing a neat furrow through a pirate's face, including his right eye. He toppled back, shrieking and clutching at his wound. Not a single drop of blood had touched de Luna's finery, and he turned to regard Bachir who was still scrambling to his feet amidst the detritus of the table.

'Gentlemen.' The Pirate King addressed the scowling mob closing ranks behind him. 'Your captain is not a wise man. He is not even a good captain. Will you follow him, or will you follow a king?' The air was charged with aggression, many of the other patrons taking the opportunity and cover of the brawl to settle some scores of their own. Giraldo made one last bid to puncture the tension and dispel the violence before it boiled over. 'Or do I need to make my point clearer?' He drew a dagger that perfectly matched his blade and quirked an eyebrow.

'These men are *mine*, maggot! *Kill him and his gold will be ours!*' Bachir bellowed at his crew. 'We'll *all* be kings before the sun sets tonight!'

Geraldo sighed. *Perhaps I* am *getting too old for this,* he thought to himself.

Then the tavern exploded into chaos.

Giraldo banished the maudlin thought and leapt up onto the bar.

He briefly crossed the sword and dagger across his chest in mock-salute and looked down at Bachir, who had drawn a massive cutlass and was pushing his men ahead of him through the brawl. Giraldo wrinkled his nose in distaste at this display of cowardice. 'And you call yourself a captain?'

Bachir shot him a black look and pushed closer. The Pirate King stepped and spun along the length of the bar while tankards and bottles sailed past. He kicked the first man who dared to approach directly in the face, sending him sprawling back into his fellows, then flipped from his perch and landed among them. Boots, clubs and knives descended on him from all sides, a directionless maelstrom of violence that had already spilled out of the tavern and into the market.

None of the weapons, none of the men could touch him. He slipped through the press of bodies like a ghost, his blades wounding, crippling, but never killing. He was a flying ribbon of colour moving through a sea of the ugly and the drab. A bell started ringing outside, summoning the governor's guard, and Giraldo smiled as he ducked a flying stool. It seemed he had outstayed his welcome in Mahón.

Bachir's men had grown less interested in him as their numbers dwindled and they became bogged down in the brawl, but Bachir himself seemed determined to have the Pirate King's head. He cut down a man who stumbled into his path and cuffed another aside as he pushed through the throng. His eyes were wild with hatred; he was beyond reason, possibly even beyond sanity. He was certainly beyond good taste and style.

'Captain Bachir!' a voice yelled above the clamour. 'The *Hermione* is leaving! She's weighed anchor and is putting out to sea!'

'Your crew have abandoned you, worm!' Bachir roared. 'They must despise you as much as the rest of us! I might even let them have your head once I've finished with you!' He shoved through the crowd, his cutlass raised to strike Giraldo down.

The Pirate King sighed and sheathed his weapons. The fight continued, but a strange pocket of tranquillity formed around him. The combatants seemed to avoid the space in which he stood, naturally, falling to his sides without notice. Bachir pushed into the space and stood before Giraldo, splattered with blood, chest heaving. Before he could strike, de Luna's hand snapped out and tapped the burly captain on his barrel chest.

'Enough,' he declared quietly.

Bachir stopped and his eyes bulged. He let go of his sword, and it vanished beneath the feet of the surging mob. 'Enough,' Giraldo said again. Bachir opened and closed his mouth, but only a strangled gurgle escaped his lips. His eyes rolled in panic and he clawed at his throat and chest with shaking hands.

'Help... me...' he managed to choke out to one of his men, who had finally made it to his side. He pawed at the pirate's shirt, his jaw working uselessly a few more times, then vomited a great torrent of water.

Bachir's man pushed him away, staring in horror at his captain. The unfortunate captain sank to his knees, still clutching uselessly at his neck. Cords of muscle stood out like hawsers and veins bulged beneath his skin. All around him the fury of the brawl abated as more people turned to watch what was transpiring.

'Enough,' Giraldo declared for a third—and final—time. Bachir threw back his head and opened his mouth, and water fountained out. He stayed that way for a few heartbeats, like a piece of living statuary, then his eyes rolled back in his head and he toppled to the floor where he lay in a spreading puddle of brine. Water continued to bubble from his dead lips.

'And now, if you will excuse me,' Giraldo de Luna said, dropping a bow before the stunned crowd like a street magician at the end of his trick, 'I do believe my ship is leaving.'

The effect of his calm statement was somewhat spoiled by the sounds of renewed fighting outside as the guard finally arrived to break up the disturbance. Pandemonium resumed, and the Pirate King seized the opportunity to make his exit. He slipped through the mob and back out into the sunshine, where he took a moment to brush a fleck of dust from his shoulder. He walked confidently, unchallenged. Then he saw the gang of armed guards pushing toward him and, tipping his hat to them, set off at a run.

He barrelled across the market and out onto the quay, heading for the pier where the *Hermione* had been anchored. He could see her, sails billowing, as she pulled toward the open water. He gauged the distance. It was a long time since he had attempted anything *quite* this ambitious. *Maybe,* he thought, *I'm too old for this. Maybe this will be the time that my magic fails me.*

There was only one way to know.

Behind him, several of the guard were in hot pursuit. It seemed that the governor's understanding did not stretch to civil disorder and brawling. Giraldo made a mental note not to return to Mahón for at least a year. A few bribes, a word in the right ear and everything would be all right again in time. An arrow whistled past his ear and buried itself in one of the pier posts.

Maybe two years.

Three, at the outside.

With an athletic leap, Giraldo de Luna dived from the end of the landing stage just as the first of the guards reached for him. They skidded to a stop, not quite keen enough to follow him into the water, but brought up more bows to pick him off when he surfaced.

There was no splash. There was no sound of de Luna's body hitting the water. Instead, a few seconds later, the guards saw the lean figure of the Pirate King as he sprinted across the surface of the sea towards his departing ship.

Ripples spread out beneath his boots and marked his passage across the waves. The guards fired from the pier, but de Luna laughed and spun as he ran and their arrows plunged harmlessly into the water. Giraldo ran as hard and as fast as he could until he was jogging alongside the *Hermione*.

'Permission to come aboard, Tohias?' Giraldo hollered up to his grinning first mate, who was already leaning over the side, the rope ladder in his hands.

'One of these days, Captain, I'm not going to let you back on board,' he called down before dropping the ladder. Giraldo swung himself easily onto the lower rungs and clambered up with the ease of years of practice.

'Perhaps,' he said. 'But not *just* yet.' He raised his head to the sea air and inhaled the fresh, clean scent of freedom. There was another scent there, too; the second pressing matter of the day moved to the top of his mental list.

'Set course for Genoa,' he said, quietly. 'We need to be ready to receive our guest.'

TEN

The Alps
Switzerland

THE MOUNTAINS OF Switzerland were nothing like the hills of Tagan's homeland. She clung to the neck of Warin's horse form as the beast made its way through the narrow passes. They had climbed to an altitude where a mist of cloud gathered below them, and she could not shake the sensation that she was flying high above. It was equal parts exhilarating and terrifying.

She was not as cold as she might have expected, despite the sudden drop in temperature. After a little practice, her growing ability to conjure fire from nowhere was certainly proving itself to be useful on this journey. Whenever they stopped for the night—be it in the edges of the vast spread of the Black Forest or the rocky outcroppings that protected them from the worst of the weather—she was able to provide them with warmth and a means to cook their simple camp food. In that way, at least, she felt she was contributing.

Mathias had found the ability to change into a horse increasingly simple and could now take on the form with the ease that Warin demonstrated. He trailed behind them now, his hooves picking carefully along the path. They had passed huge lakes of clear water reflecting the blue of the sky like a mirror, seen mountains perpetually crowned with snow and followed rivers along deep defiles that the sun never reached. It was an experience that left her feeling dizzy and light-headed, and more than a little gleeful. She could not remember ever feeling so free of responsibility in her entire life. Something about the wonder and thrill of travelling numbed the dread of what had become of her home.

Warin picked up speed as the path began to curve away and down.

Tagan felt the brief sting of disappointment as they passed through the cloud bank and back out into the clean Swiss air. The threat of snow was heavy in the clouds, which now loomed above them, dark and threatening. Just clouds now, and no longer something wispy or ethereal.

They were heading southwest, following the sweep of the mountains and keeping well above the floor of a broad valley. Sometimes when they stopped for the night they would see the lights of civilisation below, but Warin insisted they keep to his route. When pressed on the subject, he claimed repeatedly that it was more direct. Tagan was beginning to harbour suspicions that he was not being entirely truthful with them.

The path beneath them began to widen out and Warin increased the pace. He was pushing himself hard today. She felt it in the play of the horse's muscles across his neck and flank, and in the heavy panting of both horses as they ran for all they were worth. She couldn't get rid of the faintest tickle of guilt that she was not contributing to their efforts. The days of riding had already made her legs and back ache, but she knew that it would pass. Their food was meagre, and although Warin hunted and provided meat for the fire, amidst the mountains, pickings had not been good. All three of them had lost weight and were tired, even Tagan.

She reached her arms more tightly around Warin's neck and hugged him fiercely. 'We need to stop for a while,' she said quietly. 'Mathias is getting left behind.' It was true; the pony was entirely failing to keep pace. Warin snorted, tossing his magnificent mane, and dropped into a gentle trot before stopping altogether. The pony caught up a few minutes later.

Tagan slid off the horse's back and crossed to Mathias. She patted his neck gently. 'We have to stop,' she said. 'We can't keep up this pace. It's killing you both.'

Warin shifted form first, Mathias following his lead. The fierce man folded his arms across his barrel chest and studied Tagan. 'It's not killing us,' he said, defensively. 'It is just hard work. Isn't that right, boy?'

'I don't know,' he said. 'I've never been a horse before. Am I supposed to have this burning in my chest?' Sweat rolled off his forehead and there was a pallor to his skin that did not look at all healthy. Tagan put a hand to his cheek and frowned.

'You're running a fever,' she said. 'I think maybe you have caught some illness in the mountains.' On cue, Mathias sneezed, startling all three of them. He grinned sheepishly, then sneezed again. Tagan tightened her lips and set her jaw.

Mathias knew that look.

She turned to the Shapeshifter. 'Warin, he's ill and needs warmth and rest. We aren't like you. We haven't lived our lives like this. We've barely been beyond the borders of our village before. He needs to stop. There is no way we can keep this kind of pace up. Is there no other way to find this Pirate King?'

Warin studied Mathias for a few minutes, and the gruff exterior melted away under a look of genuine concern. 'If he is unwell, then he should not shift. Human illnesses can sometimes... I don't know the word... change, when you are in animal form. Become something worse.' He studied the pair. 'I cannot hope to carry you both. Let's find somewhere to rest for now and I will think on what to do.' They had never heard him speak so kindly. For a moment, suspicion flickered into Tagan's eyes, but she saw that Warin's kindness was not forced.

'Thank you,' she said, crossing to him and taking his gnarled and dirty hands in her own. She stood on tiptoe and kissed his cheek, where she could find a patch of skin beneath the wild beard.

'Get on with you, girl.' He pushed her gently away, but he seemed pleased. Fire, after all, was not her only magic. 'Get the boy as warm as you can and stay safe. I will be back before night falls.' Without waiting to explain further, he shifted into horse-form and set off at top speed. Tagan watched him go and felt a sliver of fear in her heart. She fought it down and turned her attentions to Mathias, who was sniffling pitifully. She needed to concentrate her efforts into caring for her betrothed.

'I can see a cave a little way up the cliff side,' she said, offering him her hand. 'Let's go inside.'

He wrapped his fingers into hers and let himself be led up the hill a little way. She watched him carefully. There were high spots of colour on each cheek and his eyes were far too bright. Whatever he was suffering was probably nothing serious, but enough to lay him low for a while. And *he* was the one with the knowledge of plants and herbs and healing poultices. But she did not let her concern show. She watched him carefully as they walked, still hand in hand, to the cave.

The cave, once they stepped inside, clearly barely deserved the name. It was large enough for the two of them to take shelter, as long as they kept huddled close together, and at least it was better than sitting on the freezing ground outside. She made sure he was as comfortable as he was likely to get and conjured a small fire to keep them both warm and to light the tiny space. There was no wood for her to burn, but it didn't matter when she could manipulate fire however she pleased. She selected a flat spot on the floor, and within a few short moments a small, cheerful fire was crackling on the stone.

Just the sound was comforting. She had conjured a number of cooking fires during the days of travel, but this was different. This was a fire purely for warmth and protection. She felt her affinity with the element swell as she listened to the gentle pop of the flames. There may have been no wood to burn, but Tagan knew how a comforting home fire should sound.

Shadows flickered and danced on the walls, and she watched them for a while until her eyes grew heavy with a weariness she had been denying for a few days. She curled around the already-sleeping Mathias to wait for Warin's return.

There was nothing more she could do.

Bavaria
Germany

WEAVER AND HIS knights came to a stop at the brow of a grassy hill. Below them, a dark, rolling forest stretched northwards as far as the eye could see. It was periodically studded with lakes, rivers and crags, and the ten knights stared at it uncertainly. If the people they sought were hidden within those woods, it would take a hundred men a lifetime to dig them out. The Lord Inquisitor peered at the forest for a long time and then slowly turned in the saddle until he looked south.

'They were here,' he declared after a while. 'They passed this way.'

The knights shared a puzzled look but did not argue. After the episode in the farmhouse, they had been increasingly wary of Weaver, not entirely convinced that they weren't following a madman. Once they left France behind, they had slowed their pace and both man and beast had been grateful for the respite. With no certain way of replacing them, they could not longer afford to be so hard on the animals.

Weaver pointed to the forbidding mass of the mountains that lay to the south. 'There. They have gone south. If we make haste, we should be able to catch them before they reach the peaks.'

The Lord Inquisitor spurred his mount and they once again began to ride.

The Alps
Switzerland

WHEN TAGAN WOKE, dusk had long passed and stars twinkled in the sky beyond the mouth of the cave. The magical fire had burned out not long after she had fallen asleep, and she was shivering in the cold night air. She reignited the fire and turned her attentions immediately to Mathias. The chill could be dangerous. Much to her relief, he was still sleeping, and the heat of his fever had subsided a little. She kissed his cheek softly and drew her shawl more tightly around her shoulders.

Warin had promised to return before nightfall, and he had not made good on that promise. She didn't believe for a second that the gruff man had abandoned them to their fate in the mountains. She *wouldn't* believe it. There was some other explanation for his prolonged absence. Everything would be fine.

She stretched over Mathias to reach the bag that she had carried with her from Warin's camp in the forest, and rummaged through it. There was a little cold meat left over from a kill a day or two before and some flat fire-baked bread. She ate them hungrily and took a sip of water from the waterskin. The hills had been hard to traverse, but at least had offered fresh water from the many little rivers and streams. They could survive long enough to cross the mountains. The thought of it calmed the roiling anxiety in her gut.

Mathias continued to sleep, but he responded well enough when she shook him gently to make sure that he *was* simply sleeping and hadn't passed into unconsciousness. He grumbled and curled up tighter, muttering something about 'five more minutes,' and her worries melted still further. He had just caught a cold or something of that ilk. She remembered the time her father had been ill with a similar thing; he had been certain his days were numbered.

She patted his back fondly and squeezed past him to take a look out of the cave entrance, and gasped in delight. It was the first time that she had truly looked up into the night sky since they had left the confines of the forest. At every stopping point, as they travelled through the hills and valleys, they had been in some way sheltered: clumps of pines, overhangs... But from the cave on the side of the cliff, her view of the diamond-studded night sky was completely and utterly unobstructed.

Not a single cloud spoiled the view of the thousands of twinkling stars decorating the velvet sky. She stared up into the beauty of the heavens and all of her worries melted away. She instinctively felt drawn to the power of the world and all that made it such a glorious place. A fleeting understanding of her own tiny insignificance filled her soul, but rather than bringing despair in its wake, she felt intense gratitude.

I may be as nothing next to the heavens above me, she thought, *but I am here, nonetheless.*

'Tagan!'

Warin's voice. She turned to see the red-haired man stomping up the side of the hill towards her. She pulled herself out of the cave entrance and waved to attract his attention.

'Over here,' she called, watching her breath ghost in the air before her. Warin nodded and made his way across the grass and rocks to her side.

'How is he?'

'He will be fine,' she said, reassuringly. 'He just needed rest, I think.'

'Good. Come morning, we need to be on the move again. We have not so far to go. I have made a change of plans. De Luna will come to us.' He wrinkled his nose. 'Once we are together, we can increase our speed. We will be much quicker.'

Tagan looked at him and saw a flicker of concern in his eyes. 'What is it?' In the depths of her soul she was afraid of the answer, but she asked the question anyway. 'Is something wrong?'

Warin shook his head. 'I am worried for the boy, nothing more,' he said, but Tagan was not entirely convinced. He changed the subject before she could pry further. 'I feel I should warn you about de Luna and his particular brand of nonsense, as well.'

'Nonsense?'

'You are a pretty girl. Giraldo de Luna likes pretty girls. You should beware of that.'

Tagan flushed at the unexpected compliment. 'I am engaged to be married,' she said, perhaps just a *little* more primly than she would normally have gone for. 'I am sure he will understand that.'

Warin smiled flatly. 'Perhaps,' he said.

Hampton Court
England

'I UNDERSTAND WHAT you are saying, Father, but why must I go?'

At nineteen years old, the future King Richard the Sixth was a startlingly attractive man. Thanks to his mother's blood, his hair was a deep, rich auburn and his eyes were green as ocean pools. The young women at court—and some of the older ones as well—already found themselves watching his every move. Slim, but with the promise of filling out to mirror his father's muscular build, the young prince was popular amongst the people of his country.

For much of his youth and young manhood, the prince heeded the impassioned words of his father. He knew the importance of destroying magic across the country. He believed all that the King said and he never questioned. At least, he had never questioned *before*. Now, however, he had doubts.

'Magic is an affliction of the isle that must be purged. I know. I do not need to *see* it.' He did not whine. It was a simple statement of fact and one that had been taught to him since he was old enough to understand. King Richard lamented the thoroughness of his son's education every bit as much as he lamented what he was doing. At that particular moment he lamented a great many things. He felt wretched.

'Very true, boy, but a swordsman does not learn his skill through study alone. He masters his art by *doing*.' In his heart he wanted his son to make an argument so compelling that he had no choice but to agree, but he knew the prince too well. Young Richard would not be able to resist the surprise that was going to be offered.

It was the surprise that came *after* which the King dreaded.

'Are you suggesting that I should perform magic?' The prince offered no change of expression and his voice was neutral. His deadpan response did not impress the King, who scowled at him.

'Don't be obtuse, boy. You know what I mean. Experience tempers a man, gives him wisdom. You should witness magic for yourself. Feel its power. In so doing, you will better understand the wickedness of its nature.'

The prince gave a huge sigh and King Richard felt a twinge of annoyance, despite his desire to lose the argument. He did not like the sting of defiance, even from his own son.

'But Father, what of the banquet? The dance? There are already so many plans. Father, I don't really want to spend my birthday in a field staring at some filthy magi grubbing through the dirt for worms to sacrifice.'

'It is not a field, Richard,' the King replied. 'It is the oldest site of power in this country. Perhaps even the world. There will be a gathering of magi unlike any that has happened in England since the birth of our line.'

'So why not simply have the Inquisition remove them before it can happen? Why wait until my birthday to have it done?' Now he *was* whining.

The King gave his son a brittle smile before he paced the length of the room and back. 'Because they only gather there on that day, and it will be easier by far than hunting them individually. And, Richard'—the King drew a deep breath and cursed himself inwardly—'because Isaac Bonnington assures me that the *Lionheart* will be completed by then.'

The prince's eyes widened. 'You want me to command the *Lionheart* during the attack?'

King Richard nodded, and for a moment did not trust himself to say anything. He felt a lump in his throat. 'Yes,' he replied huskily. Then he cleared his throat and continued with more certainly. 'Yes. I want you to witness the truth of magic for yourself, and I want you with me in the *Lionheart*.'

Prince Richard gave his father a huge smile. 'Then the King shall have what he wishes.' His insouciant air was frustrating at times. What the King would have given to have been so free from care.

Richard's heart sank like a stone at the boy's delight. He had known his son would not be able to resist the offer. He had lied about the magi. There had been no magic in Salisbury since the rise of the Inquisition. All that would be there would be his son. In a powerful stone circle. At dusk.

On the day of the solstice.

The Alps
Switzerland

MATHIAS'S BRIEF INDISPOSITION had more or less passed, come the dawn of the next day, and he found himself subject to gentle teasing from Tagan and slightly less gentle mockery from Warin. They had resumed their journey, this time in human form, at a slower pace. He bore the teasing with good grace, occasionally laughing along mechanically, but without much humour. Tagan walked beside him, her fingers laced through his, and did her best to lift his flagging spirits.

Warin stomped ahead of the pair, occasionally muttering under his breath. His mood, although sour, was less aggressive than it had been. Tagan watched his stoop-shouldered back and her eyes grew thoughtful. There was a new urgency to the mage's manner and while he seemed happy enough to walk, she got the sense that if it were not for Mathias's health, he would have been running.

'Where are we heading?' The question came from Mathias—the first time he had spoken since they had left the cave—and Tagan started in surprise. The narrow cliff path called for concentration and careful steps. None of them had any great urge to step badly and ride the scree to the bottom.

'A lake. Big one,' Warin said over his shoulder. 'De Luna will meet us there.'

'Can he shapeshift as well?' Mathias was curious. Warin shrugged.

'After a fashion, yes. His is the power of the oceans, the seas and the rains.'

'He can turn into a fish?'

'No, not precisely.' Warin stopped to look at Mathias. 'You will see soon enough. Now come along.'

Genoa
Italy

THE WINDS HAD been fine and the tides favourable, but then, de Luna reflected, they always were. He stood on the prow of the *Hermione* as it slipped into Genoa harbour and he smiled, Mahón already forgotten. He had no doubt that there would be new opportunities to make a little coin, renew a few old friendships and make some new conquests. A gust of wind plucked at his hat and he laughed. Then something arcane tickled his senses and the smile fell from his face.

A single leaf floated on the breeze and Geraldo snatched it out of the air like a striking snake. He turned it over in his hands and examined its surface, then he pressed it to his face and inhaled its scent. Crisp and fresh. Clean, mountain pine.

'Red,' de Luna breathed. He looked over his shoulder at his first mate. 'Take her in, Tohias. We will unload any who wish to leave here, take on board supplies and then head straight back out to sea. Make it quick. As quick as you can.'

'Captain?' Tohias looked utterly mystified. They had not even dropped anchor yet.

'Back out to sea, Tohias. Be ready to receive guests.' With that, he dived over the side and into the harbour.

He didn't make a splash when he hit the water, simply vanishing beneath the waves and melting into their embrace. He became a shadow beneath the crystal surface, a liquid blur that could only be glimpsed out of the corner of the eye. The kind of shape that could be mistaken for a dolphin, perhaps. A fleeting vision that gave rise to legends of merfolk.

For Giraldo the change represented the ultimate in freedom, the rare chance to be completely at one with his magic. He felt the colossal tug of the tide, the caress of the wind across the surface, the hidden currents lurking in the unknown depths, and he revelled in it. The power of the ocean was unlike any other in this world. He flashed through the water, escaping the harbour, and flowed upstream at the speed of thought. In his mind's eye he saw a huge bow-shaped lake flanked by mountains, a place he had not visited for many years.

The river narrowed steadily and became a stream. He raced through the alpine foothills, leaping up waterfalls and through deep, underground ways, ever higher, until he could go no further. He scattered shoals of fish, which reformed behind him, unfazed by his passing.

His essence erupted from a spring high on the mountains and became snow, the shock of his arrival sending an avalanche down the slopes to bury forests and valleys below. He briefly emerged from the ice as he crested the mountains, his lower body nothing more than a whirling blizzard. He laughed with the release of it all and his voice echoed around the peaks. Then he was beneath the surface again, nothing more than a ripple that plunged toward its destination.

* * *

Lake Geneva
Switzerland

'It's beautiful!' Tagan exclaimed as they descended a grassy hillside. The lake was huge, and even from their elevated position they could not see its entire length. 'How big is it?'

'Many leagues.' Warin replied gruffly. He glanced over his shoulder at her and nodded. 'But do not worry, we do not have to walk around. De Luna should be here.'

The Shapeshifter was peering past her, as if looking for something. Tagan glanced over her shoulder, but only grass and the dark crags lay above them. 'What are you looking for?' Her curiosity was piqued.

Warin turned back toward the lake and shrugged. 'Nothing,' he muttered absently. 'I thought I heard something. But clearly I did not.' For whatever reason, this seemed to irritate him.

After a day of travel and another night of rest, Mathias had recovered considerably. Warin produced a pouch of herbs from somewhere within his leathers and brewed them up over one of Tagan's fires. It had smelled terrible and tasted worse, but the young man began to feel better within minutes of drinking it

'I assume you know where we are meeting him, then?' Mathias said with a grin. 'Because if it was just "the big lake," then we're going to be looking for each other for a while.'

Warin grunted in what Mathias chose to believe was amusement rather than irritation. 'You don't need to worry, he will find us.'

Since the night in the cave, the Shapeshifter had been surly and withdrawn, or as Mathias had said to Tagan the previous night, *more* surly and withdrawn. She smiled, but she didn't laugh, and Mathias was forced to admit that something was obviously bothering their curious new friend.

They continued down the hillside in silence until they reached the lake shore, a quiet pebble beach disturbed only by the gentle lap of waves and the wind in the trees. The mountains beyond the expanse of water were massive, their tops draped with snow and their steep flanks dark and rugged.

'Did you really mean for us to cross them?' Mathias said, gesturing to the cyclopean peaks.

Warin nodded. 'Yes. The sea lies beyond them.'

'But now we won't have to because your friend is coming to get us?'

'Yes, that is what I hope.'

'You hope?'

Warin turned to Mathias with a look of exasperation on his face. 'Yes, I hope. I sent him a message that I want to meet him, but I don't know how long it will take. He travels the seas and the seas spread far. If he is close, then perhaps he will come soon. If not, then we wait.' He shifted uncomfortably and looked up the hillside again. 'For as long as we can.'

'But you don't want to wait, do you?' Mathias said. He picked up a stone and threw it out over the lake. It arced through the air and then plunged into the water with a satisfying splash.

What happened next brought a small scream to Tagan's lips. A shimmering figure rose from the mirrored surface of the lake; the unmistakable shape of a man, tall and well-built. The shape was completely translucent, and she could make out the trees and mountains behind it. She clutched onto Mathias's arm and stumbled backwards.

The water man took a few steps forward until its feet met the lake shore and then began to fill in, assuming colour and texture. Transparency became flesh and skin, and even clothes shimmered into being. The process travelled upwards, beginning at the legs and ending with the face and head. A handsome face, Tagan could not help but notice from her vantage point behind Mathias. The face broke into a huge grin and Giraldo de Luna, the Pirate King, caught Warin the Red, the Shapeshifter up in an exuberant hug.

'Red!' There was genuine pleasure in the greeting and Tagan smiled a little at the embarrassed expression on Warin's face. 'You old dog, how have you been? How many years has it been?'

'Not nearly enough,' came the curt reply, but none of them missed the affection in the brown eyes, or could ignore the warmth in the tone. 'You're still as ugly as ever, I see.' He wormed his way out of Giraldo's embrace. 'Glad you could spare the time in your busy life to join us.'

'Wouldn't have missed this for all the gold in the world. An invitation from my old friend Red! I knew it was coming, and when I got your leaf... how could I refuse?'

Warin shook his head. 'You always were an odd one.'

'Are you going to introduce me?' Giraldo's eyes had flicked to Mathias briefly and lingered just that little bit longer than would normally be considered appropriate on Tagan. 'These are two fine young people you bring with you.'

'The boy is Mathias. The girl is Tagan. His betrothed.' Warin said the word sternly.

'Betrothed? Ah, my disappointment knows no bounds.' Giraldo stepped forward and took Tagan's hand in his own. He brought it to his lips and kissed it gently. Her face instantly went bright pink and an unexpected giggle left her. Giraldo held onto her hand for a little longer. 'I smell the flame on this one, Red. Is she...?'

'Blessed with the spark, yes. Now let go of her hand. You're making the girl uncomfortable.'

Tagan opened her mouth to say that it was all right, but no words came out. Instead, she took her hand from Giraldo and put it awkwardly behind her back. She suddenly wanted to giggle, and she was not normally much given to giggling.

Mathias watched the entire exchange with a strange expression on his face. Giraldo examined Tagan with indulgent amusement for a moment or two longer, but when he turned to Mathias, the levity was gone, replaced by something entirely more serious.

'It is a great and grave thing you do.' Giraldo studied Mathias, taking in everything about the young man in that intense glance.

'How... you know about our journey? Has Warin already...'

'Journey?' Geraldo's face split into a grin again. 'I was talking about marriage. It is a very serious thing, yes? You must promise to make her very happy, Mathias...?'

'Mathias Eynon,' he said and rolled his eyes. He kept his voice pleasant, but the distrust was apparent. 'And you are Giraldo de Luna. Your reputation precedes you, sir.'

The Pirate King burst into a fit of infectious, raucous laughter. Mathias couldn't help the slight smile that tweaked the edges of his lips. Eventually the laugh settled down and he wiped eyes that were completely dry.

'My reputation? What have you been telling the boy, Red?'

'The truth,' was the response. 'What else do I know?' The Shapeshifter's words had silenced the pirate, although he still chuckled quietly as he studied Mathias thoughtfully.

'You know,' he said, 'you remind me of somebody I once knew when I was young. He was a good man. Maybe even a great man; and I don't know many of them, to be sure.'

Further discussion was cut off by the thunderous report of hooves. Mathias turned and looked back up the hillside they had only recently descended to see a group of horsemen bearing down on them. Warin cursed quietly and Tagan glared at him.

'You knew we were being followed.' Her tone was accusing; the Shapeshifter did nothing to deny it.

'I felt in the earth that there were men at our backs, but we were ahead of them. I had hoped to be gone from here before they arrived. It seems we are not so fortunate.'

As the men drew closer they saw that the horses were in terrible condition, their flanks lathered in sweat and painfully thin. Their riders were little better, their eyes ringed by dark circles and their cheeks hollow. They charged with a grim determination, though, and when the final rider came in sight, Mathias immediately understood why.

'That's an Inquisitor!' His eyes widened in fear and shock. It was impossible to be sure behind the mask, but Mathias suspected that it was the same one he had seen at the stone circle in Wales. The man who had probably killed Wyn.

Giraldo sniffed and drew his weapons. 'They don't look like much, do they, Red? What do you say? You take the five on the left and I'll take the five on the right?'

The horsemen spread out as they approached, forming a line that the magi could not hope to escape on foot. The Inquisitor hung back and slowed his steed to a more sedate pace, cantering along behind his warriors.

'Warin,' Mathias hissed to the Shapeshifter. 'I think that's the same Inquisitor that was after us at home!'

Warin's head snapped around and he fixed Mathias with a look of such primal ferocity that the young man shrank back in shock. 'The one that killed Adelmo?' He shook his head and snarled. 'And destroyed the circle?'

Mathias nodded.

There was an inrush of air and Warin was gone, and in his place stood an enormous red-furred bear. The beast reared up on its hind legs to tower close to ten feet in height. It opened its mighty jaws and bellowed a challenge at the oncoming warriors. The sound was deafening, and a couple of the horses reared in terror, throwing their riders to the ground.

Giraldo looked askance at the massive animal as it crashed back onto all fours. 'I'll take that as a "yes," then.' He turned to Mathias and Tagan and flashed them a dazzling smile. 'Don't worry. Just stay out of the way and we will have all this sorted out in a moment. We have them outnumbered, after all.'

Warin took off at a lumbering run, his massive bulk quickly gaining speed as he charged. Giraldo, by contrast, looked as though he were out for a casual stroll as he walked toward the horsemen. It was a ludicrous sight, the great beast and the peacock preparing to make war on trained warriors, and Mathias could not help but fear for them. He felt small and powerless, and he hated it. Tagan slipped her hand into his, and together they watched their friends prove their fears baseless.

There was a tangible moment of terrible calm before the impact, a frozen tableau of peace before the explosion of violence that followed. Warin surged into the first of the horses, knocking it to the ground. A second horseman tried to strike at him as he did so, the sword missing his hide by a whisker. The first knight rolled to his feet and turned just as the bear lunged over his thrashing horse. He had a heartbeat to look shocked before one of the bear's massive paws struck him in the chest, hurling his body into the air, trailing blood.

Giraldo leapt between the two closest horsemen, his sword and dagger flickering faster than they could raise their weapons in defence. The Pirate King balanced nimbly, one foot on each steed, as their owners flopped limply from the saddle. They were not dead, but they would also require substantial care to get back on their feet. Giraldo hopped onto the back of one of the vacant horses and from there sprang at the next.

'They could really do it!' Tagan's voice was breathless. Her awe at the prowess of the two magi eclipsed her horror at the violence taking place yards from where she stood. Warin swatted another warrior from his horse, clamped his jaws around the screaming man and shook him like a rag doll until the struggling stopped. He and Giraldo seemed invincible.

Then the Inquisitor galloped from behind the mêlée with a pistol drawn and trained directly on Mathias. Tagan saw him. There was no time to cry out; without even thinking, she stepped in front of the man she loved and spread her hands in denial.

The pistol roared.

Warin and Geraldo turned at the sound of gunfire and were just in time to see Tagan blasted backwards into Mathias and the pair of them driven into the lake by the impact. A cry of very human denial escaped Warin's lips as he once again assumed human form. He barged one of the unhorsed knights aside and dived into the water. De Luna was there a moment later and vanished beneath the surface.

The Lord Inquisitor cantered to a stop and drew his second pistol. Then he waited.

He waited a long time.

ELEVEN

The Island of the Seer
Denmark

THE ISLAND WAS remote enough from the mainland that it offered privacy, but still allowed those who dared to petition for her services to make their way there. The difficulties travelling to the island presented were manifold and thus, visiting the seer was the last, desperate act of those poor souls who sorely craved the benefit of her wisdom and her remarkable skills.

The weather at this time of the year did not make the crossing from the village on the mainland a pleasant experience. The coracles that had to be rowed across the choppy, treacherous waters and navigated into the rocky cove were small and unreliable. Local legend said that only those with honest and entirely unselfish need could make it to the seer's island alive.

The sky that morning was a leaden grey, threatening another deluge of cold rain that would soon become sleet and snow. A sliver of silvery-gold outlined the dark clouds, but it was the only hint of daylight in an omen-heavy sky. The wind raced across the caps of the waves, whipping them into foam, and howled mournfully around the jagged coast. Strange, twilight shadows haunted the cliffs and sighed in despair at the little vessel bobbing in the sea.

The boat's single occupant tugged at the oars, riding the crest of another violent wave that seemed determined to send him back to the mainland, but his resolve was strong. He was trying to reach the Seer's island for good reason, and he would get there whatever it took. He was Brynjolf Gellirson. Over many a tankard of good ale, he had boasted that he feared nothing. Why, then, was he so scared now?

The rising gale dragged the swell into something more than he could handle and he felt the balance of the tiny boat starting to slip from his control. Still Brynjolf rowed, purpose setting his jaw in a grim line. He had too much at stake to give up now. Other, lesser men would have been beaten by the elements and allowed the tides to carry them away, battered and defeated. It happened often. Even the most determined and the most desperate, the strongest and the most able would struggle against the storm for hours, even days, but fatigue or despair would eventually overtake them. Crushed and exhausted, they surrendered themselves back to the tides. The winds would slowly drop and the gentlest of sea breezes would carry them back to the coast.

Not Brynjolf. He would not be turned back. It had taken every ounce of courage he possessed to make the attempt on the Seer's island. He had never shied away from a challenge in his entire life, and he was not about to start.

'Seer!' He screamed to be heard over the wind. It blew his long flaxen hair about his face and whipped it into his eyes like sharp twine. 'I will not be defeated! I must speak with you!' The boat shuddered beneath him, banking so sharply that he was flung to its wooden bottom. He got splinters in his cheek and the sting was exacerbated by the salt water. His eyes blurred, and he struggled to get back to his feet.

'Eyja!' He poured his heart and soul into his cry, and prayed to the gods—to whom he at least swore quiet allegiance—that she would hear the desperation that had driven him out here.

As he screamed the Seer's name, there was a momentary break in the cruel weather. The wind hesitated, and buoyed by the change, Brynjolf tried again. 'Eyja, please! I *must* see you!' He cringed, anticipating the storm's return. But to his surprise, the gale died abruptly. There was no gradual decline from hurricane to breeze; just the merest whisper of an autumn zephyr that brought a hint of winter to Brynjolf's senses. The sea calmed as though the maelstrom had never been. The waves remained foam-tipped, but the surface became calm enough for him to row to the sanctuary of Eyja's cove.

You are a brave man, Brynjolf Gellirson, to use my name so freely. Brave, or foolish. Which are you?

Her voice came on the gusts lapping the waters around the coracle, as he secured it against the pull of the tide. It whispered in his ears, in his thoughts, and above all else, in his soul. Her voice was gentle, the caress of a quiet lover, and he felt his anxieties and troubles float away.

Legend would have had him believe that Eyja, the woman who over time had simply become known as the Seer, lived in a dark cave, hiding from a world that had wronged her. It came as some surprise to him to discover a neatly kept little cottage with careful thatch, nestling within the shelter of the cliffs rising on the island's west side. The dwelling showed no signs of the weather, and could have been built that very morning. It was made of rough, uncut stone and smooth, pale wood, and was startlingly devoid of bird droppings. This seemed even more peculiar when one took into account the vast number of seabirds congregating on the shore. Hundreds, perhaps thousands of them, their voices raised in angry, squawking dispute. A never-ending battle for supremacy.

Brynjolf began walking up the pebble beach that led to the Seer's cottage, his steps hesitant and uncertain.

Don't be afraid, Brynjolf. You have come this far. Do you think I would harm you now? Do you fear that I will cast you down to the rocks and leave you broken? Or perhaps you believe the tale that I dine on the flesh of those who drowned in their attempts to reach me?

He didn't respond. He had heard the tales, and did not relish the idea of finding out if any of them were true. He faltered now, afraid to enter the woman's sanctuary and lay his problem before her. It was the final test. Elements could be defied, wind and sea overcome by strength or skill, but there was no greater enemy to a man than his own heart.

Brynjolf set his jaw and buried his doubts. His despair was too great to turn back now. He felt the hesitance in his steps melt away and strode with purpose to the door of the cottage. He did not allow himself the time to dwell upon what he was about to do as he pushed it open. Taking a deep breath, he stepped into the incense-laden air.

Immediately, a sense of peace stole over him, a feeling he had long forgotten, and he breathed more easily than he had done in many days. He could feel the weight of his worries rise from his shoulders, lifted into the curling smoke and carried away from him.

The windows of the little cottage were small and dim, and the grey light filtering from outside barely illuminated the pale haze. Brynjolf glanced around the interior. Everything was swathed in shadow and heady scent, making him feel as though he was caught up in some kind of dream. A *good* dream, though. He couldn't remember being so relaxed.

'What brings you to my threshold, Brynjolf Gellirson?'

He could hear her, but he could not see her. Whilst this was more than a little perplexing, he found he did not mind. To hear the Seer's voice was like listening to a choir of heavenly voices working in harmony, many-layered and tantalising. It was musical and lilting, low in pitch, reminding Brynjolf of being a younger man, when first he'd looked for love. Thinking of such things reminded him sharply of his reasons for battling the gale to reach her.

'Seer, I need to beg a favour of your gift of foresight. The future of my line is in doubt, and my standing in the village weakens.'

The shadows in the corner shifted and a figure emerged. The Seer was tall, and although she seemed slender, the heavy robe she wore hid her figure. The hood was drawn up and over her face. All Brynjolf could see of her features beneath were a few wisps of pale blonde hair and a glimmer of eyes the colour of rock pools after a storm.

'The future of your line? Your woman has lost another babe?'

Brynjolf wondered how she could possibly have known that, but then reminded himself of whose house he stood in.

He did not know how easily she read people, their expressions, their choices, and the way they stood. He also didn't know how frequently she moved amongst the people of the coast—unknown and unseen—and listened to the tales and the gossip.

She sought always to avoid the use of her power if she could. It was not as folk believed it to be. She did not scry, or read the fates in a bowl of water, or bloody entrails or sodden herbs. It was a blade that cut two ways.

In the many years she had lived here, she had bestowed her gift on fewer than a score of people.

'Four she has lost now,' confirmed Brynjolf. 'And she is carrying a fifth. The healers say that all is well, that she is carrying as she should, but the fifth moon approaches. Each babe has been lost at this time. I must know, Seer. Will this child live? Will it live and continue my line? Will she give me a son? I cannot bear to lose another.'

It was the unspoken that moved the Seer. Brynjolf's words seemed selfish, that he cared only for his continued status amongst his people. But she heard the tremor in his voice, saw the light of fierce love and loyalty in his eyes. He was here for his wife just as much as he was here for himself.

'Calm yourself, Brynjolf,' she said, and her tone became kinder, softer. He took a deep breath and looked up at her, tears in his eyes.

'I would give all that I have to see this child live.'

The Seer closed the distance between them and put a long, slender finger to his lips. He fell silent, startled by the gesture.

'Be careful what you wish for, Brynjolf. It may yet come to pass. Now sit. I will make tea. We will talk, and together, you and I, we will look at the future.' She took her finger from his lips and steered him gently by the shoulder down into a chair by a small table. Then she reached up and pushed back her hood.

Her beauty was breathtaking. To believe the women of the village, the Seer had to have seen at least sixty winters, yet she did not look to have seen more than thirty at most. Her skin was alabaster pale with the faintest hint of rose touching her cheeks. There was not a line, not a wrinkle to be seen. The skin looked soft and plump and flawlessly smooth. Her grey eyes were mesmerising and he could hardly bring himself to drag his attention from that stormy gaze. Her long, white-blonde hair, freed from the hood, fell about her elfin face; the small, pointed chin and the exquisite rosebud lips. She seemed more a child's doll than a flesh and blood woman.

Brynjolf gazed up at her, his eyes wide and adoring, and she gave him a very slight smile before reaching over and gently pushing his jaw closed. 'Close your mouth, Brynjolf, I have no need of a fly catcher.'

Embarrassed, he looked away and focused on the hazy smoke

rising through the shafts of light slanting in through the window whilst the Seer moved around her cottage. Her movements were light and graceful, and there was an elegance to her as she filled two cups from the kettle hanging over the cook fire. She crumbled pungent herbs into the water and carried them to the table.

'Chamomile and vanilla,' she said, by way of an explanation. She pushed a pot of clear honey towards him. 'Add as much or as little as you need to blunt the bitterness. It will calm you. Then we will talk.' Again, that little smile that brought more light to him than any of the windows. He nodded and put a spoonful of honey into his tea, copying her lead. A tentative sip surprised him with its taste.

Halfway down the cup, he could already feel himself begin to calm. Even the simple act of sipping the tea served to relax him, and the Seer knew her remedies well. She set down her mug and reached over to catch Brynjolf's free hand in both of her own. Her hands were as soft and smooth as the skin on her face, contrasting with Brynjolf's calloused and worn hands: hands that worked ropes and trawled nets. Hands that built and shaped and gave so much to the village in which he lived. He was a hard worker, a kind-hearted man in a strong, healthy body. He worked too hard sometimes, often more hours than were good for him, but everything he did, he did for others. There was nobility in his bearing and strength in everything he did.

In another lifetime, she might have said he had a Viking spirit. But that age had passed. The memories and the legends lived on, but the world was not what it had been.

He looked up into her eyes, puzzled by the sudden contact. She was examining his hand thoughtfully, tracing a finger across the lines of his palm and concentrating hard. Her expression was neutral and unreadable.

'Your wife carries a boy-child,' she said, quietly. 'The son that you both yearn for. The infant who will bear your name and continue your line. How far back can you trace your ancestry, Brynjolf?'

'Many generations,' he replied, captivated by her words and filled to the brim with joy at the news his wife carried a son. The joy was quickly pierced with fear as he remembered his reasons for his journey here. 'My son...' he began.

'Hush,' she replied, mildly. 'Be still. I need you to close your eyes for me, Brynjolf. Close your eyes and breathe deeply. Relax. Let your body rest for a while. You are safe here. Safe and protected from the world beyond this door.' She continued in this manner for a little while and he did everything as instructed, closing his eyes and inhaling the sweet-smelling smoke deeply. He could feel himself slipping deeper into the dream that had crept upon him as he had entered.

He felt the softest of breezes caress his face, and in his imagination, he fancied that he was riding the prow of his fishing boat, looking out to sea and fighting back ancestral memories that urged him to become something more than just a fisherman. A small smile touched his lips.

A fey white light played about Eyja, and everything that Brynjolf had been and could ever be stretched out before her. A million—and more—moments of joy, pain, laughter and sadness. The Seer, the Weaver, She Who Sees—all these were names by which she had been known during her life, and all of them spoke truth. She could read the lives of those few who came before her and, if the need was great, redirect the winds of fate to alter what would be. But the cost was equally great.

The cost was *too* great.

For every life saved, another would be lost in its place. For every misfortune prevented, another must be suffered. Men and women had come to her, begging on their knees for her intervention. She had given it, and they had thanked her and left with joy in their hearts. Then she would force herself to watch and endure the consequences. The Seer hated the thing which others called a 'gift.' It was a curse, nothing more.

But this man, this kind, selfless man, had come to her in desperation. She had rarely met anybody so deserving. She would do what he asked and she would explain to him the price. Sadly, she knew before she even spoke that he would willingly pay it.

'Brynjolf,' she said, in that same hypnotic tone. His eyes did not open and she knew he was caught in the moment. 'Brynjolf, the fates played out the skein of your life long ago, and if it were to remain unaltered, then your son would not live. No, do not grieve for him, not yet.' She stroked a hand down his arm gently. 'Listen to me. He can be spared. What you desperately yearn for can be yours, dear Brynjolf, but it must come at a cost.'

'I would give all that I have,' he whispered dreamily, echoing his words from earlier. The Seer sighed gently and wiped away the tears that glistened in her eyes.

'Are you sure of that, Brynjolf? It is... a high price to pay.'

'Tell me, Seer.'

She told him. And he accepted, just as she had known he would.

Genoa
Italy

MATHIAS BOBBED TO the surface, gasping for air, and floundered across to the unmoving body of Tagan, floating ominously face-down a few feet away. He put his arms around her carefully and turned her over.

'No, no, no,' he said and his tone was filled with a desperation a young man should never have to give voice to. He touched a hand to her face, his expression contorted with a terrible grief. 'This isn't happening. She can't be dead.'

A moment later, Warin spluttered to the surface. Water streamed from his hair and beard, and his expression was thunderous. The Pirate King emerged more gracefully until he stood easily on the surface of the sea. His gaze went immediately to Mathias and Tagan, and then to the prow of the ship bearing down on them.

'Are you trying to drown us? Where are we?' The Shapeshifter's rage was a terrifying thing. Then his eyes fell upon Tagan and his protests died instantly, snuffed out by concern.

'Welcome to the Mediterranean,' Giraldo said grimly. He stepped lightly across the waves and crouched beside the two young people, his expression grave. He gently prised Mathias's hands off Tagan and gathered her up in his arms.

'Get on board,' he said. 'We can do nothing for her here. I have her, lad. Don't fear what we don't yet know for sure.' He nodded towards the rope ladder that the crew had lowered down the side of the boat, and Warin propelled himself towards it, climbing up with wobbly hesitation. Mathias paused for a few moments, then nodded and swam to join his mentor, climbing the ladder with no more grace.

Giraldo came last, holding Tagan in his arms. He shifted the young woman's weight to his shoulder as he swung easily up the ladder, then set her down on the deck of the ship, lying on her side. She lay there, unmoving, and as Mathias looked over her anxiously, it appeared she was also completely unharmed.

'No wound,' he said, bafflement evident in his tone. 'But she took that shot that was meant for me. She...'

Tagan coughed weakly, and a mouthful of water gushed up from her lungs onto the deck. She coughed again and opened her eyes, blinking slowly. Her gaze sought out Mathias immediately, and when she saw him, standing close by, only then did she start to cry. Her betrothed knelt by her side and helped her to sit up; she threw her arms around him and buried her face in his shoulder.

'Tohias, fetch brandy for our guests. Quickly, now,' Giraldo ordered his first mate calmly. 'Dry clothing, too. We can find something for them all. Get to it.' He turned his attention back to the tableau before him, as did most of the crew of his vessel. Warin simply stood, dripping sea water onto the deck, his face grim.

'Why did you do that?' Mathias's voice was choked with tears of his own. 'You stupid woman!' He wasn't angry at her; in truth, he wasn't angry at all, but still reeling from the horror of seeing her fling herself in the path of the Inquisitor's shot.

'All I could see was that I was going to lose you,' she choked out between sobs. 'All I wanted to do was stop it from happening. I just did what felt right.'

'You could have died!'

'So could you!'

They went on in this vein for a little while until Giraldo knelt down beside them, taking one of Tagan's hands in his own. Her tears continued to flow, but she stopped sobbing as she looked up at him, then down at her hand. The palm was covered with silvery spots.

'You could have died,' the Pirate King said, 'but you did not. Look, Tagan. Look at your hands.'

She unhooked her arms from around Mathias's neck and did as Giraldo said. Both were the same; flecked with a silvery metal. She stared at her hands in confusion and uncertainty.

'What exactly did you do when you threw yourself in front of Mathias?' Giraldo's tone was gentle, filled with quiet wonder.

'I just wanted to save him,' came the artless reply. 'I stepped in front of him. I put my hands up...'

All eyes fixed on her hands and Giraldo gave her a half smile. 'You certainly saved him,' he said.

Warin spoke up, his voice gruff and carrying a tinge of respect that had not been there before. 'You melted the bullet before it could strike. Your magic is a lot more powerful than I felt it to be, Tagan.' He looked over at Giraldo and the two exchanged nods. Mathias didn't understand the gesture, but sensed that something important had passed between them.

'Come,' said Giraldo. 'She can use my cabin while she is here. There will be brandy and warm clothes. Then hot food, hmm?' His voice was soft, coaxing and decidedly hypnotic. The more Mathias thought about it, the more he agreed. He helped the sniffling Tagan to her feet and followed Giraldo to the captain's cabin.

The Island of the Seer
Denmark

After Brynjolf left, Eyja stood atop the highest cliff, watching the tiny boat as its sailor pulled back towards the mainland. Brynjolf's acceptance of what was necessary to ensure his son's survival was easier to bear than most. He would have a few years, enough to see the child grow a little. It was more than most received. Her last two visitors had drowned in the course of their journey home, caught in sudden squalls that blew up out of nowhere. Those for whom they had petitioned had lived, for what little comfort that may have brought.

With eyes as sharp as a raptor's, she watched the distant figure pull the boat up onto the shore and run joyfully towards the village. He would soon be celebrating the birth of his new son. There would be a great feast in celebration. Much mead would be passed around, and in his happiness, he would forget to invite Eyja. She would remain as she ever was; apart from the people, shunned until the next time they needed a boon. She felt no bitterness at this, it had ever been thus.

Isolation was her refuge, her protection from the world and its infinite possibilities. When she walked among the people, robed and hooded, she saw their lives stretched out before them, the decisions they would make and the consequences of those decisions. Every possible future mapped out again and again and again, an impossibly complex weave, as changing as the winds. She insulated herself against it, but the temptation was constant.

A twitch to help a starving child, a nudge to spare a loving mother on her sick bed. It was so easy to do, and it made her heart ache to have the power to change everything, but have to force herself not to.

Every night she stood on the cliffs, her perfect face upturned to the heavens, allowing the winds of the Danish coast to chill her blood, and every night she peered into the tangled knot of possibility that surrounded her future. Always it was in flux, countless threads of possibility branching into ever more threads... and so on until they extended far beyond her reach.

Tonight however, one of those threads shone brightly. She carefully followed its path to where it joined many others and became bound, a pendulum cord upon which one future hung. She sighed softly as she withdrew her vision, her path chosen.

'At last,' she said to the air. 'It has been too long.'

The breezes around her lifted her long blonde hair around her exquisite face and, drawing the cloak tightly around her body, she allowed her whole being to become one with the wind.

* * *

The Desert
Morocco

A FLAME FLARED brightly in the cool dark of the tent.

Outside, he could see the moon beginning to rise over the dunes, bringing a smile to his face. It would not be long now. He could feel it in his bones. The little fire flickered and danced, scattering weird shadows around the expansive pavilion. It illuminated the piles of rugs and cushions, shone from polished gold and reflected in the goblet of dark wine beside him.

The old man rolled the fire around his hand and then pressed it into the bowl of tobacco. Thick, heady smoke immediately began to rise from it, and he put the stem between his teeth. He took a long draw on the pipe and leaned back, his eyes closed, and breathed the night air of the desert.

He could wait. He had already waited a long time.

Genoa
Italy

THEY HAD RETREATED to Giraldo's cabin and dried off, and were now gratefully sipping on the brandy he had insisted that they sample for what he called 'medicinal purposes.'

'That man was an Inquisitor,' Mathias said, coughing a little as the fiery liquid burned a trail down his throat.

'Strange, though,' pondered Giraldo, 'that he should try to kill you and not me.'

Warin made a noise and grumbled softly. 'Everything in this world is not always about you, despite what you may believe.'

Giraldo's expression was one of exaggerated hurt, but he continued, unperturbed. 'As hard as it may be for you to believe, Red, I do expect the sun to rise even if I am not there to see it. No. I mean why would he shoot for Mathias and not your hairy, obvious self... or me? We were the ones attacking, after all.' He put the question to Mathias. 'What do *you* think? What's your secret? What's the *attraction*?'

Mathias felt the faintest of smiles tug at the sides of his mouth. It was hard not to be caught up in Giraldo's energy. He considered his answer for a moment. 'I can't be entirely sure, but it could have been the same man I saw in Wales. He could have been hunting us since then. It's... the kind of thing they do.'

Giraldo frowned. 'This Inquisitor is a very determined man, to chase you all the way from England. Those men he had with him wore the livery of English knights. They looked half dead, and so did their animals. How did he know where to look?'

Mathias shrugged and shook his head. 'He is good at his job. They hunt down those they consider their quarry. They are very good at finding people. To be perfectly honest, I'm still not sure how we got away. I remember falling into the lake, and then it felt like a current was tugging me along, as if I was in a river. Then... then we were here.' Giving the thought voice did not make it seem any less ludicrous.

Giraldo sketched a bow, sweeping the floor with his feather-plumed hat. 'I am not just a pretty face, lad. I have many tricks up my sleeves.' He winked at Tagan, who coloured again and suppressed a smile.

'If one of your Inquisitors and his knights can track us through the forest and over the mountains, then that can only mean that they came across France.' Warin had clearly been giving the matter some thought, and he made the pronouncement in a dark voice. 'That can only mean one thing.' There was a grim pause as he allowed the information to sink in.

'War,' Giraldo said quietly.

Warin nodded and gulped some of the brandy.

'Then what, precisely, are we supposed to do now?' Mathias looked from one to the other. 'Is this what Wyn was afraid of? Isn't war precisely what Melusine was trying to achieve?'

Giraldo hissed between his teeth at the mention of the demon's name. 'Please don't use that name on my ship. *Hermione* is a gentle lady and I would not want her soiled.' He sipped his own drink and gave a small sigh of appreciation. He swirled the liquid around in the beautiful crystal-stemmed glass and then spoke carefully. 'I think we need to talk to... her.'

Warin glared daggers at him, and pointedly looked the other way.

'You mean She Who Sees?' Tagan replied, reading Warin's reaction.

'That is one of her names, though she has many. She lives alone, far in the north, a long way from here. We will be many weeks at sea.' Giraldo looked thoughtful.

'Can't you just... do what you did before? Take us there quickly, like you did in the lake?' Mathias asked.

'Sadly, no. I cannot do that,' Giraldo replied apologetically.

'Why not?'

'Because I have never been there. I would not know where to go. No. If we wish to find her we must look for her. In this, we will be no different from the others who seek her.'

'And how, exactly, will we do that?' Warin turned back to the conversation, his expression controlled, but unreadable. 'If England has gone to war, the Channel will be thick with their navy. Your boat will not be so lovely when she is full of holes, eh?'

'"Ship," please,' Giraldo corrected, his voice pained. 'She is a *ship*. And my delightful lady of the sea will see us safely through. The English will never catch her.'

He said the words with a great deal more confidence than he felt.

Lake Geneva
Switzerland

CHARLES WEAVER STARED at the still surface of the lake for several long minutes before he finally holstered his pistol. He was certain that at least one of the targets had eluded him. Despite his best efforts here, the hunt would have to continue. He steered his horse away from the shore and back to where Sir Anthony was helping one of the fallen knights to his feet.

The three men who had been unhorsed by the man in the ridiculous hat were only wounded. Two sported lumps the size of eggs on their skulls, but apart from an appalling headache they would live. The third, however, had been left blind. Blood seeped from a deep gash that split his face from ear to ear. It was to this man that Sir Anthony attended.

Those who had been savaged by the bear had been less fortunate. Three knights and two horses lay sprawled in death, their torn bodies cooling in the afternoon sunshine. Weaver looked down at them through the slits in his mask and silently commended them for their service. They had not been mercenaries who spilled blood for coin, but bold, brave knights who had given their lives in service to their King.

'My lord,' Sir Anthony said evenly. 'Sir William is gravely wounded, and he can ride no further. What would you have us do?'

The Lord Inquisitor turned from the dead men to look at Sir William. It was painfully clear that his days behind the lance were over, and should he return to England, he would live out the rest of his life a broken man, reliant on others to tend to his needs. Weaver did not know if Sir William was married, and neither did he particularly care. At his age he could well have a son in training as a squire; if so, he would certainly never see the lad's face again.

'Sir William,' Weaver rumbled. 'You have done a great service to the Crown, but now it is ended. Your wounds are grave, we are far from home and our prey yet eludes us.'

'My lord,' Sir Anthony protested. 'You surely cannot mean to continue? We have no idea where the magi have gone.'

'On the contrary, I know exactly where they have gone; and more, I know exactly where they are going. We may yet run them to ground. But we must leave immediately and ride hard for the west.'

'Lord Inquisitor...' Sir Anthony began to protest again, but the wounded Sir William pushed him gently aside, standing unaided.

'Lord Inquisitor Weaver, it has been my honour to ride at your side.' He spoke with great formality. 'But I will not hinder you in your duty, nor will I burden these good knights with my care. I would ask that you inform the Lady Margaret that I died well in my service to King Richard, and...' His voice faltered for a moment, but he set his jaw and continued. 'And tell my son that his father will always proud of him.'

Weaver dismounted and walked to where the man stood. 'It shall be as you say. Your courage does you credit, William Lyttle. The King himself will hear of it, I promise you.' Without further hesitation, he drew his dagger and plunged it into the knight's heart in one swift, fluid movement. Sir William grunted quietly and slid from the blade.

'Bury the dead,' Weaver ordered, looking down at Sir William. He bent to wipe the blade of his dagger on the grass and slid it back into its sheath. 'We must move quickly, but no Englishman's grave should go unmarked.' He turned to look at his surviving knights. 'Then we ride.'

Ten miles outside Paris
France

Your majesty.

Sir Thomas Thirwell was seated behind a table at the rear of his pavilion, quill in hand. Outside, the afternoon sky was black with smoke and heavy with the acrid stink of alchemical fire. The roar of cannons and the cries of the artillery crews as they worked filled the air, along with the clatter of armour and muffled sounds of impact.

Progress has been swift and the army of King Henri is driven before us.

There had been no further resistance, and the army had marched unopposed across the French countryside, laying waste to anything arcane—and plenty that was not. Most of the people in the towns and villages surrounding Paris had retreated within its walls before the gates had closed. Those that hadn't were now dead or gone, and only scorched ruins surrounded the city.

The King's court magi have sealed Paris with their powers, and have warded the city against attack, but it weakens with each passing day.

The first shots fired had been repulsed with flares of pallid light, but as the siege ran into days and then weeks, the magic faltered. The cannons began to strike stone instead of spells, and gradually the defences had begun to crumble. Sir Thomas believed King Henri's magi must surely be worn down to nothing...

The end was near.

Upon my honour, the city will be yours before year's end.

Sir Thomas Thirwell.

[illegible]

[illegible] among the [illegible] in a pit, and [illegible]

[illegible]

TWELVE

November, 1589
The Hermione
Off the coast of France

THE WEATHER REMAINED fine for the majority of their journey, apart from a single, unexpected squall that blew up as they plied the Portuguese coast. They had all been soaked through as they worked up on deck, apart from the Pirate King, who—perhaps unsurprisingly, given what they had seen of him—was apparently immune to the depredations of the weather.

It was a useful time for them all. For Mathias and Tagan, it was an opportunity to practise the new talents they had discovered. Warin and Giraldo both seemed to relish an opportunity to guide the pair of them. After the first few days around the Pirate King, Mathias slowly began to let go of his suspicions and relax. Tagan allowed Giraldo to flirt with her, but it soon became apparent that was all there was to it.

The days were filled with a combination of arcane lessons and an endless parade of tasks that seemed to need doing on board a ship. Giraldo's attitude from the start was that there were no passengers on the *Hermione*, and he found work for all his new guests that kept them busy during the day and ensured they slept well at night. Even Warin had a job, and it was one that surprised both Mathias and Tagan.

'You're working in the *galley*?' Mathias laughed, without truly knowing why. Warin tightened the straps of the decidedly off-white apron.

'Did you taste that muck we ate last night? The man doesn't know salt from sugar. I have cooked for you before. Is it really that surprising?'

Mathias had to concede that he had a point. It was still entertaining, however, to witness Warin barking orders at the ship's boy, a fifteen-year-old Spaniard who didn't speak a word of English or German. Somehow, the two managed to communicate, and the quality of the ship meals improved radically.

Tagan proved to be remarkable with knots and rope work, and she could more often than not be found beneath the shade of a sail rigged on deck for the purpose, netting in her lap, or stitching torn sails and clothing. She had adapted to life on board the *Hermione* as if she had been born to it and proved, very early on, that she could drink with the best of them. That endeared her to the ship's crew, whose early hesitation about a woman on board soon gave way to a kind of rough affection. Mathias didn't fear for her safety. He suspected that after a couple of weeks in her company, every one of Giraldo's crew would leap to her defence in a heartbeat.

He spent a lot of his own time climbing the ship's rigging, or scrubbing the decks, or generally fetching and carrying as others dictated. He didn't mind at all. Indeed, he welcomed the chance to keep busy. It took a lot of the worry from him and gave him other things to think about. Hard work and good food filled his body out to more of a man's shape, and light brown stubble, so pale as to be barely visible, speckled his face most of the time.

It was however, the lessons in magic that Mathias and Tagan came to love the most. Tagan's tuition was, by its very nature, limited. Giraldo had suggested that the conjuration of fire on board a vessel sealed with tar and carrying kegs of gun powder might not, in all senses, be wise. It was hard to argue with the logic and as such, they had not attempted to replicate her feat of melting bullets in flight.

Lessons took place early in the morning, usually after the crew had risen and after the night-watch had gone to their bunks. They had been travelling now for five weeks and Mathias was well used to the routine.

'Good morning, lad.' Warin lounged amidst the ropes on the ship's deck, a pipe in the corner of his mouth. Sweet-smelling smoke curled from the barrel as he sucked at the rich tobacco that Giraldo had finally deigned to share with him. 'Ready for practice?'

Mathias nodded, and Warin's eyes shifted to Tagan. 'What do you think, girl? You proud of him yet?' In the weeks of travel, Mathias's ability to shapeshift had grown gradually faster and smoother, and entirely less convoluted. Tagan smiled.

'I was proud of him to begin with, Warin,' she said. The gruff man wrinkled his nose and waved dismissively. She laughed.

'Both of you, this morning,' said Warin, getting up from his rope-throne. 'We must start to teach you how to pool your magic with mine and de Luna's... if he ever arrives.' He said this last in a louder voice. 'Wherever he might be.'

'He's up here, Red,' came Giraldo's voice and there was something tense in his tone. All three of them looked up to watch him swing down from the rigging with the sort of casual grace that Mathias could only ever hope to attain. Unless he changed into the thing Warin had called a 'monkey' again, of course.

That had been fun.

'No lessons today,' said the Pirate King, landing on the deck with a soft-booted thump. 'We're entering the Channel.'

The Channel
Between England and France

THE EARLY MISTS had not cleared in the cool morning, and pale, ethereal fingers curled around the prow of the ship, wreathing the figurehead in an intangible disguise. The *Hermione* had dropped her sails and the crew took to the oars, sculling slowly as they approached.

'Port side, Captain!' the lookout in the crow's nest far above them called out, his voice clear and strong. Giraldo moved to stand by the deck rail. He looked out across the water and drew a breath.

The broken hulk of a ship, bearing the tattered remnants of a torn French flag, only two of the fleurs de lis still visible. loomed up out of the mists. Giraldo's face was grim as he studied the damage to its hull. The fog lifted briefly and Tagan put a hand over her mouth as the first bloated corpses became visible. They were floating amidst a maze of broken ships and wreckage that had once been the French fleet.

Worse than this grisly sight, somehow, was the silence. The only sounds were the slap of the water and the creak of wood as the wrecks settled. Tide and weather had worked on the remains, dragging them from the site of the battle, but it was clear that King Richard's ships had exacted a terrible toll.

'It's horrible,' Tagan whispered, her eyes bright with fear and compassion.

'It is war,' said Giraldo, pragmatically. 'Slow us down, Tohias. We need to negotiate this graveyard.' His own face was strained. They all knew from the tales told around the dinner table each night that Giraldo de Luna did not take lives lightly. To witness such slaughter, such horror was anathema to them all. Even Warin, a hunter by nature, looked on the carnage and shuddered.

Progress was excruciatingly slow. More than once, the *Hermione* snagged her hull on a piece of wreckage, or her oars became fouled by sails or the remains of the dead. More bodies bobbed to the surface, and Tagan could no longer look at the wreckage. The very tangible evidence of war was appalling and alien to her.

Mathias glanced at her as she moved away from the rail, his eyes filled with concern and sympathy. He was finding it no easier. He had been raised a man of the country, to whom life was precious. A man whose only plans had been to marry the girl he loved and bring beautiful, happy children into the world. War was not something he had ever thought to see.

'All French, Captain,' said Tohias, who was carefully studying the ships. 'Not an English ship amongst them.' His thickly accented Spanish voice cut through the grim scene cleanly.

'Richard's fleet must be exceptional,' observed Giraldo. 'It looks like the French made a fight of it, and they would have had magic on their side. To see this much destruction does not bode...'

'Ship to starboard!' The cry came from above. 'Approaching.'

'A survivor?' The Pirate King squinted through the mists.

'No, Captain. It's flying English colours.'

Giraldo cursed furiously. 'Tagan, get below decks,' he ordered.

'You can help with the guns, but carefully, yes?' He unsheathed his blade and hurried to the prow. Mathias went to Tagan's side, and she gave him a quick, fierce hug. There was no time for words; she hurried below, where the gun crews were rushing to their stations.

Warin watched the captain, incredulity written on his features. 'Going to put a pinhole in the side of the ship are you, de Luna? Fat lot of use you will be with that pig sticker. We need to get out of here. If they did all this'—he gestured to the grim surroundings—'then I don't think your little boat is going to worry them much.' Mathias couldn't be entirely certain, but he suspected that Warin was actually having whatever passed for fun in his strange world.

The muffled roar of a discharging cannon sounded from the approaching vessel and the whistle of a projectile hurtling towards the *Hermione* became the only thing that mattered. Every sailor on deck threw himself flat, braced for an impact that did not come. The cannonball plunged into the water bare feet from the hull, sending up a plume of steam and water.

'They're firing on us,' said Giraldo, so outraged that Mathias felt a sudden, crazed urge to laugh. 'How *dare* they? We have not even run up the colours!'

'Still finding their range,' retorted Warin. 'I don't think we will be so lucky next time. Now, can we go?'

'I believe you may actually be right for once, my hairy friend.' Giraldo nodded and sheathed his rapier once again. 'I need your eyes. Guide my ship through this wreckage. I am going to go and have a talk with the captain of that ship about his conduct.' His eyes flared bright aqua and without another word, he dived into the sea. Mathias stared at the surface, shocked by Giraldo's sudden departure. Then he saw a fast moving shape beneath the waves, knifing its way toward the attacking vessel.

The wreckage had been difficult to traverse before, but at least the Channel had been calm. Within minutes of the Pirate King leaving the *Hermione*, it became entirely less benign. The dark waters began to ripple, then churn, and waves began to rock the ship. Bodies and wreckage stirred, unpleasantly animated by the sudden surge.

'Steady as she goes!'

'Mind out, mind out... there, now! To port! To port!'

Warin's voice called out and was repeated to Tohias at the helm, a raucous chain of cries and confusing commands that overlapped and intermingled. The sea grew more violent and Mathias gripped onto the rail as the *Hermione* pitched to one side. He was flung hard against Warin as the deck tilted back in the other direction; the man was like a rock. The Shapeshifter grabbed him around the waist and hauled him upright, before thrusting a rope into his hands.

'Tie up, boy!' Warin shouted over the growing swell. He never took his eyes off the sea ahead, but clapped Mathias on the shoulder when he'd finishing winding the rope around his waist.

'At least it's not raining,' Mathias said. 'That would *really* be bad.' Warin glanced sideways at him, but before he could say a word, the first raindrops began to fall. Mathias spread his hands helplessly. 'What? It wasn't *me!*'

FROM THE DECK of the British fighting ship *Vanguard*, Charles Weaver watched the passage of the *Hermione* through the field of debris. The return journey to the occupied ruins of Dieppe had been less cruel and far less fraught. They had only needed to replace their horses once, and the Lord Inquisitor felt that they had enough time to spare the beasts the alchemical broth.

He had chosen a ship built for grace and speed rather than one of the King's new ironclads, as the monsters lacked the element of surprise. The *Vanguard* had then spent a week prowling the Channel, waiting for its prey, despite her captain's protests. The man had wanted to head south to hunt the pirate vessel, but granted foreknowledge, Weaver knew that his quarry would pass this way and that the mire of wreckage would slow them.

Now, he was angry. The gun crew of the *Vanguard* had disappointed him with their poor aim. With the element of surprise lost, the magi were attempting to flee, their ship weaving a slow retreat through the shattered hulls.

'Fire again,' Weaver demanded, 'while their broadside is presented. I trust you can manage to hit them this time?'

There was a roar as the pirate ship returned fire, her guns speaking in almost perfect unison. Plumes of water exploded around the *Vanguard*, wood splintered and voices howled in agony as the hull was punctured in several places.

'I said fire!' the Lord Inquisitor bellowed. 'Was that unclear?'

The *Vanguard* had at least twice as many guns as the *Hermione*, if not more, and even with the Channel growing choppy it should have been impossible for her to miss. But the ship lurched hard to port just as her cannons thundered into life, spoiling the *Vanguard*'s aim and ensuring she hit nothing but sea. Weaver was flung hard against the railing and found himself staring down at the black waves. To his surprise a face stared back, the face of the graceful man with the ridiculous hat.

A name sprang unbidden into his mind, and he knew, with a sudden surge of hatred, who this man was. He roared the name into the growing gale.

'Lunus!'

THE RAIN CAME down harder, and storm clouds piled together into thunderheads that grumbled and growled in rage. A sudden flash lit up the English ship's mast, but there was no accompanying crack of thunder. Nonetheless, voices on board the ship could be heard raised in alarm.

Another flash. Still no thunder. Mathias stared in confusion. Several of the Spanish sailors were making warding gestures as they worked, making the sign of the cross or pressing their lips to silver pendants.

'*Fuego de San Elmo!*'

Mathias did not know Spanish, but he knew that sailors believed very firmly in signs and omens at sea. They seemed anxious and continually glanced up at the darkening sky as if expecting it to fall upon them at any moment. As far as omens went, Mathias was not encouraged.

Ephemeral fire licked the mast of the English ship, pale and obviously without heat. Mathias stared at the phenomenon and sensed the change in the air like hot metal in the forge, or the sharp tang after a storm. But the storm seemed to be growing rather than receding. A familiar tingle tickled his senses, the feel of powerful magic. A thrill ran through him and he lifted his head to the darkening skies.

AT FIRST, IT was hard to make out the shape of the woman amidst the steel grey of the storm clouds. She was wearing a woollen dress of the same shade, and a darker grey cloak that billowed out around her as she soared. Then her hood fluttered down around her shoulders and the pale skin of her face and the white-blonde of her long hair streaming behind her made her obvious. Those who laid eyes on her could not tear their gaze away.

Her voice was raised in a strange kind of song, although the words were in a language that few had ever heard before. Her voice was clear, ringing out through the skies that bore her aloft, and as her fluting soprano rose to an impossibly high pitch, the wind tore into the *Vanguard*. Sailors on deck were thrown from their feet and several were hurled overboard and into the rolling waves. The survivors struggled to recover and crawled on hands and knees back to their positions.

'Eyja!'

Bursting from beneath the waves, Giraldo let out a cry of delight. His own voice, a rich baritone, rose to join with Eyja's, a perfect harmony that rose and fell with the swell of the storm. The gale rose and clawed at the *Vanguard*'s sails, tearing them to shreds and plucking sailors from the spars. The foremast splintered and crashed down onto the deck and there was a loud, ominous cracking from the hull as the sea tossed it about.

Flotsam was scooped from the waves and dashed against the vessel. Lengths of flailing rope, spears of broken wood and shards of debris riddled the ship's prow and flanks, wounding men and savaging the stricken craft. None of it touched the figure standing at the prow with his hands locked on the rail. He stood unmoving, as if rooted to the deck, and stared up at the storm, the flash of lightning reflected from his mask.

The hurricane did not touch the *Hermione*.

Mathias was caught up in the spectacle of it all. He had witnessed feats of power from Warin and Giraldo and even watched, awed, as they had combined their talents. But this was something else. He glanced at Tagan, who had emerged from below, and her eyes were wider than he had ever seen before. She was gazing up at the woman suspended in the air with wonder and more than a little apprehension.

Giraldo's crew seemed to have forgotten their earlier worry once they realised that the bad omen was actually on their side. They were pointing up at Eyja, or down at Giraldo as he stood amidst the thunderous waves, and calling out things in their own language.

Warin, on the other hand, was staring up at the woman in the skies with a wistful, eternally sad expression on his face. He did not lend his voice to the ensemble that was gradually forcing the English into retreat.

He just watched.

Despite his wonder, Mathias felt a sudden pang of sympathy for the gruff Shapeshifter. He had never seen anybody look so forlorn or so lonely. There was little time to dwell upon it, however. With a shout and a raucous laugh of delight, Giraldo grabbed hold of the ladder at the side of the *Hermione* and swung himself back up onto deck.

'Be ready to add some sail and... well, hold onto something,' he said and the laughter in his voice was infectious. His enthusiasm and delight caught hold among the crew, and they obeyed their captain's order instantly. 'We're heading south! Pay attention! Easy as she goes, now.' He moved to take a place by Tohias's side at the helm, and gave the first mate a huge grin. 'Prepare to come about!' He patted Tohias's shoulder and let out a bellowed command.

'Hard to port!'

The *Hermione* wallowed for a moment, and the deck groaned alarmingly as Tohias spun the wheel in a blur. The ship heeled over to one side and Mathias held fast to Tagan as the spray foamed over the rail. Then the turn was complete and the sails snapped tight.

'More!' Giraldo urged. 'More!' He laughed as the *Hermione* leapt away from her pursuers and left them foundering in her wake.

Travelling with them in the dark skies overhead, Eyja floated with ease and grace, always staying between them and the wounded *Vanguard*. A silent protector. Silent and beautiful... and exceptionally deadly.

Their speed was such that they soon left the English ship behind, a dwindling dot, lost amidst the storm. Slowly, the gale abated and the rain eased until it was nothing more than another autumn squall. Giraldo looked up into the skies, where patches of pale blue were starting to appear amidst the clouds, and grinned. The grey-clad figure was slowly descending toward them.

'We have another guest on the way, my friends,' he said, clapping Tohias on the back. 'Set a southerly course, the winds will see us true.'

'Where are we headed, Captain?'

'We should know soon enough,' came the reply. 'But for now, *away* will be good enough.'

Giraldo's eyes and those of everyone aboard *Hermione* were fixed on the slender woman, who was carried to the deck on a gentle breeze. She landed perfectly, her blonde mane falling around a face of ethereal loveliness that drew a sigh of admiration from every man present. Even Tagan stared.

Beside Mathias, Warin made a sound so soft that it was barely audible. It had become apparent what the reasons for the Shapeshifter's reluctance to work with She Who Sees actually were.

HER SPEAKING VOICE was lilting and musical, as though she were still singing, and Mathias was captivated from the moment she began to talk. The three powerful magi were sitting so close that they were almost touching. Almost—but not quite. Mathias had expected at least Giraldo to embrace Eyja in the same manner he had greeted Warin, but there was some unspoken respect between them. He had contented himself with simply dropping a deep bow before her, as though she were royalty. Giraldo's eyes had danced with delight and affection as he looked at her, whilst Warin's were filled with that deep sadness.

Tagan sat with Mathias, leaning into him. Her hand slid into his and she sat possessively close to him. The constant stares of admiration that Eyja drew from the crew had clearly made her anxious.

Warin, Giraldo and Eyja spoke together for a while, including no others. Their voices were kept low and their heads were bent together, as they discussed some matter to which no other was party. Every once in a while, Eyja's head would rise and she would glance at either Tagan or Mathias. Nothing in her stormy eyes gave away what she was thinking.

Eventually, their council was complete. Giraldo and Warin rose, the latter stomping over to the young couple. 'She wants to meet you,' he said, gruffly. 'Go and talk to her.' Giraldo also moved away, leaving Eyja seated serenely on deck. A stiff wind continued to fill the sails of the *Hermione*, carrying her steadily south. The skies above them were still scattered with cloud, and the air was chill and sharp as they retreated from the Channel.

Mathias and Tagan, still hand in hand, approached the woman who had appeared so fortuitously and she smiled up at them. It reassured and soothed, and yet there was a sadness in her eyes.

'Mathias Eynon,' she said in her lilting voice. 'And Tagan Stradling. The honour is mine.' To both of their surprises, Eyja stood gracefully and dropped a curtsey before them. Mathias flared bright pink, but Tagan simply nodded her head politely. Not for the first time since this unlikely journey had started, Mathias could not help but admire his betrothed's ability to absorb the extraordinary.

'You are She Who Sees,' said Tagan, and despite her calm demeanour, her voice was filled with apprehension and awe. The blonde woman nodded.

'Yes,' she said. 'That is one of the names by which I am known. I prefer to go by "Eyja," if it pleases you to use that instead; it is less unwieldy. Please, sit with me a while. I would hear your tale as you tell it. Warin and Giraldo have given me their parts in what has taken place and it grieves me deeply to hear of the loss of your adoptive father. My condolences, young man.' She took Mathias's free hand in her own and bowed her forehead to it. He knew, without understanding, that somehow her grief at Wyn's death was every bit as real as his own.

'Thank you,' he said, unsure of what else he should say. 'He was a good man.' He felt a peculiar calm steal over him, and he settled down on the deck. It was not until several minutes later that he realised she still held his hand whilst Tagan held the other. If Tagan cared, she didn't let it show. She was gazing up into Eyja's face. The two women's eyes were locked in a silence that was too deep to intrude upon.

'You are quite lovely,' Eyja said, breaking the silence first. Her own free hand came out to caress Tagan's freckled cheek gently. 'So full of life. So full of love.' There was something ominous in the tone she used. 'A beautiful couple who must be suffering at the hands of a future neither of you understand. But please, have no fear. When we find Akhgar, the one you call "the Wanderer," then we will be strong enough to bring this all to an end. Have courage. Have faith.' The hand stroking Tagan's cheek came down and took the blacksmith's daughter's fingers into her own.

'There now,' she says. 'We are joined, the three of us. Always trust in the power of a circle, children. In a circle, all are equal. There is great strength in that. You have learned this, I think?'

'The stone circles,' said Mathias. He couldn't unlock his eyes from her face. 'Warin called them the bones of the earth. He said that they have a great power.'

'More than you know,' said Eyja, moving her gaze back to Tagan. 'They are the source of all magic. It is through them that we are... gifted as we are.'

Mathias felt a twinge of apprehension at the way she paused, as if a great gulf of meaning lay behind the words, just beyond his reach. He wanted to ask this beautiful, mysterious woman what was happening, what they were going to do, where they were going to go.

'Hush,' Eyja pre-empted him. 'We sail south to Morocco, where we will find the Wanderer. Now leave us, Mathias,' she said, her eyes still on Tagan. 'I must speak with Tagan alone. There is a truth that only she may know, at least for now.'

'But...'

'Leave us, please.' Eyja's voice was commanding, and he reluctantly got to his feet, letting go of both their hands. Tagan didn't even look up at him. She reached out to Eyja with the hand that he had freed and held onto the Seer's hands as though her life depended upon it.

Portsmouth
England

THE HEAT IN the forge was incredible, and the ring of hammers deafening. Isaac Bonnington walked the length of the royal armoury, his gaze roving over the machines, armour and weapons in production and inspecting them with a critical eye. The war was underway, and demand to keep the army supplied was soaring.

The sudden and unwelcome order to launch the *Indomitable* had deeply concerned the engineer; she had left Portsmouth with several decks still unfinished. Regardless, the reports that she had crushed the French fleet had allayed most of his concerns. Now that the *Indomitable* was queen of the seas, he had time enough to work on the *Lionheart*.

Isaac turned away from a work gang labouring at one of the furnaces and made his way toward the builder's hall. Lines of filthy workers smudged with soot and streaked with sweat shuffled past, their ankles bound with iron manacles. The overseer at their back barked at them to stand aside, but Isaac waved a hand absently.

He tried not to dwell on the human cost of his industry. It had once distressed him greatly, many years ago when Richard had first introduced industrial servitude, but he had learned that there was nothing he could do to make a difference. The King had made it quite clear, on the one occasion that he had voiced his concerns, that if Isaac did not want to be the Royal Engineer, there were others who would happily claim the honour.

Isaac had chosen to be pragmatic. He might not have been able to release the workers from their bondage, but he did ensure that they were provided with clean water to drink, and occasionally he would acknowledge younger workers who showed promise. He would hand-pick them and arrange engineering apprenticeships that saw them released from the work gangs and given the possibility of a future. It was an extraordinarily generous thing that he chose to do, and the best he could manage under the circumstances; and it effectively negated some—but not all—of the guilt the work gangs gave him.

He approached the huge double doors to the builder's hall and nodded to the guards on duty, who unlocked the smaller hatch at the base of the doors and waved him inside. The noise of hammers increased, along with the rhythmic cries of the pulley teams as they worked the ropes. Isaac straightened and dusted himself down, then cast his eyes over the machine taking shape. Even unfinished it was still magnificent. The alchemical engine was the latest innovation to come from the unfathomable mind of the King, a poorly-rendered sketch improved upon and brought into the world by Isaac Bonnington. He watched a huge cannon being lowered slowly into place with a mixture of awe and terror.

When the *Lionheart* was complete, when the fruit of his labours was brought to bear, all nations would crumble before the unstoppable might of England.

THIRTEEN

The Hermione
The Atlantic Sea

THE WINDS REMAINED steady and mild for the remainder of the journey. It became quickly obvious that Eyja was able to command the skies without any apparent effort and the *Hermione* did not have to endure any more rain, even with the steady approach of winter. Command and control, it seemed, were parts of her talent. Mathias had been impressed by Giraldo's easy charm and his ability to manipulate with the right word or phrase; Eyja, he learned very quickly, was able to achieve the same result with little more than a smile.

He also noticed that the smiles rarely reached her eyes. It bothered him. He felt a deep sympathy for this strange, quiet, beautiful woman. Tagan had become her constant companion and he noticed the change that had come over her. She was less impulsive than she had been, more thoughtful and considered in what she said. She'd rather self-consciously tried to make herself look a little more presentable, and had spent time repairing the numerous tears and snags in the only dress she had. The rest of the time, she made do with sailor shirts and breeches that were far too big for her, but at least protected her modesty.

Until Eyja's arrival, Tagan had remained quietly apart from the crew during the day, understanding—but not necessarily appreciating—the superstitions surrounding women on board. Now, however, wherever Eyja walked, Tagan was always a step or two behind her. It had a clear effect on her confidence, and it made Mathias glad to see her smiling again.

By the fourth day of the journey south, Mathias was beginning to enjoy the routine once more. The daily training sessions with Warin had paid off and he was able now to slip into animal forms with little thought and far less effort than when he had first tried. Giraldo, in turn, was teaching him the basics of handling a sword, with which he was proving to be far less proficient.

'You don't think ahead,' laughed the Pirate King after Mathias had ended up on his backside for the fifth time in a row. 'You need to anticipate. Learn to read what your opponent *might* do, whilst you deal with what they *are* doing. Did you never play chess?'

'No,' replied Mathias, a little sullenly. The humiliation of constant defeat was starting to play on him and it was affecting his performance, not to mention his mood. It wasn't entirely true; Wyn had tried to teach him to play chess once or twice, but despite his intelligence and his patience, Mathias had never had much of a talent for strategy.

'Perhaps you should start.'

'*More* training? Isn't this enough?' Mathias brandished the wooden sword fiercely enough to elicit laughter from the Shapeshifter, lounging amidst ropes and nets watching the sparring. Mathias turned on his mentor, a spark of irritation in his eyes. 'You aren't helping, Warin.'

'Swords. I never had any interest in the weapons of men. You've seen what I can do. Who needs man-made weapons when you can have claws or teeth? The boy isn't a natural warrior, de Luna. What are you hoping to accomplish with this farce?'

Giraldo shrugged his slender shoulders. 'It is a distraction. The boy has taken to brooding.'

Brooding. For no very rational reason, Mathias was annoyed by Giraldo's words. What did this *peacock* know of his worries? What did Giraldo de Luna know of uncertainty and homelessness? Time on board the ship was giving him time to think, allowing events to catch up with him. To dwell upon what had happened. And yes, he reluctantly admitted, to brood. Acknowledging the truth did not improve his temper.

Other men might have turned to insult or given vent to their anger. Mathias simply set down the training sword and walked away. But the ship was not that large. There were not many places he could walk to.

But he walked anyway.

* * *

The Vanguard
The Channel

IT HAD TAKEN some time to organise the crew in the wake of the damage caused by the magically conjured storm. Following the departure of the *Hermione*, the storm had slowly abated and work had begun to make the vessel seaworthy once more. The *Vanguard* was heavily damaged; one mast was broken, and the hull breached in several places. Debris was dragged from the water and used to patch the holes, and boards were sealed with pitch to keep the waves at bay. Replacement canvas was brought up from the hold and used to make what sails they could. Battered and bruised, the ship limped into Portsmouth harbour three days later.

The Lord Inquisitor was unimpressed by the delay.

With the entire fleet anchored off the coast of France, the only vessels available were cogs and fat-bellied cargo barges. None were suitable for the pursuit of the fleeing *Hermione*, and he could feel her slipping away with each passing day. Weaver demanded the men work faster. Work gangs were drafted in to speed the repairs, and worked day and night removing the guns from the damaged decks.

When the *Vanguard* slipped back out into the channel a few days later, she was a shadow of her former self. If Isaac Bonnington had seen what had become of his beautiful ship, he would undoubtedly have wept.

'My lord, surely it would be wiser to return to the fleet?' The *Vanguard*'s captain, an increasingly stressed man by the name of Henry Hudson, was trying desperately to convince the Lord Inquisitor to change his mind. 'She's in poor shape. Any further damage will see her at the bottom of the sea. And even with fair winds and every strong man at the oars, we cannot hope to catch a ship propelled by magic. We...'

Weaver turned slowly on the spot to glare at Hudson through the slits in his mask and the captain's words died in his throat. The six knights accompanying the Lord Inquisitor stood at his back, their own expressions fixed in steely determination.

'Never presume to tell me my business, Captain Hudson,' he rumbled menacingly. 'Here are my orders and you will see fit to obey them. You will set your men to the oars and they will row harder than they have ever done before. We are going to make up as much lost time as we can. When we reach our destination, *then* you can do what you want with this ship. Not before. Is that quite clear?'

The unfortunate captain found his mouth had suddenly gone very dry. He swallowed thickly. 'Yes, my lord. Might I ask about our course?'

'Set her to the south, Captain Hudson,' Weaver said. 'We are heading to Morocco.'

December, 1589
The Hermione
Morocco

For the past forty years, the Portuguese had insisted on referring to the port as Casa Branca. The military fort standing strong and proud on its overlook above the port kept a close eye on the many vessels passing through on their way to exotic eastern lands. Quick action put a stop to the worst of the pirate raids.

'Anfa,' Giraldo said wistfully as the *Hermione* made her way up the narrow channels leading to the busy port. 'She will ever be Anfa to me. I had some fine times here in days gone past.'

Seeing Warin roll his eyes and sensing that the Pirate King was about to embark on one of his lengthy tales, Mathias made a quick move to forestall it before it began. Warin's patience, always thin to begin with, had started to fray in the time it had taken to sail to the coast of Morocco. He had little wish to bear witness to another blazing argument between the pair.

Even with the onset of winter, the weather had grown hot as they travelled further south. For both Warin and Eyja, used to more temperate climes, the heat was oppressive. Eyja adjusted to it more quickly, but Warin seemed to visibly wilt as the heat sapped his stocky body of strength. Mathias thought on this as he asked Giraldo about the sights and spectacles of the approaching town.

'Give it a few days,' he said mildly. 'Warin is a solitary creature, rough and full of bluster, but he will adapt. It is what he does best.' Mathias shrugged and focused on the remarkable sights before him.

The young man pointed to a high tower, with a domed top and intricately worked detail in rich turquoise. 'What is that place?' He was captivated by its beauty, by its clean lines, as it stood at the waterline, waves lapping lightly at its base.

'That's a mosque,' said Giraldo, happy to be the guide in this instance. 'It is where the people of Anfa go to pray to their god.' His usually cheery expression grew serious. 'We have timed our arrival well. When you first hear the call to prayer, it can be something you never forget.' His expression grew wistful. 'I know I have never forgotten it.'

The mosque loomed larger and larger as the *Hermione* passed by, and all eyes were drawn to its magnificence. The white buildings that made up the port city were so brilliant, so different from anything that Mathias and Tagan had ever seen.

'Whatever else happens,' said Mathias in a low voice filled with wonder, 'I will always be glad for seeing this.'

The *Hermione* became a bustling hive of activity as the crew made ready to drop anchor. Voices rose and people ran around the deck, winding in rope and trimming the sails. Eyja, her heavy cloak neatly folded and slung over one arm, seemed perfectly comfortable in the warmth of the late afternoon sun as she joined Mathias, Tagan and Giraldo at the rail.

'Anfa,' she said, wrinkling her nose slightly. 'So... *dusty*. Why he ever chose to stop wandering in this part of the world...'

'Who knows why he does anything, Eyja?' said Giraldo. The mysterious exchange meant little to Mathias. 'Where's Warin?'

'In your cabin, making the most of the shade, or so he tells me.' Eyja smiled fondly. 'Once we land, he will join us. What is our plan, dear one?'

'There is a tavern in Anfa where we can spend the night,' he replied. 'Tomorrow, the *Hermione* will leave. If the Inquisitor really wants to find us, and he seems remarkably good at doing that, then I would prefer it if he didn't find my lady of the sea. He's unlikely to catch up to her. And besides, my Tohias can run circles around that English ship. If someone could see fit to give them a good wind out of port tomorrow morning, they should get enough of a head start to get clear.' He gazed up at the ship's figurehead and sighed. 'I'll miss her, but... well. Needs must, as the saying goes.' He grinned. 'Tohias is no doubt sick of me bringing him into port only to send him away again, but he is my first mate for a reason.'

Eyja smiled her dazzling smile and inclined her head. 'It will be as you ask,' she said, before returning her attention to the port city. Her arms stole across the shoulders of Tagan and Mathias. 'Tonight,' she said, 'you will see what free people do with the gift of magic. You will see the wonder that King Richard the Lionheart hoped to bring to his people so many years past.' She raised her head and inhaled the dust and riotous scents of the port town.

THE *HERMIONE* DOCKED without further ceremony, and despite a few suspicious glances from the locals, there was no trouble. A portly man with a deep voice and skin tanned darker than Mathias or Tagan had ever seen before approached them, speaking in a language that sounded similar to that he had heard used amongst Giraldo's pirates.

'Portuguese,' murmured Eyja. 'That is Anfa's port master. Giraldo will soon deal with him. Just watch.'

The clink of coins was slow and deliberate as Giraldo pressed them into the man's palm. He smiled with all the considerable charm at his disposal and the port master smiled back, displaying a mouthful of dazzling white teeth. Or mostly white—the gold caps in his mouth stood out startlingly.

The port master turned from Giraldo and dropped a ridiculously over-exaggerated bow. 'Welcome to Anfa, travellers!'

Eyja nodded politely and smiled at him. Tagan followed her

mentor's example and smiled as prettily and nicely as she could muster. The port master made an expansive sweeping gesture towards the town.

'Where is Warin?' Mathias looked around. Giraldo shrugged.

'He said he'll follow on later. Let him be; he has one of his bad moods upon him. He will get over it. Come. Come see the town. You will never have known anything like it.'

His excitement was undeniably infectious, and they followed him eagerly as he led them into the white-walled Moroccan town. It felt oddly enclosed once they stepped through the archway that Giraldo led them through, and the day, already fading to dusk, seemed to become a little darker. But it was not in any way threatening.

The smells hit them first: roasting meats and sweet, burned sugar that lingered in the nostrils and lured them towards the traders plying their wares. Both Mathias and Tagan were used to markets and had even experienced a travelling fair, but this was something else entirely. The closest market stall was trading meat of some kind, sold in big, succulent-looking slices.

But the trader did not have any kind of campfire or grill set up to cook his wares. Instead, he was roasting the steaks with short bursts of fierce fire that he seemed to conjure from his own fingertips. Mathias felt the tingle of magic and Tagan clapped her hands together in delight.

'He is like me,' she said excitedly. 'He conjures fire! Oh, look!'

Already the mage was forgotten as Tagan's attention was caught by another trader, a woman selling fine silk cloth. The beautiful fabrics were a vast array of colours and designs, and before their eyes, she was passing her hand over the weave and altering the shades to her customer's tastes.

'It used to be better. It used to *thrive*,' complained Giraldo, apparently heedless of the packed *souk*. He half-closed his eyes and allowed memories of past glories to surface. Nobody noticed.

Everywhere they looked, they saw magic used in different ways. Some obvious and remarkable, such as the woman selling the silks; others more mundane but no less extraordinary. A young boy carried a pail of water on a cushion of air before him. Eyja gave him the sweetest smile as he passed her. An obviously wealthy merchant, given his fine attire and arrogant bearing, had employed a young woman to conjure gentle winds to keep him cool in the evening heat. A train of robed monks followed a softly glowing cross as it led them on their long pilgrimage to the Holy Land. They maintained a soft chant, musical and tuneful, and with each rise in pitch, the cross glowed just a little brighter, fed by their magic and their faith in equal measure.

'It's wonderful,' breathed Tagan, turning in circles where she stood. 'So much life. So much *colour*.' Before anybody could stop her, she had raced over to the woman with the silks and found herself caught up in a conversation in halting English. Giraldo walked over behind her, smiling ever so slightly, as he watched the country girl with no experience of the world beyond her village communicate well with a complete stranger.

'Her work is beautiful, isn't it?' Giraldo said something to the woman in Spanish and she tipped her head to one side, giving the Pirate King a huge smile. She said something back in a fast, fluting voice and passed her hand across the piece of fabric she was holding. The cloth became a deep, arterial scarlet. She held it up and studied Tagan critically, then passed her hand across it again, and threads of glittering orange and yellow were worked into the red silk. It caught the light breeze, flickering like a forge fire. Her eyes grew round and wistful.

'That's so beautiful,' she said, breathlessly. The woman smiled and stood, tying the piece of silk around Tagan's waist.

'Beautiful silk for a beautiful lady,' she said in halting English. Tagan began to shake her head and untie the sash, but Giraldo stopped her.

'She is giving you the fabric as a gift,' he murmured softly. 'Perhaps there is something you could do for her?'

'But I couldn't make anything so beautiful.'

'Really?' Giraldo's smile never slipped, and Tagan nodded thoughtfully. She closed her eyes for a moment and after a second or two, a tiny flame sat in the palm of her hand. She teased the small flame, stretching it out and shaping it until she had crafted another fiery butterfly, just as she had done for Mathias on that day back in Wales, which felt so far away and so long ago now. She opened out her palm and the fiery creature fluttered free. The trader laughed delightedly and clapped her hands, even after the butterfly had faded to a smoky memory.

'There. You have pleased her. A gift for a gift.' Giraldo linked his arm into Tagan's. 'This is how a community thrives with magic at its heart. Do you see now how grey, how poor, England has become for the lack of it?'

Before she could respond, the noise in the market fell to a hush and the strangest sound began to thread through the crowd. A haunting, but beautiful sound; a male voice, raised in song. Tagan did not understand the words, but there was something strangely uplifting in them. Around them, the market place began to close down, traders moving away.

'What is that?' She didn't notice the tears on her cheeks until Giraldo gently wiped them away.

'The *adhan*,' he replied. 'It is the call to prayer for these people. They live in harmony with the gift of magic, the bounty of nature and their faith. It is the ideal envisioned by so many... so long ago.' He sighed softly. 'Come. Let's get a few hours sleep in a comfortable bed. We have a hard journey, come the morning. We leave at dawn.'

'Where are we staying?'

'I know a woman who owns a tavern.' Giraldo's grin was wicked. 'Well, *sort* of a tavern. Eyja's not going to approve, put it that way.'

The Vanguard
The Atlantic Sea

SEVERAL MEN HAD died under the strain of the ruthless pace set by the Lord Inquisitor. With each death, one of the knights had taken the empty place and continued the relentless pull of the oars until even the Lord Inquisitor went to an oar and rowed alongside them.

'My lord, this can't go on. We can *not* keep this up. Not unless you want to have a mutiny on your hands. The men are exhausted.'

Hudson had finally found his courage and made his stand before the Lord Inquisitor. Weaver's heavily muscled arms hauled at the oars. Though stripped to the waist, he still bore his mask, and the captain tried not to let his eyes linger on the scars that laced the other man's body.

'We will not stop, Captain.' Weaver rumbled. There was no obvious strain in his voice. 'But work the men in shifts. Feed them, rest them, water them, then put them back to work. We *must* reach Anfa as quickly as we can.'

'Yes, my lord.' The captain scurried off to be the bearer of somewhat good news for the first time during this arduous trip, leaving Weaver pulling on the oar.

Anfa
Morocco

DAWN WAS NO less hectic than dusk had been as the party emerged from what the Pirate King had referred to as a 'tavern.' Giraldo was right. Eyja was not impressed, although she had been the model of decorum whilst they had stayed in the raucous lodgings that Mathias rather innocently noted aloud seemed to house mostly young women. His comrades' laughter had embarrassed him straight to bed, where he had slept better than he had done in the weeks since leaving home. No dreams plagued him, and when he woke, he was refreshed and eager to make progress.

Of the Shapeshifter there was still no sign. It did not appear to bother either Eyja or Giraldo, although given the slightly self-satisfied expression on Giraldo's face as he emerged from one of the larger chambers, it was possible that very little would bother him this day. Mathias caught the briefest glimpse of more than one soft body lounging on the bed behind the door as the Pirate King blew an extravagant kiss through it and closed it firmly. Tagan, it seemed, was enjoying the luxury of a proper bed and was still sleeping.

'You have never changed, have you, Giraldo?' Eyja gave him a disapproving look, but there was indulgence in her sparkling grey eyes.

'Would you want me to?' He took up a piece of fruit and bit into the flesh hungrily. His expression was filled with a boyish charm that Mathias wished he could muster. He had never known anybody as flamboyant as Giraldo de Luna, and despite his initial distrust and even dislike of the man, he had grown fond of him over the weeks.

'Warin hasn't arrived,' Mathias put in cautiously. 'I've been looking out for him, but... nothing.'

'Red will turn up when he wants. He doesn't like crowded places.' Giraldo dropped into a chair and put his booted feet up on the table. Eyja pushed them off again.

'Show a *little* respect,' she said and this time there was no amusement in her voice. Giraldo shrugged and sat properly. He drained all the juice from the orange and then ate the pulp. He licked his lips clean and hungrily ate a handful of dates. Mathias shifted uncomfortably.

'Weren't we... leaving at dawn?'

'A man should not travel on an empty belly. The miserable old bastard won't mind waiting a little longer.' Eyja quirked a perfect eyebrow.

'That is *certainly* not respectful,' she scolded. 'And you really believe he's waiting?'

'Of course he's waiting. It's what he does best these days. Besides. Isn't he about ten thousand years old now?'

Mathias had no idea who they were talking about, but the last statement made his jaw drop. Eyja laughed lightly.

'Oh, Giraldo. Look at poor Mathias's face!' She stood up, cupped Mathias's chin in her hand, and kissed his cheek. 'Don't listen to his ridiculous lies. The old man can't be more than five thousand years old.'

Somehow, that was not any better.

'Who are we talking about?' Mathias asked. He had naturally assumed that the Wanderer bore his title because he wandered.

'Akhgar,' Giraldo said. 'I forget the rest of his name, but it has something to do with his ancestors. He is very old and very wise. It is said that he has taught magic to more people than any other mage in the world.'

'Ibn Atash,' said Eyja softly. 'Akhgar ibn Atash. It translates, more or less, as "Sign of the fire, son of the flame." I have not seen him for many years.'

'Did he teach you magic?' Mathias paused in his restless fidgeting. 'Did he teach Warin?'

'Yes,' said Eyja. 'At least in part. It was Havard who had the talent for teaching.'

'Havard?' Mathias did not recognise the name.

'Yes,' Eyja replied softly. 'That was the name by which I called him. Warin knew him as Adelmo. Giraldo...'

'Ramon. To me he was Ramon. And to you, Mathias, he was Wyn.'

'Wyn taught all of you magic? I never believed the stories about his travels.'

Around them, the brothel was starting to come to life. The moody, hazy lighting of the previous night was replaced by bright sunlight as curtains were pushed aside and the morning sun of Anfa streamed in. Dust particles twirled and glistened in the light and a long silence settled over the breakfast table, broken only by the voices of the residents as they began their daily chores.

Finally, Mathias asked the question that had been plaguing him since he had stood in a stone circle in Wales.

'Why me? Why *us*? Tagan and I, I mean.'

Eyja stroked Mathias's hair back from his face. 'He cared for you and he was running out of time,' she said quietly. 'So he saved you. And he saved Tagan because you care for her. Not all of us have been so fortunate.'

A shadow passed over her face and Mathias could not tell whether it was fear, pain or regret, but it did not feel right to pry. He shifted impatiently again. 'So when are we going to leave to meet this Akhgar?'

'Soon, dear one. Trust me.'

And he trusted her. There was no way he could not. By the time Tagan emerged from her room, looking more relaxed and happy than he had seen her in a long time, he had forgotten his worries and simply looked forward to the trip ahead.

* * *

ANFA IN THE early hours was every bit as lively and colourful as it had been the previous night, and the small party moved through the market place slowly, squeezing past the press of bodies. Giraldo bartered for several skins of clear, fresh water from the town's well. They purchased food and heavy wraps that Eyja assured them would protect their noses and mouths from the desert sands.

Still there was no sign of the Shapeshifter. Even the ever-patient Eyja seemed to be growing concerned by his lingering absence. They arrived at the port in time to see *Hermione*'s sails unfurl as she put out to sea.

'You don't think he's abandoned us, do you?' The question came from Tagan, who was wearing the scarlet silk gift from yesterday around her head. The look was faintly exotic against her fair skin, and it became her.

'No,' said Eyja after a moment. 'Warin is here in the city. He is just... sulking.'

'Why is he sulking?'

'Too long at sea and too many people,' she replied, glancing briefly over at Giraldo, who shrugged. 'Warin loves the wild and has little time for people and their cities. Once we get out into the desert, he will soon change.'

'So will I,' muttered Giraldo. He patted the waterskin. 'Fortunately, I can conjure more as long as we have at least a little. So don't drain these skins too quickly.'

Mathias reassured him that there would be no danger of that. He had already tried a sip of water from the skin and it tasted faintly of goat. 'How are we going to cross this "desert"?' He had asked what the unfamiliar term meant the previous evening; Giraldo had said that it was like an ocean of sand. Mathias had never imagined such a thing, but had seen so many extraordinary things over the course of his journey he was losing his ability to doubt.

'Take a look over there.' Giraldo nodded his head towards a small, dusty compound. Mathias saw horses there, beautiful horses with the most perfect lines he had ever seen. Heads held high and arrogantly, they looked at the world around them with a kind of sneering indifference. Mathias considered them with a practised eye. They pranced and shook their shining manes, and he could tell just from looking at them that riding the creatures would be a nightmare.

'We aren't taking those,' he said, with such conviction that Giraldo grinned.

'Damn right, we aren't,' he said. 'We're taking those.'

Mathias followed the line of Giraldo's pointing finger and stared at a creature he had never seen before.

'What are *those*?'

'Camels,' came the cheerful reply. 'Come on, take a look.'

The Sahara Desert
Morocco

IN A SWELTERING tent at the edge of the desert, Akhgar ibn Atash looked up and smiled. They would be here soon. They would arrive and he could rest. He had wandered for so long, he fancied that he could not even remember what it was like to be still. To be at peace. Soon he would be free of the burden. He set down his pipe and tapped the ash from the bowl.

'Send out some riders,' he said to the young man who sat with him. 'They will be here soon.' To a man as long-lived as Akhgar ibn Akash, *soon* was a relative term.

'Yes, *effendi*.' The young man bowed deeply and backed out of the tent into the blazing heat of the oasis.

THE CAMELS WERE evil-looking creatures. The animal nearest Mathias lifted its head in a bored manner and chewed idly as it fixed him with a look of faint indifference. There were six of them, some sitting and some standing, but all with that same look of veiled malevolence directed towards the people standing nearby.

Mathias stared into its eyes. The smallest of smiles crossed his face as recognition dawned.

'Warin?'

The camel let out a grunt and shook its shaggy head slightly. Then, ever so slowly, it closed one long-lashed eye and winked at him. Mathias's small smile broke out into a huge grin and he started to chuckle softly.

Eyja sighed and shook her head. 'I can't say that I'm surprised. Still, at least we have found him.' The camel turned its head to Eyja and knelt on its front legs, a startlingly respectful gesture. She patted it on the nose with a wry smile.

'These are strange animals,' Mathias called over his shoulder to Tagan, who was standing back fearfully, 'but they won't hurt us. Come over here.' He beckoned her closer and she came to stand beside him. She slid her hand into his and looked at the camel.

'They call them the "ships of the desert,"' said Giraldo as he also joined them. 'Nothing near as wonderful as the *Hermione*, of course...' He stared deep into the eyes of the camel that was Warin the Red and smirked. 'But they'll do. Not as comfortable as my lady either. Still... needs must.' He turned to the trader, and a swift exchange took place in smooth, easy Spanish. The clink of coins sealed the deal, and within minutes, they were on their way.

Within a few minutes more, both Tagan and Mathias had fallen off their camels, unused to the swaying gait of the hump-backed animals, so very different from the horses they had grown up with.

Time ticked on and as they rode, each step just as uncomfortable and jolting as the last, the city of Anfa shrank away behind them. The greenery that thrived here, kept alive by the breeze from the ocean, began to thin out, and by the time they had learned how to hold on to the camels comfortably, Tagan and Mathias were introduced to the most arid environment that they had ever known.

There were six camels in the party: Warin and five more, one for each of the riders. They moved at a steady, easy pace. Giraldo's incessant chatter of the morning slowly began to fade as the heat of the day began to take hold. He sat, slumped on the back of his camel, staring out at the vast, rocky plain that stretched ahead of them. Eyja leaned over and squeezed his shoulder gently.

'It is not for long, dear one,' she said to him in a soft voice. The

Pirate King raised a brief smile, then hung his head again. He seemed to be wilting in the heat, and Mathias couldn't say that he was particularly surprised. He could feel the stifling, still air sucking all the breath from his lungs. Beside him, wobbling dangerously on the back of her mount, Tagan looked as pale and wan as Giraldo did. Only Eyja seemed in any way comfortable, although even she had to periodically reach up to wipe sweat from her pale skin. On her instruction, they were all wearing the wraps that they had picked up in the market. Mathias had gone to remove his outer laying of clothing, but Eyja slapped his hand back.

'No,' she said. 'Stay covered. Otherwise you will burn. There is a small oasis beyond this ridge where we can rest. I believe we will find Akhgar beyond that, at the edge of the desert. If we hurry, we should be able to get there before nightfall.'

Even as she spoke, the thick, stifling air freshened a little, stirred into a cooling breeze by her magic. Even Giraldo perked up, sitting forward on the back of his camel and brightening enough to start whistling a cheery tune.

They made a strange caravan, travelling through the desert heat, but with the magic of the winds and Giraldo's water, they made it to the oasis. The shade of the trees was a blessed relief and they slid off the camels, welcoming the cooling shadows gratefully.

Tagan and Giraldo both melted slightly, and sat underneath the trees, their eyes closing as the parched air sapped their strength. Warin refused to change back from his camel form and simply sat on his haunches with the other beasts, chewing his cud contentedly and giving them all the evil eye.

'Eyja? Why does Akhgar... the Wanderer... why does he not come to us?' Using the unfamiliar name felt awkward on Mathias's tongue. 'I mean, Wyn sent us to Warin, but he felt us coming; and you found us, and so did Giraldo, in a manner of speaking.' He paused, running the complexities of their connection around in his head. 'Why is Ak... why is the Wanderer so different?'

'You will understand more when you see him, Mathias.' Eyja reached over and stroked the young man's soft hair, made damp with sweat, from his face. The soft, boyish looks he'd borne in

Wales had gone. His cheekbones were sharper, more clearly defined, and the weeks of travel and hardship on board a ship had hardened his body into something leaner than it had been.

'Why do you all have so many names?'

'Names have power. At least, true names. For those with magic, knowing a person's true name can give you power over them. You must guard yours well, or another could use it against you one day.'

'So Eyja is not your real name either?'

'No, but it is closer than "She Who Sees," though I suppose there is a certain amount of accuracy in that title.'

'So what should I call myself if I'm not allowed to be Mathias?'

Eyja looked as though she were about to speak, but instead she frowned in concern. She closed her eyes and turned her face to the cloudless sky. Mathias could feel the tang of magic on the edge of his tongue, felt the hairs on his neck start to prickle. Her eyes flared open again.

When Eyja spoke next, it was not in the gentle, maternal tone she usually used, but hard and urgent.

'Wake them,' she said, gathering her skirts together and standing. 'Our stubborn shadow has made up for lost time and is on our heels. We must move swiftly.'

FOURTEEN

The Vanguard
The Mediterranean Sea

'WHEN WILL WE make landfall?'

Charles Weaver's patience was all but exhausted. The makeshift oar deck of the *Vanguard* was littered with the hunched bodies of men, rowing mechanically, their eyes hollow with weariness. They rowed as if their lives depended on it—and in a very real sense they did. Those who could take it no more were cast overboard without ceremony. In their wake followed every scrap of cargo and furniture that Weaver deemed unnecessary: leftover ammunition, the fittings from the captain's cabin, even rails and spare rope were pitched over the side in an effort to coax more speed from the ailing vessel.

It proved to be a shrewd move. The captain looked up from the navigation charts into the masked visage of the Lord Inquisitor and was able to give him an answer that he sincerely hoped would please him more than the last.

'At this speed and bearing, my lord, we will make Anfa within the next three hours.' Weaver's knuckles turned white around his oar and the captain noted the dried blood that flaked from beneath his hands.

'Excellent,' he said. 'We will catch them yet.'

Hampton Court
England

KING RICHARD STARED at the scroll held between his hands. He felt numb and lifeless, and his heart was as heavy as a stone. For all intents and purposes, he could be dead. He *would* be dead, and all would fall to ashes, unless the demon had some greater plan of which he was unaware.

'Father?' Prince Richard leaned over to touch his father's arm gently, alarmed by the pallor of the King's face. 'Father, what dire news ails you so?'

Richard handed the scroll wordlessly to his son, and slumped back in his chair and stared into space as the prince read aloud.

'*Sire,*' read the boy. '*Word has reached us that the Vatican has dispatched its army to aid the French. We seek to verify this news, but have little reason to believe to it be anything less than the truth.*' The prince looked up, his face contorted with horror, and stared at his father. 'The magi of the Vatican Army are legion,' he said.

'Do you think me some kind of fool?' Richard snapped. He controlled his temper, immediately contrite. He could not afford to upset the boy. Not now. Not with the solstice only days away. He continued more calmly. 'Yes. With the magic of the Vaticae, the army will reach Paris by the end of the year.'

The Templar Magi of Holy Rome fielded a force unlike any other. Powerful magi and extraordinary warriors alike, the militant order of the Church were charged with the protection of the faith. This drove them to feats of great strength and heroism the like of which the rest of the world could barely comprehend. Richard been led to believe that they would not rise to the invasion of France, and would seek only to defend their own borders. Richard had not planned to confront them until his power was consolidated in Europe, and even then only once his armies were fully rested and resupplied.

Now it seemed he had miscalculated.

'Their combined might against our armies...' The young prince allowed the words to drip from his tongue slowly. 'Even with the *Lionheart*, we would not stand a chance. Without more men and more weapons, defeating them would be impossible.' He cringed, anticipating retribution from his father. He was surprised, therefore, when Richard simply sighed and shook his head.

'It would be difficult, my boy,' he said. 'Difficult, but nothing is impossible. The price of that victory, though...' He fell into a deep brooding silence as he stared at the boy whom he loved more than anything in the world. The words of the demon came back to haunt him again.

When the sun sets on the day of the solstice, young Richard must stand within the circle at Salisbury. I will hold your pact fulfilled, and your line will endure forever, as was promised. England will have a king unlike any in history, and all will fall before him. What more could any father ask?

There were two paths open to him now; he could taste them, like blood in his mouth.

Victory. Defeat.

Two paths. And the cost was great for both. If the army were defeated, then there was every chance that the Vatican would turn its attention to England and look to bring the wayward child back to the ways of the parent Church. The House of Plantagenet would be broken. England would once again fall under the influence of the arcane, and all that they had worked for—a century of rule—would have been for nothing. Plantagenet would be a forgotten name, consigned to the annals of history. He would be the shame of his forebears, and his descendants, should they be permitted to live, would do so in ignominy and exile.

But victory came with a different price. He lifted his eyes again to look at the young prince.

'*A king unlike any in history,*' he murmured, beneath his breath. That was what Melusine had called him. Somehow the idea chilled him to the bone. But what father would not want greatness for his child? The King put his head in his hands, misery settling about him.

What price victory?

What price?

The Sahara Desert
Morocco

THEY MADE SWIFT passage. The knowledge that Weaver and his men were close on their heels had a remarkable effect on even Giraldo's lethargy. The camels proved to be remarkably swift when spurred on and with Warin at their head, the sands of the Sahara Desert passed in a dusty haze behind them.

But after an hour's hard riding in the oppressive heat, the camels faltered and slowed. This came as some relief to Mathias and Tagan. The long ride in the mountains had been difficult and arduous, but at least the climate had been bearable and the animals they rode were familiar. The camels had a longer, bumpier gait that jarred them with every stride.

'We cannot tarry,' said Giraldo, urgency in his tone. 'I have never known a hunter like this Inquisitor. He must have run men and beasts to death to get here. And he always knows how to find us! How can a man know such things without the gift?' His voice had lost all of its airy lightness, becoming threatening and dark. 'How?'

'Oh, Giraldo, please,' said Eyja. 'You are frightening the children. Everything will be just fine. Have a little faith in your friends, will you?'

'A little faith,' he retorted. 'One is presently a camel, one is too old to leave, and the other... the other is...'

A long, awkward pause.

'Do continue,' Eyja said in a pleasant, tinkling voice that rang in the air. '*What* am I?'

It was past midday and the desert air was hazy with the heat. Giraldo seemed to be steaming ever so slightly in his saddle.

The pirate's silence dragged on a little further, passing beyond the merely awkward and into something else. The two clashed silently and Mathias's eyes moved from the one to the other, waiting on the outcome.

He never got it. Tagan's voice rose in panic and she pointed back the way they had ridden. 'Look!'

They looked, all of them. Even Warin-as-camel turned his head to the cloud of dust on the far horizon.

'They are coming,' said Giraldo in a grim tone. 'We have sat bickering for too long.'

'Oh, shut up, Giraldo.' The camel vanished as Warin took human form once more and stomped over to stand beside Eyja. He offered a hand up to Eyja, helping her climb down from her own beast.

She thanked him demurely and brushed her hands lightly across the front of her gown.

'If beasts and blades and storms do nothing to turn this man from his course, perhaps we should test his resolve with all three at once. Warin, will you join with me? Set your will against this foe once again?'

Warin nodded, his expression dark. 'This Inquisitor has done enough. I will kill him if I have to.'

The two of them clasped hands for the briefest of moments and then turned their attention to the oncoming plume of dust.

'FASTER!' WEAVER DUG his heels into the horse's flank. 'We are upon them!'

Sir Anthony and his remaining knights followed in the Lord Inquisitor's wake. Within minutes of leaving the *Vanguard*, they had thrown gold at the horse merchant and taken his best and swiftest creatures, the beautiful Arab horses that Tagan had so admired earlier. Seven riders had left Anfa. One had been thrown barely two miles from the city gates, unused to riding such skittish animals. He had landed badly, breaking his ankle, but had waved the rest of them on and turned awkwardly to return to the town.

'My lord, look.' One of the riders pointed ahead where the tracks that marked the group's passage were no longer half-buried by the shifting sands. 'We are gaining on them.'

'Then be wary. I will not let this quarry escape. Not again.' They pushed on, the sand scouring their skin and the sun baking their backs as they rode. After the gruelling ride across France, the return journey and the storm at sea, the knights were as eager as Weaver to end the chase.

Almost as eager.

Unlike the knights, the Lord Inquisitor showed no signs of flagging; even his time behind the oar did not seem to have fatigued him. It was as though he'd passed beyond the limits of mortal flesh. Charles Weaver seemed beyond pain and weakness, driven to the point of obsession.

And he seemed, by turns, to be utterly ruthless and startlingly kind. Sir Anthony could not decide what was the real Charles Weaver.

'My lord!' This time, the cry was not one of triumph, but of horror. Weaver raised his masked face and looked to where the man pointed. A wall of sand was moving towards them at an impossible pace.

'Sandstorm!'

IT HAD BEGUN as nothing more than a handful of sand. Warin squatted down and gathered up a scoop of the hot Sahara dust in his rough, calloused hands. It did not trickle between his fingers, but held its shape in his cupped palms, like a tiny, ochre pyramid. He held the gathered sand before him and lifted his arms slowly to the sky. Eyja touched his arm gently and her voice lifted in the sweet soprano Mathias had heard her use on her arrival in the English Channel. Her call to the winds was answered by a skirling sirocco that plucked streamers from the dunes and twisted its way around Warin. The grains shifted gently, changing from mere sand to something living.

'Beautiful,' breathed Giraldo, his earlier irritation seemingly forgotten. 'It has been so long since I watched the two of them work together. So very beautiful.'

'I prefer "practical,"' grunted Warin, who crouched again and set the tiny dust devil down on the ground before him. It spun gracefully, twisting from side to side and growing in size and strength.

At first it was a dervish of sand, hovering a fraction of an inch above the ground, but as it grew, it began to take on shape and form. The arcane wind was something more than just a storm, although as it began to rush toward the pursuing figures it became very apparent that a wall of sand was building in its wake. Creatures became distinguishable within the body of the storm. Limbs. Ears. Tails.

'Wolves,' breathed Tagan softly. Of course it would be wolves.

The sand-wolves threw back their heads and howled, a sound like the cry of the wind across dry rocks and bone. It filled the air like a mournful dirge and raced ahead of the growing dust-storm like a harbinger of doom. It built up speed as it moved across the dunes, a wall of razor-sharp sand billowing behind it.

'Will it hurt them?'

Giraldo and Mathias turned to Tagan, who was staring after the disappearing sand-wolves. 'It depends how quickly they find shelter,' replied Giraldo carefully. He sighed softly. 'Probably,' he admitted. She nodded.

'Good,' she said. 'After what men like him did to Wyn... to every mage dragged before a trial... to Mathias's father... they can feel our retribution. At our hands, the Inquisition will suffer for their folly.' The words were archaic and decidedly un-Tagan. Mathias felt something curdle deep in his soul as he stared at her.

Giraldo, however, studied the young woman's face carefully. 'We are close to our destination,' he said. 'It tells.'

'What do you mean?' Tagan had turned away and was looking out to the east, her eyes cool and calm, her expression neutral. She did not seem to be completely her usual self.

'Akhgar,' said Giraldo. Tagan turned her head in his direction slightly and inclined it in the briefest of acknowledging nods.

With a sudden release of energy that set all of Mathias's senses buzzing, Eyja and Warin relinquished control of the storm. Both of them looked immensely wearied by the magic and leaned heavily against one another for support. Giraldo looked them over with a practised eye. 'They will be fine. Two minutes to rest and then we need to move. Time is precious. My friends, Akhgar is near.'

As HE REGARDED the approaching storm, Weaver reluctantly conceded that they must take cover. They rode hard, desperate to reach the comparative shelter of the nearby dunes. The horses, sensitive to the urgency of their riders, became even harder to control and the men struggled to steer them.

The storm struck minutes before they all reached the edge of the dune and for a fleeting moment, Charles Weaver swore he saw the body of a vast, glistening wolf in the heart of the wall of sand that lashed against his armoured body and bounced off his masked face. The protection, minimal though it was, meant he fared better than two of his knights and most of the horses. The screams of man and beast rose in the howling winds as the sand blinded them and scored bloody tracks in their flesh. One horse, maddened by the horror, threw and trampled its rider before disappearing from view, galloping off as fast as its legs would carry it. The noise and the chaos were terrifying and Weaver's men huddled in the lee of the dune, helpless to defend themselves against the eldritch wind and biting sand. They pulled their cloaks about them and waited as the desert threatened to swallow them whole.

Charles Weaver roared his defiance right back, something greater than resolve glittering in his eyes.

'WHAT DO YOU mean, the Wanderer is near?' Mathias reached out and caught Giraldo's arm. 'What's wrong with Tagan?'

'Nothing is wrong,' replied the Pirate King. He looked down at Mathias's hand on his arm and frowned slightly. Mathias reluctantly released him. 'Tagan's connection is to fire, yes? It is natural that Akhgar would reach out to her.'

Tagan smiled at Mathias and he felt, rather than saw, that she was still the woman he knew.

'We are ready to travel,' Eyja said, in a voice paled with weariness. 'The storm should delay them, but given the persistence of our foe we should certainly be away.' Giraldo helped her to climb back onto her camel. The animals had stood chewing contentedly, barely even paying attention to what was going on around them.

Warin shifted form once more, hanging his head slightly with his own weariness, and the party set off at a loping gait. The day had passed into afternoon and the sun's relentless heat continued to sap their collective strength. But for Giraldo's ability to produce water on a whim, they would surely be as dead as the skeletal remains they passed; unfortunate animals and travellers who had lost their way among the dunes.

Mathias rode his camel as close as he could to Tagan, concern for her still nagging at him. He reached over to touch her hand with his own and she swung her head to look at him. The smile she gave him was as warm and sweet as ever it had been, and yet there was a strange sadness in her eyes that worried him. He squeezed her hand once more and released it, riding on in continued silence. The camaraderie of Anfa had dissolved with the discovery of their pursuers. Now there was a sense of terrible urgency that Mathias realised had always been there.

The desert was vast, and silent. As they travelled, Mathias began to understand just why camels were called 'ships.' The endless desert was just like the seas across which they had travelled; both were treacherous, and both were blessed with their own aching beauty.

It was the treachery that came first and foremost to Mathias's mind when he suddenly found a spear levelled at his face. They hadn't even seen the five men in sand-coloured robes rising up from the dunes to form a threatening circle around them. The lead tribesman said something in a language that Mathias did not understand.

It seemed the other thing the desert shared with the seas was pirates.

FIFTEEN

The Sahara Desert
Morocco

MATHIAS HAD MADE many assumptions since the beginning of his journey; assumptions based on his own inexperience and lack of understanding. When he had learned that their destination was an oasis, he had imagined something similar to the one they had stopped at earlier: a small pool of water with a few palm trees standing limply beside it. Nothing could have prepared him for the lush green wilderness where Akhgar ibn Atash and his tribe made their home.

The camp was based in a hollow between two dunes that sparkled in the dying remnants of the afternoon sun. As they rode closer, Mathias leaned towards one of the dunes and took a handful of sand. Tiny fragments of glass glittered amongst the silvery-gold grains.

Mathias had never seen so many tents. A veritable town surrounded the crystal-clear pool at the heart of the oasis. Everywhere there were signs of life. Men, women, children, and animals large and small roamed between the tents, living peacefully amidst the beauty of this unexpected paradise. Water was being drawn from the pool and the smell of cook fires made the young man's stomach rumble. It had been the better part of a full day since they had last eaten, and only now did he realise how hungry he was.

With a delighted cry, Giraldo took off at full speed towards the pool of water, nimbly dodged a small huddle of children playing at its edge and dived into its crystal depths. There was such joy and exuberance in his laughter as the children turned to join in with the stranger splashing them that even Warin, now changed back to human form, cracked a smile.

The leader of the warriors who had brought them to this place, a swarthy man with long, gleaming hair falling around a sun-weathered, sand-beaten face, spoke a few words to Eyja, pointing towards first one large tent and then another. She nodded and replied to him for several moments.

'He says that Akhgar will send for us when he is ready. Until then, we are free to relax in the shade of that tent there. We could all use a little food and rest.'

'But what of the Inquisitor?' Mathias could not shake his concern, and it put a childish tremor into his voice that shamed him. 'If he is alive, he will be right behind us.'

'They will not find this oasis,' said Warin. 'It is protected. It is... hidden. Do not worry about it. Not for now. Eyja is right. You need to rest and eat.' He grumbled slightly and put a hand to his stomach. 'Actually, so do I.'

Tagan looked up from the back of her camel. 'I am tired,' she said and her voice was tiny. Concerned for her health, and even more for her strange behaviour, Mathias reached up to help her down from the animal. His arm stole around her protectively and he drew her close to his side.

'You need some sleep, my love,' he said softly, and she leaned into him gratefully.

Giraldo was perfectly happy where he was and so they let him be. The remaining four headed towards the tent that had been indicated by the tribesman and entered gratefully into its cool interior.

Sumptuous was not a word that Mathias had ever had cause to use, but it applied perfectly to the interior of the colourful pavilion. Hand-woven rugs in threads dyed the most glorious shades decorated the floor. Silk-covered cushions littered the ground, offering places to sit or rest. A long, low table was covered with food—fresh and dried fruits and cured meats of all kinds, some familiar, others less so.

'Mathias, settle Tagan comfortably. She looks exhausted.' Eyja took charge. 'Water first, I think, and a little of the fruit if she feels she can manage it. Then you will eat, too.'

Warin was critically examining the laden table, his nose wrinkling amid the whiskery beard. 'Delicate,' he complained, snatching up a handful of dried figs and cramming them in his mouth. 'No real food here at all.'

It didn't stop him, Mathias observed, from taking his fill. He accepted a goblet of crystal clear water from Eyja and gave it to Tagan, who sipped it gratefully. He took a goblet for himself and drank deeply, thankful to be free of the hint of slightly rank animal that had tainted the water they'd drunk since leaving Anfa.

Tagan settled down amidst the cushions and closed her eyes with a little sigh. Eyja knelt beside her, putting a hand to her forehead. Mathias hovered anxiously.

'Do not fear for her,' said Eyja, not looking up. 'She suffers in the heat. A little sleep, a little more water and she will be fine.' She stroked Tagan's tangled curls gently as the young woman fell asleep. 'She is very fair-skinned. The desert is not the place for an English rose. More exotic flowers grow here. But none so tough.'

'They are Welsh,' said Warin, bringing a bubble of laughter to Mathias's lips. For the first time in several days, he finally allowed himself to relax.

The Royal Armoury
England

PRINCE RICHARD HAD never been keen on London. He had always enjoyed brief visits to the city that was his future kingdom's capital, *brief* being the operative word. He had been raised on a country estate and his heart belonged there. The city was loud and busy and filled with people, noise and sulphurous stench. When his father had announced their destination, however, his interest had been renewed. He peered out the windows of the carriage as it made its way towards the docks.

'You have not met Isaac Bonnington before, have you, son?' King Richard sat opposite his son, studying him with a rare intensity.

'The Royal Engineer? No, Father, I have not. But you have told me of his great works, and of course I have used some of his weapons.'

The prince, like his father before him, was a keen hunter and had utilised a Bonnington mechanical bow on his last expedition. The intricate clockwork weapon allowed him to loose his arrows faster and with more deadly impact than ever before. 'He will be there? It will be interesting to meet him, I think.'

'Yes,' replied the King, staring at his son for a little longer before he also turned to look out of the window. 'It will. You will like what he has created for our armies. If he manages to get it working in time, then it may give us the strength to stand against Rome.'

There was no point in relaying his doubts and fears to the boy. To do so would raise his suspicions. His time with his eldest son might be short. There was no point in filling it with portents and fear.

Beside the carriage rode six of the Royal Guard, resplendent in the blue and yellow livery of the King's armies, the black rose emblazoned on their tabards. The horses beneath them were decked out in the same colours. They created an impressive tableau as they passed through the East London street. People stopped what they were doing, and for once in their dull, grey lives lifted their head to appreciate the riot of colour that moved past them.

'Is the *Lionheart* really as impressive as he has claimed?' the prince asked as the carriage turned down a narrow lane towards a huge foundry. The King's reply came with a small smile and a shake of the head.

'It is beyond imagining,' he promised, gratified by his son's interest in Bonnington's work. So few people had believed in the nervous, eccentric engineer when he laid his plans before the royal court. But King Richard had commissioned the project. He, at least, had believed in Bonnington's genius.

IN THE WHOLE of English history, there had never been anything like it. Prince Richard could see, as he walked around the massive hull, where Isaac Bonnington had drawn some of his inspiration, but there were mechanisms that he had no hope of ever understanding. Steam vents wheezed, expelling white-hot air from numerous places around the central carriage.

Carriage. That was the only word that Prince Richard could think of to describe what it was that he was looking at. In its most basic form, it resembled the very vehicle in which he and his father had arrived into the workshop. But it was at least four times as large and covered with metal plating. Pulleys and chains looped around its eight wheels and disappeared into apertures beneath its bulk. A pair of bulky chimneys huffed soot into the air of the workshop, and it sweated a reek of sulphur, pitch and hot iron.

The windows of the carriage were barely more than slits all around the sides, situated just above the carriage's most prominent feature.

'There are six guns on either side,' said the excited little engineer as he walked the King around it. 'And two more at the front and back. The armour is strong enough to repel heavy cannon fire and is coated with an alchemical lacquer of my own devising that should repel the base elements.'

King Richard stared at the vehicle. It was unlike anything he had ever seen, and yet he was not afraid of its appearance. He had seen the work of the Royal Engineer in the mighty ships that set sail from docks around his kingdom, and each ironclad he had been commissioned to produce had been successively larger and more deadly. But this was something new. This was something that the French and Roman armies could not expect. With all their magic and all their arcane might, this vehicle had the capability to destroy them before they approached.

Across the vehicle's hull was inscribed the name that King Richard had chosen.

Lionheart.

'I call it a *cannonade*,' said the engineer, delighted by the impressed looks of father and son. 'It's not strictly accurate of course, but it is as close an approximation as I can manage.'

'How does it move?' Prince Richard was examining the peculiar machinery at the *Lionheart*'s rear. 'Have you refined the alchemical engine in some way?'

'Indeed, your highness, though I could not have done it without your father's original insight.' Isaac moved away from the King to stand before young Richard. The prince towered over him and had to fight down an overwhelming urge to crouch slightly so the engineer didn't have to squint up at him. 'This vehicle, like many of our ships, is self-propelled. All she needs is water in the reservoirs, some tanks of dragon's breath and a crew to drive her. I have yet to master the art of making the engine work in reverse.'

'Forwards is all we need,' said King Richard, stepping across to join them. 'We will drive the *Lionheart* across any army that dares to invade our shores. We will literally crush the enemy as they stand before us.' He rested a hand on the cannonade's cold metal hull. 'Your last message stated that she is ready to go into service. Is this correct?'

'Yes, your majesty.' Isaac bowed deeply. 'She has performed beautifully in all her tests. A skeleton crew have been put together.' He indicated the *Lionheart* in a sweeping gesture. 'She can carry sixteen gunners, two drivers and a further twelve passengers.'

'Good,' said King Richard. 'Then assemble the crew and make her ready to leave. We are going to put her to the test. How fast can she move? How long, Master Bonnington, would it take her to travel thirty leagues?'

'Under the best conditions and with a constant supply of fuel...' Isaac's eyes rolled up as he calculated. 'Perhaps four hours at the most.'

'Four hours?' Prince Richard was incredulous. 'Nothing moves that fast!'

'The *Lionheart* does,' replied Isaac with unquestionable pride. 'And she will.' He turned back to the King. 'Where do you plan to take her?'

Richard looked over at his son, who had gone back to studying the *Lionheart*. Even as the words left his mouth, he felt the chill of fear.

'Salisbury,' he said. He looked down at the little engineer. 'To the circle of stones. And we need to be there soon. In our continued efforts to rid the country of the taint of magic, the Inquisition has uncovered a plan by the magi to conduct some kind of rite at the site. The *Lionheart* gives us the perfect weapon to put an end to it.'

'She will be ready to roll'—Isaac chuckled at his own joke—'within the hour, your majesty.'

'Be sure that she is,' replied King Richard, oblivious to the attempt at humour. Isaac deflated visibly. 'The safety of our kingdom depends on this creation, Bonnington.' The King took a small satisfaction from the look of alarm on the engineer's face. It took his worries, for a moment, off his more pressing concerns. But only for a moment.

The Sahara Desert
Morocco

AKHGAR IBN ATASH sent for the party after night had fallen. Eyja gently woke Mathias and Tagan from the heat-induced slumber in which they had been indulging. The first thing that Mathias noted was the intense chill in the air. The days in the desert might have been dangerously hot, but the nights, it seemed, could be just as cold. The extremes confused him, but he drew his tunic more tightly around his body as they stepped out into the night.

A huge fire was burning, around which many of the tribe were variously sitting talking, or eating from a communal cook pot. Delicious scents wafted up at him—a soup or stew of some sort in the black cauldron, and spiced flatbreads cooking on the stones. After the hostility of the day and the nightmare of the chase, it was friendly and welcoming, and as the group crossed the oasis, Mathias wondered if, when this was all over, maybe they could stay among these people. It was a glorious dream, if one which he sadly realised was most likely impossible.

Tagan walked beside him, once again holding his hand. She seemed much improved. Careful attention from the ever-present Eyja, who had thus far treated both young people like they were her children, had speeded her recovery.

'It has been a long time,' Giraldo said. For once, his jovial nature was subdued. He had assumed a serious air that was reflected in the faces of the others. Eyja and Warin walked behind him, keeping pace together, but all three had their eyes locked on the tent as they approached it.

The warrior who had greeted them out in the desert stood by the entrance, and bowed his head respectfully as they approached. 'The Wanderer bids you welcome,' he said. 'He will see you now.' He lifted the flap of the tent and they all ducked in beneath the canopy.

The interior was every bit as extravagant and luxurious as their own had been. The air was heady with the scent of sweet jasmine, which made Mathias feel light-headed and dizzy, and the heat from the pot-bellied fire in the tent's centre was stifling. A hole in the roof kept the air inside clear, but a single thread of smoke trailed out towards the frail figure lying amidst the cushions.

All eyes followed the thread, and all eyes looked upon the face of the man known as the Wanderer. His sun-darkened skin was shrunken with age or illness, but his raisin-black eyes were bright and intelligent. He turned his head from one guest to the other and then he smiled, revealing a mouthful of white, strong teeth.

'You have come at last, then. Welcome, my friends. Welcome.' He fell silent, as though the small speech had worn him out.

There was a long pause, and then Eyja took the initiative, moving forward and kneeling beside the ancient, wizened man amidst the cushions. 'Dearest one,' she said warmly and carefully embraced him. 'It has been so long. Too long.' Akhgar's wrinkled old hands closed around her and slowly she helped him to a better sitting position.

'Still so quick to manhandle me,' he grumbled and for a moment, a smile flickered onto Mathias's lips. He sounded so very much like old Wyn. 'You look well, girl. But then, you always did.'

'I do hope you're not expecting me to respond in kind,' she said with a gentle reprimand in her tone. 'Because I am a poor liar. You should have sent for us sooner, foolish old man.'

'Why would I ruin my twilight years by surrounding myself with women I can never have, endless complainers and colourful fops? Speaking of which...' His twinkling, old-man's eyes took in Warin and Giraldo, who stood a little way back. 'Ah, there they are. In an ever-changing world, it is good to see some things remain as they must be. Come over here. Let me take a closer look at you.'

It was clear to both Mathias and Tagan that Akhgar was the undisputed senior of the four magi, despite his frail appearance. Even Warin, usually so sour-faced and dour, had a smile on his lips as he knelt before Akhgar, taking the old man's hand into his own. Giraldo knelt the other side and also laid a hand on Akhgar's shoulder.

When the four of them touched, a shock of arcane power radiated from them like a wave, all but knocking Mathias from his feet with its sheer might. He gripped onto Tagan's hand with his own, unable to take his eyes off the scene before him. An amber nimbus played about Warin, followed by glows of red, blue and white from Akhgar, Giraldo and Eyja. The glows expanded, twisting and joining, until the four were bathed in a light so bright that the two young people could no longer look at them.

There was such terrifying beauty in the sight that Mathias could feel tears prickling at the back of his eyes. A low hum began, soft, musical and deeply moving. It slowly built to a melodic crescendo that dragged the darkness out of Mathias's spirit and gently caressed his soul with the promise that all would be well if he would just let it.

Warin was first to break the bond, stepping back and clearing his throat loudly and perhaps just a little over-dramatically. Giraldo grinned and also stood back, leaving only Eyja embracing the old man amidst the cushions. Eventually, she too rose and for the first time since she had breezed into their lives, tears streaked her cheeks.

'So soon?' It was all she said. Akhgar stroked the back of her hand and smiled up at her.

'You knew it must come to pass in time, little bird,' he said to her. 'But do not weep. Do not grieve for me. My time in this life is done, but my time in the next is just beginning. Now dry those tears and help me sit up. I would see these children from the land of the Lion.'

Mathias and Tagan took a hesitant step or two forward, their hands still clasped. Akhghar's rheumy old eyes peered at them with startling intensity.

'This is what time brings me?' He shook his head. 'They are so young. Too young, yes, for what lies ahead.'

'They are both proven,' said Warin. 'They are both brave, strong of heart and spirit. Youth is a blessing, old man. Or is it so far away now that you forget its wonders?'

'Mind your tone, Warin,' said Giraldo, quietly. 'Remember to whom you speak.'

'Don't fret yourself, boy,' said Akhgar, waving a hand in Giraldo's direction. 'I have ever preferred directness. To answer your question, no. I have not forgotten my youth. The world around me has changed. I have travelled so far, but I can travel no further. The spirit is willing. The spirit is *ever* willing.' He sighed heavily. 'But the flesh, alas, can take no more. My time on this plane is done.'

Tagan chewed her lip and looked at Mathias. 'Excuse me, sir? But... but just how old are you?' Truly, she had never seen anybody so very old and wizened as the tiny, frail figure before her. He turned those berry eyes on her and gave her a crinkled smile.

'I stopped counting centuries ago,' he said. 'I was an old man when that arrogant boy, Richard the Lionheart, marched at the head of his righteous army on the town of Jerusalem. I gave him my aid and I gave him the gift.'

'Richard the Lionheart?' Mathias spluttered. The ludicrousness of the suggestion was quelled somewhat by the grave expressions of the magi. It was obvious that they believed the old man's claim.

'Yes. A good soul at his core, but filled with pride. He burned from within, driven by outrage at the sacking of the Holy Land. The war between the Christians and the Saracens... ah, it was a sight to behold. Protected by their shields of faith? So the tales would come to say. It has never been my place to question the faith of man. Religion, for good or ill, is its own form of magic and something I do not touch.' Akhgar fell silent, trying to catch his breath. Tagan let go of Mathias's hand and moved to the old man, kneeling beside him and lifting up the goblet of water by his side. This close to him, she could smell the sourness of dried sweat on his skin and feel the unnatural heat that radiated from within. She gave him a shy smile. If he was as old as he claimed—and the suggestion was that he was even older still—he deserved her respect. Thus had she been raised.

Mathias's heart swelled with pride and love. This was the woman he loved. This was the woman he would marry when all this was done. They would go back to Wales, live simply and happily. Maybe raise a family, if things went to plan.

Wales. The rains and the green fields seemed a world removed from this exotic place.

Akhgar took a sip of the water and gave Tagan a piercing look. She did not even flinch, but remained at his side. He took a breath and continued. 'Protected by shields of faith, yes. But there were other shields in place on that army. Magical shields. Richard saw the value of the gift and he begged me to teach him the secret. The lands of Europe would flourish, he told me.'

'And so they did,' said Giraldo, picking up the story. 'The cities of Europe grew and prospered as the gift spread to them all. Paris. Rome. Madrid. All the great cities embraced the wonders magic had to offer them, and most saw the benefit. Even England flourished for a time. The jewel in the crown of the west; the source of the great gift. But as often happens with such things, the gift fell into the wrong hands.'

Warin interjected next. 'The gift was meant for all, not just the few who were already rich. Those in power sought to take back that which could not be taken. When they understood, they turned instead to oppression. It was the beginning of what you have come to know today. And it is too easy for power to corrupt. Where corruption finds root, worse things follow.'

'Demons,' Mathias breathed quietly.

'As you understand them,' murmured Eyja. 'Henry Tudor bartered for power on the field of Bosworth, but it was not power for himself that he desired. A noble soul, but misguided. Melusine betrayed him when she forged her pact with Richard. Henry's magi were defeated and the battle lost. To this day, nobody knows what became of Tudor, not even us.' She smiled. 'He was extraordinary, in truth. To have the will to deny Melusine's lure is remarkable. You are very like him, Mathias.'

For some reason, this made Mathias deeply proud. His spine straightened.

Eyja continued. 'Henry was strong. He was noble and pure of

spirit. Without the meddling of the demon, his victory would have been certain. Your home land would have gone on under the rule of a different bloodline. That is important.'

'The power Melusine wields is tied to the House of Plantagenet,' said Akhgar, picking up the story now that he had been granted time to catch his breath. 'The deal she struck with Richard that night has led to this, the birth of her pure vessel, though the word could not be more misleading.' The old man began to cough and Tagan once more lifted the water to his lips. He took another sip and then waved her away.

'What does she plan to do?' It was, perhaps, the first time Mathias had asked the question that had sat at the forefront of his mind since the day Wyn had told him of the demon and its machinations. 'And how can we stop her?'

'A demon cannot walk freely in this world. They are creatures of magic, and are sustained by magic. Melusine needs a body through which to wield her power, but no mortal mind can willingly bear such evil. But through the pact forged by King Richard, her taint has been slowly growing in the royal line, and all the while she has whispered in the ears of English kings. For generations she has worked to ensure that the power of the arcane cannot pose a threat to her. And young Prince Richard is the fruit of her labours. He is her perfect vessel,' said Warin. 'Through him she will wield the might of a nation and her power will not be fettered by the veil between worlds.'

'Enough,' said Akhgar. 'I must rest again. But I would speak with this one.' He reached out a hand to Tagan's cheek. 'Her kindness pleases me and I would learn something of her skill with fire.' She started and he laughed throatily. 'I can smell it on you,' he said. 'Don't be alarmed. Now go on, all of you. Leave us in peace.'

'Tagan?' Mathias's concern could not be hidden from his voice, but she got to her feet, crossing to him and kissing his cheek fondly.

'I will be fine,' she reassured him. 'I will see you soon, my love.'

Reluctantly, Mathias let the others lead him from the tent. His last sight of Tagan was as the flap of the tent fell back into place, obscuring her from view as she knelt down beside the oldest man he was ever likely to meet.

* * *

I CAN SMELL it on you, he had said. Strange words, perhaps, but she knew precisely what he meant. There was a distinctive scent to the old man that made Tagan feel comfortable in his presence. It was the smell of the forge, she recognised. The smell of burning wood and coals that she had grown to love over the years. It rolled from Akhgar in waves. It carried every kind of wood smoke, from the pines she had seen in Germany to the leafy woodlands that surrounded the village back home. She felt *right* sitting here with him.

His eyes had closed again and she respectfully sat in silence, not wishing to disturb him. Pouring another cup of water, she took a drink of her own and patiently waited for him to address her. In time, he woke from his brief doze and fixed his watery gaze on her.

'Tagan,' he said. 'That is your name?'

'Yes, sir,' she said and she felt a little shy.

'Tell me what you have learned of my brethren,' he said. 'Of Warin, Eyja and Giraldo. Don't worry about sparing their feelings, either.' He added the last with a gentle chuckle, presumably to suggest he was joking. Tagan knew that he wasn't.

'The elements,' she replied without hesitation. 'Their magic is strong, but it is tied to the elements. Warin told us when we met him that he was a child of the earth, just as Matty... I mean, Mathias is. Giraldo's magic is stronger whenever he is near water and Eyja seems able to speak with the winds. You smell like the forge. You are like me... or I am like you.' She flushed slightly and looked down at the backs of her hands. She was startled to realise how dirty she was and fought back the urge to hide her hands behind her back. The years of working in the forge had accustomed her to a griminess that she worked hard to keep away, but now she was reminded how long it had been since she had properly washed.

'You are most observant, little one.' Akhgar shifted his position slightly on the cushions and gave her a tired, crinkled smile. 'Fetch me some of those dried fruits, if you would? There is something we must discuss. I have been waiting for your arrival.'

'We got here as soon as we could,' she said, following his pointing finger and gathering up a silver platter laden with dried fruit. She recognised the dates, which she'd encountered in Anfa, but the other fruits were unknown to her. Akhgar urged her to try something and she selected what she learned was a sugared fig.

'I don't speak of waiting for all of you now, though I knew you would come,' said Akhgar, clearly delighted at her response to the delicious sweet treat. 'I mean that I was waiting for *you*, Tagan. You and your gift. You are my... salvation.'

Fear stirred her to wariness and she did not look up to meet his gaze. Instead, she squirmed uncomfortably beneath his piercing stare. He seemed to be studying her intently, scrutinising her in a way that made her skin crawl.

'Stop,' she said, after a few moments. 'What are you doing?'

'I have no desire to frighten you, little one,' he said and the weakness in his voice was gone, replaced by something deep and powerful. 'I have something to share with you, and I am struggling to find the best way to word it... to give you the gift without you being afraid.' He gave another of those crinkly smiles as she looked up, puzzled. 'The four of us are not simply magi. You must have worked that out by now?'

Tagan hesitated, but sighed, nodding. She chewed on her lip for a moment or two. 'I have,' she admitted. 'I think I've suspected it ever since we met Warin. I don't think Mathias has, though.'

'No,' he replied. 'Mathias has a different path to walk from you. It was providence that brought you together; fate that saw you both born to the world at the same time. You are the first child so gifted with fire that I have met since I found Akhgar.'

She looked at him then. *Properly* looked at him. 'You're not just... one person, are you?' She felt a little thrill of fear run down her spine, but it was fear of something momentous and unknown, rather than genuine dread. 'You are... like a demon. That is what Eyja meant when she talked about names.'

'Yes, child,' said the old man. 'You can call me Ignus, but even that is not my true name. There is much I need to say, and if you would hear it, I will tell you. I will give you a choice at the end of it. Both ways will be equally grave.'

Tagan's fear slowly melted away as she listened to Akhgar speak. It was hard to be afraid of the old man lying on the cushions before her. His manner, his voice, everything about him made her comfortable. He reached out to take her hand in his own and looked up at her.

'Will you hear me out?'

'Yes,' she said without hesitation, and he nodded in approval. 'Yes, I will listen.'

Akhgar took a deep breath and began to speak. As his tale unwound, the voice telling it grew gradually stronger and surer. 'This body is dying. Akhgar has carried my presence for many centuries. He has far outlived the years which should have been his, and that was the gift he received for agreeing to be my vessel. Longevity—but not immortality. Akhgar is a proud man. It has brought him joy to see his children, his grandchildren... his descendants grow and prosper. I was fortunate to have found such a soul. The others have not been so lucky. Eyja has known three bodies in her time, Giraldo more. Warin... well, he is different. The form he has taken this time is certainly unusual.'

Tagan listened just as she had promised she would, but when Akhgar paused, she spoke up. Her question was carefully worded; she was dealing with things she simply did not understand.

'How does it work? You said no mortal mind could hold a demon and survive.'

'No mortal mind can bear the *evil* of a demon, but that is a word made by men to label something that they do not understand. Do we seem evil to you? Akhgar willingly accepted me, and I have been bound to him ever since. There have been times in his life that he has asked me to withdraw. When he was with his wives, for example.' The old man chuckled again and then laughed even harder when he saw just how pink Tagan went. 'I have the ability to give him back to himself at any time. As he aged, of course, it became easier for me to continue speaking on his behalf. But he is always there.' Akhgar tapped the side of his head. 'He is always here with me.'

'What happens if he dies?'

Akhgar's smile faded a little at the question. 'If the flesh dies, then I cannot endure in this world. I would be banished back to the Aetherworld,' he replied. 'There I would be hunted by evils that I hope you never have to know. They would seek to destroy me. You must understand by now, Tagan, what it is that I am going to ask of you.'

'Completely,' she said. 'But you told me I have a choice. If one path is to... is to accept you into my head, or my heart, or whatever part of me it is that you would inhabit, what is the other?'

'I will teach you all that you could know of magic,' he replied simply. 'In the blink of an eye, before Akhgar's time is over. Once I am a freed spirit, I cannot remain. I would be gone just as surely as the man before you. I would teach you what I know and hope that it is enough to bolster the work of my siblings in thwarting Melusine's plans.'

Tagan sat in silence for a moment and nibbled absently at another fig. 'It was going to be simple,' she said, in time. 'I was going to marry Mathias, have his children. Live happily. That's how it was supposed to be. It's not going to happen, is it? Whatever I choose, that dream will be forever that. Just a dream. If I accept you into my life, I become a host to something I can never hope to understand. If you teach me what you know, my skills with magic will be needed... elsewhere.' She knew, even as she said so, that that would be the case. The words that Akhgar—or Ignus—spoke were as nothing to the words he did *not* speak.

'You are wise for your age, little one.' Akhgar let out a rasping, painful breath. 'I will not force this choice upon you.'

'No,' she replied. 'No, you will not force the choice upon me, I accept that. But...' Her eyes filled with shimmering tears that pooled for a moment before falling down her face, streaking the grime on her cheeks. The old man's skinny fingers traced the line of the tears and he nodded.

'I know, Tagan,' he said, softly. 'And for what it's worth, you will never be alone.'

She cried for a while, tears of sorrow for the death of an impossibly old man she had known for barely an hour masking the grief she felt at the impending death of her own sense of self. Everything she had believed in, all that she had worked to achieve... everything lay in tatters. Her wedding dress would never be finished.

After the grief was spent, she sat up straighter.

'I have made my choice,' she said.

THE CHILL OF the desert night was forgotten around the homely warmth of the communal fire. People had been gathering there since the sun had sunk below the horizon and the flames licked into the star-studded night. The heady scent of the flowering blossoms on the trees around the oasis filled the air. Someone passed around a bottle containing something that made Mathias's head swim after only two sips. Giraldo, however, was happily swigging from the bottle and holding court with a group of young women who were hanging on the Pirate King's every word.

Warin and Eyja sat quietly together to one side of the fire, talking in low voices. Mathias watched them for a little while. They did not touch, not even the gentle brushing of hands that Eyja seemed so fond of to show support and empathy with others. He could feel the sadness in both of them. They were coping with their friend's failing health in one way whilst Giraldo, now leading a rousing bout of singing with his new-found friends, was handling it another way.

For his own part, he felt as though his innards had turned to ice. It had been in the look Akhgar had given Tagan. Something was happening; something was changing and he was completely powerless to prevent it.

That was the one thing all this had made him realise. Just how little control he had over his own life. Back home in the village, everything was so clear. Back there, he had been one of the educated, one of the lucky. Someone who would rise to a position of authority and leadership. He had welcomed it.

Once, he and Wyn had talked about his dead father. The man put to death by the King for practising magic. The memory of his tears that night had never faded, and neither had his sense of outrage, his desire for revenge. Wyn had taken that anger and tempered it.

'One day,' he said to the young Mathias, a child caught between grief for a mother he had adored and rage for a father he had never known. 'One day, you will recall how you feel right now. When that day comes, lad, you will turn all that anger into a force for good.'

He was at a crossroads in his life. He didn't need Wyn by his side to tell him that. Everything was crowding in on him. It was arrogance to believe that he was the centre of the universe, that everything pivoted on him... but Warin had called him the *waagehenkel*: the Fulcrum. The balance. What, he wondered exactly, was it that he was balancing?

Staring into the flames, Mathias allowed himself to relax. He could hear Wyn's voice in his mind, just as clear as if the old fool had been sat beside him.

Accept what comes, Mathias. You cannot change it, after all.

The fire stretched up into the desert skies, and he followed the track of the smoke as it spiralled away into nothingness. Around him, he could sense the contentment of the people. Such harsh lives they led, but everything was made that much easier by the use of magic. How the rulers of his home had come to such a bleak place beggared belief.

He only became aware that Tagan had left Akhgar's tent when she moved into his line of sight, going first to Eyja and Warin. She knelt behind them and spoke in a low voice. The pair nodded and rose, going to fetch Giraldo, who left his drunken party singing sea shanties happily.

Then she came to him.

'He wanted to say goodbye to them,' she said to Mathis by way of explanation. 'His life is now measured in hours.' Her eyes were heavy with weariness, and she slid onto the ground beside him and ducked into the protective circle of his arm.

That chill within his body became, if possible, even colder. 'Then he isn't coming with us?'

'He can't, Mathias. He is so old. He is dying.' There it was, laid bare. The thing that all of them had avoided discussing—or even mentioning—since they had seen the frail old creature lost amongst the silken cushions. She leaned into his chest and drew a long, slow breath, and he let his fingers run down her hair. Despite their situation, and despite barely understanding anything, he knew that this whole affair had brought them closer together than even marriage might have done.

Such irony, he absently thought, considering how they had begun this journey standing in the heart of a stone circle long used for marriage.

'Don't worry, Mathias,' she said. 'His magic is great. He has taught me all that he knows. I can help the other three when the time comes.'

'But you were barely in there for more than an hour. How can...'

'Didn't you sense his power, Mathias? So strong. He passed on his knowledge to me in a way I can't start to explain. He took my hand in his and I just... *knew.*' She smiled and removed herself from his embrace. 'The knowledge of so many years is mine now. All that there is to know about fire is mine. What I had has become so much more. Watch.'

She reached out a hand towards the fire in the camp's centre and a long plume of flame stretched free and streaked across to her hand. She shaped the flame into a ball of fire that did not quite touch her flesh and tipped her head to one side as though considering what she should do. Then a genuinely sweet smile touched her lips.

'Butterflies?' She whispered the word with the faintest hint of amusement. 'Very well.' She clapped her hands together and a thousand or more fiery butterflies broke forth from between her fingers, fluttering around everyone seated by the fire. They all called out in delight, some of the younger children racing around attempting to catch them. Whenever they succeeded, whenever other hands touched the shapes, they simply faded away into ethereal smoke. Mathias watched, entranced, remembering that day—long ago, now—when she had concentrated so hard to produce a single butterfly to impress him.

'You are wonderful,' he said with disarming honesty. 'Will you marry me?' Of course, he had asked her that years ago. But now, when the words came out of his mouth, he had never wanted anything more.

In response, she gave him a bright smile. Mathias was so captivated that he failed to notice how the smile didn't reach her eyes.

Sixteen

The Sahara Desert
Morocco

The sandstorm blew itself out after a few hours, but it was the loss of the horses that caused the greater delay. The men shook themselves loose of the sand piled atop them and blinked owlishly in the evening sun. They had lost another of their number. Blinded and wounded by the flying grit, he had become mired beneath the shifting dune and subsequently buried alive. All trace of the fleeing magi had vanished, but it did not matter, Weaver knew where they were going. Wrapped in their cloaks to ward off the growing chill, the Lord Inquisitor and his dwindling band of warriors pressed on into the night.

Nothing was going to stop them now.

Dawn at the oasis brought a return of the stifling heat, sucking the moisture out of the air. Mathias had woken before the sun, nestled amidst cushions on the floor of the tent where they had waited before. A thin blanket had been drawn up around his ears—by Tagan, he presumed—and he lowered it sleepily. He and Tagan were the only ones still sleeping. Eyja, Warin and Giraldo were conspicuous by their absence. They had only come back once during the night, and he had been deeply touched by the grief he had seen in their faces.

His thoughts turned immediately to Akhgar. Had the old man died in the night? That would explain their continued absence. He sat up and rubbed at his eyes sleepily before he reached over to gently shake Tagan, discovering that she was already awake.

'I woke ages ago,' she said. 'I just couldn't sleep.'

'Shall we find the others?' He stood up, and despite having slept on the floor, his body was free of the customary gripes and pains he'd suffered on their journey so far. The discovery was pleasing. He felt stronger for it.

She climbed to her feet and nodded, reaching up to tie her hair back. It had grown longer and far more unruly over the weeks of their journey and it suited her. It made her features softer, more feminine. Instinctively, he reached across and stroked a stray strand back from her face, and she turned away from him a little.

'Don't,' she said, quietly and he dropped his hand, perplexed. She shook her head. 'I'm sorry,' she added. 'I just didn't sleep that well. I am a little out of sorts this morning. Yes. Let's find the others.' As if to make up for her reaction to his touch, she slipped her warm hand into his as they stepped out into the morning.

It was as though the night had never happened. Activity around the oasis had clearly resumed some time ago and people moved around with the comfortable ease of routine. Mathias wondered for a moment why it was that the camp seemed smaller, until he saw one of the gaudy pavilions collapse. People were packing up their tents.

'Where are they going?' He asked the question aloud and Tagan shook her head.

'I don't know,' she replied. 'But I am sure we will find out. Come on.'

She tugged at his hand gently and pulled him towards Akhgar's tent. The tribesman still remained at his post, and lowered his eyes respectfully as the two young people approached.

'You are just in time,' he said in his thickly accented voice. 'The Wanderer's time draws near. Soon he will sleep.' He sounded saddened.

'Thank you,' said Mathias. 'You are sure we are..?'

He left the question hanging and the tribesman flashed him a faintly indulgent smile. 'Truth tell, my friend, I think the Wanderer has been waiting for you, yes? In you go.'

They returned his smile, not quite so brightly, and ducked into the tent. The mood and the atmosphere were very different from the reunion that had taken place there the previous night. There was a sadness that permeated the air, and a sense of solemnity. Eyja immediately moved to Tagan and smiled.

'He has been asking for you since he woke,' she said softly and the young woman nodded.

'Yes,' she said, gazing over at Akhgar. The old man's breathing was shallow, his lungs rattling in a way that suggested every rise of his chest might be the very last. 'I will go to him now.' She squeezed Mathias's hand gently and crossed to the dying elder. Eyja studied Mathias's face momentarily as though looking for some sort of reaction. Seeing none, she relaxed a little.

'All will be well, Mathias Eynon,' she said. 'I have seen a world where your strength and spirit reforge that which was broken. Your purity of spirit, your love and your sense of duty will lead you to great things.'

She Who Sees. For the first time, Mathias understood the name by which she was known. 'You really are a seeress,' he said. It was a statement of fact, not a question. 'Wyn once told me of the power of the seers. He also told me that people fear them.'

'People fear the truth, Mathias. They live their lives in denial. When someone learns a great truth it is a cause for change, and change can be painful.' She suddenly put her arms around him and drew him into an embrace. 'Remember that, during the times ahead. Sometimes the truth is hidden by those who would spare their loved ones pain.'

He did not understand her words, and yet he felt the weight of them. He glanced over to the dying Akhgar. Tagan knelt at his side, his hand in hers. She stroked his brow and held a cup of water to his parched lips. He spoke in a quiet voice that Mathias could not hear. After a moment or two, she looked up and beckoned him across.

'He wants to talk to you,' she said quietly. 'Come over here.'

Feeling decidedly uncomfortable, but filled with compassion of his own, Mathias obeyed, kneeling beside Tagan. He had barely spoken with the old man the previous day, content to let the magi tell their tale and have their reunion, but now it seemed that there was some final wisdom he wished to impart. As he looked down into the fading light of the old man's eyes, Akhgar smiled up at him.

'The Fulcrum,' he said. 'The balance on which events turn. Do you understand this name, Mathias Eynon?' The words wheezed, every syllable taxing the poor, wizened creature.

'No, sir, I don't,' he admitted. 'I understand very little of what is going on, to be honest. All I have come to learn is that... people are depending on me for some reason. Wyn depended on me. Tagan depends on me.' She smiled at him. 'I take my responsibilities seriously. This must be what Wyn saw in me.'

'Your aura is golden,' said Akhgar. 'A protector's light. Do not let it dwindle and die out. You must look after Tagan. Will you do that for me, Mathias Eynon?'

It could be mistaken for the dying ramblings of an old man, but Mathias knew that Akhgar was something more. He gave what he hoped was a reassuring smile. 'I have taken care of her since we were children. I see no reason for that to change.'

'Good. Then there is one less thing for me to die worrying about.' He leaned back and closed his eyes, that same little half-smile on his face. 'This has been a good life. A long life. A hard life, yes. But a life that has granted more reward than I could have hoped for. My children, and their children, and *their* children beyond them live on. Akhgar ibn Atash's name will not be lost.' He let out a deeply contented sigh and the hand closed around Tagan's briefly tightened.

He did not draw another breath.

IT WAS STRANGE to grieve for a man he had hardly known, but Akhgar's death touched Mathias nonetheless. He retired to a quiet part of the oasis—difficult, with so much going on around him—and he let the tears come. He wept for all he had lost in his young life. For the death of a father he had never known, the loss of a mother who had never really recovered and the horrific loss of the man he had come to love as a parent. So much lost.

But he had also gained. Tagan, a woman he loved beyond life itself. He had made new friends who had never treated him as anything but an equal despite the fact that he knew he was anything but. He had travelled, and he had seen things he could never have imagined.

In the strangest way, the death of Akhgar ibn Atash freed Mathias from the chains of his past. He felt the strangest sense of liberation, gradually severing the last ties to a childhood that had been spent never quite understanding where he belonged in the world. Akhgar's simple words had given him a sense of responsibility unlike anything he knew. In another man, the feeling might have been crushing. In Mathias Eynon, it lifted him to new heights.

After Akhgar's death, Tagan remained in the tent for a little longer, helping Eyja arrange the old man's body for the funeral rites that the other three said they would perform. She seemed calm and composed, carrying herself with quiet pride. When she emerged, her eyes sought out Mathias and both women came to join him by the pool. Tagan seemed subdued.

'It is the winter solstice today,' Eyja said by way of greeting.

Mathias was startled by this. 'I hadn't realised how much time had passed. When we left Wales, it was late summer. So far away.' Not for the first time, he felt a pang of terrible homesickness. The stark beauty of the desert was undeniable, but Mathias yearned for the greenery of his childhood.

Eyja sat down on one side of him and Tagan on the other. 'You will have noticed that some of Akhgar's people are leaving the oasis for a while,' she said, as they watched them strike their tents. 'They came to celebrate his passing, and now that he is gone, they have no reason to remain here. They will return to their hard lives out in the desert.'

Mathias didn't question it. He nodded. 'To celebrate the life of a man as long-lived as Akhgar,' he said softly, 'is a wonderful thing. It still seems incredible, that his magic could sustain him so long. But aren't they going to stay for his funeral?'

'No,' said Eyja. 'Only his closest family, those born of his bloodline, will remain for the cremation.' She smiled. 'Born in fire, ended in fire. It is a most beautiful and fitting end for a most remarkable man.' She looked out across the water and let out the smallest of sighs. The sound was not unlike the whispering of the wind in the trees, and it brought memories of home even more sharply to Mathias's thoughts. 'When the funeral is done, we must make ready to return to England.' She gazed up at the sky and her expression grew serious. 'It must be done before the day is ended, or we will be too late and Melusine will have exactly what she wants.'

THEY WERE CLOSE, he could feel it. Weaver and his men had marched through the night, and with the return of the sun had come the scent of magic on the wind. Anfa had been difficult enough; its blatant use of the arcane had made his flesh crawl with contempt. Magic was a disease that needed to be burned out. Only the urgency of his mission had prevented him from putting the town to the torch for its crimes.

He had weathered the sandstorm better than his men, who were down to their last dregs of water, but his fine clothes and armour were now made tattered and ragged by his journey. Only his mask and his will to succeed remained unblemished.

The same could not be said of the men trailing behind him. They were hurt and exhausted, their skin burned by the sun and scalding sand. Only the invincible drive of the Inquisitor kept them moving, pulled along in his wake like a line of pilgrims swaddled in rags, bound for the tomb of a saint.

The sun was high in the sky and had already begun its descent when a pillar of fire blossomed into the cloudless expanse. Birds, serpents and less recognisable shapes twisted and cavorted in the flames. Its source could not be more than a few leagues distant.

'We are close,' he murmured. 'The magi reveal themselves, and will be brought to judgment for their crimes.'

His words put a little steel back into the listless men and they picked up the pace.

'I BRING THE gift of water. Water nurtures us before birth, sustains us in life and cleanses our bodies in death.'

Giraldo's was the first voice to speak, breaking through the stillness of the morning. He knelt before the body of Akhgar, now laid upon the ground beneath the shade of a palm. In his hands, Giraldo held cupped water from the clear pool. Not a drop leaked between the gaps in his fingers. He raised his hands high and let the water trickle on the length of the body. 'May your spirit run with the tides.' He lowered his head respectfully and stepped back. Warin, his red beard combed neatly for once, took his place.

'I bring the gift of earth,' he said and there was a catch in his voice. Akhgar's death had touched Warin far more than Mathias could ever have imagined. 'I bring the gift of earth,' he repeated, in a stronger voice. 'From earth we are born and to the earth we return.' He knelt by Akhgar's body and scooped up a handful of sand, and laid his palm out flat. 'May your return to earth bring you the peace you have earned, my brother.' He let the sand trickle, just as Giraldo's water had done. Then he rose to his feet, choked back a sob and allowed Eyja to step forward.

'I bring the gift of air,' she said in her melodious voice. 'Air is all around us. Our first breath is the world's gift to us when we are born and the world takes our final breath in payment at the end of our days. In sharing every living breath with the world, we become a part of it. In this way, what we are lives on beyond death.'

As she spoke, the faintest of breezes rustled the leaves above them and she too knelt before Akhgar, leaning down to place a gentle kiss on his cold dead cheek. 'You were the best of us,' she said. 'And you were the wisest, my dear Akhgar. You will not be forgotten.'

She rose to her feet and turned to Tagan, who was wearing the beautiful red silk from the market in Anfa around her head and face. All that was visible of her were her eyes, bright with unshed tears as she stepped forward to do what had been asked of her by the man lying on the ground.

'I bring the gift of fire,' she said, her voice trembling on every syllable. 'In fire our spirits are forged and in fire our mortal bodies are consumed.' She reached up a shaking hand and brushed away tears. Eyja laid a hand gently on her shoulder, and Tagan took a deep breath before she knelt down beside Akhgar. The next words she spoke came in a much stronger voice.

'My gift is your gift.' She reached for the dead man's hand and closed her fingers around it. 'In fire we are bonded, and in fire your memory will burn on.' Mathias watched her, not truly understanding the ritual, but caught up in the solemnity of it all. Even as he watched his betrothed, she drew forth a single flame from nowhere and held it in the palm of her hand—much as Warin had held the sand and Giraldo the water. She tipped up her hand and the single flame slid onto the body. It caught light on the cloth in which Akhgar had been wrapped and Tagan stepped away, closing her eyes and willing it to burn stronger and brighter.

Within moments, the body of the Wanderer was engulfed in a magical flame that burned with more intensity than anything Mathias had ever seen before. It consumed the body, the blinding flames shrouding the sight. There was no pungent stench of roasting flesh, only a faint hint of slightly acrid smoke that tickled at Mathias's nostrils. The heat was incredible, and yet it did not burn or even singe him, despite his proximity.

Tagan remained where she was, focusing her efforts onto the cremation fire and winding the flames into ever-more exotic shapes and patterns that Mathias could never hope to name. Time passed; he had no idea how long. The shadows cast by the sun had moved, but it was impossible to gauge with any accuracy. Tagan finally drew a long, shuddering breath and opened her eyes.

'It is done,' she said and her knees buckled slightly. Mathias was there in a heartbeat to steady her, his arm around her, and she smiled gratefully and more than a little sadly at him. 'I'm afraid that was just the beginning, my Mathias,' she said in a voice he did not recognise. There was something so venerable in her tone, in the sad way that she looked at him. He drew her in protectively and kissed the top of her hair. She smelled, as she ever had, of flowers and freshness. But the scent of smoke was stronger than it had once been. Her display of magic had, truth be told, frightened him a little. Her power was now something beyond him, and deep down he felt a genuine fear that he was going to lose her.

'You did well, Tagan,' said Eyja. She, Giraldo and Warin moved to stand with her. 'The time has come.' She smiled at Mathias and the expression mirrored Tagan's perfectly: that same slightly sad look. 'It is time for you to go home. It is time for us to come with you.' Her expression was hard steel, a far cry from the usual benign smile. 'The time has come to put an end to the evil that blights the line of kings.'

CHARLES WEAVER AND his beleaguered knights struggled up the bank of the final dune and stared down the other side. The wind tugged streamers of grit from the surrounding dune crests to collect in the broad, dry depression, which was empty and entirely devoid of life. Sir Anthony sagged, certain that the elusive magi had once again managed to slip from their grasp and strand them in the desert.

Weaver, however, saw none of this. He looked down on an oasis.

A sprawl of tents sat around a bright, clean pool fringed with leafy trees and people thronged the canvas avenues, carefully collapsing their bright pavilions in preparation for travel. A thin ribbon of smoke curled from somewhere near the heart of the camp, the last residue of the fire they'd seen. The whole scene rippled with a peculiar haze, as if it were being witnessed through poorly made glass. The Lord Inquisitor felt the familiar prickle of magic and turned to the despondent knights.

'We are upon them,' he stated simply. 'Do not let your eyes be deceived by arcane treachery. We have run them to ground and will deliver the King's justice.'

Despite their doubts—and their private opinions of the Inquisitor's sanity—the knights drew their weapons and advanced down the dune.

HOME.

Back to England, then perhaps to Wales. The thought filled Mathias with a joy that he could not put into words. He had travelled so far in the past months. He had come such a long way from the hills and hollows of his childhood. Here he was, amidst the burning sands of a foreign desert, surrounded by some of the most powerful people he was ever likely to meet. He was fortunate—or cursed, depending upon your point of view—to have experienced so much in so short a time. He had grown.

Home.

The word sent such a thrill of happiness through him that for a moment he was able to forget the gravity of their situation—one he still did not fully understand. All he knew for certain was that soon the journey would be over.

Home.

'How will we get there?' His question was a simple one: childish in many ways, he knew, and he suspected he knew the answer. It was confirmed with Warin's reply.

'A sending, much as Wyn did to bring you to me. There are enough of us now that it will be a simple matter. With the three of us...'

'Four,' murmured Tagan. 'I can do so much more than I once could.'

'I am corrected. With the four of us and the power of this circle, we will be able to transport to the great circle in England in the blink of an eye.'

'The great circle?'

'Stonehenge.'

Mathias nodded. He knew. Somehow, he had always known. 'But how far will we have to travel to reach the nearest circle? You said yourself that we are running out of time...' He looked at Eyja and stopped speaking. 'What? Why are you laughing at me?'

'I am not laughing at you, dear one. The answer to your question is simple. We will need to travel...'—she took three paces until she stood at the edge of the oasis pool—'about this far.'

'The water?'

'The whole oasis. The pool is merely the arcane centre and the strongest focus. We will perform the sending from here, just as soon as we are prepared'—the Seer exchanged glances with the others—'and as soon as some things are made clear.' She lowered her eyes, unable to look at him, but he reached over and touched her arm.

'Eyja,' Mathias said softly. 'I understand enough. A demon means to sit upon the throne of England and use that power to drive all magic from the world. The same demon has twisted the line of kings and seen the rise of the Inquisition. It needs to be stopped.'

She looked up at him and cupped his chin in her hand. 'You are a fine man, Mathias Eynon,' she said. 'Whatever comes next, I want you to know that.'

Her words made Mathias a little uncomfortable, so he shrugged and gave her a slightly embarrassed smile. 'You said something needed to be made clear,' he said and there was a forceful manner to his tone that startled even him. 'So what else do I need to know?'

Whilst around them the tribe continued striking camp, Mathias and the magi sat together beneath the shade of a palm. Mathias looked at them, so contrasting, so familiar and yet all still so strange to his eyes.

'As I understand it,' he began, 'we're going to interfere in Melusine's plan to take Prince Richard as her own.' He paused, then gave a weak smile. 'Actually, that's about as much as I know.' He looked to Eyja. With the death of Akhgar, she seemed to have become the leader of the group, a position that had moved seamlessly and without question from the others. She straightened the skirt of her gown primly before she began her explanation.

'If left unaided, Richard will be unable to resist the lure of Melusine. She will take his body and walk the land of men with her power unbound.'

'How powerful is she, exactly?' Mathias asked, remembering the alluring and terrifyingly awful presence that Wyn had shown him in his illusion.

Eyja closed her eyes as though speaking the reply somehow pained her. Somewhere at the back of the camp, a voice was raised briefly in a shout. Giraldo glanced over and his brow furrowed. 'Speak fast,' he said. 'I think our time is running out.'

'She is mightier than any one of us,' she said. 'An insidious force that can turn, break or corrupt this world and recast it in an image of Hell worse than any described in the texts of the Church.'

Laid so bold and bare it was horrific. Somehow, Mathias had

always known that the truth that Wyn had spoken of would be hard to bear. Something so terrible that it could not be named. He felt the weight of responsibility press down on him and he felt the eyes of the three magi on him, trying to gauge his reaction to the news. He looked around the small group, his eyes resting last of all on Tagan. She looked back at him, implacable, expressionless. Hopeless, even. As though she had given up.

I am losing you and I don't know why, he thought. He tried to put all his love and desire into a single look and thought he achieved the faintest of smiles. He nodded at Eyja.

'Then how can we defeat her?' he asked, though he was not at all sure that he wanted to hear any more answers.

'She is greater than any one of us,' Eyja repeated, 'and she cannot be slain in this world, not in a way you can understand. But we do not need to slay her. Together we only need to keep her from taking the prince. Even if...' She paused, and a note of regret entered her voice. 'Even if it means we have to kill him.'

Mathias nodded, but his expression was fierce. 'We should try to save him,' he said emphatically. 'None of this is his fault. It is not even King Richard's fault, from what you have told me.'

'You have a noble heart, young Mathias,' Eyja said. 'It shall be as you say. There is, however, one other thing you must know.'

It felt like any further revelation might be one too many, but Mathias continued to listen.

'When we arrive, the veil between the worlds will be at its thinnest,' continued Eyja. 'It is possible that other things may be drawn to the circle by the lure of the prince. Be wary of anything you see. Guard your mind.'

The shouts on the edges of the oasis grew louder, accompanied by screams. Giraldo was first to his feet, his sword drawn. 'They're playing my song,' he said, with a wicked grin on his face. 'I believe the King's hounds have found us.'

'*Your* song?' Warin also got to his feet. 'I still have a matter to settle with that man.' With a whisper of magic, the form of the wolf was once more there before them, hackles raised and teeth bared. Warin turned his muzzle towards Mathias and bowed his great head.

The instruction was quite clear, and with an elation that he wasn't entirely sure was appropriate, Mathias also shifted into wolf form.

'Tagan, come with me.' Eyja moved to stand beside the girl. 'You and I must begin the spell of sending. We will have very little time to complete the rite. Follow my lead. You have been through a sending before, but this will be more powerful. There will be no gentle passage of time. This will be *instant*.'

'Like the way Giraldo transported us to his ship?'

'Much like that,' Eyja replied. 'Only with greater control.' Giraldo grinned at her. 'Simply do as I do and follow the words of the chant. The earth will answer, it knows the way.'

Eyja looked over to the far end of the camp, where the screams had become shouts of defiant fury. The orange light of fire blossomed as the first tent was put to the torch. Eyja's beautiful face grew grim. She waited no further, and with her hand in Tagan's, led the young woman into the water of the pool. It was not deep, coming barely to their waists.

'We must hurry.'

Salisbury Plain
England

THE *LIONHEART* HAD not been designed with the comfort of its passengers in mind. It was a weapon of war, not a carriage for nobility. As a consequence, the King and his son were feeling uncomfortable and cramped by the time the vehicle had reached the expanse of Wiltshire.

For Prince Richard, what had begun as something of an adventure had rapidly become a nightmare as he had discovered motion sickness. He elected to abandon the claustrophobic belly of the *Lionheart* and ride outside with the guards, leaving King Richard alone on the velvet-cushioned seat. Left alone with his thoughts, Richard fell to brooding. The entourage was making excellent progress and the navigator was certain that they would reach the henge within the hour, shortly before sunset.

For the first time in his life, he felt utterly helpless. Events had spiralled beyond his control, and he could see no way in which he could save both his son and his country. A knot of bilious hatred for Richard the Third formed in the King's belly, but it quickly faded. If Tudor had won at Bosworth, what would the world have become? A nation of weaklings, reliant on magic and subservient to a church that beguiled them with mysticism.

How would history remember him, he wondered? Would he go into the books as a king whose rule saw the extermination of magic in his own country and across Europe? Would they remember him as the man who finally conquered the combined might of France and Rome? Would he simply be forgotten in the tidal rush of adoration that must surely go to his son, when all that Melusine promised for him came to pass?

Would his son even be the boy he knew? The demon was bound as surely as he by the pact that had been made, but what exactly had been the terms?

So many questions. Questions that the King could never hope to answer, even with the best of intentions. Instead, he closed his eyes and drew a shuddering breath as the *Lionheart* rattled on toward the shadowy horizon.

The Sahara Desert
Morocco

WEAVER'S MEN WERE hopelessly outnumbered by the press of warriors surging to protect the collapsing camp. The Lord Inquisitor had commended the knights for their courage in service to the Crown. Then he had given them all but a few of his remaining phials of alchemical fire and departed.

The knights put the phials to good use, hurling them into the forest of canvas as soon as they breached the illusion that surrounded it. Sir Anthony led the charge, his once noble visage reduced to that of a hollow-eyed wild man. He side-stepped the first spear thrust that came his way, cut the tribesman down and pushed deeper into the burning camp. Surprise, confusion and the impetus of the charge carried him further than he expected.

He cut down another warrior rushing past on his way to confront another of the knights, and then circled a burning pavilion as he descended toward the pool. He could see two figures standing in the clear water with their arms raised, a gentle glow spreading beneath them.

He heard a scream to his left, and turned to see Sir Martin fall with a spear in his chest. The knight fought on weakly, thrashing on the ground until two more blades pierced his body and he lay still. Something finally withered and died inside Sir Anthony at the sight, and a killing rage rose up in him, sweeping away his pain and the fatigue of the long journey.

He charged between the burning tents, cutting down any who stood in his way, his sword running red with the blood of the slaughter. He thought he saw one of his fellows between the press of bodies, the man surrounded and fighting for his life, but then he was lost from view.

The shrill cry of a child grabbed his attention and he saw a young boy standing beside the fallen body of his father. The distraction was enough that he did not see the great, red wolf until it landed on top of him and crushed him to the ground. The beast growled and glared down at him with feral rage, but there was an unsettling intelligence in its eyes. Sir Anthony rolled and hurled the animal away before it could strike, its jaws snapping mere inches from his neck.

He did not know if red wolves were natives of the desert, but there was something unnatural about the creature. He raised his sword in front of him as the animal circled him.

The second wolf came from behind him, not nearly as large or as strong, but powerful and quick enough to knock him off balance. He stumbled, and sharp jaws fastened around his arm. Sir Anthony cried out in agony as the beast tore at his flesh, but before he could stab the animal it released him and circled away again.

Blood dripped from his wounded arm and the knight turned slowly, keeping the wavering point of his sword before him. He could still hear the sounds of battle and could faintly make out a lilting, jovial voice among the shouts of the desert folk.

The wolves circled him. One huge and red, the other sleek and dark. Both carried themselves with more certainty than animals had any right to.

'Abominations,' he hissed.

The red wolf blinked, and in a moment became a massive bear. It could only be the shapeshifter who had killed his fellow knights on the shores of the lake. The great, red-furred beast reared back on its hind legs and roared, the sound drowning out the din of battle and the screams of the dying.

Sir Anthony's last thought was of home. Then the bear fell upon him like a living mountain.

Warin and Mathias shifted back into their natural bodies and looked down at the fallen knight. He was thin and ragged, his eyes sunken and his skin burned and raw. Whatever noble bearing he had possessed when he began his journey had been lost upon the way. Now he was just a man. Warin leaned down and closed the dead eyes.

'He did not deserve to die,' the Shapeshifter said sadly. 'Not really. He was only a pawn. But all will be like him if the demon has her way.'

'There is no time to lose,' called Eyja from the centre of the oasis pool. The water was rippling out in concentric circles from where she and Tagan stood, and she held a hand over the surface. 'Giraldo, Warin, come quickly. Mathias, you too!'

Warin and Mathias ran to the water's edge, closely followed by Giraldo who emerged from between the tents. They plunged into the oasis and Giraldo and Warin immediately mimicked Eyja's stance, their hands out before them, palms down. The ripples came larger and faster until the whole pool was a churning, frothing mass that climbed up around the people standing inside its embrace.

'Mathias, Tagan, hold onto each other.'

They already were. The moment he had moved into the waters, they had clasped hands, in equal parts exhilarated and terrified by what lay ahead. As they stood together, the water rose higher and higher. To their hips. Their waists. Their chests.

The sounds of the burning camp, the wails of the dying were

fading: as though they were falling away. Mathias could feel Tagan's hand still clasped in his and he knew, somehow, that everything would be all right. They were still together and they could weather any storm.

Just before the moment of darkness came, the very moment when they stopped being in one place and reappeared somewhere else, he felt something that filled him with absolute dread: fingers closing around his tunic.

Seventeen

21st December, 1589
Stonehenge
England

By three in the afternoon, the sun was already beginning its slow descent in the west. It had been a mild day for the time of year, but now that night was coming, there was ice in the air. It told in the spill of blood across the skies of southwestern England: in the crimson hues that tinted the edges of the few clouds scudding gently above in the clear sky. With nightfall would come a sharp, biting frost and a starry night.

The ancient site of Stonehenge was enough to take the breath away. Even those not gifted with magic found it awe-inspiring. Prince Richard, riding on the outside of the *Lionheart* with the men of the Royal Guard, drank in the sight before him. He waited eagerly for his father to disembark from the vehicle.

The final few miles of the ride had been particularly unpleasant for King Richard. The *Lionheart* had juddered uncomfortably across tracts of farmland, uneven and nauseating. He had voided the contents of his stomach three times and the inside compartment of the war vehicle stank of vomit. He was glad beyond words to escape its confines as he stepped down to greet his son climbing down from the guards' bench.

Again came that terrible despair. How hard would it be to just tell his son the truth? Melusine had told King Richard on countless occasions that he was the man upon whose shoulders the future of the English throne rested. In his arrogance, he had always taken this to mean the war with France. But now he feared exactly what it was that the demon wanted with his son, and what it might mean for the future of the throne.

'Father?' Prince Richard had been jabbering away to his father as they walked the perimeter of the circle.

'I'm sorry, my boy. I was... thinking.'

Something about the place made both of them reluctant to walk between the stones, to enter the circle within. Perhaps it was the strong sense of the arcane that emanated from the stones themselves. King Richard could not help but be moved by the sheer beauty of the monument, captured by the dying rays of the winter sun. The very stones appeared alive with an inner, fey light that no stone should possess.

Cautiously, he reached out a hand to touch one of the nearest menhirs, fully expecting a warmth to reflect the amber glow coming from it. But his hand touched nothing but cool, unyielding stone. Implacable and solid. Just like his reign over England had been. The analogy entertained him for a few moments until he remembered watching the men working the quarries. Stone could be broken. It could be hacked and shaped and made into something new, something entirely different.

King Richard snatched his hand back, a wild, discordant ringing of fears sounding in his mind, and the reality of his situation became more and more stark with each passing minute.

'It's quite remarkable,' observed Prince Richard. Not for him his father's doubt and hesitation. 'They say that this site is as old as England itself. Why is it, Father, that when you have sought to oust the use of magic in this country, you allow this place to stand?'

Why indeed? It had never seemed necessary, when the magi themselves were hunted by the Inquisition. For a while the circles acted as a lure, bringing practitioners of the arcane from the lands around, and the Inquisition had waited in ambush at the solstices to round them up. The site beyond the borders of Wales had been the first to be destroyed, but when Richard had realised that they *could* be destroyed he had briefly entertained the thought of pulling down the henge as a way of defying the demon.

Melusine had, quite forcefully, advised otherwise.

'There was never the need. They were useful hunting grounds for the Inquisition,' he said, eventually. It was close enough to the truth to be acceptable. 'This site is heavily steeped in magic, but it is kept under watch at all times. No practitioner has been allowed to set foot inside the circle proper since the time of King Richard the Third. No practitioner, but... well. This is a part of your introduction to what it means to be king, my boy.'

'What do you mean? I thought we were here because of some magi?' Prince Richard turned his head slightly, studying his father. He had not missed the melancholic tone.

'When I was a boy, my own father brought me here.' The lie came smoothly. 'Together, we walked its perimeter. Alone, I stood inside. I felt the true evil of magic. It... it helped me to understand why it is that the so-called "gift" is an insidious, terrible thing that must be cast out. You are here today to experience that for yourself.'

As the sun gradually began its final descent, sinking into the western horizon until only a sliver of daylight remained, King Richard the Fifth, the Unyielding, the man known to his subjects in whispered tones as the Demon King, raised a hand. Around the perimeter of the circle, the guardsmen began to light candles. His breath was visible in front of his face as he spoke to his son.

'You are of age, Richard,' he said. 'Tonight, you will become a man.'

Tonight, came a slithering female voice at the very back of his awareness, *he becomes* mine.

HE IS FALLING.

No, not falling. Moving forwards. Backwards. Sideways. Every conceivable direction and several he has no name for. He is everywhere at once, and he is nowhere. He has ceased to exist in a way he understands. Mathias is a simple man; he could not have envisaged a world beyond his own. He glimpses wide open spaces so vast as to defy comprehension, colossal trees and oceans of stars. He slips between the world of men and the hazy shades of the Aetherworld.

He feels as though the very world around him has been pinched tightly together. Turned inside out. He is suddenly acutely aware of the utter insignificance of his being. How could he not be aware of such a thing in the face of the overwhelming power of the three magi... and Tagan... who have brought him to this place of alien beauty?

He can still feel an unwelcome presence nearby, riding close to his own. He tries to shake free, but the grip is like a vice. Resigning himself to it, and to the problem it will very shortly pose, Mathias lets the spell embrace him and carry him onwards.

'STEP INTO THE circle.'

King Richard shook off the creeping horror of the whispers in his thoughts and smiled in what he sincerely hoped was an encouraging and winning manner at his son. 'Don't be afraid. You need to feel the taint of magic's power so that you may fully understand why we must do... what we must do.'

'Father, I...' Prince Richard's handsome young face was a knot of conflicting emotions. The last sliver of daylight marked the skies above the ancient ritual site. In a few short minutes, the moment would be nigh. Sunset on the shortest day. An hour and moment ordained by a man long dead.

With a fierce, sudden passion, Richard Plantagenet loathed his ancestor. Had the snivelling coward given any real thought to what he was doing when he had succumbed to Melusine's wiles all those years before? Had he even *cared* that one hundred and more years later, a father was being forced to part with a much-loved son for the sake of the throne of a country that they might no longer control? Richard doubted it very much. Richard the Third's only interest had been in glory. He had been victorious at Bosworth. The Plantagenets had won the throne, but they had bartered away their freedom. He could waste no further time. He took the prince by the arm and pushed him forward until his feet were inside the circle.

The last of the light fell beneath the horizon. The stones around the circle, the vast and silent monoliths that had been there since the land was young, gave off that same faint amber glow, but this time, there *was* something else. At the far end of the henge, opposite the confused Prince Richard, a figure shimmered into being.

There came a low thrumming sound, an insistent buzz, as though the night had suddenly filled with noisy insects. The King put a hand to the closest stone and this time it *was* warm to the touch. It vibrated with powerful, ancient magic that would not be denied. He felt his heart begin to pound; heard its incessant beat in his ears, a counterpoint to the pulse of magic that throbbed deep in the earth beneath his feet.

The hazy, indistinct figure began to take on a frighteningly familiar shape. Unquestionably female, it took three sure strides toward the prince. Prince Richard, his eyes locked on the shape, took three decidedly faltering steps of his own. His eyes took on a faraway look as a will much greater than his own seized hold of him.

There was a crack in the song of the stones, a discordant note like tearing fabric. The air within the circle shivered in anticipation and King Richard's heart stopped for a moment or two. When it began again, it pounded in a staccato rhythm of fear and hope.

Not now.

His thoughts were wild. Perhaps the demon had been wrong? Perhaps his son was not the one she had been waiting for? He stared in abject disbelief as reality bent in the most peculiar way within the circle, and six figures were disgorged to join the ethereal form of Melusine and the mesmerised prince.

THE FALLING STOPPED as abruptly as it had started, and Mathias staggered forwards, dropping to his knees as his feet hit solid ground. The hand clutching the back of his neck released him as Charles Weaver, the Lord Inquisitor, also tumbled to the ground. His four friends, Mathias could see as he raised his head, scrambling to his feet, had not fallen. They landed lightly, with dark, ominous expressions.

The contrast between the heat of the desert and the winter chill of England made Mathias gasp, and he sucked in a deep breath, grateful for the cool, sharp air of his homeland. He tried to orientate himself, muddled by the effects of the spell. The towering slabs of Stonehenge were completely unmistakable and it was dusk. The sun had not long gone down and the sky was a deep, rich blue, speckled with the first suggestion of stars. But darkness would come soon; literally, from what he had come to understand.

The figure of Melusine took on a more solid form as she continued to walk towards the now utterly captivated Prince Richard, but now her way was blocked by the new arrivals. The ragged form of the Lord Inquisitor staggered to his feet and went for one of his guns, still intent on bringing justice to the magi. Without thinking, Mathias threw himself bodily at the man.

The Royal Guard looked uncertainly from the scene unfolding within the henge to the King, who was backing away toward the hulking sides of the *Lionheart*. Richard had no idea what was happening, but the serpentine hiss that issued from the circle as Melusine was denied her prize filled him with dread. The circle was a door, but she was empowered by blood; and right now, there was none to be had.

Mathias swatted Weaver's hand away from the gun at his belt, but the Lord Inquisitor was quicker by far. His other hand smoothly plucked a knife from beneath his cloak. The blade licked out and Mathias twisted away, but not before the razor edge nicked him. It slashed through the fabric of his shirt, piercing the skin beneath, and spattered crimson drops across the dry floor of the henge.

Richard cringed and fled back to the cannonade. The blood soaked into the ground and, feeding from the gift, Melusine took solid form.

The world held its breath.

MATHIAS'S FOCUS WAS very much on dealing with the wild attacks of the Inquisitor. Until recently, he had never even *seen* an Inquisitor; now, it seemed, he could not be rid of them. Even masked and with his attire tattered and worn he still recognised the man from the lake. It was the same man who had killed Wyn, and of the same Order who had put his father to death. He jumped back as the masked Inquisitor slashed for him again, the blade passing within an inch of his face. He wondered, wildly, why it was that none of his companions was helping him. From the corner of his eye he could see the four of them standing very close together, heads bowed so that they were all but touching each other and a fey light building around them. Tagan did not even seem to notice his struggle.

It was like walking through a nightmare. The distraction nearly killed him. The Inquisitor lunged and it was only Giraldo's lessons that saved him. Mathias twisted and the dagger slid past his chest, opening another wound. He grabbed the bigger man's arm before he could withdraw and hauled with every ounce of strength he could muster. Weaver let go of the knife, which tumbled to the ground. The Inquisitor rolled smoothly and came up with another short blade between his fingers, which he flipped at Mathias with a flick of his wrist.

Mathias threw up his hands, willing the blade away, and the expected pain of the weapon never came. The throwing knife bounced harmlessly from the craggy stone that suddenly sheathed his arms. Mathias stared in wonder at the sudden manifestation of his magic and turned to confront the Inquisitor once again. The brute was already moving, sword in hand, and Mathias once again had to defend himself, fending off a flurry of blows with his stony arms. On the third strike he was able to turn and deliver a clumsy punch directly into the man's masked face.

The Inquisitor rocked back under the blow and staggered. Mathias was shocked by his own success and failed to follow up on his assault. The masked man cast his gaze around the circle and it fell upon the Royal Guard, who were caught between the desire to flee and their duty to their King.

'Open fire!' Weaver roared. 'Kill them all!'

Obedience was immediate.

The air filled with the bark of gunfire and the gathering gloom lit up with muzzle flashes. The shots passed around the magi and seemed not to touch the demon at all. The air around her was filled with a shimmering haze, as if it were repulsed by her presence. She could no longer reach the prince, but she beckoned to him, and he staggered toward her once again. A stray shot from one of the Royal Guard clipped the young man's thigh, but he did not notice.

Weaver snarled in rage and snatched one of the remaining phials he wore at his waist. He flung it between the prince and the demon with a bellow of fury. A gout of alchemical fire halted the prince in his tracks, the demon obviously unwilling to risk her prize, and Melusine hissed again before she retreated from the flames. Evidently, the alchemical fire was a threat to her.

The air was still filled with gunshots and the bright flash of weapons discharge, but they paled into insignificance beside the roar of the *Lionheart* as one of her fore cannons spat flame. Fire belched in a spreading cloud toward the demon and the magi. Mathias felt the tremendous wash of heat roll over him, singeing the hairs on the back of his arm. He ducked and rolled just as Tagan turned from the group. With a simple wave she turned the flames aside and the cannon guttered and died.

Mathias looked to the woman he loved and did not recognise her. A corona of yellow and orange light was boiling off her and her eyes had become smouldering pits, bright with power.

There was a clank from the *Lionheart* as a different cannon was engaged and a deafening boom thundered from its maw. The cannonball sped across the circle directly at the demon. Melusine snapped her fingers with apparent disdain and the projectile shattered into shards of spinning iron. She finally turned her attention from the prince, whirling to face the *Lionheart*. King Richard's pale face was just barely visible through the aperture that looked out from the vehicle's prow.

'You dare defy me now, worm?' The liquid allure of her voice was gone, replaced with an awful, echoing roar. The Royal Guard stopped shooting and screamed, some of them turning their guns on themselves. With a screeching noise of buckling metal, the cannon that had just fired on her crumpled in on itself.

The true voice of the demon scrabbled at Mathias's mind and he felt blood drip from his nose, but something warded him from its full horror, allowing him to stagger drunkenly to his feet. He turned in time to see the Inquisitor's gun coming up, and for a second he imagined this must have been what it was like for Wyn.

Time stood still.

'You must release us,' four very different voices said in unison.

The sudden silence was shockingly loud. Mathias looked into the fatal darkness of the Inquisitor's pistol, but nothing happened.

'There is no time left,' the voices said again. 'You must release us, Mathias Eynon.'

Mathias turned away from the Inquisitor to see Tagan and the magi looking at him. They were all haloed with light, their eyes burning with barely contained power. Eyja took a single step forward. Her white gown billowed in a nonexistent breeze, and Mathias felt cool air wash over him. A tumble of thoughts and sensations rushed through him; the sirocco that races across the desert, the gale that drives the snow around high peaks, the fury of the storm at sea. It was like standing in a silent hurricane.

'I am Nimbus,' Eyja declared, in a voice most decidedly not her own. Snow gusted from her mouth and lightning crackled at her fingertips. 'And this magic will not last long. You must unbind us, so that we may drive out the evil that threatens the world.'

'I don't understand.' Mathias stared at the magi. 'You... you are all like her, aren't you?'

Giraldo came forward, though he did not step, but *glided*. The smell of brine and the crash of waves rolled from him and water bubbled up from the earth beneath his feet. 'I am Lunus. And you are right, Mathias, but we are also nothing like her.' A translucent finger jabbed towards Melusine. 'Have you ever thought us evil?'

Mathias shook his head. Out of the corner of his eye he saw the perfect visage of the demon twitch in fury. Whatever enchantment Eyja had woven, the creature was fighting it. 'No,' he said, and he did not feel any malevolence in the entities before him, simply a wild energy struggling to be free. 'But... why didn't you tell me?'

Warin approached and his tread was like boulders falling from a mountain. He reeked of rock dust, and when he spoke it was like the grinding of millstones. 'Would you have listened to a demon, boy?' There was still something of the Shapeshifter in that voice, but it was hard to make out. 'I am Dolus. While we are very different in nature, we are kin to the creature you call Melusine.'

Mathias didn't want to accept what that meant. He didn't want to see the fourth figure that approached and all that it meant to him. His very existence was in pieces, and all he knew was gone. Despite his agony, both physical and mental, he turned to Tagan.

She was looking back at him, but not with the eyes that he knew and loved. She looked at him through the smoking orbs of something otherworldly. Heat poured from her flesh and blackened the ground beneath her feet. The ethereal magic did not touch Mathias.

'I am Ignus,' she said. 'The living flame. Tagan has become my vessel. I am sorry, Mathias Eynon. I am sorry there was not more time to prepare you for this.'

Mathias shook his head, tears forming in his eyes. 'Why her?' he croaked weakly. 'Why would you take her from me?'

'There is no time,' Lunus said urgently. Melusine twitched again, and her form shivered unnaturally.

'I have not taken her. That is not what we are, or what we do. Tagan understood the nature of what we must do and she gave her body to me, but only you can unbind us to fight the evil of the sixth.'

'The sixth?'

Sound began to intrude on the silence once again. The echoes of screams as the Royal Guard lost their minds. The groan of metal from the *Lionheart*. The crack of a gunshot.

'The creature you call Melusine is only sixth among eight great powers that seek dominion. But we cannot explain now. You must release us, quickly!'

'I don't know what you mean. What do you want me to do?' Tears streaked Mathias's face as he looked at the woman he loved. She was still as he had always known her, but she was no longer Tagan.

'Tagan is still here,' the crackling voice declared. 'She always will be. But a part of her still clings to you, to the life you wanted, and I cannot force her to let that go. Only you can do that.'

Mathias nodded slowly, and then again more firmly. There was every chance that he would die within the next few minutes; the pain of loss would be fleeting. Suddenly, he welcomed death. The hereafter would be free from this terrible agony.

He raised Tagan's hand to his lips and gave it a last, gentle kiss. 'I understand,' he said sadly. 'I release you from your promise to me, Tagan. We are no longer betrothed, you and I. You are bound to another now, more surely than you could ever be to me. Do what you must do.'

Tagan smiled at him gently and reached out a hand to stroke his cheek. His heart felt as though it were tearing itself apart with the pain and knowledge of what he had done. She was no longer his.

But then, a voice in his mind asked, *was she ever yours to begin with?*

Mathias closed his eyes and reality snapped back into place. There was a shot, but no stab of pain, no sudden oblivion. Mathias opened his eyes to see a fist clenched in front of his face: Tagan's hand. As he watched, it opened, to reveal a small, lead ball.

The metal hissed and spat and ran between her fingers, and the woman he knew became something else entirely. She doubled in size and her reddish skin cracked to reveal molten veins webbing her entire body. Her legs became back-jointed and cloven, and a crown of horns sprouted from her brow. Her dark hair became a mane of fire that spilled down her broad back and Mathias, for all his grief, found the creature oddly beautiful.

Warin was gone and in his place stood a wolf larger than any bear. Its flesh was stone that flexed and bulged as it moved, and its fur was slivers of shining crystal. A pair of yellow gemstones served as eyes, and obsidian fangs filled its cavernous maw. The wolf of the earth snarled, a sound like an avalanche, and sprang toward the demon.

'Don't look at her,' the voice of Eyja said in his mind. She was now an avatar of living lightning. A gale whipped around her, and a skin of ice formed on the ground beneath her as she followed the others toward the swelling form of Melusine. The lower half of Giraldo had become a raging tidal vortex and what could be seen of him was blue-skinned and fluid. 'We can ward you from her presence and her voice, but the sight of her can shatter even the strongest mind.'

Mathias turned away and caught only a glimpse of something

both serpentine and chiropteran. It was enough to freeze the blood in his veins

The terrible sounds of battle thundering from behind him were unlike anything he had ever heard, but he had no time to dwell upon them. Weaver had cast aside his pistol and, heedless of the chaos unfolding nearby, lunged for Mathias. The Inquisitor's meaty fist sent Mathias sprawling into the prince, who was still dreamily shuffling toward the conflict, oblivious to the danger around him, and knocked them both to the ground.

Mathias shook his head to clear the ringing and looked up to see the Inquisitor towering over him, yet another blade in his hands. Then there was a crack of displaced air and Weaver was flung across the circle to smash into one of the standing stones. He hit it with such force that Mathias was briefly sure the impact must have killed him, but the masked man groaned and struggled to rise.

Mathias didn't know whether one of his former companions had just saved him or whether it was a happy accident, but the fury of the conflict that he could not see continued to escalate. The scorch of fire from Ignus's flames, the gust of ice winds from Nimbus as she passed... the scents of the sea and the forests... every sense was being assailed by the mighty battle occurring. He concentrated on keeping the young prince pinned beneath him, conscious that he was Melusine's prize and that she could not be allowed to take him.

Beneath his weight, Prince Richard squirmed and twisted, trying to break free from Mathias, but to no avail. Everything was so frenetic that Mathias's head was spinning. Something huge rushed past and went sprawling into the stones. Dolus got to his feet and shook himself from head to tail, then, with a howl of fury, the wolf of the earth bounded back towards Melusine.

Weaver struggled to his feet and retrieved his sword. It seemed to Mathias that nothing could stop the Inquisitor. He seemed invincible, implacable, something more than human. Not for the first time, Mathias wondered how it was that he had managed to hunt them so relentlessly and so successfully. The Inquisition was said to have spies everywhere, but it had to be something more than that.

He had killed Wyn. He had tried to kill Mathias and had nearly killed Tagan. He had spent the lives of his knights in order to make his way through Akhgar's camp and it seemed that he absolutely would not stop until all of them were dead.

Mathias had had enough.

He climbed to his feet; roots sprouted from the earth in his wake and bound the struggling prince to the ground. Then he became the wolf. Not the small, sleek animal that he had been before, but a feral hunter, a predator to match a predator. He gathered his powerful legs beneath him and charged at the Inquisitor. A shot rang out and scored a bloody line down Mathias's hide, but then the huge, shaggy animal forced the Inquisitor to the ground and Mathias's wolf body stood atop the fallen man like a conqueror at the top of a fort. The animal growled furiously and long jaws snapped at Weaver's throat. The Lord Inquisitor thrust his arm into the wolf's maw and grunted as it drew blood, savaging his flesh. It was too close to stab with his sword, but he pummelled the creature with the hilt of the weapon until it released him and sprang away.

A titanic maelstrom was beginning to engulf the henge. Hurricane winds roared about the stones, lifting bodies into the air and rocking the *Lionheart* in which the King cowered. Rain slashed down and the bellow of thunder had become a constant background sound. Fire fell from the heavens and lit up the night with an infernal orange glow.

The next time the wolf sprang, Weaver was ready. He turned on his heel and dragged his blade across the hind leg of the animal. The shock of the wound forced Mathias back into his own body and he stumbled, streaked with blood from his injuries. The pain was excruciating, whichever form he took. He dropped to his hands and knees and gritted his teeth against the agony.

Weaver came at him again, a ragged, masked monster trailing blood, but refusing to die or surrender to human frailties. The blade came up and Mathias, on his hands and knees, suddenly imagined his father lying upon the block. The thought struck him like a blow and his pain, fear, loss and anger crystallised in that instant.

The blade came down in a beheading arc.

Mathias caught the sword in a fist suddenly as hard as diamond. He squeezed and the blade shattered. Then, with a bellowed cry of pure rage, his other fist crashed into Weaver's jaw. The impact lifted the big man off his feet, tore the mask from his face and flipped it into the air.

Weaver fell to the ground with an unearthly shriek that pierced the din of battle. He thrashed and rolled as if he were in the grip of a seizure, clutching at his exposed face. Mathias glimpsed cold, cold eyes between the scrabbling fingers and then, in front of him, the man began to age. His hair went white and his face became lined and weathered. In the space of a few seconds, Charles Weaver gained decades.

The mask arced through the air, an innocuous, inanimate thing that bounced a few times before rolling to a stop before Melusine. Something more terrible even than the demoness burned within its simple design and sick, greenish light burst from it. Made weary from her struggle with the otherworldly magi, Melusine was hurled against the stone perimeter of the henge; the softly glowing stones pulsed and repelled her, the world beyond still anathema and unattainable to her unbound form. The hurricane winds drove her back into the crackling pillar of light that spilled from the mask's inner face.

Melusine's shrieking roar shook the earth and one of the ancient warding stones around the henge cracked from top to bottom. The sound grew in pitch and Mathias began to scream, sure that his mind would break under the onslaught. A single, sibilant voice spoke a word in his mind. Then there was a great rushing of wind, like the inhalation of something impossibly vast, and then sudden, shocking silence.

Mathias got to his feet and limped to where the mask lay, ignoring the titanic forms of the magi. He stared down at the vile thing, which now lay inert and lifeless. It seemed to be nothing more than roughly fashioned iron. A crack ran down its length, splitting the metal. Mathias dragged the tips of his fingers over it; the artefact was warm, but swiftly cooling. He did not know what had happened.

'A power greater even than her was bound within that mask,' the tectonic voice of Dolus rumbled, voicing the answer to the question he had not asked.

They turned their attention to Charles Weaver, who lay curled and shrivelled on the ground. He raised his withered face to look at them.

'Mercy,' was all the man said, a hand outstretched toward the fallen mask. 'Mercy.'

For a long, drawn-out moment, Mathias simply stared at the old man; but, despite everything he had done, he pitied the Inquisitor. He nodded and kicked the mask over to Weaver, who grabbed it and hugged it to his chest protectively. Then the mighty Lord Inquisitor bawled like a babe. Disgusted, Mathias turned his back.

The four magi were shifting and changing, resuming their human forms, but Mathias would not let himself look at them. Instead, he turned his attention to the young Prince Richard, still sprawled in the dirt. He knelt down by the unconscious youth and put a hand beneath his head, lifting him gently. The roots unwound from the prince's body, freeing him.

'It's over now, your highness,' he murmured. From the corner of his eye he saw the amber glow of the henge fade back to the grey of inert stone. He saw the shape of King Richard rush from the ruined *Lionheart* towards them, and he looked up into the eyes of his King.

A jolt of connection ran from the one to the other: a sense that they had been waiting for this moment their entire lives. The King stared at Mathias and Mathias returned the look. This was the man whose rule had brought about the death of a father he had never known. The man whose decision to wage war on the arcane had led to his mother's early end. A king whose ambition to end magic had led to so much hurt and suffering, and whose armies had brought war to the shores of France.

But more than anything, he saw the eyes of a man who had been deceived, and a father whose love and concern for his son were entirely genuine. 'He is well,' said Mathias to the King. 'It's over.'

King Richard the Fifth, Scion of the House of Plantagenet, Heir of the Demon King, stared down at his son and shook his head. 'Not yet,' he said. He looked back at Mathias. 'But it will be soon.'

Epilogue

26th December, 1589
The Feast of Saint Stephen
Wardour Castle, Wiltshire
England

Prince Richard, heir to the throne of England, was struggling. He recalled travelling to Stonehenge with his father on the *Lionheart*, but beyond that, he could not remember what had happened between then and when he had woken two hours ago in the home of one of the court's nobles.

Through cautious explanation and his own fractured memories, he was piecing together what had happened. The *Lionheart* had failed in the most disastrous and devastating manner possible. Even now, he was told, members of the Royal Guard were accompanying Isaac Bonnington as he worked on picking through the wreckage of the vehicle to try to find what had happened. The Royal Engineer was in terrible disgrace over the shoddy workmanship, he was told. But it was all second, third-hand information. He needed to speak to his father.

'My boy.' As though he had summoned the King by thought alone, he turned to see Richard standing in the doorway. 'It is good that you are awake.' Prince Richard sat up amongst the goose down pillows and gave his father a weary smile.

'Father,' he said. 'What's happening?'

'There was an accident,' came the reply. The King pulled a chair across the room to sit beside his son. He took the young man's hand into his own. 'You have no idea how close you came to being killed, but you were saved at the last. There are new advisers to the court and they prevented a planned attempt on your life.'

'They tell me the *Lionheart* proved to be faulty.'

The King nodded and looked sombre.

'I'm sorry, Father. I may not remember much, but I know what the machine represented for you. What it could have meant for the war with France...'

'The war is over.' The King closed his eyes briefly. 'For now, at least. I have sent word to Paris. We are withdrawing our army and we will fortify the isle. I hope that we will be able to talk terms with the Vaticae. I don't want to see more men die.'

'But the cause, Father.... to rid Europe of the magic taint...'

'No,' said King Richard, cutting him short. 'No. Magic is not what I believed it to be. There was much I did not understand about the magi. Much that has haunted us from our past that has now been put to rest. We will need their counsel in the coming months, particularly if Rome comes to our shores. This is a new England, my son. A new world to which you have woken.'

'Will you tell me what happened?'

King Richard studied his oldest son for a while. 'Perhaps,' he said. 'But when the time is right. In the meantime, rest and get well. You will need all your strength.' He held onto his son's hand for a little while longer. For the first time in his life, he did not feel Melusine's presence in the back of his mind, and in the strangest of ways, he mourned her. Just as his people faced a new and uncertain future, so did he.

Willow Tree Farm
Amesbury, Wiltshire
England

THE FARM HAD once thrived, a place of bustling activity. Hard work and determination had brought the place to prosperity from little more than a shack in a field, inherited from a long-dead grandparent. Now, though, it was abandoned, and the fine stone farmhouse had fallen into a state of disrepair. The farmer had been a practitioner of petty magic, using his talents to grow crops that were lush and bountiful. His discovery had brought his execution and his execution had brought the ruin of his family. They had abandoned the farm, fleeing to the borders of Wales for fear of further persecution.

The shell of the farmhouse was intact, although the state of repair was poor. Cracks in the walls that would once have been patched by the farmer went unattended and it was likely that within a few short months, the roof, already sagging visibly, would collapse. But for now, it was a peaceful, anonymous location where five people met.

Five days had passed since the defeat of Melusine. In that time, Mathias Eynon had forsaken the company of the magi. King Richard had all but begged the four to attend him. To discuss the future of the nation. 'To atone for the errors of my past,' as he had put it. They had all agreed, and Mathias had been asked to come as well.

He declined. He wanted to be alone. It had taken five days for him to finally agree to this meeting.

King Richard had provided accommodation for the young man, who, as far as he was concerned, had saved his son from a fate worse than death. The room of the manor house in which he had been staying was far more opulent than anything he had ever known, but he had been unable to get comfortable. The bed was too soft, the temperature too stifling, the food—delicious and plentiful though it was—too rich. The Yuletide festival had left him feeling sickly and drained. After months of struggling just to survive, and a lifetime of toil and simple living, Mathias was poorly suited to the sudden life of nobility.

He arrived at the farmhouse first. The one concession to his new status had been an exceptionally welcome change of clothes. Gone was the simple tunic that had kept him warm for so long, replaced with an extravagant weave of dark green thread that suited his colouring well. He set a fire in the ash-filled grate and watched for a while as the kindling caught and the flames began to lick up against the back of the fireplace. Mathias stood with his hands close to the welcoming warmth and let his mind wander. It was a strange kind of luxury that still felt odd.

There was so much to say and so much that he did not want to say. More than anything, he felt utterly alone. He, who had travelled in the most extraordinary company, was the only one who did not belong. He watched the flames for a while, adding a log from the dusty pile beside the grate, and turned away from the fire.

'Hello, Mathias.'

He had not heard Eyja enter the building, and yet her sudden appearance did not startle him in the least. Everything about her appearance was as he had remembered from the first moment they had met. The white-blonde hair, the gentle expression, the exquisite, doll-like beauty of her porcelain features. She smiled warmly at him.

'Nimbus,' he said, and she looked pained.

'Please,' she said. 'Not you. Never you. We are friends, you and I. I am Eyja to you and that is who I will always be. Nimbus is the... other part of my life. She is powerful and she is wise, but she is not who I am here.' She placed a hand over her heart. 'Nimbus is *part* of who I am.'

'I don't need an explanation,' said Mathias in a curt tone. 'I agreed to meet you.' He looked over her shoulder. 'Are the others coming?'

'They're already here,' she replied. 'They are outside. Waiting for you.'

'Then tell them to come in,' he said. 'It's far more pleasant by the fire than it is standing in the frost.' Without another word, he turned back to the hearth. He couldn't understand quite why it was that he was so angry at Eyja. She had never shown him anything but kindness. He took a deep breath and faced the door. Faced them all.

The others, when they came in, were less silent than she had been. Warin stomped, as he did everywhere, and the old floorboards protested loudly as he entered. Giraldo was whistling softly and tunelessly. And Tagan...

Tagan walked in last, wearing a simple gown dyed a deep, berry red. Her black hair, which had grown so long over the months of travelling, was caught behind one ear by a white winter flower. He had never seen her looking so feminine, and his breath caught in his throat. She had her eyes lowered demurely, but she glanced up at him when she felt him staring at her.

'Hello,' she said in the voice that he knew and loved. Or at least that he had thought he loved. To hear her speak that one simple word broke his heart. He didn't reply to her, but simply stared. The look they exchanged was charged with an unspoken question, a single, desperate word.

Why?

But no answer was forthcoming. Warin moved in between them and the look, the moment of connection was broken.

'Well now, pup,' said the Shapeshifter, clapping Mathias on the arm roughly. 'You left in such a hurry the other day. Don't you think that was a little bit rude?' Warin scowled, his voice gruff, and Mathias smiled faintly.

'Forgive me,' he said. 'I had a lot on my mind.' Warin snorted in response and hauled Mathias in for a rough hug. As a concession to time spent in the royal court, Warin had made an effort to tidy up his beard, but it was likely to go back to its usual haywire self at any given moment. He clung to the man for a few moments in silence, his worries temporarily forgotten.

'So sentimental,' said Giraldo. He dusted the thick layer of grime from a chair lying on its side and righted it before dropping down in it, his legs hanging over the arms nonchalantly. He flipped Mathias a salute and an easy grin. 'How are you, lad?'

'I've been better,' Mathias replied. He knew he sounded petulant; frankly, he didn't care. His shoulders sagged as guilt immediately filled him. 'At least I'm clean,' he admitted reluctantly. 'I was starting to get a little fragrant.' The luxury of being able to immerse himself in clean, warm water had been perhaps the most welcome thing that had come with the return to normality. Not that he could ever return to normality. Not knowing what he now knew. Eyja brushed a stray lock of hair out of his eyes.

'You could do with tidying yourself up a little,' she observed. 'Now that you are living amongst nobility.'

'Only until the turn of the year,' said Mathias. He reached up and caught Eyja's hand, pushing it gently but firmly away from him. The single gesture conveyed so much about his new attitude and new approach. 'Then I'm returning home. This has all been remarkable. The journey and saving the kingdom. But...' He looked briefly at Tagan, who did not raise her eyes. 'Whilst others may have changed, some of us have lives to go back to. The village was not completely destroyed in the attack. Some of the people escaped and are trying to rebuild their lives.'

'My father? Have you found out if...' Tagan finally spoke. When she raised her head, her eyes were bright with unshed tears. It was a question to which she had yet to get an answer. Learning of their home's destruction had hit both of them hard. Tagan, despite the changes that had come over her, had been distraught. They had tried—thus far in vain—to discover the fate of her father. With the destruction of the circle, there was no swift way to reach the Welsh village.

Mathias studied her for a moment. He had to fight down the urge to cross the room and take her in his arms. 'A messenger brought news yesterday,' he said. He kept his voice as neutral as he could manage. 'Your father was wounded during the attack. Apparently he led the fight against Weaver's men. Tagan, he's dying.'

'I should go to him.' Tagan set her jaw determinedly. 'I should... explain...' The other three exchanged glances, and just for a few moments, Mathias found that he could forget they were there. His focus was completely on his former betrothed, the way she looked, the way she carried herself. Everything about her that was so familiar. Anger reared in him.

'And what will you tell him, Tagan? What will you say to him? How will you explain what you are?' Mathias waved a hand at her. 'Will you tell him that you can't stay because you answer a higher calling? Will you tell him what you've become? Do you truly care?' He bit his lip. That last had been unnecessary, and he regretted it the second the words left his lips. She shook her head, upset but calm. The calm that he had come to depend upon over the past months.

Tagan took a step towards him, but he shook his head. Her hand, which had reached to touch his arm, fell to her side. She let out a gentle sigh. 'He doesn't need to know the whole truth,' she said. 'If he is... dying, then I would not bring that hurt upon him. At least if he sees me before he passes, then it may bring him some comfort.'

There was no arguing with that. Mathias closed his mouth tightly against a harsh retort, and shrugged. It was the best he could manage. 'Fine,' he said. 'It's not as though I would deny you the chance to say farewell. What right do I have?' The bitterness ran deep. Tears tracked down Tagan's face, but he hardened his heart against the sight and turned to Warin.

'What is it that you wanted to speak with me about?' It hurt more than anything to turn his back on his crying betrothed... no. He must learn to let go.

'About what happens next,' said Warin. Gone was the gruffness, and in its place was a quiet, carefully spoken man. 'Your role in this is not yet finished.'

'Oh, it's finished,' asserted Mathias and he folded his arms across his chest. 'I have nothing left to give.'

'That's not *quite* right,' said Giraldo, unfolding from the chair and standing. 'You still have something to give.'

'What is there?' retorted Mathias. 'Between the three of you, I have given all I had. Or that I could ever wish to give. I want to go home to Wales, and I want to...'

'Forget about us? Dear one, you can't do that.' Eyja's voice was sad. 'Don't you think all of us would choose that life if we could? Warin has his forest, Giraldo has his oceans and I have my island. In our own way, we have hidden from the world. We can go back to those lives, but we can never give up what we are. The decision to bear the spirits within us is not made lightly.'

'What does that have to do with me?'

'Everything,' said Warin. 'There is one who needs your help. The one who set you on your path in the first place.'

'Wyn?' Mathias's brow creased. 'I don't understand. He's dead.'

'He was only Wyn to you. I told you that I knew him as Havard.

Remember the names, Mathias. To Warin he was Adelmo. He is the Protector. The Warden. The Shield-Bearer. The Light in the Dark. He was also a father to you,' said Eyja, diplomatic to the last. 'But we need to get him back. He needs to return to this world. He needs his vessel.'

'You mean me, don't you.' It was statement, not a question. 'I worked it out after Stonehenge. I realised that was what my role in all this was supposed to be. For a while, after Tagan'—he looked at the young woman—'after Tagan changed, I thought maybe the whole thing had been entirely for her benefit. That I was just an extra body. The speed with which she accepted the role she has taken...' He looked at her again and his heart thawed just a little. 'The old man in the desert knew she was coming. How he selected her to be his vessel with so much distance between them defies me—and no, it's all right.' He held up a hand. 'I don't need an explanation.'

He ran his fingers through his hair, which fell straight back into his eyes. It had grown so long now and the look suited him. He had also chosen not to shave in the past few days, and was beginning to sport a beard. 'I suppose I've realised that none of this has happened by accident.'

'Not true. All right, maybe it's a *little* bit true,' admitted Giraldo. 'Except that things did not quite begin as they were supposed to. If they had, then this would be a lot simpler. It was nobody's fault.'

'There is no blame to be apportioned, but if Wyn had not grown so fond of Mathias—and I can understand why he did—perhaps matters would have become clearer far sooner.' Eyja offered the young man one of her soft smiles. 'You do understand, don't you, Mathias?'

'Completely,' he replied and there was a weary resignation underlying his tone. 'I was supposed to be the vessel for the Warden. When Wyn died, his demon... passenger... was returned to whatever place it is that you come from...'

'The Aetherworld,' said Warin, his tone grim.

'...and this Warden's spirit is back where it came from.'

'Indeed it is.' Giraldo took up the explanation. 'Without a vessel, he can't return. In the Aetherworld, he is being hunted as many of us are. We can't leave him to the fate that awaits him if the enemy tracks him down and gets her claws into him.'

'I thought she was dead.' Mathias looked from one to the other. 'If she is still out there somewhere, then what in the name of... what has all this been for?'

'Melusine has been banished back to the Aetherworld,' said Eyja. 'But it is difficult, if not impossible, to destroy one of our kind in this world and she was but the sixth among them. Sixth, among the eight. We have asked for this meeting with you, because we need your help. The Warden needs your help.' She smiled and there was nothing of humour in the expression. 'You are his intended vessel, Mathias. That's the truth of the matter. You can't avoid it forever. And you can't run from it. Please. We are asking you. We are *begging* you. Help him. It is something only you can do.'

He looked at them, from one face to another, his mind a whirl. His eyes met Tagan's and remained there. He knew what his answer must be, but he could not put it into words.

Stonehenge
England

IT COULD NOT be denied that sunrise across Salisbury Plain, as it fell across the ancient stone circle, was a breathtaking sight. It was a place of peace and reflection, a place of ancient power and magic that enchanted and ensnared in equal measure.

Charles Weaver stood amidst the battle-scarred stones of the ancient monument, the broken mask in his hand as he looked around at the devastation littering the area. The *Lionheart*, the extraordinary machine that had held so much promise, lay at the circle's edge, nothing more than a shattered, ruined hulk. The explosion that had seen its demise had lit up the December sky for miles around, and it was a wonder, people said when dawn had broken and the true extent of the devastation became apparent, that more damage had not been done.

A huge crater marked the site of the vehicle's end and its debris littered the circle inside the stones and the surrounding plains. Of the Royal Guardsmen who had accompanied King Richard to this place, this 'testing ground' as it was called, nearly all had died. The monument itself, of course, remained intact.

Strangely, of all those who had survived, not a single Royal Guardsman retained memory of the events. Only King Richard, Charles Weaver and five other people would ever know the truth of what had transpired.

The Inquisition was no more. One of the first things King Richard had done—after ensuring his son was well cared for—was to send orders to seize the Tower. All the current inhabitants were expelled. This new England had no place for the hunters of magi. The Inquisitors had scattered, hiding from the retribution that would follow once the loss of their power became known.

Weaver turned the mask over in his hands. He had not put it back on since the battle of the henge. It had been a part of his body for so long, and to have been free of its constraints for five days... it was longer than he could remember. His anonymity had been assured. Nobody knew the face behind the mask. But the loss of its magic—a magic he had not even known he carried—had hollowed him out, leaving nothing but the husk of a man in its wake. He had not slept in the last few days and his heart pounded constantly whenever he thought of the mask lying in the circle.

Without it he did not know who he was. He turned the mask over in his hands and looked at its inner surface, where tiny, living script once squirmed and whispered its secrets. The rays of the dawn light shimmered on its surface and for a moment, just for a fleeting second, he thought he saw the script move once more. But it was a dead thing. He was free of its influence. Free of whatever had whispered instructions to him.

Without it, he supposed, he could be anybody he wanted to be.

He lifted the mask until the rising sun shone through the eye holes and he smiled in sudden understanding. The mask *was* who he was. Even without the Inquisition, it made him powerful. A faint ripple of green ran across the inside surface and he thought he heard a whisper, just on the very cusp of hearing.

Closing his eyes, Charles Weaver put the mask on and turned his back on the rising sun. As he set the east to his back, he opened his eyes again.

Something inhuman looked out from within.

END

ACKNOWLEDGEMENTS

Huge thanks to Dave and his understanding, patience and the Veneer of the Week. A shout-out to everyone in LoA, CTO and the Lost Praxeum, for hours of endless distraction. And special thanks and all my love to Ben, who puts up with my tantrums and moments of self-doubt with the kind of patience and stoicism I probably don't deserve.

ABOUT THE AUTHOR

An NHS worker by day and a writer under the cover of night, Sarah's first novel *The Gildar Rift* was published by the Black Library in 2011. Since then, she has written several other novels and short stories set in the grim-dark worlds of Warhammer. *Heirs of the Demon King: Uprising* is her first full-length original work. Other works include tie-in fiction for World of Warcraft and several original tales for an assortment of publishers. Sarah lists her hobbies as reading, writing, reading about writing, writing about reading, online gaming and writing about online gaming. She needs to get out more.

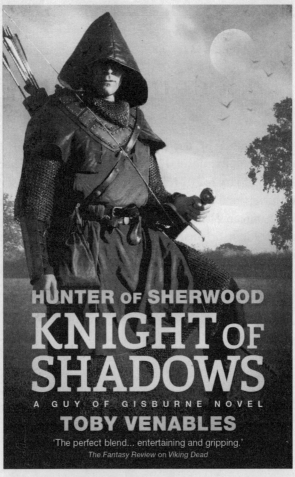